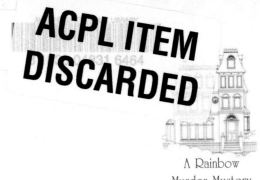

A Rainbow
Murder Mystery

Rave Reviews for the Ben Candidi Series

Pharmacology Is Murder

"First-time novelist Dirk Wyle skillfully pairs the tone of the hard-boiled mystery with the intricate scientific detail common to the medical thriller. The result is an excellent whodunit . . . a first-class mystery that combines elements of Michael Crichton, Patricia Cornwell, and even Edna Buchanan."

> — *Booklist Mystery Showcase*
> American Library Association

"When the chairman of the pharmacology department of a Miami medical school is murdered, Dade County medical examiner Geoffrey Westley recruits Ben Candidi to infiltrate the department as a student and gather information. Candidi's venturing forth from his houseboat may be more hazardous than he thinks."

> — *Publishers Weekly*

"Wyle demonstrates a breezy style, a flair for drawing vivid and memorable characters with just a few deft strokes . . . I've found myself thinking about it and admiring it in retrospect over and over again."

> — **Best First Detective Novel** — **1998**
> *Lofgreen's Detective Pages*

Biotechnology Is Murder

"Dirk Wyle . . . is a sure winner. His character Ben Candidi is just finishing his Ph.D., but Ben packs more punch per square inch than most veteran detectives . . . a timely plot with larger than life characters with which the reader has an immediate affinity. Ben Candidi is the young Jack Ryan of the biotechnological world."

— Shelley Glodowski, *Midwest Review*

"Nifty, light-hearted and deadly."

— Edna Buchanan, *Garden of Evil*

" . . . a potent mix of science, business and crime."

— *Publishers Weekly*

Medical School Is Murder

"Wyle creates Ben as the playful idealized man: Mensa member; looks like Frankie Avalon; can fight like a pit bull; has a steady relationship with the beautiful Rebecca while tossing off adversaries with stumbling panache and outwitting the evil administration."

— Shelley Glodowski, *Midwest Review*

Amazon Gold

"Scientist Ben Candidi would like nothing better than to escort his soul mate, Dr. Rebecca Levis, on her Amazon expedition to provide medical care to a nearly extinct tribe . . . But Ben needs to return to his laboratory in Miami to complete his project of studying how new technology can aid in drug development. You would think that his research would be mundane compared to the Amazon, but when it comes to Ben, who's starring in his fourth adventure, excitement is never far away. All the while, transmittals from Rebecca come less frequently . . . and his research leads to startling conclusions that have him fearing for both their lives. Wyle has given the hard-boiled thriller a scientific twist, making his novels pleasing for both their intrigue and their intellect."

— *Booklist Mystery Showcase*
American Library Association

Dirk Wyle

BAHAMAS WEST END IS MURDER

A Ben Candidi Mystery

Rainbow Books, Inc.
FLORIDA

Library of Congress Cataloging-in-Publication Data

Wyle, Dirk, 1945-
  Bahamas west end is murder : a Ben Candidi mystery / Dirk Wyle.— 1st ed.
    p. cm.
  ISBN 1-56825-100-9 (pbk. : alk. paper)
  1. Candidi, Ben (Fictitious character)—Fiction. 2. Pharmacologists—Fiction.
  3. Drug traffic—Fiction. 4. Bahamas—Fiction. I. Title.
  PS3573.Y4854B34 2005
  813'.54—dc22

                        2004028313

Bahamas West End Is Murder
A Ben Candidi Mystery
Copyright © 2005 Dirk Wyle
www.Dirk-Wyle.com
ISBN 1-56825-100-9

Published by
Rainbow Books, Inc.
P. O. Box 430
Highland City, FL 33846-0430
www.RainbowBooksInc.com

Editorial Offices and Wholesale/Distributor Orders
Telephone (863) 648-4420
Email: RBIbooks@aol.com

Individuals' Orders
Toll-free Telephone (800) 431-1579
www.BookCH.com

⊗The paper used in this publication meets the minimum requirements of the American National Standard for Information Sciences—Permanence of Paper for Printed Library Materials, ANSI Z39.48-1984.

First edition 2005

11 10 09 08 07 06 05   5 4 3 2 1

Printed in the United States of America

DEDICATION:

To Gisela, Karl and Ellen,
who helped sail the *Gizmo II* around the Bahamas —
a right good crew and a right good family, too.

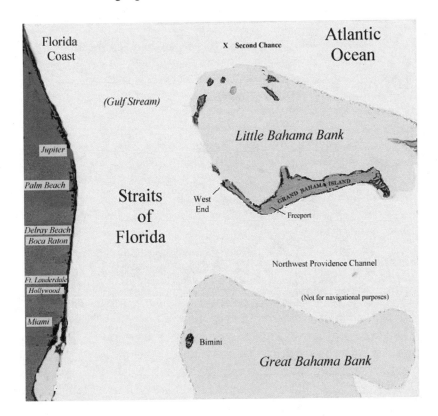

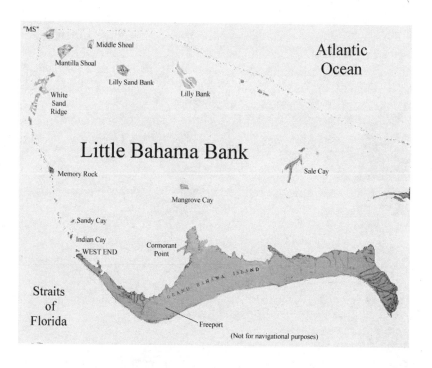

"MS"

Middle Shoal

Mantilla Shoal

White
Sand
Ridge

Lilly Sand Bank

Lilly Bank

Atlantic
Ocean

Little Bahama Bank

Memory Rock

Sale Cay

Mangrove Cay

Sandy Cay

Indian Cay

WEST END

Cormorant
Point

GRAND BAHAMA ISLAND

Straits
of
Florida

Freeport

(Not for navigational purposes)

Lucky 13　　　　　1

"Sunrise 6:45 a.m., Latitude 27° 39.6', Longitude 79° 0.8', heading for the Little Bahama Bank, 13 miles due south."

I made the notation in the *Diogenes'* log one minute after sunrise. I made it promptly, then pushed aside the hand-held GPS satellite navigation unit and marked the position on our two-by-three-foot chart of the Little Bahama Bank. I had no idea how important the notation would become — one minute later.

My plan was to approach the Little Bahama Bank at a point between the Middle Shoal and the Lilly Sand Bank. I called up the revised course to Rebecca.

We had left the Chesapeake Bay eleven days earlier and were at the end of a difficult November passage. Our tired, sleep-deprived bodies longed for the tranquil waters of the Bahamas — the *baha mar* or shallow sea, as the Spanish explorers called it. What a pleasure it would be to toss out the hook into the 12-foot water of the protected Bank, hoist up the yellow quarantine flag and sleep all day and night!

Or so we thought.

The weather was cooperating, now. The sky was blue and cloudless. A warm, 10-knot breeze filled our three sails from behind and pushed us along at a respectable five knots. One-foot waves overtook us slowly, lifting our stern gently and nudging us along. Yes, off to the west that virtual river called the Gulf Stream was sweeping northward out of the Straits of Florida. But here, shielded by the Bank, we didn't have to sail against it. In fact, an eddy current from the Gulf Stream must have been helping us along. The GPS said we were approaching the Bank somewhat faster than the knot meter said we were moving through water.

I was below deck, in the cabin. Since the *Diogenes* is a 36-foot sailing yacht, tradition allows me to call this space the "main salon," but it seemed horribly cramped at the time. I was sitting at the dinette table where the charts were laid out. I looked up the companionway or cabin entrance to catch a glimpse of Rebecca. Standing in the open cockpit behind the wheel, my soul mate was looking ahead with helmsman's concentration. Her straight black hair was pulled back into a ponytail, her usual style when engaged in serious work. Her fine-featured, narrow face was still showing evidence of our rough days in the Atlantic. But a couple of restful days would erase those strain lines from her lovely face. Her yellow foul-weather jacket reminded me of the days and nights of bone-chilling wind and relentless spray that she had endured without complaint. But the wind was warmer now. Her jacket was open and could soon be taken off. In a few minutes, the rising sun would be warming her svelte, athletic body.

Within two hours, I thought, we would be anchored in protected water, enjoying the first day of a two-month, between-jobs, Bahamas vacation.

But that was not to be.

"Cabin cruiser dead ahead." Rebecca called the information down to me in a helmsman's style. She has an expressive voice that makes full use of the soprano register. "Approaching at trawling speed. We'll pass it on the starboard."

"Well, it's our lucky sign," I called back with enthusiasm. "Wave to them for me."

When Rebecca spoke again, she sounded worried. "Nobody's waving back, Ben. And it looks real low in the water."

I came up with binoculars and looked it over: a big cabin cruiser, probably 40 feet long, trawling slowly in the water but with no outrigger poles or fishing lines. Nobody at the high outdoor steering station, the "flying bridge." And nobody standing in the cockpit, the open area in the back that serves as a platform for fishing. The navigation lights were on, unnecessarily now that the sun was up. And the boat *was* deep in the water, like it was carrying a heavy load up front. The steady stream of water shooting out the side told me the bilge pump was going full blast. And that could only mean that the boat was taking on water — lots of water.

I felt my throat tighten. "You're right, Rebecca, it's sinking."

I reached through the companionway to the radio attached to the ceiling of the cabin. I grabbed the mike and switched on Channel 16. "Forty-foot cabin cruiser on the northwest end of the Little Bahama Bank, this is the thirty-six-foot, two-masted sailing vessel the *Diogenes*.

You are low in the water and seem to be in distress. Please acknowledge! Over."

There was no response. We had just passed it, and now I could make out its name on the transom — *Second Chance*. The name was close to the water and the city of registration was partially submerged. From the tops of the *m*'s and *i*'s, we could just make out that it was from Miami. The exhaust ports were submerged; the exhaust was coming up as bubbles and froth. The tub was dangerously low in the water.

"*Second Chance, Second Chance, Second Chance!* This is the *Diogenes*. You are in deep distress. We are going to board you."

No response.

"How are we going to do it?" Rebecca asked, her voice cracking.

And that was exactly what I was asking myself. Our hard-bottomed inflatable was stowed on the deck, upside down between the bow and masthead. It would take too long to untie and launch it.

"We have to do this vessel-to-vessel," I said. "We'll take down the sails and motor up. We'll do it all in one maneuver."

In one fluid move, Rebecca leaned and reached towards the engine control panel. She pushed the button. The *Diogenes'* inboard diesel cranked, then sprang to life. She threw the motor into gear. "Ready into the wind, Ben."

I answered with a nod.

Rebecca threw over the wheel, the boat turned into the wind, and the big Genoa headsail came flapping inboard. I loosened its halyard and went into a frenzy, pulling down on the fluttering sail while making my way over the inflatable and stuffing canvas between the stainless steel tubes of the bow "pulpit."

Clambering back to the mast, I pulled down the fluttering main sail and tucked it under the bungie cords strung on the boom. No time for the third sail fluttering behind on the mizzen mast. The stern of the *Second Chance* was coming up too fast.

Rebecca slowed the engine. "What are you going to do, Ben?"

"Got to find the leak and plug it," I said, between breaths. "When you get to within ten yards of the boat, slow down, match its speed and inch up. I'll jump from the bowsprit."

I started for the bow.

"Ben, use your head!" Rebecca screamed. "Get a life jacket and a lifeline."

"Okay."

"And take the hand-held VHF."

"Good thinking. I'll call you on Channel Sixteen." I scrambled down to the cabin, got the stuff and raced back to the pulpit. I tied the hand-held VHF marine radio to the life jacket, put it on, and tied a 12-foot length of shock cord to my waist. Tied the other end to the halyard that raises the Genoa.

"Ten feet and closing," I yelled. "I'm calling out the distances from the bowsprit."

The *Diogenes'* bowsprit increases the boat's length by three feet. Besides increasing the sail area and making the boat look more nautical, that pole serves an important function: To its tip is attached the so-called forestay cable that keeps the mast in place. Bang off the bowsprit and your mast will come crashing down.

"Eight feet," I yelled.

The tip was eight feet away and chopping up and down with two-foot amplitude. The boats were out of sync in the waves.

"Five feet," I yelled.

I climbed onto the pulpit and inched my way out on the bowsprit, holding the forestay for balance. I checked that my safety line wasn't hung up somewhere. Rebecca's face was drawn tight with concentration and concern.

"Four feet," I yelled back to her.

Four feet ahead and between two and four feet below me, as we bobbed in the waves. The cabin cruiser's transom was too narrow a target to land on. I'd have to jump *over* it and land in the open cockpit. Timing myself to the next surge, I leaned forward, curled my toes, and jumped with all my might.

As in a bad dream, I flew over the yacht's transom and over the length of its cockpit, coming down on my side. I dropped a shoulder and pulled in my head as I rolled. The life jacket absorbed most of the shock and something else took care of the rest — a man's body.

I pushed away from him fast enough. Something else helped me to my feet. It was the lifeline, tugging at my waist, dragging me back and lifting me as the mast of the *Diogenes* receded. I untied that line a second before it could drag me overboard.

I turned and took stock of the situation. The man was lying in a small pool of blood in front of the door to the main salon. Lifeless. Nothing my physician fiancée could do for him. I stepped over him, opened the door and looked down on a chaos of floating cushions and sloshing water in the main salon. I pulled the radio to my face and squeezed down on the transmitter button.

"Rebecca. Maintain station at about twenty yards. There's a dead man aboard. The main salon has two to three feet of water. I'm going below. When you get a chance, take photos that will show how low the boat is in the water."

"Roger," she replied, affirming my request.

I threw the bulky life jacket to the floor of the cockpit, descended into the wash, and waded to the indoor steering station. The electric switches on the control panel were less than a foot above water and were getting sloshed periodically by the indoor waves that were running back and forth through the boat. With the voltage indicators showing 13.4, the engine's alternators were still making electricity. The ammeter told me that the boat was using five amps.

I flipped a toggle switch labeled "bilge pump" and the needle on the ammeter didn't change.

That was bad news: There was no additional bilge pump, and the one that was working already couldn't work any faster.

Only one way to save the yacht — find the leak and plug it.

But how to find it? Grope around in the wash? Swim around the outside, looking for holes? No, I would work the problem backwards:

The murderer wanted to scuttle the yacht. The fastest way for him to do that would be to cut a hose leading to a through-the-hull connection.

I waded forward and two steps down to the "head." The water was up to my chest. I opened the door, took a deep breath, pulled myself down, and groped around the toilet. The salt water flush line was intact, the effluent line was intact, and there was no back-flow through the toilet bowl. Came up for breath and did the same thing around the sink. Everything was intact.

I elbowed my way out of the head and waded back to the kitchenette near the companionway and did the same thing for the sink. Everything intact. Hell! Only one place left to look for a severed hose — in the engine room. The access door was halfway submerged near the companionway steps. It opened to reveal a pair of diesel engines, submerged almost to the top of their fan belts. Movement of the belts and wheels frothed the water before me and sprayed the ceiling of the squat compartment. But it was amazingly quiet. Immersion in water had decreased the engine noise — and was threatening to drown the engines, too. Every few seconds one of them slowed and shuddered. Their air intakes were just a few inches above the average water level and were getting splashed regularly. The engines were choking like a couple of caged lions in a sinking Roman galley. And by opening the door I was letting waves roll into the compartment, making things worse.

Probing carefully in the froth, I found the raw water hoses and ran my fingers along them as far back as possible, turning my head to avoid the fan belts. To trace the hoses the rest of the way, I crawled over the motors, taking care to stay away from the alternators and whirling belts. Followed the hoses all the way down to their seacocks. Everything was intact. Found one spare seacock, and it was closed.

Damn. No leak to be found in the engine room. Where was it, then?

I climbed back over the engines and back into the main salon. Closed the door and returned to the cockpit where the hand-held radio was squawking a hailing message from Rebecca. I squeezed down on the transmitter button. "Rebecca, I'm having trouble finding the leak."

"Where have you been?" Her naturally high voice rose to a horrified screech. "You haven't responded to page for ten minutes." Under pressure, she was reverting to hospital jargon.

"I was in the engine compartment. The water was too high to take along the radio."

"In the *engine compartment?*"

No time to tell her the whole story. "Can't find any torn hoses or open seacocks. The bad guys must have made a hole somewhere. I'm going to inspect the hull."

"Don't go over the side. I forbid you!" She screamed it so loud that I heard her voice through the air.

"Okay, then I'll have to inspect it from the inside. Over."

"*Diogenes* standing by."

I climbed back into the main salon and felt my way along every submerged section of the hull I could lay hands on, cursing the boat maker for leaving all those sharp fiberglass spines on the unfinished surfaces. One of the engines was sputtering badly. After 10 minutes of groping, my bloodied hands found the leak. It was on the port side, in a compartment under a bench near the dinette table. Water was welling up through the compartment like a Florida spring. And in the subdued light under the table, the compartment was filled with a light-blue glow. I dunked my face and saw it better: one hand-sized hole, and three finger-sized holes, all aglow in ocean blue. Viewing it from inside that black box with water streaming past my face, the ocean seemed unstoppable and infinitely deep.

The weak engine sputtered again and almost died.

I staggered to the galley, tore open a drawer, and found what I needed — a steak knife. Grabbed one of the floating cushions, ripped it open, and cut off a big piece of foam. I rolled it tight and stuffed it down the compartment, wedging it in as best I could. Held my breath and moved my hands around inside the compartment, testing for flow. My patch was working. Must have slowed the leak down to one-third.

The sick engine was getting sicker. Nothing I could do for it; opening the engine room door might let in a wave that would kill it. I thought about increasing the revs, but that might dig in the stern and drown it for sure. What was keeping the stern afloat, anyway, with those heavy engines in back?

Nothing to do but pray. No, too early for that. Nothing to do but be objective.

With the knife, I slashed marks on the wall along the waterline. I started the timer function on my watch. Time and water level were two things I could measure objectively. I went topside and leaned over the port rail to check the bilge pump output. It was still fighting, putting out a steady stream of water.

The sick engine's cough was starting to sound healthier. I waved to Rebecca, giving her thumbs up. She waved back.

I knelt down to inspect the crime scene: one tall, heavy-boned, muscular man lying facedown in a small pool of blood. This time I noticed the gunshot wound in the back of his head, obscured by his thick blond hair. I rolled him at the shoulder and found what I expected: a gunshot wound in the chest. His muscular arms were lightly tanned, like you might expect for a weekend boater with a desk job. His face and neck were red, from sunburn. He was probably handsome before, with that broad forehead and those widely spaced eyes. Now they were glazed over and bulging from their sockets.

With both engines sounding a lot better now, I turned my attention to the proximate cause of death. It wasn't a full bleed-out, so the chest shot must have stopped his heart. During the six years that I had worked as a lab tech with the Miami-Dade County Medical Examiner's office,

I learned a thing or two about cause of death. And after three years spent in a pharmacology Ph.D. program, I'd learned a lot of systemic physiology. And Rebecca is always teaching me something new about medicine.

Something was under the man's stomach. Rolling him at the hips, I pulled out a pair of night vision goggles. Lifting them carefully and putting them up to my face, I saw a solid wall of eerie green. They were still on — maxed out by the daylight. I clicked off the switch and put them down.

I gave Rebecca another thumbs up and climbed the ladder to the open steering station on the roof of the cabin — the flying bridge or "flybridge," as it is usually called. On the floor I noticed more blood. The victim had received the chest shot up there. Then he had fallen to the deck where his assailant delivered the *coup de grâce*.

The flybridge had a control panel just like below. The gauges said that the alternators were still making electricity. The tachometers said the revs were around 800. The readings on the oil pressure gauges were about right. The knot meter registered about two knots. The autopilot was engaged and holding the course straight.

Now for the big question: Were we still sinking?

I went back to the main salon and checked the water level against my marks. The bilge pumps had dropped the water level six inches. I checked the timer function on my watch. Only three minutes had elapsed. That was strange because it felt like so much longer. I waited another minute and checked again. Yes, the bilge pumps were dropping the water level two inches a minute. The situation was under control.

I picked up the radio on the way to the flybridge. After taking a look around, I squeezed down on the transmitter button. "Candidi to *Diogenes*. Switch to Channel Thirteen."

Channel 13 is used for short-range conversations with bridge keepers. On our equipment, Channel 13 was set to transmit with only one watt of power — enough power for close-in conversations and impossible to hear several miles away.

"*Diogenes* to Candidi, over to Thirteen," answered Rebecca.

She made the switch and said, "*Diogenes* on Thirteen. Sounds like a serious situation. Go ahead, please." She sounded real professional.

"I can rescue the boat, but that's all I can rescue."

"I copy that," Rebecca answered, affirming that she heard and understood my message. "I guessed that, too."

"Let's scan the horizon for other boats."

Extending a dozen feet over the flybridge was a "tuna tower," a framework of aluminum tubes that come together to form a platform and lookout station. The elevation of the tuna tower provides a definite advantage in locating fast-moving schools of those fish. The elevation also offers an advantage in locating boats that might be just below the horizon.

I climbed the tuna tower and did a 360-degree sweep with the naked eye. No boats in view. One hundred yards astern, Rebecca was doing the same thing, using binoculars.

Climbing down, I noticed that the yacht had a cylindrical radar antenna. The unit had a small display mounted on the flybridge control panel. The radar was on and the screen was showing two big green splotches. The one in the center was the *Diogenes'* radar reflector and the one at the bottom of the display must have been the water tower that marked our destination, the town of West End. And the scope was showing a lot of little blips that couldn't have been boats. It was showing a lot of so-called false returns. The signal amplification was turned up too high.

My hand-held radio was amplifying a lot of static, too. But Rebecca killed it with her carrier signal when she squeezed down on the transmitter button. She waited a second or two before speaking. "No boats on the horizon, Ben."

"Good. That's just as well. Good guys can't do anything to help, and I don't want the bad guys to hear." I told her what I'd seen and done. "You didn't broadcast any distress signals, did you?"

"No. The only information that went out on Channel Sixteen was what you said about the dead man on board. Then we talked about the leak. What are we going to do, Ben?"

"Bring this smudge pot to the marina at West End, Grand Bahama Island, and call the police."

"Maybe we could use our cellphones?"

"You can try, but I don't think they will work. When we left Washington I didn't request activation for the Bahamas. And the Florida coast is too far away to get reception."

The Florida coast was about 70 miles west of us.

"I'll try them anyway."

"Okay. If you get the Bahamian police, be sure to tell them that we found the boat in International Waters and that we are going to file a salvage claim in Miami. That's where this boat is home ported."

"Hold on and I'll try right now," Rebecca said. I listened to static for a few minutes while she went below to get her cellphone. Then she came back on and said, "You were right, Ben. I can't get any signal."

"Did you take the photos?"

"Yes. They'll show it sinking. I also did a work-up in our log."

I love Rebecca's physician lingo.

"Great. Could you go below and find my cordless drill, a screwdriver and a collection of screws? Self-tapping would be best. When you get them, come along side and toss the stuff over to me. If all goes well, I'll have the boat pumped dry in another twenty minutes. But before we turn around and get underway, I want to put on a patch with solid backing."

"Sure, I'll get your tools. I'll also give you a fever thermometer for a time-of-death estimate."

"Good thinking."

"Roger. You'll have your tools in a few minutes. What do you want me to do after that?"

"I'd like you to take a look at the chart on the table. Figure a course around the 'MS' marker — the course should be about two-seven-zero — and then down along the western edge of the Little Bahama Bank."

"You don't want to go straight south and over the Bank?"

"It's too complicated when each of us has a boat to steer. And too difficult to eyeball. Too many shallow 'sand bores' and 'fish muds' to watch out for. And the eastside approach to West End is a tricky channel. No, I want to take it on the outside, along the west edge of the Bank."

"But we'll have to fight the Gulf Stream."

"We'll hug the edge of the Bank where the water's about forty feet deep and there won't be much problem. The bottom contours are fairly regular. Use the depth sounder as your guide. I'd like us to make seven knots. Once we get level with Grand Bahama Island, we just turn ninety degrees to the left and head into West End."

"Roger that. Are we going to keep our radio transmissions like this, all the way?"

"Roger. I'll put out the word to West End just before we pull in there. That way it will be too late for the bad guys to do anything."

"Okay, Ben. Stand by for your tools in about five minutes."

I went below and made another three-minute mark on the wall.

Spent some time picking floating debris out of the water so the pump would have less chance of getting fouled. There was so little debris that I wondered if the boat had been lived in. And no marijuana or cocaine floating around. No paper money, either. The lowering water revealed no more corpses and not much paraphernalia, except for an old radio direction finder dish and a hand-held radio, both waterlogged.

The front face of the main salon was dominated by a large, clear, slanted window that gave good visibility for the indoor piloting station. The sides also had large expanses of tinted glass. When I noticed the *Diogenes* pulling alongside, I went to the cockpit to receive the tools. Rebecca threw them over in an inflated, knotted garbage bag. She'd wrapped the things in a clean white sheet, which I could use to cover the corpse when the time came. She'd also included two sandwiches, an apple, a plastic bottle of water, paper napkins, my hat, my Polaroid sunglasses, and a tube of sunscreen lotion. That girl thinks of everything.

It took the pump 22 minutes to clear out all the water. After it did, it shut off and was able to stay off most of the time. By opening an access hatch in the floor, I was able to verify that it was a single pump, operated by a float switch.

My jammed-in rubber foam plug was doing a good job at two knots, but a more robust one would be needed for travel at seven knots. I selected another cushion and cut up a new piece of foam for the sturdier design I had in mind. Went to the head and removed the toilet seat cover to use as a solid backing. Before starting, I laid out all the tools on the bench. Got a face full of water while pulling out the old plug and inserting the new one. But the foam rubber made an excellent fit and the four screws held the plastic backing tightly to the hull. They were easy to screw in, once I drilled the tap holes.

With that done, I opened the door to the engine compartment to find the two lions roaring loudly. I removed the oil caps and made a quick inspection of the innards of those diesel, overhead-valve engines. Flowing over the rockers and tappets was a stream of hot, clean-smelling, yellow oil. No milky emulsion of oil and seawater like I'd been worrying about. Good. The *Second Chance* would return to port under its own power. The alternators were looking healthy, but I didn't want them crudding up with salt as they dried out. I went to the sink in the galley, got a pan of fresh water, and splashed them down.

Taking the victim's temperature required loosening his pants for anal insertion of the fever thermometer. While waiting for it to come to equilibrium, I noticed a light pattern of finely divided blood spatter on the cabin door. Studying it for a couple of minutes, I saw that it fit perfectly with an executioner's shot to the head.

I called in the temperature to Rebecca.

"Good, Ben. I'm writing it down. Check his jaw and appendages for stiffness."

"Jaw is not movable. Arm is very hard to move."

"Good. My preliminary estimate is that the death was about eight hours ago. But please check the temperature every half hour. That will improve our estimate. You can check for stiffness again, in another hour — on another limb."

"Roger that. You can change course whenever you are ready. Put on seven knots as soon as I fall in behind."

I went to the flybridge and made careful note of several things. Most important was the yacht's course on autopilot. It was 35° (northeast by north). Next was the RPM on the engines (unchanged) and our speed in the water, which was now 2.9 knots. Riding higher in the water, the yacht was now moving 0.9 knots faster than before. I punched out the autopilot, then changed the course and speeded up to fall in behind Rebecca. The patch held well at seven knots.

Leaning back in the captain's seat, I congratulated myself for rescuing a valuable yacht and performing a crime scene investigation to professional standards. As I sat there, steering the boat's wheel at one spoke using a paper napkin as a glove, my body slowly came down from an adrenaline high. But my brain didn't relax. How lucky that the boat was 13 miles out when we discovered it. That put it in International Waters, one mile outside the Twelve Mile Limit. My brain was running all over the place, trying to remember facts about salvage law, estimating the value of the yacht, and calculating how big a salvage fee I could claim.

Luckily my free hand didn't fumble around much during that brainstorm. When my eyes settled on the seat next to me, they made a shocking discovery: Lying in the crack of that seat was a long-barreled revolver — cocked and pointed at me.

A Good Citizen's Duty 2

I punched in the autopilot and used the paper napkin to pick up the gun and let back its hammer. It didn't smell like it had been fired, and all the visible chambers were loaded. Maybe the victim was an unlucky hunter who was killed before he could get off his first shot. I put the revolver in a drink holder under the console and went back to the routine: steering, thinking, and taking rectal temperatures on schedule.

It took an hour for the "MS" marker to come into view and another hour to round it and start heading south along the western edge of the Little Bahama Bank. Off to the right, the Gulf Stream water was as blue as the sky above us. And 20 to 40 feet below me, the bottom glided by — a patch of grass here, a patch of sand there, punctuated by chimney-shaped sponges and brain corals ranging in size from a picnic table to a VW bug. Occasionally I could make out a snapper, a yellowtail or a brightly colored reef fish. My Polaroid sunglasses did such a good job of blocking surface reflection that the water seemed to have no surface at all. It felt like flying over a landscape of green, beige, red, brown and blue hills and valleys, which rose gently to our left to meet a silvery horizon.

The bottom contours were so regular that Rebecca needed few adjustments to our average course of 165°. Here on the edge of the Bank, the Gulf Stream wasn't fighting us more than one knot.

With little to do but follow Rebecca, I spent the time thinking about the crime we'd discovered. Why does a man go trawling at 2.9 knots at night without fishing line but with night vision goggles and a cocked revolver? Was it a drug deal gone bad? Was he the buyer or the seller? Was the revolver his only armament? Why hadn't he taken a rapid-fire weapon? Was he doing the deal alone? Did he have a partner or sidekick? If the sidekick was the one who did it, how had he gotten off the boat? The stern didn't have any davits for hanging a dinghy or inflatable boat behind. My inspection of the front deck didn't reveal any shackles, straps or tie-downs for an inflatable, either. And why would the murderous sidekick take the chance of lining up the shot for the front of the chest when it is so much safer to shoot a guy from behind?

Well, when the police identified the victim and his boat and started interviewing people, they should be able to test the murderous sidekick theory for us. Correction: They would check it for *themselves* because Rebecca and I weren't going to get involved.

The alternate theory would be that the victim was out alone and was attacked by a boat full of bad guys. They pulled up to him, knocked him down with a chest shot and sent one man aboard to deliver the executioner's shot. The fact that they'd chosen to sink the boat with a tight pattern of shots at the waterline said many things about them. Either they were stupid, or they didn't know much about boats, or they were in a big hurry.

Hell, if I'd wanted to scuttle this yacht and make it look like an accident, I would have laid a wrench on the bilge pump float switch so it couldn't turn on, and I'd loosen the aviation clamp on one of the raw water hoses and pull off the hose. That would take the boat down in 15 minutes. Barracuda and shark would scatter the body parts and nobody would know that a crime was committed.

I went back to speculating about the victim's intentions until Rebecca asked for another temperature reading for the time of death calculation. That got me wondering whether it would be possible to deduce the time of the attack from how long it took for the yacht to flood to the level we found. The principles were simple — a race between the leak and the pump. The pump has only two speeds: off and full speed. If the leak were slower than the pump there would have been no problem. The pump would click on when the water rose an inch or two, and would click off when it had pumped it back down. And the water would never rise above the bilge.

If the leak is faster than the pump, the boat will sink. If the leak is a lot faster, the boat will sink in a short time. If the leak is only a little bit faster, the boat will take a long time to sink.

I spent some time thinking about how I could use calculus to compute how long the race had been going on. Then I thought up a simple experiment that I could do, once we got the *Second Chance* to safety.

While eating the lunch that Rebecca made for me, my thoughts returned to the other calculation I had made:

We were going to earn $100,000!

The calculation was easy. This smudge pot had to be worth around $200,000. A salvager who saves a boat from going down can claim 50 percent of its value. Now $100,000 would be a nice chunk of change – enough to keep this biomedical scientist and his physician fiancée going for a couple of years. Between jobs, as we were, we could use the money. I had given up my job at the U.S. Patent and Trademark Office and Rebecca had given up her fellowship in world health at George Washington University.

Actually, I'd given up the Patent Office job a couple of months earlier and had accepted a research assistant professorship at Bryan Medical School in Miami. After I'd worked hard there to start a career in laboratory research, the effort sort of exploded in my face. But that's another story. After the dust settled, we sailed out of Chesapeake Bay, planning to take a two-month vacation cruising the Bahamas before looking for work in Miami. My long-range goal was to build up a pharmaceutical consulting practice. Rebecca's plan was to find a job in an emergency room or to do family medicine in a small group practice. Her true passion, third world medicine, she would pursue in her spare time.

My black-haired, green-eyed soul mate called me on Channel 13 for another temperature reading. After giving it to her, I praised her piloting and her corned-beef sandwiches. She reminded me to put sunscreen lotion on my face and neck. I thanked her for thinking of me and keeping me on track.

I meant it sincerely. That slender, Manhattan-bred lady was the best thing that ever happened to this mid-sized, oversexed New Jersey Italian. Several years ago, she had rescued me from a downward spiral toward the life of a boat bum. She had shown me how to get useful work out of my high-voltage brainstorms. And, in appreciation, I had shown her a kind of love that she'd never experienced before. And now, with Rebecca in her late twenties and with me in my early thirties, we were lifetime partners.

Once we completed this salvage, our partnership was going to be $100,000 richer.

Of course big chunks of cheese invariably attract nibblers. It would be a shame to have to spend any of that money on a Bahamian lawyer. But I might need one if Bahamian bureaucracy asserted authority over the yacht. The best way to avoid pests is to leave nothing that will attract them in the first place. I spent some time formulating oral statements that I would make to the Bahamian police and customs officials. I worked them up as a half dozen sound bites that would reveal me as an expert on maritime law who would stoutly defend his rights:

"Were it not for the dead man on board and the need to bring the crime to the *immediate attention* of the nearest police authority, we would have taken the salvaged yacht directly to its home port of Miami."

I practiced laying in a respectful pause and viewing the official with a diffuse gaze.

"It is, of course, unnecessary to say that the Bahamian Government has no jurisdiction over my salvage claim."

I practiced waiting him out until he backed down. And I practiced a response if he turned argumentative.

"Of course I would be glad to render a written statement to that effect, if I were furnished with the name, title and address of the responsible official on the Bahamian side."

I practiced those sound bites until they rolled off my lips with ease. Eventually I stopped pacing. I sat down and went back to thinking.

Maybe I didn't really have to deal with Bahamian authority. Palm Beach was only 60 miles to the west. The rubber foam on my patch was fluttering, but it was holding well. The bilge pump was clicking on only once every 10 minutes. The engines were doing fine and the gauges said we had plenty of fuel. We could make the Port of Palm Beach in about 11 hours. We could hand the murder investigation over to the Palm Beach Sheriffs Department. They would investigate the murder professionally.

Or would Palm Beach complain that my actions had caused an intolerable delay? Would they accuse me of obstructing justice? West End was only four hours away. Maybe International Law actually required us to go to the nearest port with police authority, even if the crime was committed in International Waters.

Where had the murder taken place, anyway? When we discovered the yacht, it had been coming from southwest by south. That direction took in a slice of the Little Bahama Bank and then the Straits of Florida. I hadn't found any charts on board, but I didn't really need any right now. I knew this part of the Bahamas like the palm of my hand. In fact that was exactly how the Little Bahama Bank looked — like the palm of my *right* hand. I held it in front of me, horizontally. My thumb formed the north side of the Bank. Beyond it was the Atlantic Ocean.

My little finger formed the Grand Bahama Island, which lies on the south side of the Bank. And the rest of my palm and fingers was the Bank, a big expanse of shallow water, six to 18 feet deep. Beyond my fingertips, to the west, were the Straits of Florida and then the Florida coast. It wasn't a bad map, my flattened hand. The place where we'd found the *Second Chance* was half an inch north of the last joint of my index finger. At the present moment, we were at the tip of my longest finger, at the western edge of the Bank. And at the tip of my little finger was our destination, West End, so named because it was on the western tip of Grand Bahama Island. The Island is long and narrow. On my improvised map it took in the little finger and the edge of the hand that delivers a karate chop.

I stared at my improvised map for a long time, trying to figure out where the *Second Chance* had been eight hours before we found it. If it had been traveling straight and steady all that time, it would have started out between 16 and 23 nautical miles southwest by south of where we found it. That would be on the pad of my longest finger. That would put the murder on the Little Bahama Bank, inside Bahamian jurisdiction.

A problem with that simple calculation was that it had the yacht moving over a lot of shallow water — sand bores and fish muds — where it should have run aground. Another problem with that straight-line calculation was that it didn't take into account the influence of wind, tides and ocean currents. The night before, we'd had a strong northwesterly wind that weakened and shifted to northerly before dawn. The wind would have been pushing the yacht southeastward, bending its course. The murder could have taken place in the Straits of Florida.

Staring at my hand again, I factored in the currents this time. In the middle of the Straits of Florida, the Gulf Stream flows northward at about four knots. Along the edge of Little Bahama Bank it moves at only one knot. Where the Gulf Stream passes the northern edge of the Little Bahama Bank there would probably be eddy currents. Taking all this into account, I got a much different result: The murder was probably committed in the Gulf Stream, 10 to 20 miles due west of West End.

I was proud of having done these vector calculations in my head. But I would have been happier if the result had been 13 to 23 miles west of West End. That would have put the murder completely outside of Bahamian jurisdiction. I was about to launch into a new set of calculations to see if the result could be moved a few miles westward when I stopped myself:

No, Ben, you can't do that. A scientist lives by a code of intellectual honesty. And the scarcer the facts and the more complicated the calculations, the more important it is that you keep to that code. West End is now only 30 miles away and you must lose no time in turning the crime over to police authority. Do your good citizen's duty.

Basta! Enough! That's what my Italian grandfather would have said.

My eyes returned to my hand. It was shaking. And while wondering why, I came up with an uncomfortable thought: Had the murderer operated out of West End? What would the murderer think when he saw me pulling in with the resurrected *Second Chance*?

I scanned the horizon. There was one sport fisherman about 10 miles to the west. And West End's water tower was now emerging before me like the tip of a ballpoint pen held at arm's length. It was still far away.

As the day wore on, I thought more about the crime. Eventually I came up with an idea for a new calculation. I punched in the autopilot and went below to get a small drill bit. Probing with it carefully in the chest wound, I found that the hole pointed upwards at an angle of around 30 degrees. I took another temperature reading for Rebecca, then went back to the flybridge. Before calling her, I took another look at the radar display. It was showing two big blotches straight ahead. The outer one was the West End water tower. The other was the *Diogenes*. And the rest of the screen was pocked with false returns. I turned the unit off.

I got Rebecca on Channel 13 and told her about my calculations and my plans for dealing with Bahamian authorities. And I said that the murderer would feel threatened by us. "We're going to keep a low profile when we arrive."

"I agree," Rebecca said.

"We won't tell the people about our temperature measurements, the vessel's course, or my calculations. We'll save that for the police."

"Roger that."

"We'll tell the police about our qualifications. They'll need to know that for their investigation. But we shouldn't let people know that you're a physician and I'm a scientist. The less they know about that, the better."

"I agree, but if we give them a complete lie then we'll seem all the more suspicious if they find out."

"I agree. I'll say I'm a patent evaluator."

"Good. They may not ask me, but if they do I'll say I'm a world health policy evaluator."

"And since we're coming into radio range for West End, even for one watt, we won't be able to talk like this any more."

"Roger. But keep calling in the temperature readings as long as you can."

Rebecca had never been to West End. I had sailed into it once, a couple of years before I'd met her. I told her about the shoals and currents around the channel leading into the West End marina and how I wanted us to maneuver, once we reached its mouth.

"When are you going to tell them we're coming, Ben?"

"When we are abreast of West End."

"It seems clear to me, Ben."

"I'm going in there as the salvage master of the *Second Chance*, which I am returning to its home port in Miami. Officially, the only reason I am stopping at West End is to turn the body over to the nearest police authority."

"I read you loud and clear, Captain."

"Great. From now on we monitor Channel Sixteen. I'm over and out on Thirteen."

"Over and out, Ben."

Over the next hour or so, the West End water tower grew from the size of a pen tip, to a thimble, to a red and white mushroom. And it was all too soon that we came abreast of it. At 3:17 p.m., I threw over the wheel. The low November sun moved from my shoulder to my back. Although we had been in transit over seven hours, I hadn't thought enough about the salvage work at the dock and dealing with the people at the marina. Well, I would just improvise. That's how I do my best work, anyway. I picked up the hand-held, now set for Channel Sixteen, and squeezed down.

"Ben Candidi calling West End Marina." I repeated it three times, paused, and repeated it three more times.

"West End Marina to Candidi. Please switch to Channel Twenty-Four." The voice was Bahamian, female and businesslike.

"Negative. Please stay on Sixteen and listen carefully. This is an emergency. I am two miles west of you and am approaching. I am at the helm of the sport fisherman yacht, the *Second Chance,* which I discovered and salvaged in International Waters several minutes before it would have sunk. I am requesting a temporary berth."

"You are salvaging the *Second Chance.*" She said it as a statement but meant it as a question. And there was no question that she knew the vessel.

"Affirmative. And I will need to be directed to the shallowest berth you have. I will need men and four dock lines. Additionally, I am requesting that you call the Royal Bahamas Police Force and have them dispatch a homicide detective. When I boarded the vessel, I found a man aboard, dead from gunshot wounds."

"I copy both requests." She said it professionally, with not a trace of excitement.

"One further request. I will be followed in by the thirty-six foot sailing vessel, the *Diogenes,* captained by my partner, Rebecca Levis. Please have someone give her directions to the *deepest* berth you have, and give her help with docking."

To complete the story, I told the marina manager that we had sailed here directly from the Chesapeake Bay.

My message was received by many people. There were a lot of three-second announcements of boat names and channel numbers – listeners announcing to their buddies that they were ready to talk on other channels about what they had just heard.

Rebecca dropped behind as I lined up for the channel. To the right was a rocky seawall; to the left was a large expanse of flats where the water was knee-deep. Rebecca was following about 300 yards behind. For the last minute of approach to the channel, I concentrated on depth and currents. Then I squeezed down.

"Candidi to *Diogenes.* You'll be okay. You will have at least seven feet of water. In the channel, watch for a left-going, two-knot cross-current. I'm having to steer against it by ten degrees."

"I copy that, Candidi. I don't want to end up like the boat to port."

A glance to the left confirmed what she was talking about — the careened, stranded and sun-bleached hull of a full-keeled sailing yacht. The wreck stood in front of a small mangrove island, 400 yards up the flats. Straight ahead was another distraction — a couple of bikini girls on Waverunners, buzzing around in the channel. They should have stayed away and hung to the side, like the dark-haired man with the yellow Waverunner. He slid in close enough for me to see the tattoo on his shoulder, but he didn't get in the way.

I moved through the channel past the entrance to the modest-sized "commercial harbor." The only sign of commercial activity there was a couple of stacks of pallets. The yacht harbor was the second right. I decreased the revs while closing on the buoy that marked the end of the channel, then executed a sharp right into the marina channel. Although I had been here many years before, I was still amazed at the depth of the cut and the steepness of the coral banks on either side. A row of Australian pines towered on either side. The fuel dock was 100 yards ahead on the right, where the channel opened up into the marina basin.

The marina basin was as I had remembered. It was rectangular, with docks on the seawalls to both left and right side, and with one long wooden dock projecting toward me, dividing the basin and creating two water lanes from which to choose. All the slips were laid out perpendicular to the docks. Quarters were close.

The attendant at the fuel dock gave me hand signals toward the right lane. This required a sharp turn to the right and then to the left to get around a big trawler tied up at the end of the center dock.

Although less than half of the marina's three dozen slips were occupied, it seemed horribly cramped — like a campground that specializes in recreational vehicles. As I completed my turn and my open cockpit area passed the trawler's stern, I heard the first comment: "Oh, God. They killed him." The words were spoken in a New York voice by an old guy sitting at the upper steering station of the trawler.

Obviously, our sheet did not hide the outlines of the human body.

Straight ahead, at the end of the lane, were a bare seawall and the marina office. Standing at the edge, a well-dressed Island woman was motioning me to come forward.

On the next boat to my left — a large Hatteras — a pretty blond-haired woman was waving to get my attention. She gestured to the end of the lane, where I was heading. "Steve's slip is over there," she yelled, with Southern-accented concern.

Obviously, the Island woman was the marina manager. She gestured for me to take the final slip on the right. Like all the slips along the west wall of the basin, it consisted of a narrow dock jutting out from the seawall on one side and two poles to define its other side. Two local guys were standing on that last dock, holding ropes for me. Getting into that slip required a sharp turn to the right in close quarters. As I counter-rotated the props, I sensed the apprehension of my soon-to-be next door neighbor standing on his mid-size Bayliner. Meanwhile, my across-the-lane neighbor was standing on the bow of his large Bertram with a boat pole in hand like he was ready to fend me off, if necessary. He was middle-aged and wore his gray hair in a Caesar cut. As my boat slowly rotated on its axis and my transom turned toward him, he peered down on it as if mesmerized. But he snapped out of it as soon as I completed the maneuver and began to inch forward into the space between the dock and the two pilings. He jumped off his boat and onto the large dock. He ran along the seawall, past the well-dressed marina manager and toward my dock.

The two dockhands were standing by, ready to throw ropes.

"Don't anybody come aboard," I yelled to them. "This is a crime scene."

Caesar Haircut stood at the edge of the seawall, ready to push back my bow if I didn't stop in time.

A couple of seconds with the props in reverse brought the boat to a halt in the right place. What a relief to put the throttle levers in neutral! I scrambled below to secure two starboard dock lines. The guys handed me two more lines to throw over the pilings on the other side. After securing those lines, I repeated my keep-off-the-boat order on my hand-held radio. It was eerie, hearing my voice from several directions in the marina. It seemed like everybody was tuned into Channel 16 with the volume up high.

Caesar Haircut had stationed himself at the base of the narrow dock that I shared with the Bayliner. He kept himself busy holding back onlookers.

With regal bearing, the marina manager worked her way through the gathering crowd and addressed me. "The police are on their way." Her voice was the same as on the radio. "Is there anything else I can do?"

"Yes, I would like to hire these two men," I answered, making eye contact with the older of the two dockhands. "Sir, I'm ready to pay you and your buddy fifteen dollars an hour, starting right now."

"No problem," he said. "My name is Edgar." He was middle-aged, healthy, and seemed to have enough muscle for the job.

"Great. My name is Ben. I saw a stack of pallets on the dock of the commercial harbor. Bring them here. I need to get them under the boat to stabilize it."

"No problem." He spoke with an Island accent, but with the hard undertones you might expect from a foreman.

"And if you can find some rocks to weight the pallets down, that would be good, too."

Edgar and his younger buddy went off in the direction of the pallets and the dockmistress went off in the direction of her office. It was time to thank the paunchy middle-aged guy with the Caesar haircut and the Bertram. "Thanks for the help with crowd control."

He waved a big hand and a pudgy forearm in a quarter arc. "Think nothing of it. My name's Wade. Wade Daniels."

It was a stroke of luck that he'd stepped in because a crowd was growing. They were a fifty-fifty mix of boat owners and Islanders, fanned out along the bend in the seawall in front of the marina office. From ten yards, they all had an unobstructed view of the *Second Chance*'s damaged port side but couldn't see the white-shrouded dead man. However, a lot of people had crowded the top deck and bow of Wade Daniels' Bertram, and they were looking down on my cockpit, seeing everything. There was no time to think about public relations. I had a salvage job to complete.

Looking over the port rail, I was pleased to see the rubber foam was still bulging through the hand-sized hole in the hull, just below the waterline. The depth sounder said there were three feet of water under the hull. A glance at the barnacle-encrusted pilings holding up the dock told me that the tide was rising and had another foot to go before it crested. That would probably take two more hours. Sunset would come in about two hours, with darkness shortly after that.

Edgar and his buddy deposited a couple of pallets on the seawall and went off to get more.

While checking the rope locker, I looked up to see Rebecca coming up the dock. With no visible change in her bouncy stride, she negotiated the four-foot drop from the dock to the yacht's cockpit, throwing in a couple of steps along starboard rail to ease the transition. She threw an arm over my shoulder, leaned into me for a kiss, and spoke to me in a semi-whisper.

"Everyone was so focused on you, Ben, that there was nobody to help me dock the boat. But don't worry, I didn't scrape anything."

"You did great." I kissed her on the cheek.

Continuing in a soft voice, she said, "I agree with you about keeping it low key, but I *should* take a look at the body to assess blood pooling."

"Right," I said.

She peeked under the sheet to examine the corpse.

I knelt beside her. "And you can sign off on my observations."
I didn't notice the flashing lights. I didn't notice him, either, until he stepped aboard.

3   Bahamian Constabulary

"Sergeant Leonard Townsend of the Royal Bahamas Police Force," he announced with an unfriendly voice in baritone register. I looked up to see a muscular Bahamian staring down at me. He cut a handsome figure in his uniform: blue pants with a red stripe down the side like the U.S. Marines; semiautomatic pistol snapped inside a black leather holster at his side; and a closely fitted white shirt. It was a seersucker weave, with narrow and closely spaced vertical blue stripes. Chevrons on each arm confirmed his rank.

Sgt. Townsend shifted his stare to Rebecca. She let go of the shroud as if on command.

Getting to my feet, I noticed that Sgt. Townsend wouldn't have any height advantage. He was about five-nine, just like me.

I took a deep breath and answered with a full voice. "We found the body. That is, I found the body. I'm Benjamin Candidi. This is Rebecca Levis."

Rebecca rose and stood at my side.

I waited a few seconds for Townsend to offer his hand, which he didn't. He didn't say anything either. I used the time to look around. On the dock stood Townsend's sidekick — a younger, thinner guy in tennis shoes, a blue jumpsuit and police ball cap. And at the head of the dock stood a dark blue jeep, its engine running and red emergency light flashing. The gold crest with velvet-fitted crown painted on its door matched the symbols on the Sergeant's shoulders. And a cloth bar pinned through the Sergeant's shirt at pocket level identified him as "1444."

"You found the body like this?" he asked, with skepticism.

"Just like this, right where it's lying."

"Exactly like this?"

"Yes."

Sgt. Townsend responded after a long silence. "*Covered* like this?"

"No," I replied, perhaps a bit too impatiently. "I put it on. It's our sheet. Rebecca threw it over to me." I waited for Sgt. Townsend to nod or say something. "It's unused and clean. It seemed the decent thing to do."

How irritating when they use silence as an interrogation tactic.

"And why were you on this yacht?"

I looked around and saw plenty of spectators, but all were too far away to hear. Most of them were standing along the seawall, on the two-foot-wide strip of concrete that capped the basin's rough coral wall. Those people definitely wouldn't hear. Wade Daniels was still doing crowd control at the head of the dock, keeping people away but looking toward us most of the time. He wouldn't hear if we kept our voices down. The Sergeant had been talking loudly. Maybe he was feeling competition from the engines, which were also operating at baritone frequency.

I turned sideways to the guy and moved a little closer. Speaking in my natural tenor range, I didn't have to raise my voice to compete with the gurgling diesels. I tried for an earnest expression. "Sergeant Townsend, we discovered this yacht foundering in International Waters, thirteen miles north of the Little Bahama Bank. We discovered it at six forty-five this morning while *en route* from Washington, DC. When I boarded the yacht to rescue it from imminent sinking, I discovered the body. I made temporary repairs that reversed the flooding." I looked for a nod of approval and received none, not even a blink. "Look, we have diverted our salvage operation to bring the body to you, as the nearest police authority capable of investigating the murder."

"I see."

Sgt. Townsend stepped forward and knelt, forcing Rebecca to step back. He used his left hand to lift the shroud carefully, not more than one foot. I glanced around, worrying that someone might see underneath. No, the people on the seawall couldn't see over the yacht's rail and the people on Wade Daniels' yacht were looking down from the wrong angle.

Sgt. Townsend frowned, then pointed a stubby finger at the victim's bare rear end and the protruding thermometer. He shook his head. "You found the body exactly like that?"

I answered him on the bounce. "No, it wasn't a rape-homicide. I pulled his pants down to insert a fever thermometer."

Deftly Rebecca dropped to one knee and retrieved the thermometer, snapping it into a small plastic case she'd brought along. Returning to her feet, she said, "He did it under my instructions. We did it to be able to give you a time-of-death estimate."

When Sgt. Townsend responded with a silent stare, Rebecca pretended not to notice. "I'm a medical doctor and he's a scientist. We recorded temperatures every half hour. The measurements indicate the death was eight hours before we found the body. That makes it ten-forty, last night."

Sgt. Townsend dropped the shroud and rose to his feet. "Are you a specialist in forensic medicine?"

"Estimating time of death is part of the standard medical school curriculum in the United States." She answered neutrally but she blinked under the force of his stare. "And Dr. Candidi has made a lot of careful observations that you should hear."

Slowly, Sgt. Townsend turned his dark brown eyes to me.

Exerting considerable willpower to maintain a relaxed posture, I turned to the side and drew a step closer. Standing at short range would give me an excuse to ignore his eyes. "Look, Sergeant, there are a lot of people watching us and I don't want them to see me pointing a lot of things out to you. I'd just like to tell you the facts right here and now and then *you* can confirm them."

"Very well."

I told him how I'd jumped onto the boat and salvaged it. I told him about the position of the body, about finding night vision goggles, and the cocked pistol on the seat on the flybridge and that he could find it up there in the drink holder. I told him about the blood spatter from the head shot and that I believed that the chest shot came in at an upward angle. And I told him that the autopilot and the navigation lights were on.

Townsend said nothing while I gave him the facts. But I didn't let his silent treatment jar me, either. I just told the story at my own pace. Nods from Rebecca told me I was doing okay. When I finished, Townsend pulled out a little notebook and made some notes. When he closed the book, I had more to say:

"Here's what we think happened. The victim was standing on the flybridge with a loaded and cocked pistol. The murderer shot him in the chest from below. The victim dropped the pistol onto the seat up there and he fell to the cockpit floor. There, he received an executioner's shot to the back of the head. Then the gunman got off the boat and tried to sink it by shooting holes in it at the waterline. And he would have succeeded if we'd come half an hour later."

Sgt. Townsend shook his head. "I would be very careful about making interpretations. They can cause you a lot of trouble."

Was I dealing with a crooked cop who had a stake in this matter? "I don't completely understand. Could you explain what you mean?"

Sgt. Townsend looked at the crowd on the seawall and threw a glance at the people on Wade Daniels' cabin cruiser. "It can be dumb to be too smart."

"And that's exactly what I meant when I said that I didn't want to show you around this yacht in front of all these people. And that's why we're not going to tell them that Dr. Levis is a physician and that I'm a pharmacologist. And we don't want you to tell anyone anything, either. Just your superiors. For all we know, the murderer is looking at us right now. My unofficial story is that we don't have any idea how it happened."

"That's right," Rebecca added. "We're going to tell people that Ben was too busy keeping the boat afloat to even *look* at the body."

A small smile came to the Sergeant's face. "You are both very wise. And since we do understand each other, I will make it very easy for you. I am designating this yacht as a crime scene. I am asking you to step off this boat and stay off of it."

Rebecca took that as a command and made for the dock. But I held my ground and answered loudly. "Sorry, Sergeant, but the boat is still in danger of sinking. As the salvage captain, it is my right and duty to stay with the boat."

He turned to face me squarely. If physical intimidation was his game, his body gave him a definite advantage over me. His arms and upper body carried twice the muscle, his chest was huge, and he had the neck of a wrestler. His big head and heavy-duty, square-set jaw were intimidating, too. But I didn't think he would dare to lay hands on me in front of all these people. I stared back at him, trying to act curious as to what he would say.

He took his time answering. And when he did, he answered loudly as if speaking as much to the crowd as to me. "Very well, Mr. Candidi, you may stay on the boat to complete your salvage. However, you must help enforce my order that *nobody* else comes aboard."

I retreated one step and shouted back at him. "Nobody else except for Rebecca Levis."

He didn't answer. He knelt over the dead man, reached under the shroud and searched pockets, finding nothing.

I glanced at the crowd. Most of them were watching me. I played the role of the worried salvage man, leaning over the side and starring at my foam rubber patch. Soon a few of them started pointing it out to their neighbors.

Sgt. Townsend moved to the main salon. I watched him through the door. He moved around with a sure-footed walk, making a quick, efficient search. He had excellent eye-hand coordination, and, considering his stout build, he had a remarkable ability to position his body for tasks at any level. He was all muscle and no paunch.

I shouted in to him. "Where you are standing, the water was up to your waist."

"As I have already noticed," he answered.

On the edge of the seawall, the pile of pallets was growing. I yelled to Edgar, "I'll need a lot more to hold up the boat."

Edgar understood, and so did the crowd. With that taken care of, I went inside the main salon to check with Sgt. Townsend. His search for personal items had turned up nothing but a couple of changes of clothes hanging in a forward locker. Mounted on the wall behind a piece of clear plastic, we found a Coast Guard Documentation Certificate. It bore the same number that was painted on the bow. The certificate listed only a corporation with a Miami post office box as the boat's owner and operator. Townsend wrote it down, and so did I.

Reflected daylight was strong enough to keep anybody from seeing in through the three big windows. Away from public scrutiny, Sgt. Townsend seemed a little more friendly and maybe even approachable.

"Sergeant," I said, "when you find this guy's name and address, I would appreciate your giving it to me. I'll need that for my salvage claim."

"How big a claim are you making?" He was still playing the boss man, but curiosity was starting to show.

"For fifty percent of the boat's true market value, plus expenses."

He smiled like he knew better. "I wish you luck. What do you need to do to complete the salvage?"

"I need to brace the boat to lift the port side a few inches out of the water. Then I'll lay on a fiberglass patch. With a little luck, I can have it finished by tomorrow. But, like I said, I will need my partner here to help me."

"Very well. Just be sure you don't disturb anything." He moved toward the door. "Now, I need you to turn off the engines. I want to speak to the crowd."

"Sorry, but I can't do that. I need electricity to keep the yacht afloat and I don't know if the batteries can hold a charge."

"Very well."

He went out to the open cockpit and made a full-throated announcement for all to hear, saying he was a police officer, that the man under the sheet had been murdered, and could anyone identify him.

Wade Daniels, the crowd-control volunteer, walked up the dock. With slow eyes, he surveyed the open cockpit. "It is probably Steve. It's his boat."

The Sergeant pulled back the sheet just enough to reveal the victim's face.

"That's him," Wade Daniels said. "Poor guy."

Sgt. Townsend dropped the shroud. "What's his last name?"

Wade Daniels' eyes were amazingly still. "I don't know. He's only been here for a week or so . . . on this boat."

Sgt. Townsend resumed his address to the crowd on the seawall, saying that if anyone had information about the man who captained this boat, please see Constable Walker. That was the name of his sidekick in the blue jumpsuit.

When no one came forward, the Sergeant gave the cockpit a good looking over and went up to the flybridge. Rebecca returned with a load of things from the *Diogenes*. It was as if she had read my mind. She brought a diving mask, diving light, tools, scissors, fiberglass cloth, resin, catalyst, paint brushes and a can to mix it up in. She even gave me money to pay Edgar and his buddy who had now assembled a big pile of pallets along the seawall. Two uniformed customs agents were standing impatiently at the end of the dock, wanting to go home. I asked Rebecca to take care of formalities for herself and the *Diogenes*.

Sgt. Townsend left the boat and walked to the crowd, apparently to interview people about the victim.

Before starting work, I flipped on the cabin and deck lights. It would be growing dark soon enough. I stripped down to my Jockey shorts and let myself over the port side. The water came up to my chest. The bottom was about four inches of ooze on top of rough coral rock. That would be just right for stacking pallets under the boat. Edgar and his friend were still standing by their pile of pallets and stones. As I waded toward them, the water got shallower. They handed me down a pallet and I weighted it by jamming in stones. Getting it settled under the stern was no trouble. Soon I had a whole column of them under the port side of the stern.

Night was coming on fast but the deck light helped some and the marina had a few widely spaced streetlights. A dozen spectators remained, watching the lit-up *Second Chance* from the bend in the seawall.

I had almost completed a second column on the starboard side when an orange-and-white ambulance arrived with flashing red lights. A stretcher team got out and Sgt. Townsend conducted them aboard. Their movements rocked the boat and that helped me to snug in the last pallet. I secured the column with rope.

Rebecca was watching from the dock. "Ben, you be careful under there. It could shift and trap you."

"I'm being careful. I've even been careful about breathing around the diesel exhausts."

"Good. What's the salvage plan?"

"I have two columns supporting the stern. I'm going to place a third one under the bow, right on the 'V.' When the tide goes down, the boat will be resting on them and the hole will be out of the water. Then I'm going to fiberglass it over. Tomorrow, when the tide comes up again, the boat will float off — without any help from the bilge pump."

Sgt. Townsend heard some of this. He reboarded the yacht and looked down at me from over the side.

"Mr. Candidi, will you please tell me what you are planning to do?"

"I'm going to patch the hole in the boat like I was just saying to Rebecca. After we're done here, I plan to return the boat to its home port of Miami and file a salvage claim. With that out of the way, I'll return here and we'll make up for lost time on our vacation. We'll sail our *Diogenes* to the Abacos and then to the Berry Islands."

"You realize that I have jurisdiction over the boat. It is a crime scene."

"Yes," I said, not wanting to argue with him in public.

I went back to work, building a column of pallets under the bow. When I finished, I thanked and paid Edgar and his friend, saying I would no longer need them. When I stepped back onto the *Second*

Chance, Sgt. Townsend was aboard, telling his Constable Walker to rig the boat with yellow tape.

"This is an official crime scene," he said, gruffly. "And all are forbidden to enter it. You may only enter as necessary for the safety of the boat. The constable will enforce it."

"Great. Could you introduce me to the constable and tell me his name?"

"Constable Ivanhoe Walker."

The Constable acknowledged me with a wide, friendly smile that included a prominent gold tooth.

"Pleased to meet you, Constable Walker. I look forward to working with you."

The Constable's smile disappeared quickly when he noticed that his boss was looking.

"You will obey his instructions," Sgt. Townsend said.

"No problem," I answered.

IDLING DIESELS throbbed and the pallets creaked and groaned at us through the hull as the ebbing tide set the boat down on its improvised cradle. Sgt. Townsend had been gone for a long time. Rebecca had just returned from locking up the *Diogenes*. Now she was keeping me company in the main salon of *Second Chance*. In a fresh blouse, shorts and Oregon rafting sandals, she sat on a soggy cushion, leaning her back against the bulkhead and resting her thin, shapely legs on the dinette table.

I was sitting on the other side of the table with screwdriver in hand, taking a break from work. I took a second to admire Rebecca's lovely face and rested my eyes on interesting contours around her thin neck and collar bone. Then I glanced down through the access hole in the bench for another look at my patch. Although I knew that the *Second Chance* was sitting firmly on solid supports, a part of my brain said that the yacht was swaying back and forth in resonance with Atlantic Ocean waves. It would take a day for this curious but well-known neurological effect to wear off. They call it "getting your land legs back."

With darkness outside and the cabin lights on, we could be observed from the outside through the yacht's big windows. But we were innocent, now. The weight of the crime had been lifted onto the broad shoulders of Sgt. Townsend. The corpse was gone, and so was the pool of blood. Ditto for the night vision goggles and the revolver. We kept the cabin door open to let in the night air.

"Thanks, Darling, for bringing me these corned-beef sandwiches. I was running on empty."

"You were running on adrenaline." A teasing smile widened her narrow face. "Adrenaline and *testosterone*."

"Are you talking about my communication with the Good Sergeant?"

"Yes."

"Give me a break."

Rebecca defends herself with *tai chi*. I prefer karate.

I flashed her a grin. "Don't forget that it was my testosterone in defense of your estrogen." I shook my head in mock disappointment. "Can't you see that he's one of your basic male chauvinist misogynists?"

Rebecca laughed. She dug her fingers into her long black hair and threw it back. "Very funny, Ben — using my lingo to explain yourself." She dropped her legs and crawled over to see what I was doing under the bench. A couple of black strands dropped over her face. "Hey, why are you loosening the screws from your patch? The hole's not out of the water, yet."

I affected a jocular mood.

"That's just it. I'm about to make a scientific measurement."

"I see."

I released the final screw and water came gushing in and splashing up. Rebecca squeaked and retreated. Feigning nonchalance, I pushed the timer button on my watch. "I'm going to measure how long it takes for the water to rise a couple of inches, fighting the bilge pump."

Water came flowing out from under the bench. It streamed across the floor to the two-by-three foot opening where I'd removed the access hatch. It fell into the open bilge and the pump switched on. While we watched the contest being played out in the open bilge I ate a second sandwich. Water rose in the bilge. Slowly it crept along the floor of the V-berth up front.

One-half an hour into the experiment, Rebecca offered a commentary. "The water's rising, but the pump's doing a pretty good job holding it back."

"Yes, the level is rising at approximately one and a half inches per ten minutes," I said. "That's about right for the boat taking eight hours to flood the way I found it."

"Ben and his calculations!"

She said it with a giddy laugh. How many times her laugh had cheered me over the last several years! That's what we needed tonight — a good laugh.

I made a face. "You want the details? Then here goes." I slipped into a parody of a high school physics teacher, increasing pitch and tempo. "Eight hours equals four hundred and eighty minutes, times one and a half inches per ten minutes equals seventy-two inches. But since the floor area that it's flooding now has only half the area that will eventually be flooded — because of the deep V shape of the hull — the final answer will be only half as many inches, or thirty-six." I gave Rebecca a frown, like the teacher had turned impatient. "And that corresponds to 'up to your ass in seawater.'"

"Excuse me," came a voice from behind us. I looked back to see a muscular guy about my age standing in the companionway, leaning with one hand against the door frame. Like me, he sported a lot of curly black chest hair. But the similarity ended there. "Can't you turn off those engines?" It was more of a demand than a request, and he made no effort to suppress his irritation. "Look, you're berthed right next to us and my girlfriend can't sleep. And the damn diesel exhaust's a bitch to breathe."

"I'm sorry, but we're still in a state of emergency. I should be able to turn the engines off when I get a solid patch on. We'll be able to start work on that in another hour."

His forearm was tense and his right hand was in a fist. "What do you need the diesels on for?"

"To power the bilge pump . . . and in case I have to ground this boat somewhere to keep it from going under."

He was handsome enough, with dark, widely spaced eyes and a broad forehead. But he didn't know a thing about charm. Like the Sergeant, he was doing too much staring and not enough thinking. "Why can't you use shore power to run your bilge pump?"

"Because the power converter's been under water. I don't know if it will work. Same deal for the batteries and starter motors that I'll need to restart the engines."

He looked away. "Well, it's a real bitch trying to sleep next to this thing."

"And it's been a real bitch for us, finding this thing." I got up, and took a couple of steps toward him, making sure to splash some of the inflowing water in the process. I extended my hand. "I'm Ben and this is Rebecca. What's your name?"

"Martin Becker." He shook my hand with a firm grip and nodded to Rebecca who was resting against the bulkhead. She nodded to him, then returned her eyes to the slowly rising water in the bilge. Becker frowned.

"And what's your girlfriend's name?" I asked.

"Beth Owens."

"And you're the one with that sleek Bayliner with the diving flag on the side?"

Rebecca winked approval of my flattery. Sure, that sleek boat would look great skimming along at 30 knots on a balanced plane in the protected waters of some bay. But caught in a winter storm in the Gulf Stream, it would be a rolling death trap.

"Yeah, that's ours," Martin said.

He was wearing a diving watch that was almost as thick as my sandwich.

"Well, Martin, we've got something in common — diving. You know, I don't think the mosquitos are too bad tonight. Maybe the solution would be to take a couple of bench cushions to that thatched pavilion where they have the picnic tables and sleep there. I'm sure everyone will understand."

Martin's eyes turned to the right and he didn't say anything. Slowly his left hand found his right wrist and clasped it. Backing down would be a long, painful process for this guy.

"Say, Martin, how did you get past the policeman they posted outside? He's supposed to be guarding the boat as a crime scene."

"The guy's asleep in his car."

"Figures. But his boss, Sgt. Leonard Townsend, is a lot more serious. And I hope you didn't touch anything, because tomorrow he's going to be dusting for fingerprints, trying to find a suspect."

Becker pulled back. "No. Didn't touch anything. I guess I'll be going."

"Nice meeting you, Martin. We'll turn the engines off as soon as we can."

After he left, I consulted my watch and measured the height of the water. I also took a good look under the floorboards and discovered a couple of fresh-water tanks that were three-quarters empty. I thought for a second. Their buoyancy had offset the weight of the diesels. And that was all that had kept the yacht from flooding over its transom and taking a rump-first dive into Davy Jones' locker. I shuddered at the memory of my crawl in that dark engine compartment. When I looked up, Rebecca gave me a wink. "This time you get a good grade on public relations."

"Thanks, but Martin didn't attack you like the Sergeant did. Anyway, we're keeping with the program — playing dumb and telling people we don't know anything."

"You know, Ben, I've been thinking that the best way to handle this would be for me to give the Sergeant a medical affidavit detailing what I found. And you could also write out a statement on the condition of the vessel. Then he wouldn't have to come back and interview us and nobody would see it."

"I agree. We unload all the karma onto Detective Sergeant Leonard Townsend."

Rebecca frowned at the water running over the floor. "What's your next step, Captain?"

"To screw the patch back in and wait for the tide to drop so the hole is out of the water. Then we will fiberglass it over. In the mean time we'll put these soggy cushions out on the dock and we'll hose down this yacht's fine wood, Formica and fabric-covered interior with fresh water. But just the parts that were submerged. We will give special attention to the electric converter, the electric switches, and the starter motors on the diesel motors."

"What do you want me to do with that satellite dish? It looks like it got soaked, too."

"It's an RDF — a radio direction finder. It's an antique. You can soak it in fresh water, then shake it out and hang it up to dry. Same with this hand-held radio that I found swimming around with it."

We discussed how to desalt the bank of electronic equipment to the side of the pilot station. It had gotten sloshed but not dunked. I thought the best treatment would be to spray the outside with a fine mist, working from the bottom up, hoping that the salt would diffuse out and that we wouldn't have to put too much fresh water in. Rebecca agreed, calling it a "sponge bath."

IT WAS WEARY work, hosing the interior as the tide slowly sank and the boat put more and more weight on our improvised platform. Luckily the interior damage was not too bad. Twenty-four hours is not long enough for saltwater to penetrate high-quality marine plywood. Luckily the electric converter was solid-state — sealed as tight as Martin Becker's diving watch. I used the hose liberally in the engine room, paying special attention to the starter motors, alternators and electric switches. Then I handed it off to Rebecca for her fine mist project with the compromised electronics modules.

After an hour or so the hole was three inches above water level. Rebecca went for the camera while I inspected the damage. No question, the shots were from the outside. After Rebecca photographed the holes, I went to work on them with chisel and hand file, preparing the jagged edges. Then we set up as a production team, with Rebecca whipping up small portions of a quick-setting mixture. I soaked the glass fiber cloth with it and laid it over the holes. And I brushed on resin. After it hardened, I let myself down in the water and waded out to apply a layer of fiberglass and resin on the outside. Alternating between the outside and the inside, I laid up a thick patch.

Luck was with us. Rebecca's search of the compartments turned up a shore power cable, which she connected. When I turned off the diesel engines, the electric converter worked. It could charge the batteries and we had lights. And when I pushed the starter buttons, the diesel engines sprang back to life. Mission accomplished! Rebecca had scavenged a hasp and combination lock off the rope locker of the *Diogenes*. We fitted them on the *Second Chance*.

After applying one final layer to the patch, I turned everything off and we locked up the boat. We walked off the dock, past Ivanhoe sleepily ensconced in a ratty-looking subcompact car, past the closed marina office, and past many darkened yachts to the other side of the marina where the *Diogenes* was berthed. Once aboard, I lay down and fell asleep instantly.

4   Local Knowledge

Olfactory stimulation was beginning to rouse me. Sunlight was penetrating my eyelids. I raised one of them — the one closest to my Timex Ironman digital watch. My sluggish brain registered 10:15 a.m.

I opened my eyes wider and they reported images: shapely legs, broad hips and a flat stomach. Over time, the images coalesced into the svelte figure of Rebecca Levis moving around in the galley area. With great effort, I raised my head. Rebecca had performed a miracle on our alcohol-burning stove — pancakes and sausage! I climbed out of bed.

"Rebecca, babe, you deserve a big kiss for this," I said. She giggled as I delivered it.

"Prepared fresh from pancake mix, powdered egg, condensed milk and sausage straight from the can," she continued, with a mixture of enthusiasm and irony.

"Well, I love you anyway," I said.

She flipped a pancake onto a plate and gave it to me. I set it down and gave her another kiss.

Before eating, I slipped into my surfer jams and climbed the ladder to the cockpit for a look around. We occupied the outermost berth on the east dock, close to the Australian-pine-lined channel through which we'd entered the day before. The *Second Chance* was kitty-corner, across the marina and wasn't visible. The view was blocked by boats tied up to the long center dock. The marina was less than half-full and some of the boats seemed unoccupied. That was typical for the Bahamas in November. There was no family trade. No kids running around the docks. Summer vacation was over and the Gulf Stream was too tricky for a fair-weather captain to bring his family over here for the weekend. No, the boat-owners here now were a couple of grades saltier — liveaboards, sport fishermen, divers and other categories. Most were independently wealthy or, at least, had sources of income that did not involve manning someone else's desk. And many would have sources of income that they couldn't talk about.

I looked to the east. Beyond a thin row of Australian pines was a vast expanse of shallow water — the Little Bahama Bank — and a long stretch of beach which was the beginning of the northern coast of the Grand Bahama Island. A mile down the coast, a lot of recreation equipment was assembled on a beach. A couple of windsurfers were gliding on the water.

Rebecca called up from the galley. "If you're worrying about the *Second Chance*, don't. I checked it out this morning and it's doing fine."

"Thanks." I leaned in and gave my dark-haired, green-eyed ocean lady another kiss. But before going below I took another look around.

Our immediate neighbor was a 20-foot daysailer with an outboard motor and a small cabin in which the occupants seemed to still be sleeping. Beyond that was a semi-covered Boston Whaler. It wasn't much over 20 feet long but it had two enormous Mercury outboards and a grossly exaggerated tuna tower that must have gone up 30 feet. Shielding my eyes with an out-stretched hand, I looked up toward the sun. A man was up there, hunched over the controls. He didn't return my wave.

Returning to the cabin, I helped Rebecca convert the bed to a dinette. I lavished praise on her culinary handiwork as she set it on the table.

"Consider yourself fortified for a big day," she said. "It will include a visit to the dock office and formalities with the customs officers. I registered with them yesterday as the captain of the *Diogenes* with no passengers. That leaves you as the salvage captain of the *Second Chance*."

"Good thinking."

Rebecca sat down with her own plate. "And I told them that you were dealing with a dangerous situation and wouldn't be able to go to them until this morning.

"Great thinking." I leaned forward and gave her another kiss.

She smiled at the attention. "What is on your own agenda for today?"

"Composing my crime scene affidavit for Sgt. Townsend. It should also be useful for pressing our salvage claim." Below deck, we would not be overheard, but I kept my voice low, anyway. "Did he talk to you any time after he tried to order us off the boat?"

"He came here when I was taking the hasp off the rope locker."

"What did he say?"

"He asked me how we found the *Second Chance* and saved it. I told him and he wrote some of it down."

"Did he give you any information on the victim?"

"I asked him and he said he didn't have any. He said he couldn't find any identification on the man. No driver's license, credit cards or anything."

"Hopefully the Sergeant has a name and address by now. In the mean time, I will make a phone call to the U.S. Coast Guard and ask them to help me get in touch with the 'S.C. Corporation' that is listed on the Coast Guard Documentation Certificate. All it lists is a post office box in Miami. And for the rest of the day, I'll put finishing touches on the repair and respond to matters arising. Which reminds me — could you call the phone company here and have them activate our cellular phones? It's called 'Batelco.'"

"Sure."

"Thanks."

"Oh, Ben, I feel a *project* coming on."

"Yes. If we pull it off right, the salvage will net us one hundred thousand dollars."

"Wow! That's great news." Then a frown came over her lovely face. "And the reason you said 'pull it off' is because there could be complications with the Bahamians and with . . . the people who scuttled the boat."

"Or complications with whomever owns the boat. It might not be owned by the victim."

The frown deepened. "Will the salvage project get us in trouble?"

"Not if I can get that smudge pot out of here quickly. Not after I get it on solid ground in Miami."

We were interrupted by a slight rocking of the boat and footsteps in the cockpit. It was Sgt. Townsend. When we both looked up, he was standing before the companionway, looking in but not saying a thing.

"Hey, Sergeant," I called up to him. "I might have given you permission to come aboard, but never with leather-soled shoes."

He was dressed like the previous evening but this time he was wearing sunglasses. "And I did not give you permission to place a padlock on the *Second Chance*," he replied tensely.

Rebecca's hand came down on my forearm. I gave her a nod as a promise to not go over the top, this time.

"It's a combination lock. Rebecca — Dr. Levis — took it off our rope locker. Consider it to be our contribution to crime scene integrity. Ivanhoe was asleep on his steed, last night." I looked for a reaction and got none. "He was sleeping in his car."

"What is the combination?"

I wouldn't tell him that because it was the same as the rest of our locks, including the one to the companionway, hanging open on its hasp just a couple of feet from his face. "We're not giving out the combination. But we'll open the lock whenever you need to get in."

"Then you must open it for me now."

"Gladly," I said, with a glance to Rebecca.

All I needed to look presentable was my Swarthmore College

T-shirt. I pulled it down over my head and got up to lead Sgt. Townsend off the boat. The people on the daysailer were up, now — a thin guy in his mid-twenties with a head of thick, unruly, dirty-blond hair and a Jesus beard, and his girl, an emaciated strawberry blond who looked a few years younger. They were dressed like hippies. He wore full-length jeans with no shirt and she had on a semi-transparent dress that was probably manufactured in India. I gave them a wave.

I also waved to the tuna tower guy as we walked past. He was sitting on a "fighting chair" mounted on the back of his Boston Whaler. Those chairs are designed for reeling in marlins and other so-called big game fish. His buddy was sleeping in a small enclosure up front. A few steps later, I waved to an older guy sitting in the cockpit of a yacht named *Engineuity*. Passing the center dock and the marina office, there was nobody to greet. The Sergeant and I didn't have any small talk for each other.

Ivanhoe was standing guard at the base of the small dock that the *Second Chance* shared with the diving couple's Bayliner. I stepped up the pace to pull ahead of the Sergeant, gave Ivanhoe a naval salute in passing, and hopscotched over the cushions that Rebecca had laid out on the dock to dry. I sprang aboard and dialed in the combination on the four embedded wheels and pulled off the brass lock before the Sergeant could catch up. I opened the door for him. Then I clamped the lock back on the opened hasp, taking care to turn all four wheels so that the combination would not show.

"There you are," I said to Sgt. Townsend as he huffed aboard. "Have fun. And let me know when you're done so I can lock up."

"I will still need the combination."

"No, that won't be necessary," I said, following him in. "I plan to be here twenty-four-seven until you are through with your investigation."

He responded with a snort. "I noticed that you have fiberglassed over the hole. Your salvage is completed."

"Negative. I still need to protect the engines from the saltwater exposure and try to rescue the electronics."

The Sergeant's mouth dropped open for a second, then his lips closed and tightened. "Very well, but you are to keep all other people off the boat. And you are not to move the boat until I relinquish jurisdiction."

"Okay. But you should do the fingerprints right away. They are decaying by the minute. And when you do get around to dusting for them, I suggest that you pay special attention around the cleats on the transom and on the cockpit's rails."

The Sergeant didn't answer and he didn't seem to agree. This was not the time to tell him that I expected to be able to move the *Second Chance* in three days. What a shame that he had made me argue with him. The Bayliner next door was open; Martin Becker and Beth Owens might have overheard.

Before leaving the Sergeant on the yacht, I took a look over the side. The tide was rising and was now taking much of the yacht's weight from the pallets. Now, the patch was mostly under water and there was no sign of recent bilge pump activity. In a few hours, I'd be able to remove the pallets.

I strolled back toward the *Diogenes*, exchanging greetings with the *Engineuity* guy. He was no transient. He had a dock box with a satellite dish mounted on its lid. The short-haired tuna tower guy's buddy was up, now. They were sitting around in their swimsuits — solid red-and-blue Speedo racing suits — too deeply engaged in conversation to respond to my hello.

I went back to the *Diogenes* to gather my documentation for the visit to Customs. Rebecca went with me. We passed the *Second Chance* and continued along the seawall to their shed. It was a couple of dozen yards inland of the fuel dock. Inside, Rebecca took me to the counter, reached into a box and pulled out several blank forms. The two agents didn't pay much attention to us. They were watching, mirthlessly, a *Seinfeld* rerun. The beat-up TV was apparently getting its signal from the coaxial cable I'd noticed strung through the trees along the way from the marina office. A big noisy through-the-wall air conditioner overrode the audio track and chilled the room down to the dew point, blurring the view of the marina through the room's one small window.

I filled out three pages of a Temporary Cruising Permit application. I crossed out "vessel's master" and wrote that I was the "*salvage* master" of the *Second Chance*. I added a footnote, stating that I had salvaged the vessel in International Waters and that it was now in transit to its home port of Miami. Another page asked for an inventory of my yacht's equipment and a statement of the yacht's value. I filled in $200,000. Then I filled out the Immigration Arrival/Departure Card, tucked it into my passport, and I handed everything to the more senior-looking official, who turned out to be the customs official. He wore a white-over-black uniform with epaulettes that were suggestive of a lieutenant in the Royal Navy. The junior-looking partner, who turned out to be the immigration officer, wore a nondescript brown uniform with small shoulder patches. She didn't look away from the *Seinfeld* episode — apparently an early one because Elaine was wearing a long, yellow, patterned dress with folded-down white socks and black penny loafers.

The customs officer said, "The Cruising Permit will cost one hundred and fifty dollars." He spoke in a soft voice that was difficult to hear over the air conditioner.

"I don't mind paying the fee," I said, handing over three fifty-dollar bills, "but I would like you to note that the vessel will not be used for cruising. I will be returning it to its home port of Miami in the next day or two, as soon as the repairs are completed."

The immigration officer chuckled — not at me but at the TV screen. She was chuckling at Kramer, who had just made a sliding entrance into Jerry Seinfeld's apartment.

"You will still require a permit," the customs officer said, making it sound like I wanted to deprive his country of its deserved foreign currency. He cashiered the three bills, took out his seal, and stamped the forms.

"That's fine with me," I said. It was fine because the Government of the Bahamas had just accepted me as the salvage captain of the *Second Chance* and had stamped its approval on my plan to take the boat to Miami.

The officer handed me back one of the stamped forms. "This is your permission-to-cruise form. You must turn it in here or at your last port before you leave the country, or you must mail it to the main office in Nassau."

"Understood," I said.

He went on to tell me that the reverse side of the form listed the types and quantities of fish, conch and lobster that I had permission to take. Then he handed my passport to the immigration officer. She stamped it and my customs form, telling me I could not engage in any gainful occupation. She said that I was to return the form when I left the country.

Rebecca and I left the Customs/Immigration shed in good spirits. She went back to the *Diogenes* and I went to make arrangements with the marina. The office was in a small, concrete-block building with a flat roof. There were three soft drink machines out front, restrooms and showers on the left side, and a bank of coin-operated washing machines and dryers behind. The office itself occupied the right side of the building and was accessible through a glass-windowed, wooden door in the center. This led to a narrow reception area with several wicker chairs. A wall-mounted TV was showing the same *Seinfeld* episode as in the customs shed. The set was on "mute" and an oversized, through-the-wall air conditioner was doing its best to fill the space with cold air and white noise.

The office was on the far side of the reception area, to the right. I walked up to the Dutch door where they transacted business and leaned in to see who was there. The manager was sitting at a small wooden desk, deeply engrossed in paperwork. I announced my presence with a light cough, but she didn't look up. Like yesterday, her wardrobe wasn't the least bit nautical. She wore a silky buttonless and armless blouse — the type that a girl slithers into. And that's what her feminine assets seemed to be doing underneath — slithering — in resonance with her right arm as she made longhand entries in her ledger book. The blouse was a chocolate brown, one shade darker than her skin. She had a broad forehead, strong cheekbones that formed a broad sloping valley beneath her dark eyes, a generous nose with broad nostrils, and a full mouth. Taut, flat cheeks descended to a gracefully rounded chin. Her straight black hair was swept back and held in place by a broad leopard-spotted band of structured cloth, a statement of pride in her African roots.

She was also taking pride in her work. I caught her with a smile when she looked up. She responded by narrowing her brow and tossing her head. I interpreted this as a warning against acting too familiar.

"Good morning, I'm Ben Candidi."

Her lips thinned and her face stiffened. She said nothing. Grabbing a clipboard, she got up and came around the desk to the Dutch door.

I added, "Thanks for the quick and helpful response yesterday."

I noticed she was a couple of inches taller than me. Her height and slenderness were accentuated by a long, straight beige skirt. The long slit on its left side revealed an attractively thin leg. The straps on her high-heeled sandals were decorated with dark glass beads.

She handed me the clipboard. "The police could come quickly because the West End station is only two miles up the road."

"And Sgt. Townsend is the desk sergeant there?"

Two small creases formed over the bridge of her nose, between those two carefully trimmed and penciled eyebrows. It was just a trace of a frown. "He is in charge of the station and the western portion of Grand Bahama Island," she said crisply. She paused, then gave me instructions at a rapid pace. "Please read the contract carefully before signing. Our rate is one dollar and fifty cents per foot per day, prepaid. Use the out-of-the-water length of your vessel, please."

She spoke like an educated Bahamian, her words well enunciated — over-pronounced, actually — and her inflection in the English style, but lacking the sharp edges and the high resonances of the Ox-Bridge standard to which some aspire. This Bahamian style often includes dropping of voice at the end of each sentence. Americans hearing it for the first time often perceive it as condescending. Although quite used to this, I still felt a gut reaction to her downward inflections on *signing, prepaid* and *please.*

"My *Diogenes* is thirty-six feet, out of the water. But I am not sure what length to write down for the *Second Chance.*"

"You need not worry about the *Second Chance.* You have returned it to its original berth which is prepaid to the end of the month."

I thought for a second. "Very well, then I won't include dockage in my salvage claim against the boat or the victim's estate. His name was Steve. What is his last name, anyway?"

"I do not recall." She said it in a matter-of-fact tone and with no hint of apology. She just stood there, regarding me with inscrutable black eyes. It was hard to tell if they moved when I cast a meaningful glance at her file cabinets. After I raised my eyebrows, she said, "I *cannot* tell you."

I turned my attention to the dockage agreement for the *Diogenes.* I signed at the bottom and filled in the required information — my name, address, home telephone number, names of accompanying persons, and name plus registration number and length of my boat. Obviously she would have gotten this same information for Steve and the *Second Chance.* We would revisit that question. I handed her the clipboard and said, "I would like to pay for eight days."

As fast as these words left my mouth, she told me my total bill. She noticed my surprise at her mental arithmetic. The corners of her mouth went up when I grabbed for my money clip.

"We also take all types of plastic," she said with the tiniest of smiles. She pulled from the wall a plastic-encased, laser-printed sheet and set it on the Dutch door counter before me. It was a rate table. She placed a long, sculpted index fingernail under the entry for eight days and a boat length of 36 feet. She copied the dollar amount onto the contract.

Chagrined, I handed her my American Express card. She wasted no time putting it through her scanning machine. She signed the contract and made a photocopy. What a cold, formal treatment I was receiving from this woman. She offered no small talk while we waited for the credit card authorization to come back. The only noise in the room was from the VHF radio: hailing traffic on Channel 16, which she monitored. She didn't show the slightest uneasiness during our silence. She just stood there, statuesque — a finely rendered and polished statue in tropical hardwood.

The light blinked, and she handed me the contract. I stared at her signature, trying to decipher a name from it. It was formed around an oversized "Z" which was connected with a light upstroke to three sharp peaks which were followed by a resonating trail of indecipherable letters which was underscored and then encircled in a final flourish. Her name was Z-M something. She waited patiently.

I tried again. "I don't have any information on Steve, and it would be a big help for my salvage claim if you could look up his last name, address and phone number."

"I am sorry, but I am not authorized to give out such information."

"But I need to contact his relatives."

"I am sure that the police are doing that," she said, with great formality.

"And I need to contact the people who are handling his business."

"I am sorry, but I cannot help you with it."

"I'm sorry, but not even having his last name leaves me — in a jam." That word has rich overtones in Jamaica and the Bahamas.

A faint smile appeared. "I am sorry, but the marina does not get involved in the affairs of the yachtsmen who berth here. As the marina manager, I do not get involved except to collect the dockage fee and to enforce the rules listed on the reverse side of the contract, which include not running engines unnecessarily at the dock and no music or loud noises after nine in the evening. If our marina service is inadequate, please let me know."

She had given me a mouthful — and perhaps some information between the lines. I glanced at the rules. Under them was written, "Zelma Mortimer, Marina Manager."

"Office hours are from eight in the morning until nine in the evening. A phone number is listed for emergencies — *true* emergencies, only."

I returned her tiny smile. "It looks like a well-run marina. I wish you a good day."

I guessed that keeping distance from things that happened in the marina was an important defense for this woman, and that formality provided a sturdy wall to hide behind.

I went back to the *Second Chance*. Sgt. Leonard Townsend wasn't there but Constable Ivanhoe Walker was, wearing the same blue jumpsuit and ball cap uniform as before. He was sitting in an aluminum beach chair under an Australian pine near the head of the dock. Behind him stood his dilapidated car which I could now identify as a 1970s vintage Toyota. Both front doors were open and the radio was on, playing reggae. I waved and smiled. He smiled back, dropped a palm frond that he had been stripping, and got up to intercept me.

"Morning, Constable," I said.

He reached the foot of the dock faster than I did, and he stood there, blocking my way but keeping his gold-toothed smile. I realized that I hadn't looked at him very closely before. He was about my size and age, but very thin. He hunched forward and seemed to favor his left leg, as if he'd been injured once. His ball cap was small and so was his head, with closely cut curly hair.

I walked up to him slowly and stopped, as if expecting a friendly conversation. "I've got more work to do on the yacht. The Sergeant must have told you."

"Yeah, he did tol' me, and he give me my orders." Ivanhoe formed his words thickly and rolled them out in the rhythm of island patois. "An' you know that you are not to take from de boat or take to it."

"Yes, and I'm taking care to not mess up the fingerprints either," I said, showing him ten fingertips.

He screwed up his face a little, and his eyes rolled up into his forehead. "An' de boat must not be moved until de A . . . S . . . P give permission."

"What is the A . . . S . . . P?"

Ivanhoe screwed up his face again. "Dat be de assistant superintendent of police."

"Oh, I see. You've got a different rank system than we have in the U.S. Is there something between constable and sergeant?"

"Yes, there be corporal."

"And what comes after sergeant?"

"A . . . S . . . P then S . . . P."

"I see. And you don't have any *leftenants* or captains?"

"No."

"So where is Sgt. Townsend's A.S.P.? In Freeport or Nassau?"

"He is in Freeport."

"Thanks, Constable Ivanhoe. Nice talking to you. See you later." I took a step around him.

Ivanhoe's smile went slack and his brow came down a bit. "Now you remember what I say about de boat." He slapped his right pants pocket. "Like we say on de Island, 'Don't try to run because I have a short gun.'"

"Meaning that you can pull out a short gun quicker than a long gun?"

Ivanhoe nodded and showed me some more gold. Then he reached in his pocket and pulled enough to expose the hand grip of what had to be a small semi-automatic pistol.

I hand-signaled my acknowledgment and went up the dock, ducking under yellow crime scene tape to step into the yacht's cockpit. Stuck onto the cabin door with adhesive tape was a photocopy of a notice warning that this was a crime scene and that nobody was to enter or disturb it.

Well, at least they hadn't sawed off my lock and put on their own. Mine was still locked onto the opened hasp as I'd left it. I walked in and checked out the repair from the inside. It had dried nicely, it felt solid to my knuckle, and no water was coming in anywhere. I went for another look at the framed U.S. Coast Guard Documentation Certificate. I'd checked the registration number against the number painted on the bow, but I hadn't checked the hull number yet. I hung upside down over the stern until I found it, molded in the fiberglass by the waterline. It checked out, too.

While hanging upside down, I noticed that the transom had a fresh white coat of paint and that the black letters spelling "Second Chance" were so new that they glistened. It seemed like the yacht had been given its "second chance" not too long ago. I did another stern-to-bow search and found nothing that would identify Steve. Since it would be another hour or so before the tide would crest, I locked up the boat and left for an errand.

Outside of the marina office building, between the soft drink machines and the showers, was a pay phone. I used it for a credit card call to the U.S. Coast Guard in Miami. I told their operator that it was the matter of bringing back the salvaged *Second Chance*, and she connected me in to a Lieutenant (Junior Grade) Michael Davis. He listened patiently while I told him about the situation, including our discovering the dead man and turning criminal matters over to the Royal Bahamas Police Force. He agreed to take the information down, but he stressed the need for me to follow up the conversation in writing. "And, sir," he stressed, "this conversation in no way relieves you of your responsibility for clearing Customs and Immigration immediately, upon your return."

"That goes without saying, Lieutenant Davis," I replied.

Those guys must have been wary of people trying to pull fast ones.

"Lieutenant, I would also like to ask for your help in getting in contact with the S.C. Corporation, which is listed as owner and master of the yacht. The certificate shows only a post office box for the address. I was wondering if you could get me a phone number for it?"

He didn't answer right away, but I heard his keyboard clicking. A minute later, he recited the corporate name and postal address that I already had. "No individual named or phone number given."

"Isn't it a little strange to have a corporation listed as a yacht's master? As its captain?"

"No, they can do it. And with the big yachts they do it all the time. They might use a different captain for every cruise."

"And with no phone number, how should we get hold of them?" I asked.

"The standard procedure is to send the owners a registered letter and wait for their reply."

"But that will take weeks!"

"And you'll have to do it yourself. Sorry that I can't help you, sir, but the Coast Guard doesn't have any duty in this case, other than recording the registration. But I will put notes of our conversation into my personal log."

"Thanks. And put me down as the salvage captain. Thanks again for the time you have spent with me."

"No problem. And remember to clear Customs and Immigration when you return with the vessel."

Being so close to the showers and restrooms, the conversation wasn't very private. During the course of it, three men and two women had passed by and any one of them could have picked up snatches of it. On the other hand, everyone knew that I had salvaged the yacht, and talking to the Coast Guard was a logical thing to do.

The next logical thing for me to do was go back to the customs shed and ask if they had an address and name for "Steve." This time the TV was playing the *Golden Girls* and the brown-clad Immigration officer was the only one there. When I asked for the full name of "Steve," she said they didn't have it.

"But you must have taken that information from him when he came here from Miami."

"Yes, but we do not keep it. We send it on to Nassau."

Public Relations 5

Deeply frustrated, I went back to the *Second Chance* where I thumbed in the numbers on the four combination wheels and opened the lock with one hell of a yank. I threw open the door carelessly, leaving the opened lock dangling on the hasp. To hell with non-productive activities. It was time to get back to salvaging the yacht. The batteries were holding their charge, and when I pushed the button the starter motors worked fine and the twin diesels fired right up. *Basta!* While the diesels were running, I sprayed them down again and washed down the yacht's interior once more, including the damaged electronics.

While spraying around the patch, I found the bullets that had made the hole. I found five of them where the hull curves and joins the floor. Banging through the fiberglass had deformed them but Sgt. Townsend and his people could still determine their weight, which would be useful as evidence. I also searched the cockpit and found one casing. That had to be from the executioner's shot. I picked it up with great care. I put all the evidence on a chart table by the piloting station.

I searched the boat a second time, from stem to stern. I looked for evidence of drug trade — a scale, paraphernalia, or even another gun. In the corner of a locker, I found a box of ammunition under a set of Bahamas charts. The charts bore no marks that would give a clue as to what "Steve" had been doing that night. Why hadn't he kept a log book?

I turned off the diesel engines.

With another half hour to wait before high tide, I turned my attention to the yacht's electronics. The depth sounder, VHF marine communications radio, and GPS navigation instrument are standard for any boat doing serious cruising. I flipped them on and they worked, just like the day before. The depth sounder gave me a lot of signals from the pallets under the hull, the VHF was working fine, and the GPS gave our latitude and longitude, within a few feet. I flipped through its functions and found no stored waypoints nor any other information that would tell me where "Steve" had been going.

Radar is also standard equipment for a yacht like the *Second Chance*. I punched its power button. The circular screen lit up with returns from the nearby sailboat masts, yacht railings, tin roofs, the water tower, and everything else that was made of metal. As I'd noticed the day before, "Steve" had the gain turned up to the highest sensitivity. After a couple of sweeps, the individual signals coalesced into a meaningless sea of green. Why had this guy been trawling slowly in the night with his radar's gain turned up so high? Was he looking for floating tin cans?

Now to look at the bank of low-mounted radio modules that had gotten badly sloshed by the high water in the cabin. I pushed the main power button and nothing came on. What a shame. Apparently the salt water had penetrated so deeply that Rebecca's fresh-water-in-a-fine-mist treatment hadn't brought it out. My theory on salt removal by capillary attraction, surface tension and dilution seemed to have been refuted. Too bad, because the label on the main unit identified it as an Electrocom Spectrum, which is top of the line. Its LCD displays stayed blank, the function buttons didn't light up and the speakers that were plugged into it didn't sound. The unit looked so sad, with an unconnected coaxial cable dangling over the top like a severed vine in the forest. I pushed the cable back so that it could do its dangling behind.

The culprit was the power button on the regulated power supply. The power supply was making a click inside every couple of seconds, and the green indicator light flashed with it. Apparently, the electronics weren't seeing enough voltage to commit to start. Or maybe a capacitor was shorting out. Or maybe the relay was too wet to function. Well, I would just let the power supply go on struggling. With a little bit of luck, the short-circuit would generate enough heat to dry itself out, or maybe the clicking relay would snap itself dry.

My attention turned to the hand-held VHF marine radio sitting on the bench. The eight hours of total immersion in salt water had obviously ruined it. But I did take a nostalgic interest in the old radio direction finder — the RDF unit — that Rebecca had sprayed and hung up to dry. Could that big dish be salvaged as a non-functioning antique? In the late 1970s, people quit using them for navigation when the price of Loran units came way down. A couple of decades later, everybody abandoned Loran when the price of the more accurate GPS units came down.

A radio direction finder is not much more than an FM radio with the antenna placed inside a parabolic dish. I pitied the pre-1970s navigators who had to wear those uncomfortable earphones and point those bulky antennaes in different directions to pick up a radio station. When they found one, they had to identify it on the map and write down its compass direction. Actually, they had to get two stations and plot their directions on the map — performing a so-called *triangulation*. The intersection of the lines gave the navigator his position, which could be off by as much as 20 miles.

Out of curiosity, I plugged the RDF unit into a 12-volt power socket and flipped it on. Its power light went on, but the dial didn't show that it was picking up any stations. Its soggy earphones didn't produce any music. I couldn't figure out what to do with the short length of coaxial cable that was dangling from it. I considered leaving the relic plugged in to burn itself dry. Instead, I pulled the plug and set it on the bench.

I didn't hear or feel him come aboard. The pallets must have been still supporting the boat, dampening any telltale rocking. It was Wade Daniels, the guy with the Caesar haircut. I first noticed him as he stood in the companionway looking at the door frame.

"Hey, Wade," I called out, "thanks for helping me with crowd control last night."

"No problem," he said, turning toward me. "But with all the excitement I missed your name."

"I'm Ben Candidi." I moved toward him, reached up and shook his hand. "Say Wade, I'd like to chat with you but we can't do it here. Have to go back onto the dock. Sgt. Townsend made me promise I wouldn't let people on board. He didn't want *me* on board, either. I had to twist his arm pretty hard to make him understand that it's my right as salvage captain."

"Are you making a salvage claim?" Wade asked, ignoring my polite suggestion but seeming friendly enough. He stood there, running slow eyes over the main salon, taking it all in.

"Damn right. I'm taking this tub to Miami as soon as Sgt. Townsend gets through with it."

Wade stood there like an insurance adjustor who had seen this sort of thing before and saw nothing to get excited about. "Looks like you had high water."

How had he gotten past Constable Ivanhoe? I showed Wade a flattened palm as a signal to turn around and get off. But I gave him a friendly answer. "Water up to my waist. If I'd found this boat any later, I couldn't have saved it."

Wade acknowledged my hand signal but didn't move back very fast as I went up the steps to enforce it. That put us at close quarters. I got a better look at him. He was wearing dock shoes, floppy blue shorts, and a nondescript gray T-shirt. He seemed 30 pounds overweight, which wasn't too bad for a heavy five-eleven frame and 50-some years. Under his T-shirt, his big chest united seamlessly with a still bigger stomach, producing an upper-body shape reminiscent of a perched owl. The impression was reinforced by a long nose and large green eyes with loose, puffy lower lids, and by the hang of his gray hair over his forehead.

"The Sergeant was very emphatic about not wanting people on the boat," I said.

Before moving back, Wade threw one last glance into the cabin. Not wanting to seem unfriendly to Wade, I stepped up onto the dock with him. Although he didn't seem the least bit athletic, he kept his balance well and he clearly knew his way around boats.

"With the water that high, it's amazing that the boat didn't sink." He spoke in middle range and sounded vaguely Southern in pleasant tones like you might hear around suburban Virginia.

"The diesels had only two inches to breathe. If they'd stopped, everything would have been lost."

"Electrical system fried?"

"No, but all of the electronics were."

Wade shrugged his heavy shoulders and then looked me straight in the face for the first time. "If you've got your engines and your electrical system, you can get it back to Miami."

"Yes, I'm just keeping my fingers crossed."

The corners of Wade's mouth turned up to produce a weak smile.

"What I came over here for, Ben, is to invite you to a fish fry tonight. You and your partner."

"Great!"

"A group of us get together a couple times a week. Around six o'clock. I guess you can imagine how you're the talk of the town and everyone will be interested to hear what you . . ."

"Sure, Rebecca and I will be glad to meet them. But after we told Sgt. Townsend everything we know — which isn't much — he instructed us to not talk to people about it. So I won't be able to tell your friends any sea stories. Not about this trip, anyway. But I'm looking forward to meeting everyone. And if you can excuse me now, I have to hose the salt out of the starter motors so the boat will start the next time I turn the key."

Wade cupped his hand over an ear. "It sounded like you have saltwater damage to a relay." Obviously he was referring to the clicking relay in the dead radio.

"And how!" I answered.

Looking around in hopes of changing the subject, I noticed a wholesome-looking woman sitting topside on the neighboring Bayliner. She had to be Martin Becker's girlfriend, Beth Owens. I waved to her but she didn't acknowledge it.

I used a stupid question to cap off the conversation with Wade. "Is that your boat there?" I pointed across the water lane to his big cabin cruiser directly behind us.

"Yes, the *Wholesale Delight*."

"Right! I remember you standing on its bow ready to fend me off while I was pulling in last night. Sorry if it seemed a little close. I'm not used to steering big motor yachts."

"No, you did good."

I reboarded and waved the guy off. "Got to get back to work."

After reaching the seawall in front of the marina office, Wade turned to me and hollered a question. "What are you going to do after you take the *Second Chance* back to Miami?"

"I'll come back here and resume our vacation," I hollered back.

"Here at West End?"

"No. Actually, we were planning to work our way eastward, to the Abacos."

With a little luck he would tell that to the other people around the marina.

The tide was now at its peak, and it was the time to get rid of the pallets. I took off my T-shirt, retrieved my mask and snorkel from the corner of the main salon and went over the side. My solid red-and-blue Old Navy surfer jams were really practical for around here: You're presentable when you talk to customs officers and you don't have to change to go for a swim. Of course, for any serious swimming or diving, I'd need my tighter-fitting Speedo-type trunks.

The *Second Chance* was floating free. I untied the ropes that held the pallets together and began the work of sliding them out and setting them on the seawall. During a pause in the work, I noticed that Beth Owens was gone from the upper deck of the dive boat and that boyfriend Martin Becker had taken her place. I caught glimpses of him through my foggy mask, but I didn't spit out my snorkel to say hi. He was watching me like he was afraid I'd mess something up. He seemed especially anxious when I worked on the side of the boat that faced his.

When I came up for air on the other side, I received a more pleasant kind of attention.

"Hey there," she called from the seawall where the crowd had stood the previous day. Actually, I had noticed her a lot earlier. Even my fogged-up mask hadn't kept me from noticing her sashaying to the showers in high-heeled sandals. And now, with the shower taken and everything tucked back in its place, she was presumably on her way back to her boat. Except that she had made a little detour for my benefit.

I spit out my snorkel, waved, and shouted back, "Good morning."

She warmed me with a big smile. "Why, you're working away like a beaver! So industrious. Taking away all that wood." She shifted her weight to one leg and tilted her hip, as if to emphasize the clever connection she'd made between beavers and wood.

I might have smiled to myself while taking off my mask. Actually I was thinking of myself as more of a sea otter than a beaver, but she didn't leave me time to say so.

"Well, I guess it's a beaver," she said with a flat-handed gesture over her chest. That was probably a half-expressed comment on my chest hair.

"I'll settle for any amphibious mammal," I replied.

She was certainly not lacking mammary qualifications. They were suspended nicely inside a floral-print half-blouse that stopped at the midriff, exposing an expanse of acceptably flat tummy. Tight-fitting white shorts completed the fashion statement. At around five-foot-three you might say she was a little short-changed in height, but since Mother Nature had issued her everything else in normal size or width, she seemed the 3-D enhanced picture of sexiness. And she knew how to put it all in motion. After throwing a defiant glance toward the flybridge of the dive boat behind me, she swung her frilly beach bag and sauntered along the seawall to a spot where we could talk without shouting.

"You know a lot about boats, I can see," she said, twisting wet strands of mid-length blond hair around a finger. "I like it when a gentleman can do everything. Then all the lady has to do is look pretty. Ha, ha."

I mumbled something in agreement and smiled back. She had such an engaging smile and so many other expressions that she could switch between.

"Where do you come from that you can swim so good? You were holding your breath so long that you got me to worrying if you would ever come up again."

"Miami."

"Oh, you come from Miamah! I guess you were swimming year round. In Beaufort, South Carolina — that's where I grew up — you can only swim in the summer. And the water's not as nice as in Miamah Beach. We visit there every once in a while. Boy, was it hot. And I'm not talking about the water, either! I mean have you *seen* some of the suits that those women are wearing there? 'Tangas' is what they call them. In South Carolina they'd arrest you for wearing something like that on the beach. That's what they call the Bible Belt —"

"The Republican South?"

"— which used to mean that you could get belted if you didn't read the Bible on Sunday. Ha, ha! No, in South Carolina a girl couldn't wear something like that and still call herself a lady. But in Miamah with all those Brazilian Ipanema girls and Latin American firecrackers . . . well, that's something else!"

"Do you live in Beaufort?"

"No, we live in Boca. Boca Raton." She paused, maybe to look me over without the self-distraction of talking. "I'm Angie. Angie Sumter."

"I'm Ben Candidi. Pleased to meet you, Angela."

"No, just call me Angie. That's what everybody does. Actually, they christened me 'Angelica,' but the only time I ever use it is when I'm signing checks."

"Who are you with, here, Angie?"

In what could have been a dance step, she fell back on her right leg and brought up a limp left hand. She was showing me her wedding ring and her big diamond engagement ring. "With my *husband!*" She said it with exclamation and feigned indignation, to which I did not react. Well, I might have cracked a smile.

Angie abandoned her pose quickly and tossed her shoulders, one at a time. "With my husband, Cal," she said, softly.

"Great. Looking forward to meeting him sometime, Angie. What's the name of your boat?"

She told me it was *Sumter's Forte*, and she spelled it out for me. "And we pronounce it 'For-Tay.' You know, like your strong point or something you're really good at."

"Right!" I said.

"And you have that two-masted sailboat with a Greek name. We saw it from the end of our dock. And you're *with* that slim, black-haired girl who looks like she could be Greek, too."

"Mediterranean anyway," I said. "Her name's Rebecca Levis. She's my fiancée."

"I *understand*." Angie's ring hand came up a few inches. Then she looked beyond me and inhaled, and the hand came all the way up and waved. "Hi, Beth, did you meet Ben yet?"

Beth had replaced Martin on the flybridge. She was hanging a blouse to dry. "Hi, Ben. Nice to meet you," she said, with shy eyes and an embarrassed wave.

"Same here," I called up to her.

Suddenly Beth was looking like something below deck required her immediate attention. Socially, she might be a shrinking violet, but physically, she seemed quite capable. She had a lifeguard's body (ocean rescue type): a strong, ovoid torso and a big rib cage for high lung capacity; short arms with plenty of muscle to clamp a guy to the side of her body; high breasts that wouldn't get in the way; and strong thighs that could generate lots of propulsive force in a scissors kick.

"Beth's like you," Angie said. "She takes to the water like a be —"

"Like a sea otter," I said, quickly.

Beth had already disappeared into the Bayliner.

"Ben, you are such a gentleman," Angie exclaimed.

"And now if the lady would grant me leave," I said, with a hint of drawl. "I must return to my underwater duties before the tide lays the boat back down on the platform."

"Well, of course," she said, as an echo. She hoisted her bag and walked off, her sleek legs and transparent high-heeled shoes making a charm-school beeline to the center dock.

There was no problem of the *Second Chance* getting hung up again, but there was still a lot of work to be done. As if by magic, Edgar and his sidekick appeared at the seawall.

"Great, guys," I said to them, "you're hired again. And hose the pallets down once with fresh water before taking them back."

Edgar retrieved the hose, and I concentrated on removing the rest of the pallets efficiently. My stepped-up activity brought hairy-chested Martin Becker to his flybridge again. With the two-foot dive flag painted on the side of his cabin, there was no question that he was into diving. And big letters on the boat's transom identified it as the *Rapture of the Reef*. Once again, he watched me intently, especially when I was working close to our shared dock.

"Careful about getting under the dock," he yelled down at me. "The cross-braces have lots of nails sticking out. Especially on my side."

I spit out my snorkel and looked up at him through my mask. "Yes, and they have barnacles, too."

Usually any mention of barnacles around docks will get a laugh out of anyone. But Martin didn't seem to have a sense of humor. He kept on staring down like a dive instructor who'd just caught me going for a two-tank dive without a decompression meter. He was athletic enough to be a dive instructor, or a weight lifter for that matter. Physically, he looked like a scaled-up, pumped-up version of me.

"Thanks again for the tip" I said.

I put the snorkel back in my mouth, blew it out, and went back to work removing pallets from the bow and from the port side of the boat. I slowed my work deliberately, making like the pallets were hard to get loose. Slowly, dive master Martin Becker relaxed his vigilance. Sitting up on his flybridge, he really couldn't see between his boat and the dock. Before removing the last pallet, I lingered in the shadow of my boat's port side and hyperventilated for a long time. Then I went for a little exploratory dive, crossing under the *Second Chance*, under the cross-members of the dock, and under the *Rapture of the Deep*. I got a good look at the dive boat's hull before returning, under water, to the far side of my own boat.

On that dive, I discovered no dangerous nails coming out of the dock. But I discovered four, through-the-hull bolts projecting from

Martin's hull. They were one-half inch diameter with threaded sides sticking out to finger length. They were under water, arranged as two pairs, about three feet apart along the centerline in the area where the bow does its important business of pushing down the water to keep the boat up on plane. And I wondered what those four bolts might be useful for — besides catching seaweed.

My helpers were much slower at removing the pallets from the seawall than I had been at setting them there. They were paying very special attention to the hose-down, acting like this would be a full-day project. I dug in the zipper pocket of my jams and handed each of them $15, saying I hoped that this would be enough for taking the pallets back to the commercial harbor and that I would soon need the hose back to desalt the cushions.

A quarter of an hour later the pallets were gone, as were Edgar and his friend, and I was standing on the dock, amusing myself with squishing fresh water into the cushions under my feet. Toward the end of my vintner's dance, Sgt. Townsend reappeared.

The uniform was the same as before and so was the commanding body language, but this time he sounded a little more cordial. "I would like to ask you some questions about your discovery."

He said it in a soft voice, and he had a spiral notebook in his hand. Alleluia!

"Fine," I said, matching his tone. "And let's get ourselves out of this hot sun." I climbed aboard and directed him to the main salon where the bare dinette benches were dry enough for him to sit. Sitting down, we were low enough in the main salon that nobody could see us through the yacht's windshield and side windows, even if they could see past the surface reflection. And since we were on the port side, the angle was bad for Martin or Beth to look down on us.

"Could you tell me, once again, the whole story — from the very beginning?" He put it to me like a polite request and tension stayed low when we met each other's eyes.

"I'd be glad to."

I told him the whole story, starting with my predawn work at the navigation station with Rebecca at the helm. I covered every detail — everything Rebecca and I had done and noted from that moment on, up to the time when he appeared at the dock. For this telling, I left out my calculations and theory.

Sgt. Townsend didn't ask me any leading questions, but he listened patiently and took careful notes. And as he did, I wondered what brought about the change in attitude. Yesterday he was ready to write it off as a routine drug murder, but today he was treating it as something important enough to consider in detail.

With my story told, I waited for his questions. But he didn't ask any. He fingered the notebook, like he was ready to close it. It was time to start feeding him conclusions:

"The holes were blasted at ten-forty in the evening."

He wrote that down and asked, "How do you know that?"

I told him about the flooding experiment I'd done at the dock, taking off the foam patch. "That time is accurate within one-half an hour."

"What else do you know?"

"As Dr. Levis told you last night, our temperature readings establish the time of death as ten-forty. That time should also be accurate within one-half an hour."

He wrote that down. "She will have to be interviewed."

"Okay, but like we agreed, Rebecca and I are trying to play this low key. We're not telling anyone that she is a medical doctor or about the temperature measurements. She's preparing a detailed medical affidavit that should be ready to be handed over to you tomorrow. Maybe that will do."

"Okay."

I took the Sergeant over to the table where I'd put the evidence: five slugs and a single casing. "These are the slugs that made the hole. They're pretty bashed up but you should be able to weigh them and compare them with the ones in the victim's chest and skull."

He pulled a sandwich bag from his pocket and put them in.

"And here is a casing I found on the cockpit floor. It is obviously the one from the execution shot to the head. Obviously it has been wet, but it is possible that fingerprints can be developed on it. I was careful not to touch it when picking it up."

Sgt. Townsend raised his eyebrows. I told him more. "Dr. Levis' affidavit will include my estimate that the chest shot was from an upward angle. That would fit with the murderer having shot the victim from the cockpit, or at least from that elevation."

He wrote that down.

"But my finding of only one casing in the cockpit suggests that the chest shot was from another boat."

He frowned. "Why do you say that?"

"Because the executioner's shot was most definitely made from the boat, and the casing accounts for it."

The Sergeant's frown deepened for a couple of seconds. But he wrote my answer down.

"Now let's talk about the shots through the hull. My observations of the holes show that the shots were angled down."

He recorded that, too.

I asked him a question. "Do you know if the slugs in the victim were from a handgun or a rifle?"

"We do not know," he said. Now, it was my turn to frown. Townsend noticed and said, "The results have not been returned."

"If it were a handgun, the shots to the hull had to be fired from a short distance."

Townsend responded with a greasy chuckle, almost a laugh. "And how would you know that?"

"The pattern was close, about the size of my hand. Only two of the shots hit outside of the pattern. It would be hard to do that with a pistol from a distance."

"And what would you say if the shots had come from a rifle?"

"I would say that the shots could have come from a greater distance."

A sarcastic smile came over his face. "And nobody has any trouble shooting on the water?"

"Rifle shots from a greater distance would have had to come from a skilled marksman on a large boat that wouldn't rock so much." After saying that, I waited a long time for him to comment. Was he inexperienced, dumb, or just unwilling?

"What else do you have to say?" he finally asked.

"It is unlikely that it was rifle shots from a greater distance because the shots seemed to be angled down."

"Very well," he said, in a tone that conveyed the exact opposite.

"I have more observations. The fact that the murder and the sabotage occurred at the same time is relevant. We can eliminate several scenarios. The simplest to eliminate was that it was done by an acquaintance of the victim and that he did it all by himself. You can rule that out by asking around whether the victim took people out and whether he carried or towed an auxiliary boat that the murderer would have needed to escape."

Sgt. Townsend didn't write any of that down. He looked to the door.

I asked, "Did he have a friend or an auxiliary boat?"

Sgt. Townsend looked pained. "Apparently not. Now, what is your next scenario?"

"The next and more likely scenario is that people unknown to him approached on their own boat, shot him and —"

"Stop right there. Why would they be unknown to him?"

"Because he wouldn't have had a cocked revolver in his hand if he really knew them." The Sergeant was getting pissed off but that didn't stop me. "As I was saying, Sergeant, people unknown to him approached on their own boat, shot him, and then boarded the *Second Chance* to dispatch him."

The sarcastic smile returned.

"But that is just theory."

"It's an hypothesis that can be checked. And the hypothesis is useful because it has implications which can also be checked. First, I didn't see any scrape marks on the *Second Chance*. You would expect them from the rub rail if a big yacht tied up to the *Second Chance* in the open sea. There'd be scrape marks even if they used fenders."

"So what does that prove?"

"If the murderer came on a big yacht, there had to be at least two of them — one to board and one to pilot the boat. Maybe he jumped on, or maybe he used a small auxiliary. And, if he used a small auxiliary then —"

"This is just speculation. You are just spinning stories on top of stories that have no meaning."

"It is called an hypothesis, Sergeant. A good hypothesis generates a theory that can be tested. My small-boat hypothesis says that if you get your fingerprint kit and dust around the inner edge of the transom by the aft cleats, you might find the murderer's fingerprints. That's where he would hold on while tying on a line from his boat. He would have to secure his boat before boarding."

Sergeant Townsend put on a stone face. "Doctor Candidi, you are not welcome to involve yourself this deeply in the investigation."

I stared at him. Maybe I was wrong to have shown him all my cards — the ones that I'd been playing in my head. Maybe he wasn't just a lazy cop who didn't want to get involved in an investigation. What if he was in tight with the bad guys? Maybe I should fear him more than anyone else at the marina. But somehow, I couldn't stop myself from telling him more.

"Just one final thing to tell you — the people who shot him know *something* about boats but they don't know all that much. They knew enough to shoot the holes in a tight pattern just below the waterline, but they didn't know enough to weight down the float switch to defeat the bilge pump. Or if they did know, they were in too big a hurry to get out of there."

Townsend had closed his eyes. "Will that be all?"

"Yes, that will be all. Tomorrow you are going to get a written statement and a medical affidavit from Dr. Levis. After that, we will wash our hands of the criminal matter."

This seemed to relax him. He got up to leave. But I needed more from him.

"Did you make any progress in identifying the victim? I need that information for my salvage claim."

"No, I cannot report any progress to you." He stepped toward the door, acting like no further explanation was necessary.

"What did the marina records say?"

"They have been transferred to higher authority. I cannot tell you."

His double-talk and stonewalling were making me mad. I followed him out to the cockpit. "Very well. It sounds to me like you should be through in two or three days so I can take the boat to Miami."

I broadcast that with a loud voice.

Sgt. Townsend stepped up on the dock and turned on his heel. "You will not take the boat until I release it as a crime scene."

He executed a quarter-turn on his heel and walked off. I watched as he passed the Constable, climbed in his jeep and drove off. I paced the cockpit, deep in thought. It was now late in the afternoon. Time to call it a day. As if on cue, my back-door neighbor Wade Daniels moved to the bow of his yacht and called to me across the water. "Remember to come and help us eat the fish. Six o'clock."

"We'll be there," I called back.

I locked up the *Second Chance* and left it.

Walking toward Ivanhoe, I realized that I had a question for him. "When the Sergeant was here with me, did anybody come out on the dock?"

"No, man," he said. "Nobody come."

"Thanks."

"No problem."

No problem except that too many people knew that I'd talked to the Sergeant for a long time.

Block Party 6

On my way back to the *Diogenes*, I caught a glimpse of a couple of girls on Waverunners speeding over the flats to the east of us. Not having seen them around the marina, I wondered where they were staying.

At the *Diogenes*, Rebecca had made everything shipshape and comfortable for lounging. She told me about having called Batelco to activate our cellphones and that we should be able to use them in two days. And she told me that Wade Daniels had come aboard to invite us to the fish fry. I told her about my conversation with the guy, and we spent some time discussing what we would and wouldn't tell people.

Rebecca told me about the cruising couple berthed next to us. Their names were Glenn Weaver and Stephanie McCallister. They were sailing back from the Abacos and would be going back to Miami in a day or two.

"I asked Wade to invite them, too," Rebecca said. She wrinkled her brow. "They're pretty inexperienced, and it would be a shame for them to be marginalized."

I glanced over to the sailboat.

"No, they aren't here right now," Rebecca said. "They're off for a walk somewhere."

"What kind of boat is it, anyway?"

"It's a twenty-six-foot Hunter," Rebecca said.

Its rail was a foot lower than ours and its auxiliary motor was just an outboard hanging off the end.

"I see they've got it locked up." Their system was the same as ours: three teak boards that fit in a slot to block the companionway, secured to the horizontally sliding hatch by a hasp and a padlock. "Always locking up would be good standard operating procedure for us, too, while we're here."

"Roger that, Captain," Rebecca said in parody. "I have already written it into the standard operating procedure. But maybe you can sand the upper edge of the top board," she said, pointing to where the teak board slotted into the entrance. "I have to finagle the sliding hatch over it to get the hasp into place."

"Sure," I said.

Rebecca handed me a cold lemonade in a can. "Now, can you tell me why you are frowning?"

I told her about my frustration in trying to find out anything about "Steve" and my suspicion that Sgt. Townsend would hold onto the boat by dragging out his investigation.

"I have a rough draft of my medical affidavit. I'll write the final draft the first thing tomorrow morning. Incidentally, I double- and triple-checked, and the time of death still comes out the same."

"Right. And first thing tomorrow, I'll work up a written statement on the salvage and probable location of the murder. It will be good to get this police thing off our desks. The *Second Chance* is in excellent shape. Ready for the trip to Miami any time."

"How long would the police be justified in holding the yacht for evidence?"

"I don't know. So far it's been dry and sunny, but the first rain will spoil their chance of getting any fingerprints off the boat. And it will wash away the blood spatter evidence, too. As soon as it rains, I'm going to argue that they give up jurisdiction."

I stepped onto the dock, hosed myself down, and returned to change into a fresh pair of shorts and a polo shirt.

It was pleasant enough to lie there on the cockpit's bench with Rebecca, watching the birds fly and the wispy tops of the Australian pines sway in the breeze as the sun got lower. I got up and took a look to the east to see what had happened to the Waverunner girls. It looked like they had returned the toys to the collection of recreational equipment that was assembled a mile or so down the shore to the east of us. With the sun behind me, I could make out a collection of Waverunners, Windsurfer sails and catamarans assembled on the beach around a prefab metal shack. I went back to sipping my lemonade and gazing at the clouds. After a while, I noticed something else in the sky — the same guy in his tight-fitting swimsuit climbing in his tuna tower.

"What's that guy doing up there, anyway?" I asked.

Rebecca opened her mouth and cocked her head. "It beats me, but he's up there a lot."

"What's he think he is? An aerialist? The man on the flying trapeze?"

"A smuggler," Rebecca said with a feisty smile. "A *grape* smuggler!"

I had to work hard to suppress my laugh, so it wouldn't carry. For all I knew, our cockpit might be focusing our words on him like a parabolic reflector.

I whispered an admonition, a parody of political correctness. "Rebecca, you must be tolerant of the Baby Boomers. They grew up with a different dress code."

Rebecca delivered a sassy answer about "letting it all hang out," and I laughed again. That was too much, and the guy did look down. I waved to him and he ignored me.

We laughed longer and harder than our inane humor deserved. We go silly like this a lot. I guess it's a good device to blow off pent-up frustration. And our jovial mood lasted while locking up the *Diogenes* and all the way to the *Wholesale Delight*.

DRESSED IN A blue golf shirt, loose-fitting white shorts, and brown leather-topped boat shoes, Wade Daniels was presiding over a shiny charcoal grill that hung over the stern. Next to him was a big ice chest full of iced-down beers. The cockpit was decked out for company, but the door to the main salon was closed. The sun was low and it was well after six, but we were the first to arrive. I shook Wade's hand, and he invited me to stick my hand in the ice chest, or he could make me a Bloody Mary.

"No, I think I'll stick with beer," I replied.

"Yes, I can understand," he said, as if there had been some significance to my choice. "That was a bad thing you came onto."

I handed Rebecca a beer and took one for myself, and we stood by the grill where Wade was fanning a charcoal fire with a piece of stiff cardboard.

"Yeah," I said, "it's not a pretty thing seeing a guy shot up like that."

Wade looked up from the grill. "How many times was he shot?" His slow eyes lingered on me with the question.

"It looked like twice, but I'm no expert. I had my hands full keeping the boat from sinking. And then all the way back my temporary plug was giving me trouble. Really had my hands full."

Rebecca affirmed that with a nod.

Wade took a couple of swipes at the fire with the cardboard. "Did they *shoot* holes in the hull?" Wade asked.

"Looks like it."

I didn't volunteer anything more. Daniels shrugged, took a couple more swipes at the charcoal fire and looked down at the deck. Okay, if he was going to ask me questions I could ask some of him.

"Did you know the guy?" I asked.

"Steve?"

"That's what I hear his name was. What was his last name, incidentally?"

Wade shook his big head slowly. "I don't know. Just knew him as Steve."

"Did you talk with him?"

"Not much," Wade said.

"Did he give you any idea why he was here? Or what business he was in?"

Wade settled his quiet eyes on me, and I just waited him out. Finally he asked, "Why are you interested?"

"Because I'm trying to get a line on him to press my claim for salvaging his boat. His estate owes me a big pile of money. His estate, or whoever owns that boat. All the Coast Guard certificate gave was a name of a some damn corporation with a Miami post office box."

Wade shook his head. "Might be dangerous. Probably drug dealing. Better stay out of it."

I puffed up and made my pronouncement. "Hell yes, we're going to stay out of it! Like I told that Bahamian police sergeant, I don't know who the guy was, and I don't know who killed him or why. I don't know and I don't care, really. I've already told that cop what little I knew. He took it all down, and that's the end of it as far as I'm concerned. But what I *do* care about is getting paid for salvaging that vessel. When that's done, we sail to the Abacos and continue our vacation."

Wade Daniels listened to me like a sleepy owl, completely expressionless except for the low set of his upper eyelids. I waited for a reaction and finally he responded with a nod. I continued:

"Drug boat or no drug boat, we're not going to walk away from the salvage claim. I put my life on the line, jumping onto a two hundred thousand dollar yacht minutes before it was going to sink. I went below, found the leak, and plugged it. And now, according to International

Law, a big chunk of that yacht belongs to me — to us, because I couldn't have done it if Rebecca hadn't been there to stay on the *Diogenes* and pilot it all the way back."

I had told my story the way I wanted to.

"Was it in International Waters when you salvaged it?"

"Yes. Thirteen miles north of the Bank and a ways east." I stopped to look at him for a second. "Say, that was a good question! Are you a lawyer?"

"No."

"What do you do, anyway?" I asked it with a teasing smile, as if to say that I knew he had to be some sort of professional.

Slowly Wade's face took on a smile. He half-sat on the rail and turned up his palms. "Wholesale appliances." He brushed his Caesar bang. "But I'm doing less and less of it, now. My partners are buying me out." His smile transformed into a grin.

"Please accept my congratulations." I said it expansively. "Think of that, Rebecca, retiring at the age of . . . what? I'd guess you're about fifty."

"Close guess. But I'm not yet completely retired or bought out, yet. Can't give up until they show me that they can run the business without running it into the ground." He had been looking at the grill, but now he turned to me. "What about you?"

"I gave up a job in the U.S. Patent Office. Now we're going to sail around the Bahamas for a few months. Then I'm going to look for a job with a technology company somewhere in South Florida."

Wade turned his head to Rebecca and winked. "And you?"

Rebecca smiled, shook her head and handled it beautifully. "I had a desk job at George Washington University."

"What did you do?" Wade smiled at her like he was interested.

"I worked on world health statistics. Maybe I'll be able to find something in Miami-Dade or Broward County."

We were interrupted by the first of Wade's other guests, a wiry, angular guy wearing tennis shoes, faded blue jeans and a locomotive engineer's cap. He boarded the boat like he'd been on it before, maybe as part of a fishing party. As he came closer, I noticed he had a closely cut moustache. It was almost colorless, like his closely cut blond hair, which was visible from behind when he turned towards the cooler.

"Help yourself, Rick," Wade said, with everyday familiarity. "The beer's cold."

But Rick had already extracted a silver can and was turning back toward us. I wondered whether it was age or the Bahamian sun that had done the bleach job on his hair and moustache. He seemed to be in his late thirties or early forties. He held the beer can and clicked open its tab top with one hand, then took a long chug while keeping his eyes on Rebecca. He nodded to Wade. Then he squared off at me, half-opening his mouth like he might have something to say.

But Wade was a bit quicker. "Rick Turner, I'd like you to meet Ben Candidi and Rebecca Levis."

I extended my hand. Rick wiped his wet hand on his jeans before shaking with me. He did it with a quick step forward and a fast arm extension, like he was handing me a tool. His shake was strong enough to work a crowbar. When we disengaged, he stepped back quickly and went back to regarding Rebecca, who had not offered her hand.

"Glad to meet you, Rick," Rebecca said.

He nodded, stared for a couple of seconds, and then returned his attention to me. His irises were light-green, with a lot of white in their texture. "I hear you guys are the ones that found that guy out there and brought him in."

"After saving his boat from sinking — which wasn't easy. You know him?"

"No. He wasn't around here for more than a week." Rick threw a glance to Wade, as if in afterthought.

"That wasn't very long. Have any idea what he was doing out there?"

Rick Turner's eyes turned up towards his hat brim. "Probably drugs." He dropped his voice like drug dealing might be regrettable but was nothing out of the ordinary.

"Well, all I saw was that someone shot him and made a hole in his boat," I said, as if in contradiction.

Rick's eyes returned to me. "Had to be dealing something." He took a big long pull on his beer.

"Probably was offloading from a mother ship," Wade added. "South Americans." He picked up a pancake turner and looked at Rick. "Ben was just telling me about how he didn't find anything on the boat and how he's having trouble getting Steve's name and address so he can move on with his salvage claim." He moved past Rick, grabbed one of two long Tupperware containers, opened it, and put a couple of fish fillets on the grill.

Rick took another pull on his beer — a Bud Light — and settled his eyes on Rebecca, once again. She gave him no reaction.

"You been around here for a long time, Rick?" I asked.

"Off and on. Spend as much time as I can here."

"Like Wade, I guess." I said it with a smile in the direction of the happy grill-tender.

"Yeah, 'cept I have to spend more time riding herd on my guys than he does. It doesn't take half as much brains to pull a wire as it does to connect it up right. Have to go back for a lot of inspections."

"Electrical contracting?"

"You got it." Rick shifted his weight and relaxed just a little.

"In Miami?"

"Hell no! Ain't nothing going on there." He noticed when I cocked my head in question. "Ain't nothing going on there if you don't '*peekie pannie*.'" Rick turned his head toward the transom like he wanted to spit over it.

I asked, "How far north up the Florida coast does a guy have to go so he doesn't have to speak Spanish?"

"Delray Beach. All kinds of good construction going on there. What about you?"

"Like I was telling Wade, Rebecca and I gave up a couple of dull desk jobs in Washington and we sailed down here to explore the Bahamas for a couple of months. When the money runs out, we'll see if we can't find a couple of desk jobs in South Florida."

This time it was Rick who cocked his head in question. But I didn't have to answer it because two new guests came aboard — the first of many. Wade moved to introduce us.

Actually Ray Vangelden didn't require much introducing. He let us know that he was the owner of the large trawler, the *Photo Finish*, which was tied up at the end of the center dock. In his late sixties, he was short, pudgy, and spoke with a friendly Brooklyn accent. He lost no time telling me that his yacht got its name from the photo kiosk business that he had developed all over South Florida. His eyes twinkled behind his bulbous nose as he told his story. He had sold his business before drugstores started offering on-site developing and before photo technology made a abrupt turn towards digital.

While Ray was explaining this, his tall, slender wife Martha gravitated to Rebecca. Wearing a long blue-jeans skirt and a loosely hanging, smock-like blouse, she seemed better dressed for land than for the water. Her mid-length auburn hair was flawlessly combed. I found it hard to judge her age. The absence of wrinkles on her forehead or crows's feet in the corner of her eyes suggested a well-preserved 45 or maybe a cosmetic-surgery-enhanced 55. She had an equestrian demeanor and seemed to look past us more than at us.

Rick Turner moved to a corner and concentrated on his beer.

After finishing what he wanted to say about the photo business, Ray scratched his big, dimpled nose and took a good look at me. "So, you're the guy who brought in that dead man yesterday."

"Yes, and as I passed your transom yesterday afternoon, I got the impression you knew the guy." I noticed that Ray was looking confused. "You're the one who said, 'Oh God, they killed him.'"

Ray scratched his forehead. "No, I didn't know him." He looked me in the eye. "But what else didya expect me to say when I look down and see a body under a white sheet?" He made it sound like a friendly argument, New York style. "I look down, and it's like you were riding into Dodge City with an extra horse and a dead man hanging over the saddle. Whadidyah expect me to say? No, I didn't know him. Just saw him around the dock. Never talked to him. Don't even know his name. I recognized the boat, though."

"They tell me his name's Steve. And that's all that I know about him. Say, it's pretty funny that we're talking about it like cowboys when we're really a couple of Northeasterners. I grew up around Newark."

"You did! Well, here's looking at you — from across the river." Ray went up on the balls of his feet so he was a bit higher than me, looked around, and saluted me with a beer can. In doing so, he noticed a big, burly guy who had been hovering off to the side. "Ben, I want you to meet Cliff Grimes."

"Glad to meet you," Cliff said, with a deep voice and a self-conscious grin, and offering a slow, heavy hand.

Ray said, "Cliff's a good friend and yacht mechanic and a good guy to know."

Cliff answered that with a good-natured chuckle and turned his eyes in the direction of a frizzy-haired, middle-aged lady in a purple polka dot house dress who was now talking with Rebecca and Martha. "That's Ethel, my better half."

"Right," I said. "You must be the owner of *Engineuity*. Clever name. And I bet you have to use a lot of 'engineuity,' working around engines."

"That's for sure," Cliff said.

As we talked on about diesel engines, I felt comfortable with these two guys. Ray was friendly and open to conversation on all subjects, and Cliff seemed friendly enough when the subject was engines. But Rick Turner, the electrician sipping his beer in the corner, would be a guy to watch out for.

Things became more complicated when two more joined the party. It was the couple from the *Dream Weaver*, the daysailer berthed next to our *Diogenes*. They made their way to Rebecca. Bearded Glenn Weaver wore blue jeans and an untucked, checker-pattern shirt with a pack of cigarettes in the pocket. It was a short pack, probably unfiltered Lucky Strike. Stephanie McCallister was wearing a Bombay-print dress and leather sandals, like before. She seemed to be doing most of the talking for the pair.

We carried on with our diesel conversation. Then Cliff shook his heavy body like a horsefly had just bitten him in the back of the neck. "Hey, aren't you the guy who found that guy who was murdered?"

"Yes, that's him," Ray chimed in.

It was time for me to make a new announcement — a short version delivered slowly in Cliff's cadence, but also for the benefit of electrician Rick, who had gotten a second beer and was now standing closer. "Yes, Rebecca and I found his yacht sinking. I boarded it and plugged the hole just in time. Boy, those poor diesels almost drowned in salt water. Had my hands full keeping it from slopping over them and getting the leak under control. Awfully terrible to see a guy shot like that. Glad when the Bahamian police sergeant came and took it all off my hands. I have no idea why they did it. Wade thinks the guy was out in the Stream, rendezvousing in the dark with a mother ship as part of a drug deal."

Ray yelled over to Rick, "Say, you were out there in the Stream that night. Maybe you saw something."

"I wasn't out there," Rick said. His light-green eyes disappeared and he took another chug.

"Sure you were," Ray said, with Brooklyn persistence. "You told me you were going out there. And you didn't come back in until around eleven o'clock."

"Yeah, okay. But I wasn't out in the Stream. I was out on the Bank, with lines out for snapper. I didn't see him or his boat. All I saw was those guys on the sailboat coming in through the channel." He pointed to our boat neighbors, Glenn and Stephanie.

"Who else was out that night?" I asked Ray, hoping for a quick spritz of information.

"Well, Wade and the Sumters weren't out. But the diving people were out until at least ten, and so were the tuna tower guys."

'I guess the diving people are Martin and Beth," I said, remembering Martin's tight-fisted complaint about engine noise from the *Second Chance*, his warning about nails under the dock, and Beth's unexplainable shyness. "Yes, I've met Martin and Beth. But who are the 'tuna tower guys?'"

Cliff's beefy face formed into a broad grin and then into a smile as he shook his head. "Can't miss them, Ben. They're the ones that have the tallest tuna tower."

"And the shortest boat," Ray added. And the two laughed together like they'd amused themselves on the subject a few times before.

"Well, probably don't do no harm as long as they both aren't up there together," Cliff said, with a chuckle.

"They've got themselves a fancy fighting chair that takes up half the cockpit," Rick said.

"Are they into sailfish and marlin?" I asked.

The three guys eyed each other for a minute while I played dumb. I caught Martha throwing Ray a command glance which she followed up by slowly turning her head to the dock. A couple of guys, dressed in Hawaiian shirts and white shorts, were walking toward us, along the seawall. As they walked up the dock, I recognized the one with the real short hair as our boat neighbor, "the man on the flying trapeze."

Ray waved to the two guys as they stepped aboard.

"Hey, Chuck," he yelled, "you were out a couple of nights ago, weren't you?"

Aerialist Chuck waved an answer that could have been yes or could have been no. Then he reached into the ice chest to pull out a large bottle of white wine and poured two glasses full.

In a low voice, Ray said that the biggest thing the tuna tower guys had brought in was a thirty-pound dolphin — the fish, not the marine mammal. Rick stepped forward to say that those guys never caught anything worthwhile on their boat. Cliff admitted to running his engine for thousands of hours but never having hooked a marlin. And I admitted to spearfishing with an Hawaiian sling.

Our foursome heated up to the topic of sport fishing, but Chuck and his friend didn't approach. They stayed with Wade Daniels who was ministering to a grill full of steaming fish fillets that were starting to smell awfully good. Rick Turner drifted off and started talking to Glenn Weaver, who was still hanging onto his girlfriend Stephanie, who was still talking to the other women.

It was getting dark but Wade's deck lights lit up the cockpit. The back of the boat was getting crowded, and heavy too. The weight of the tailgate party had dropped the stern of the boat a few degrees, and perhaps the guests sensed it. Maybe that's why the women spread out on the starboard side of the cockpit, from the ladder going to the flybridge and all the way to Wade's grill station. That put the squeeze on Chuck and his friend. They made their way to the cabin door which was behind us, on the port side. I shot them a smile when Rick made room for them to pass, but they didn't respond and nobody made an attempt to introduce me. They tried the door to the cabin, but it was locked. They sat on the rail, not too far from us, sipping wine.

Suddenly everyone's head seemed to turn at once. It was Angie Sumter, walking up the dock with swaying hips. The South Carolina belle from Boca Raton was followed by a man carrying an enormous salad bowl. He had to be Angie's husband. He was middle-aged and had the same ovoid body shape as Wade, but with less weight and more muscle. His hair was a salt-and-pepper mixture of dark brown and gray. His face was craggy.

Angie's arrival seemed to energize Wade. Our host gave Angie a big "come on over here" wave. She bathed in everyone's attention, projecting a photogenic smile as she leaned from one side to another, taking off her high-heeled sandals. She placed them on Wade's dock box and stepped aboard, receiving Wade's gallantly extended hand. She located me with a quick glance, she took a quick appraising look at Glenn, ignoring Stephanie and Rebecca, and then she returned her attention to Wade, presenting her cheek for a kiss. At close quarters, her face was still prettier than I'd noted during our earlier conversation at the edge of the seawall. Framed by a thick head of blond hair that descended in curls to mid-neck and punctuated by a turned-up nose, her face was a fascinating ensemble of playful dimples, glowing cheeks and sparkling blue eyes.

She caught me studying her, flashed a warm smile, and then settled her eyes on our boat neighbor, Glenn. "Wade, you have to introduce me to your new guests."

She said it like she was the mistress of ceremonies — which she soon became.

Wade took the salad bowl from Angie's husband and said, "Angie, this is Stephanie and Glenn."

"Well, it's certainly nice to meet you both." She said it charmingly, with a high-pitched, lilting drawl. "This is my husband, Cal. And I guess that nice little sailboat belongs to you. The one with the outboard motor in the berth next to Ben's two-masted yacht."

Angie flashed me a mischievous smile, then returned her inquiring attention to Glenn and Stephanie.

Rebecca jumped in to defend our boat neighbors and their undersized sailboat. "Glenn and Stephanie have been sailing in the Abacos. They saw a lot of interesting things."

"Oh, and you must be the Rebecca that Ben was telling me about. You look so pretty. And you sailed all the way down from up north with Ben. That must have been interesting, too."

That didn't go unchallenged. As mistress of the three-deck trawler that was the most expensive yacht in the marina, as the wife of the ex-owner of a chain of successful photo-service businesses, and as leader of the women's conversation up to now, Martha Vangelden had a statement to make:

"Glenn is an artist, Angie. He is on his way back to show some pieces at the Coconut Grove Art Fair."

"You are!" Angie exclaimed to Glenn. "What do you paint?"

"I work with wood," Glenn said. He didn't meet her eye. I couldn't see what his face was doing because of his beard, but he was opening and closing his hands.

"He's a sculptor," Stephanie said, with jittery enthusiasm. "You should see some of his pieces. Like the big dog holding the mailbox in his mouth. A *real* mailbox. And the man's face in a tree trunk. He's really good."

Glenn hunched his shoulders and half-turned away. Behind him, Rick Turner issued a snort and then slid into a smile. "You ever do any of those Jesus scenes?" The Delray Beach electrician raised his arms at his sides to explain what he meant. But he dropped them when Glenn locked onto him with a narrow-eyed stare. Stephanie's pale, freckled face reddened.

Martha Vangelden tilted her head and looked down her narrow nose at Rick. "I would guess that what you are trying to describe is a crucifix, which is a form of *religious* art." She made the comment in a strong, clear voice, with the authority of an actress on stage.

Wade killed that scene faster than you could pull the plug on a spotlight. Abandoning the grill, he put a big arm around Angie's husband and moved him toward me. With cordial enthusiasm he shouted, "Cal, I'd like you to meet Ben Candidi!"

Cal's face was creased in a mistrustful frown, but it changed to a smile when we shook hands.

It was amazing how fast Wade shifted to an outgoing demeanor. Now he was booming like a politician at a Fourth of July picnic. "Ben really knows his way around boats. Did you see how he hoisted up that boat and fiberglassed that hole in the side?"

"Yeah, that was good work," Cal said, smiling and nodding in approval, but regarding me with cautious eyes.

"Yup, he knows his way around boats," said Cliff Grimes.

"A good guy to have around," Ray Vangelden said, with Brooklyn-style sincerity.

Having gotten everyone's attention, Wade wrinkled his nose and collected up his buddy Cal with a sly smile. "Only one trouble with Ben." He winked at me as a signal that it would be a joke.

"What's the trouble with Ben?" Cal asked in a deep voice, smiling in anticipation of the answer.

"He's a Yankee!"

A lot of people laughed and so did I.

Then Rick Turner chimed in from across the cockpit. "Well, we won't hold *that* against him."

Obviously, these people had done a lot of drinking together.

I was surprised to see that Wade could be so animated. He looked around, collecting his audience with a mock frown. "Cal, do you remember that story you told me about your grandfather?"

Cal let his face go blank and shook it like he was trying to shake out wrinkles. "No, what story was that, Wade?"

The guys had everyone's attention.

"Now, you remember that story about when a Yankee pulled into your home town, rolled down his window and asked your grandfather if anything was going on."

Cal nodded and rolled his eyes up into his head. "Yeah, I remember my grandpa telling me that one." He said it in high pitch and rocked back and forth on his heels as if to set a rustic mood. Then he let himself down on the rail and rocked more, putting himself into his grandfather's proud character with a hand resting on each knee.

I felt it coming — a dollop of Southern humor.

Wade gathered everyone up with a sly smile. "And what was it, Cal, that your grandpa told that Yankee when he drove up in his car and asked if anything was going on in town?"

Cal kept rocking and turned his dark eyes suspiciously to the right and to the left.

"What did your grandfather say, Cal?"

"He said, 'Well, something's going on now, and it's *you*. Now git!'"

Half of the crowd laughed at once, and then everyone laughed when Cal picked up an imaginary shotgun resting across his legs and aimed it.

Wade glided back to the grill.

Angie exclaimed, "Cal, that's as bad as your Old Boo stories. You must have told that story a hundred times an' I *still* don't see why you think it's funny. Do you, Ben?"

Oh, hell! She was setting me up for a battle of wits with her husband. The only way to survive it would be to keep things light-hearted.

"It's darn funny," I said, with a laugh. "And what's really funny is that I heard that *same* joke about a South Carolinian rolling into New York City. You must have heard it, Ray."

With his big nose and sticking-out ears, and smiling right back at me, Ray looked comical enough. But the entrepreneur from Brooklyn didn't say anything to help.

Cal Sumter stood up, eyed me, and shook his head. "Nah, in that one he didn't pick up a *shotgun*. They don't allow them in New York." Cal made like he was sweeping with a broom. "In that one, the New York guy just got up and swept 'way the dog poop from in front of his *Eye*-Talian sandwich shop."

Rick let out a rebel yell. Everyone laughed. Cliff Grimes was shaking so hard that he spilled beer on the deck. Ethel stooped over and whisked it up with a printed silk handkerchief. And after the laughter subsided, all eyes were on me.

Poking fun at a guy who grew up as an Italian-type Yankee around Newark? Well, I had endured worse things in my life.

"You heard that one, Ray?" I asked, hoping for a quick opinion on dog poop in New York City.

But Ray Vangelden's only answer was a vacuous look and a shake of the head. Why can't you get an opinion from a New Yorker when you really need one?

I looked around to make sure everyone was watching, then boomed out, "Well, Ray doesn't know the New York story, but I do. You got it right about the dog poop, Cal. But you've got to finish the story." I laid in a dramatic pause. "Then the *Eye*-Talian shook his broom and yelled, '*malo cane!*' And Old Boo hopped into the back of the pickup truck and they high-tailed it back to South Carolina."

Rebecca graced my story with a giddy laugh and Stephanie joined in. Boyfriend Glenn stomped a work-booted foot on the deck and Martha Vangelden gave me an approving smile.

Ray chuckled and shook his head in approval. "Hey, that's very good. The hick drives through the City in a pickup truck and the deli man says 'bad dog' in Italian!"

Cal was watching me with a big old smile but serious eyes. "Sure as hell, Old Boo jumped back into the pickup truck before it drove off. He was *tied* to it!"

Angie raised a hand like she was going to swat her husband. "Now, Cal, don't you start telling any of your Old Boo stories."

In his corner, Wade had been enjoying the jovial tone of his party. Now he was loading fish fillets onto paper plates and handing them out. He handed out the first plates to the women. Ray patted me on the shoulder as he squeezed by to approach the grill. I smiled in the direction of the two tuna tower guys who had been silent through the storytelling session and were still sitting in their corner.

Wade glided through the crowd to hand me a plate with two thick slabs of fish. He put on a big smile. "Ben, you're a hoot! Darn funny for a Yankee."

"Maybe we could make that a Southern Yankee — South Florida variety," I said.

The fillets on my plate looked a little too thick and juicy for my taste. They needed more time over the flame. I waited until Wade returned to the grill, then handed my plate off to Chuck's friend in the corner. Angie handed better-looking ones to Chuck and to me. She reminded us to help ourselves to the noodle salad. While passing the women's group to do so, I caught a fragment of conversation:

"He's a scientist," Martha said.

"Well, we won't hold that against him," Rick Turner said, in the spirit of the Old Boo exchange.

Then silence.

After I loaded up on noodle salad, Rebecca caught my eye with a frown that said she was sorry but just couldn't help it.

Around Cliff Grimes, the conversation was about sport fishing and the culinary qualities of the various small fry. And as the conversation worked its way toward big game fishing, I worked my way to Rebecca, taking a place on the rail beside her. I gave her a nibble on the neck as an excuse to whisper that everything was fine.

Martha Vangelden was talking about her "involvement in the New York theater community" before she had married Ray and had come down to Miami. Stephanie McCallister said she'd always liked the plays she saw in high school. Martha resumed her role as mistress of culture, telling Stephanie and Ethel Grimes all about theater in South Florida. (If they lived in Ft. Lauderdale, the Florida Grand Opera also played there. The *Tales of Hoffmann* might be a good one to start with.) Angie listened, but did not take part in the conversation.

The final guests to arrive were the diving couple, Martin and Beth. After Wade and Cal fixed them up with fish fillets, they drifted over to Cliff Grimes and the tuna tower guys.

Figuring that I'd survived the greatest challenge of the evening, I resolved to find out more about these people, one-on-one. But first, I needed a waste basket for my empty plate. I tried the cabin door and found it locked. The wastebasket was by the cooler and the grill where Cal and Wade were hanging back, talking.

Cal welcomed me with a good-ole-boy grin that was as warm as the charcoal briquettes glowing in the grill.

"Hey, Ben, Angie told me you are a hard-working beaver, but she didn't tell me you'd be so much fun." He put a heavy hand on my shoulder.

"Yeah, it was fun trading shots with you and your 'Fort Sumter.' Are you really from Charleston?"

The grin cooled down a few degrees. "Sumter County. Farther inland near Lake Francis Marion."

"I can believe that you're dyed in the wool when you have a county named after you."

Cal shook his head and looked at the floor. "Yeah, us Sumters go way back. Cotton and tobacco."

We stood there together, chatting about South Carolina geography. And all the while, Cal's deep-set eyes kept drifting to Rebecca. Wade listened amiably, watching with sleepy eyes and offering no openings for conversation about himself.

I patted Cal on the shoulder. "I bet your grandfather did a heck of a lot more than sit on his front porch."

"Yeap, he had acres and acres of cotton and tobacco. Mostly cotton. And before he was done, he was in the milling business. Handed it over to my father, and he made a real good living with it. Cashed it out when I was in high school, and the family's been in investments ever since. I'm real proud of the old man." Gone was the jocularity of the Old Boo exchange. The serious, craggy face had returned. Maybe Cal had shot his wad for the evening. He was looking over at Rebecca and Angie again. Suddenly he turned to me and asked. "What about *your* grandfather?"

"My great grandfather came over on a boat from Italy. Came from a town near Rome. My grandfather was in the grocery business in Newark. I grew up around there and didn't go back after Swarthmore."

Cal's nose blanched when he wrinkled it. I guessed that he drank quite a bit.

"Is that Swarthmore College, somewhere in Pennsylvania?"

"Yes. Where did you go?"

"To the University of South Carolina."

We talked about college sports for a while until it seemed time for me to circulate some more. I thanked Wade for inviting us to his party.

"Glad to," Wade said. "And help yourself to another beer."

I grabbed a beer and listened to Cliff Grimes who was talking to Martin Becker and the tuna tower guys about fishing, while wife Ethel hovered at his side. After a while Ethel nudged her husband Cliff, and I received a formal introduction to Chuck and his friend.

Chuck Baker was tall, thin and gaunt-faced, with closely cut blond hair. His friend, Bill Powell, was a bit shorter and more muscular, and was dark-haired with a crew cut. Their talk quickly returned to fishing lines, marlins and fighting chairs. There was little that I could contribute to conversation on these subjects. I don't see much sport in setting a hook into the jaw of that big, intelligent fish and pulling it in over the better part of an hour. It's cruel, even if they do let it loose in the end. A much better sport would be photographing it from underneath while it feeds on a school of hatchlings, like I'd once seen on a PBS nature program. But I kept my opinions to myself.

I drifted back to Rebecca. She was still attached to the Martha

Vangelden circle, which now included husband Ray, the sailing couple, and a less vivacious Angie. Beth Owens, the shy half of the diving couple, was also there. Rick Turner stood on the periphery and Wade listened in.

Rebecca introduced me to Beth, saying she was into underwater photography. Rebecca and I were able to draw her out some, asking about her experiences with "blue hole diving." We went on to talk about coral formations, marine ecology, and conservation.

Stephanie said that it was nice and peaceful to look down and see the coral from a sailboat.

Rebecca agreed.

Rick Turner said that sailboats are okay, but if you don't have a lot of vacation time you need a power boat to get you there and back.

Martha said that fuel economy had been a big factor in their decision to buy a trawler rather than a cabin cruiser.

A trawler's hull is built according to the so-called displacement design, just like a sailboat. Its is designed to allow the water to stream around the hull smoothly and efficiently. The so-called planing hulls of the big cabin cruisers are designed to climb partially out of the water and go much faster. But big cabin cruisers require a lot of power to do this, and they waste a lot of fuel making waves. Smaller motorboats that have true planing hulls and can actually scud on top of the water are able to avoid much of this loss in fuel efficiency. They regain efficiency by making smaller waves.

After several minutes of discussion about economy, ecology and environmental impact, Rick Turner had apparently had enough.

"Heck, if you want to do something for the environment, you ought to get rid of these damn Waverunners around here. They're all over the place. They get in your way, and they make ruts on the flats." When Ray nodded in agreement, Rick raised his voice and went global. "Ain't that right, Wade? Somebody ought to do something to get rid of that damn Waverunner rental before they tear up the place." He pointed east, in the direction where I'd noticed the prefab shack and the collection of marine toys.

Rick's diatribe had attracted Martin Becker. "Hell yes, someone ought to get rid of them," Martin said. The fingers of his left hand went into his thick head of hair, and he waited for someone to agree.

Slowly, everyone's attention turned to Wade's corner. Wade raised his eyes, shot a quick glance at Rick, then looked slowly at the rest of us with a dumbfounded expression. He shrugged his shoulders. "Yeah, but a guy wouldn't know where to start."

Cal, standing beside him, shook his head like we were talking about bad weather. "They sure as hell aren't doing any good around here."

The group went silent. The tuna tower guys just looked around at everyone. Beth Owens kept her eyes on Wade, shyly but intently. Cliff Grimes looked like he wanted to say something but couldn't find the words, and Ethel just stood there, wringing her handkerchief. And Martha Vangelden stood aloof, looking from one to the other. Husband Ray finally broke the silence.

"Maybe it's doing good for the new owners. But when they tear down this place and build a tourist trap, that's when we'll forget about stopping here. We'll go straight on to Green Turtle Cay."

"That's for sure," Rick said.

Angie started to say something but cut it short after a glance from Cal. And that seemed to announce the end of the evening. Cliff Grimes said he had to get back to the *Engineuity*. Ethel followed him, picking up napkins and beer cans on the way out. Graciously, Martha thanked Wade for the lovely evening. Ray stepped up to agree with her and did nothing to slow her taking of leave. Rebecca and I held on for a few minutes, talking to Chuck and Bill but not learning much more about them. They had been around a lot of places, including Atlanta, Savannah, Tampa, Orlando and South Miami Beach. Glenn and Stephanie left, and Chuck and Bill left soon after.

By the time Rebecca and I were saying our goodbyes, Angie had stepped in again as hostess. She presented her cheek for a kiss, which I gave her after a glance to Rebecca. Cal made no move for reciprocity, although he did tell Rebecca she was the most charming doctor he had ever met. Angie told us that their *Sumter's Forte* was just up the dock, next to Ray Vangelden's *Photo Finish*, and that we were welcome to come over and visit any time. Wade responded cordially as I thanked him and shook his hand. Cal and Angie Sumter stayed with him after we left.

It was a relief to get out from under the scrutiny of all those people, whom we had to meet for the first time, all at once. When we reached the walkway, I put my arm around Rebecca and kissed her.

Rebecca wrinkled her forehead. "I'm sorry about letting it get out that you are a scientist. Martha asked if you needed a Ph.D. to work in the Patent Office. After that it just kind of unraveled."

"It's okay. No way around it. I didn't expect us to have to renounce our degrees."

"And she pried it out of me when she asked about my 'statistical work.' She's a very well-informed woman. She even knew a lot about the National Institutes of Health."

The cabin lights went off in Cliff and Ethel Grimes' *Enginuity* as we walked by.

"I don't think that we came off as a threat to anyone."

"Except to their Southern storytelling." Rebecca tickled my ribs. "How do you come up with that stuff, Ben? You were even lapsing into bad grammar!"

I laughed. "Should I have answered them like my old mentor, Dr. Westley?"

Rebecca laughed, inviting a joke on the subject.

I reached into my depths to bring up my old mentor's punctilious Oxford-Cambridge accent. "Of course the *feces* could only have been *deposited* by the Carolinian visitor or his canine *surrogate*, since even the *stupidest* and most inbred New York City *provincial* would not bear to sit in front of such a —"

Rebecca rewarded me with a musical laugh. But we both went silent while passing Chuck and Bill's tuna tower boat. It looked like they had already bedded down in the small forward cabin. And inside the *Dream Weaver*, a flashlight was shining as Glenn and Stephanie worked to rearrange their small cabin into a bedroom. We boarded the *Diogenes* noiselessly and didn't talk again until we had unlocked it and were comfortably ensconced below.

It felt good to stretch out on a clean sheet with a nice, soft cushion underneath. The air was mosquito-free and not too warm, especially under the steady breeze from the portable fan that was running happily on shore power. The fan made the air feel cool and fresh, but did nothing to diminish the pungent smell of burning cannabis that was wafting in from the *Dream Weaver* next door.

"Well, Sherlock," Rebecca whispered from across the pillow, "what do you think? Did we pass muster?"

I went for a Sherlock Holmes voice. "Yes, my good doctor, we passed muster with SAWECUSS."

Rebecca laughed. "Sa-we-cuss?"

"Yes." I spelled it out for her.

"And what does that stand for?"

"The Social Auxiliary of the West End Cocaine Smuggling Society!"

She laughed again. "But that doesn't make sense, my dear Sherlock. You've put in a *U* that doesn't belong there."

"My dear doctor, the *U* has been added to make it properly *euphonic*."

Rebecca snorted in my ear.

"And for the sake of Rick Turner," I added, in Sherlockian tone.

"Why, may I ask, does Rick Turner need the letter *U*?" Rebecca asked, playing an exasperated Watson.

"Elementary, my dear doctor — he needs a *U* to cuss."

She snorted again, then blew into my ear. I overreacted, and we both laughed a lot more than warranted by any humor in our *shtick*. But that's one of the ways that Rebecca and I keep each other amused.

"Now, in a more serious vein, Ben, do you think we met the murderer tonight?"

"I don't know. But I think we can eliminate some of them."

"I think we could eliminate the boat mechanic and his mousey wife."

"Yes. She's always with him. And if she saw him shoot someone, she'd go into catatonic trance for at least a week."

"And we can also eliminate Ray and Martha," Rebecca said. "They're too rich and upper-class. They aren't the type."

"I agree. And when he said he wasn't out that night, nobody contradicted him. With a big trawler like that, he couldn't just slip out."

"Right. And I guess we can eliminate Stephanie and Glenn," she said, gesturing in the direction of the neighboring berth.

"Yeah, a sailboat doesn't make a very good stalking boat. And the conversation had them coming in from the east, which would put them in the wrong place."

"But they're doing something," Rebecca said. "Stephanie was real uptight, and Glenn was doing a lot of looking and listening but hardly any talking. And I don't think it's just a socio-economic thing. He's mainly a carpenter, incidentally. I think they have a secret that they're afraid will get out."

"I agree. Maybe they made a score in Abaco and they're on their way to Florida with it."

"What about Martin and Beth?"

"No, we can't eliminate the diving couple," I said. "Ray said they were out that night, and I sure could imagine Martin pulling the trigger."

"I could really imagine that electrician *Rick Turner* pulling the trigger," Rebecca said.

"I'll say! Mister Impulsive, himself. And he lied about being out that night. And when Ray contradicted him, he changed it to mean that he was on the Bank and not in the Stream."

"We'll really have to be careful around him," Rebecca said. "What do you think about Cal and Angie? Could you imagine her?"

"I wouldn't rule him out because of her. He's a smart operator — Wade, too. Their Southern good ole boy stuff isn't *schmaltz*, it's lubrication to keep things moving. They are well-coordinated, all three of them. Ray said that they weren't out that night but they could be involved in it, somehow."

"And we definitely can't rule out Chuck and Bill?"

"Ray said they were out that night. They're definitely candidates."

"Funny, Ben, how they were marginalized by the group but still so integrated."

"Yes, they have *some* relationship with Wade, or he wouldn't have invited them."

Over the hum of the fan, I heard a dull clang coming from the neighboring berth. At first, I thought it was from the wind beating a halyard against Glenn's mast. Then I realized there wasn't enough wind for that. Then I realized that the mast was being struck by a coaxial antenna cable hanging inside it, and that Glenn's boat was rocking like a church bell. And from that, I deduced that Glenn and Stephanie had finished their joint and had moved on to their next course of pleasure.

"Ben, would you be interested to know which people Sgt. Townsend interviewed?"

"Very much so."

"It was Martin Becker, Cal Sumter and Rick Turner."

"And not Wade Daniels?"

"Correct," Rebecca said.

"And how did you learn that?"

"Martha told me. She's a good observer."

I was very tired. Sleep had captured my legs and was working its way through my abdomen and up to my chest.

"Ben?" Rebecca coaxed.

"Yes," I yawned.

"It *did* seem awfully strange, didn't it?"

"What?"

"That nobody said a word."

"Said a word about what?"

"About 'Steve,'" she said.

Wheeling and Dealing   7

I typed a summary of the salvage into my laptop computer while enjoying my morning cup of coffee. The sun was still not too high and the north wind was blowing at just the right speed to keep the cabin well ventilated.

Now was the time for a more rigorous version of the palm-of-my-hand calculations that I'd made the first day. Where was the *Second Chance* at 10:40 that fatal evening?

I lay the big chart on the table, clipped a clear plastic overlay onto it, and got out my collection of colored, felt-tip pens. The first step was to record on the chart how the current and wind had been pushing around floating objects that night.

I used a red marker to draw lines showing how the Gulf Stream pushed things to the north. Close to Florida, the lines were long: The Stream moved an object four nautical miles north for every hour it floated there. As I started filling in lines closer to the Little Bahama Bank, I made the lines shorter. Close to shore, I made them only one nautical mile long. At the northwest corner of the Bank, I curved the lines to the east, allowing for so-called eddy effects.

Next, I pulled out a blue marker and drew lines to show how the tide had been pushing across the Little Bahama Bank and around its edges. I covered that part of the chart with two-mile-long blue arrows pointing out to sea.

Next, I estimated how much the wind could blow a motor yacht. Early that night, the wind had been blowing southeastward at 20 knots. Later it had subsided to 10 knots, blowing due south. Soon, the chart was covered with short green arrows showing the push of the wind.

Now was time to calculate what the *Second Chance* had done under its own power and the influence of current and wind. I would work the problem backwards, in one-hour steps. I put the black marker down on the X where we had found the yacht. From it, I drew a short black line that reversed the distance that the engines and autopilot had moved the yacht during the hour before we found it. At the end of that line, I drew a red line that added the reverse of what current had done during that hour. Then I used the green pen to add the effect of the wind. The red and green lines canceled each other out.

That was where the *Second Chance* had been, an hour before we found it. I used a black dot to mark the spot.

I repeated the process with the black, red and green markers. This moved the yacht backwards for another hour, bringing it closer to the Gulf Stream.

I repeated the process again and again. As I rolled the clock backwards, the yacht slid past the MS marker and the northwest edge of the Little Bahama Bank, and it slipped into the Gulf Stream, moving backwards quickly. Coming to the end of the eighth hour, I made a big black X.

Sensing my excitement, Rebecca looked up from her medical affidavit that she was rereading.

"And X marks the spot where the murder was committed," I said, with a flourish.

"And that's right here, just like you said."

"Yes. Fifteen miles directly west of us!"

Rebecca nodded. "That takes care of Wade Daniels' theory about a rendevous with a 'mother ship.'"

"Yes, if a ship had been fifteen miles off the coast, someone here should have seen it. Tell me," I added, "how are you doing with the medical affidavit?"

"I just finished copying it. I tried the semi-logarithmic plot that you suggested, using the environmental temperatures as a baseline. It didn't make any difference."

"Good," I said. "That will keep things simple for the Good Sergeant."

Rebecca went back to her affidavit and I went back to my chart. A minute later she looked at me with curiosity.

"Ben, you said you were done with it. What are you doing now?"

"I'm redoing the calculation with slightly different speeds to define an envelope of ninety-percent certainty."

"Good old Ben! Always *pushing the envelope.*"

"'Defining the envelope,' you mean. And just for that, you can fix me another cup of coffee."

Rebecca grabbed a red marker and drew a heart on the back of my hand. I stuck my tongue out at her. She planted a kiss on my mouth.

My "envelope of 90-percent-certainty" came out as a north-south-oriented oval, which put the *Second Chance* not more than 20 miles and not less than 10 miles from us. I typed the information into my laptop computer, in which I had been composing the report. Then, I hand-copied the whole thing onto a couple of sheets of paper. Too bad we didn't also have a printer on board.

I was savoring a second cup of coffee when Sgt. Townsend showed up at our dock.

"Requesting permission to come aboard," he announced in a soft baritone.

"Granted," I answered brightly and got up to meet him. He had actually taken off his shoes. Perhaps we would get off on the right foot today. "Come below and have a cup of coffee."

He declined the coffee but accepted a place at our table.

Rebecca made room and then handed him her affidavit.

"Is this your statement that puts the time of death at ten-forty?"

"Yes," she said. "Ten-forty plus or minus one-half hour. I hope the information will be useful to you."

"Yes, thank you, Dr. Levis." He shuffled through the papers. "I do not see a reference to a time-of-death table."

"I calculated it using one degree per hour for the first three hours, then two degrees per hour for the subsequent hours. And I verified the two-degree-per-hour rate using Dr. Candidi's *measured* rate of cooling, with help of a semi-logarithmic regression analysis on his scientific calculator, taking the ambient temperature into account. The time of death was minus eight hours. If your experts want to calculate it themselves, I have included the raw data."

Sgt. Townsend returned his attention to Rebecca's report. He read it with slow-moving eyes and some movement of his mouth. I gave Rebecca a wink. She responded with a grimace that said to be careful around the guy. We waited patiently. After a while, the Sergeant's eyes drifted to my salvage report and to the chart laying next to it. And when his eyes went wide, I couldn't suppress a chess player's smile.

"What is that?" he asked, pointing to the oblong figure encircling the *X* that marked the spot.

"It's a ninety-percent probability envelope for the position of the *Second Chance* at the time when they blasted the holes in its hull." When Townsend didn't say anything, I added, "It's all explained in my salvage report. I'll give you a copy, but I'll need a written acknowledgment of receipt."

"Very well," he said, looking like I'd just given him a drawer full of mixed nuts and bolts to sort out.

"And I will unlock the *Second Chance* for you. I assume you are going to visit it."

"Yes." He sat there, staring at the table.

"We were wondering if you have made any progress in identifying the victim."

Sgt. Townsend looked up. "The body was taken to the Rand Hospital in Freeport. I understand that the U.S. State Department is working on victim identification."

I used a coaxing tone. "But in the customs hut are a couple of officials who make everyone show their passports. He must have checked in with them not longer than three months ago."

Sergeant Townsend stared at me with irritation.

I asked, "Are you sure we can't give you a cup of coffee?"

"It would be no trouble," Rebecca added quickly.

"No, thank you." Sgt. Townsend looked at my chart, staring at the first *X* where we had found the *Second Chance*.

I waited a minute before resuming my coaxing. "Zelma Mortimer should certainly be able to help. I'm sure that the Bahamas has an innkeeper's law that requires her to demand valid identification and to accurately record names and addresses of the marina guests."

Townsend shook his head. Rebecca was giving me strong signals to not push the guy too hard. But if Townsend's game was to seize the yacht and give it to someone else, now was the time to take my stand as the salvage captain.

The Sergeant was avoiding my eyes. "The investigation is being directed from our headquarters in Freeport."

I worked hard to mask my frustration, assuming an attitude of polite insistence. "Can you give me the name of the assistant superintendent of police at Freeport?"

"That would not be appropriate at this time. You will communicate through me."

"Although the weather has been sunny since we came here, it could rain any time. When it does, all the fingerprint and blood spatter evidence will be washed away. I wonder if your assistant superintendent of police is aware of that."

"That has been noted," Sgt. Townsend said, raising his eyes from the chart.

"Good. If he has already noted that, then he must agree that after the first good rain, there will be no reason for the Royal Bahamas Police Force to detain my salvaged vessel here."

The Sergeant's eyes flared and he cleared his throat. "You have no proof that you found the vessel outside of Bahama jurisdiction."

"Oh, yes, we do," I said, struggling to maintain a polite tone. "We discovered this vessel in International Waters thirteen miles outside the Little Bahama Bank and I have laid salvage claim to it, under International Law. It was thirteen miles out — one mile outside your Twelve Mile Limit."

"I agree with that, completely," Rebecca said.

"You have no *proof* that it was outside the Twelve Mile Limit."

"We have proof by a GPS reading, duly recorded in the *Diogenes'* log," I said.

To hell with politeness. This was an argument.

Sgt. Townsend smiled. "And how are you to prove that you are not making this up for your own benefit?"

"For the convenience of my salvage claim?"

"Yes."

"Because I'm a scientist and she's a doctor. We don't falsify data. We are honest — intellectually honest." I was getting loud.

Townsend took another look at my chart and then smiled. "I see that your circle includes some territory which is inside our Twelve Mile Limit."

"Oh, now you're talking about the calculated location of the attack! Well you are right. Less than one-fifth of the area inside the oval is inside your territory. Over four-fifths of the area is outside your territory. With the present information, the odds are four-to-one that the attack occurred outside your territory. Without better information on the Gulf Stream current and the wind directions that night, I can't honestly exclude your territory as the site of the crime."

Townsend smiled, like he'd thought up a good chess move. "Since you can't honestly exclude it being inside our waters, you can't honestly reject our jurisdiction."

"Regarding the criminal act. Are you trying to have it both ways, Sergeant Townsend? Are you saying that my calculations were honest but that my recorded *facts* were falsified?"

"*Our* recorded facts," Rebecca added before Townsend could say a word. "I made the GPS reading, too."

Townsend was flustered for a minute, then the smile returned to his face. "And where is your proof that the boat was sinking?"

"You demand proof?" I yelled. "You must have recorded the high water mark in the cabin when I first showed you the boat."

"And I took photos that show the boat sinking," Rebecca said. She was beginning to share my exasperation.

"You have photos? Where are they? I would like to see them."

"They're in our camera, undeveloped," Rebecca said.

Townsend extended a palm. "I will require the film as material evidence."

It was time to jump back in. "You may have *prints* from us as evidence. We need the originals for our salvage claim."

"You will give me the film. I will have it developed and have copies returned."

He was making me mad. "No, I'll take the van to Freeport and get the film developed there."

"And I will receive one set of prints," Townsend said.

"Only after you sign and annotate them as true copies received by you and that —"

"Quiet! Both of you," Rebecca exclaimed. "I'll go to Freeport, and you two can spend the rest of the day right here, butting heads."

I tried to suppress a laugh and failed. Sgt. Townsend shrugged his shoulders, turned up his palms and laughed, too. And Rebecca seemed surprised at herself.

I picked up the chart and grabbed the camera from behind the ledge along the wall. I went to the cockpit and photographed the chart in direct sunlight. Rebecca came out with the log book and our two affidavits tucked under her arm, in a cloth bag. "Make photocopies and get him to sign them," I whispered.

Sgt. Townsend came up, looking much more benign than before. "Dr. Levis, I can drive you in my jeep."

"No, thank you," she said. "We're trying to keep a low profile."

"Then I will follow the van. You should get off in downtown Freeport. There is a drugstore within sight of the bus stop. I wish us all a good day." Townsend climbed to the dock, put on his shoes and walked off.

Rebecca slipped the camera into the bag, gave me a kiss, and walked off. For the next few minutes, I sat alone in the *Diogenes'* cockpit worrying that Sgt. Townsend might snatch Rebecca's bag and destroy the evidence. Boy, if he did anything like that, I would drive that boat out of here faster than you could say "Ivanhoe."

I looked around. Luckily the sailing couple next door hadn't been home to hear our interview with the Sergeant. But the whole marina must have noticed that Townsend had paid us a long visit.

Hell, if the police were going to be no help and all hindrance, there was nothing to do but help myself. I went below and grabbed my cellphone. As Rebecca had predicted, it wasn't working yet. So I grabbed my little brown book in which I keep my credit cards, locked the *Diogenes*, and walked over to the pay phone near the bathrooms and showers. There, I called up Lt. (Junior Grade) Michael Davis. No, the U.S. Coast Guard had not, by chance, turned up "Steve's" full name and address.

While I was inquiring, Wade Daniels slid by. I waved a pleasant hello and watched him move out to the small parking lot behind the marina office and get into a faded-blue compact Chevy.

Next, I directed my inquiry to the U.S. Embassy in Nassau. Ms. Helen Cobb, public information officer, told me that the victim had not yet been identified and that the Bahamian police were investigating the murder. She listened politely to my arguments about the importance of notifying the next of kin and how easy it would be for the Embassy to inquire with the marina office.

In the middle of this conversation, Rick Turner walked by. The outspoken electrician from Delray Beach went into the men's restroom and shower. A Toyota van with right-hand steering pulled into the parking lot, and Rebecca came forward to climb into it.

Ms. Cobb listened nicely enough, but I was becoming upset with her passivity. "Can't you call Customs and find out the name and passport number of the man who took out a three-month cruising permit for the *Second Chance?*"

"We will see what our procedure allows."

No getting around it: I would have to start putting my own money into this project.

I had directory assistance give me the phone number of Jimmy

Sykes, a detective who had helped me before. I got him on his cellphone.

"Jimmy, this is Ben."

"I hope you are keeping out of trouble."

"Keeping out of it, but I seem to have a lot of it swimming around me."

I told him about the yacht salvage and my search for the identity of "Steve."

"Well, whatchu want me to do?"

"Find out who owns the S.C. Corporation whose address is post office box number five forty-seven in Miami, Florida, zip code three-three-one-three-three."

"The post office box is in Coconut Grove," Jimmy said.

"Right. Look up the corporation with Florida's Department of State and see if they have an officer named 'Steve.'"

"If I hit the jackpot, do I tell the little woman the bad news?"

"Good question. It would probably be best to tell them you are inquiring for a guy concerning his boat. You want to know the name of his insurance company and that you also want to talk to the lawyer of the corporation. You get me the info, and I'll turn it over to the U.S. State Department and the Bahamian police. They can tell her she's a widow."

"And if the corporation doesn't have any officer named 'Steve?'"

"Same deal. You are inquiring for a guy concerning the boat. You want to know the name of the insurance company and to talk to the corporation's lawyer."

"You sure you want me to take this one on, Ben. I'm gonna have to charge you straight hourly fees."

I felt more bad news coming on. "Sure. What will that be?"

"First hour for free, then two-fifty an hour plus expenses."

"Wow. I didn't know you'd gone to law school."

"Candidi the *optimist*! Wasn't that what that old Brit was calling you at the victory celebration?"

"Did Dr. Broadmoore make fun of my name to you? After I put myself out on the line evaluating that biotech company for him?"

"Risked my life" was what I really meant, but there was no way to be sure I wasn't being overheard.

"Didn't ask him about it, Ben. And I didn't ask him anything about Volt-Tare, either. But I know what an optimist is, Ben. It's someone that will walk into a roomful of bad guys. If I'm going to be risking my life sniffing out a mailbox corporation that's running drugs, you gotta give me regular pay for it."

"Okay. I read you. And you're right. Walking in a room full of bad guys."

"Working for the FBI," he sang, in wavery nasal.

"I've heard that song somewhere before, Jimmy."

"It's 'Long Cool Woman in a Black Dress' by the Hollies." Jimmy let out a big whoop, like in the song.

"Well, get it on . . . on!" I half sung.

Rick Turner came back from the men's room without his engineer's cap and with damp hair. He must have been in the shower.

I joked around some more with Jimmy before hanging up. The conversation was fun, even if it would add one thousand dollars to my salvage bill.

I waved to Martha Vangelden, who was on her way to the ladies' room and shower. The culture maven raised an eyebrow in acknowledgment.

It must have been a habit, a reflex or homing instinct: My fingers dialed a familiar number.

And I waved to Chuck and Bill, the guys from the boat with the high tuna tower. They were on their way to the men's room and shower. Bill looked kind of sick.

"Laboratory for Protein Kinase Investigation," answered the deep, friendly voice. It was my erstwhile dissertation advisor and recent collaborator, Rob McGregor, Research Associate Professor of Pharmacology at Miami's Bryan Medical School.

"Rob, this is a blast from your past," I said, echoing Rob's words of a few months ago — words that had started a conversation that had lured me from my job at the U.S. Patent Office to set up as a temporary research assistant professor in Miami. The job had turned out to be more temporary than I'd expected, and the dust hadn't settled yet.

"Ben! How's my ex-graduate student doing? Where are you?"

"On Grand Bahama Island."

"Yeah, I heard you were headed that way after you went back to pick up Rebecca in Washington. You made it okay? How was the trip?"

I decided to not tell him about the salvage project. Rob was a natural born amplifier for stories. Tell it to him, and he'd spam the whole med school with it. "Fair weather and following seas until we got a big storm two hundred miles off North Carolina coast. The wind was blowing our way but there was too much of it. Sailed for four days and nights on nothing but the storm jib. Waves were so high that the autopilot was useless. Rebecca and I had to alternate on two-hour watches."

"I thought it was supposed to be six-hour watches."

"Too wet and cold for more than two hours at a time."

"Wet wind and waves, huh?"

"Wind was so strong it nearly blew the inflatable off the bow."

"Inflatable boat? I thought your auxiliary was a little fiberglass dinghy."

"It was. But we got a good deal on an inflatable plus outboard."

"Why an inflatable?"

"You can use it as a survival raft. It floats even if it's swamped. And for protection against that, I cut and grommeted some canvas to span the top."

"Is Candidi getting cautious in his old age?"

The burly Canadian Scotsman could never resist playful jest.

"Sailing way out in the Atlantic in November is a lot tougher than sailing up the Gulf Stream in May. But yes, I am a lot more cautious. Older, sadder and wiser, too. How are things doing at Bryan Medical School?"

"The shakeup is still going on, and the dust hasn't settled yet."

Cosmic coincidence! Thinking the same thoughts, using the same analogies. "Is there any *professional* news to share with me?"

Then came the double cosmic coincidence.

"Yes, your old client Dr. Broadmoore is trying to get hold of you. He called last week. Made it sound pretty important. I told him you were planning to vacation in the Bahamas."

"What did he say to that?"

"He said, 'Capital!'"

"As head of the Broadmoore Capital Company, I'm sure that's what's on his mind. I'll give him a call. Say, tell me, how's the lab going? And how's my ex-lab going?"

"It's going great! The ex-Peterson lab is running fine under Mildred the Super-Tech. And, yes, I'll be sure to put your name on all the research papers that I will submit, based on that work."

"You'd better. I *designed* a lot of those experiments."

"Yeah, you're a real designing guy."

I sensed that it was time to end the conversation, and did so — politely, of course.

Chuck and Bill came out of the men's restrooms and showers. Bill really did look bad, like every step was painful. Both of them avoided my eyes.

I dialed Broadmoore's number and was answered by Sally, his tomboyish personal assistant who served him ably as a "results wizard." And within seconds I was connected to the wily old Brit, himself.

"Ben!" he boomed. "So glad to hear from you."

"Same here."

"Yes, I'm so *very* glad to hear from you. Knowing that you are an old Bahamas hand, I called you at the Patent Office and they said that you'd resigned to take a position at Bryan Medical School. And when I called the dean's office there — they don't seem to be organized with a central exchange as you would expect from any normal medical school — well, they seemed to be in the throws of a major upset. Anyway, they did give me a number for your colleague — Rob McGregor."

I could imagine the old boy, pacing around his dark-paneled Boston office in his double-breasted suit, his thin-soled size-12 shoes leaving deep impressions in the thick carpet, stretching the phone cord to the limit as he moved to the window for a peek at the Charles River. Like his name, everything about him was broad, including his northern English accent. Broad face and heavy-handed. But with a nose that could seek out pharmaceutical opportunity like a pig can seek out truffles. Heavy-handed, yes, but they were Midas hands.

"Yes. I'm on a vacation," I replied. Actually, it was a paid leave of absence from the med school.

"Yes, so I understand," Broadmoore said, dropping his voice.

"Please tell me, what I can do for you?"

"You can tell me exactly where you are, to start with."

I waved to Martha Vangelden. The lay of her auburn hair told me she had taken a shower. Pretty environmentally conscious of her – taking her shower here and not in her three-deck trawler that would put soapy water into the yacht basin.

"I am at West End, Grand Bahama Island."

"Capital!"

"Yes?"

"Yes, I will get to the point. I had first wanted just your advice, as an old Bahama hand, but now that you —. I will never in my life forget what a superb job you did for me on the BIOTECH buyout, homing in on the scientific truth like a bloodhound."

"My pleasure." It was another project that blew up in my face.

"I was wondering if I could *engage* you on our behalf, once again."

A chance to make some money! And what excitement I felt coming over me! I felt like a bloodhound when they wave an unwashed shirt in front of his nose and say, "Go get 'im, boy." But it would defeat my purpose to jump at this one too eagerly.

"Sure. Delighted," I said. "But I have to tell you that Rebecca wants this to be a vacation, and I have already picked up a little salvage project that will also pin me down here."

"You won't need to *travel* for me. Not very far, at least. I am offering you a chance to work *while* on vacation. Your work will take place right on the water . . . which, I know, is the very essence of your soul . . . well, at least of your heart."

"And also of my blood and lymph. Don't try to humor me."

"That was quite *good*, Ben. Blood, lymph, bodily fluids . . . and humors!" Then he cleared his throat to announce that we would now have a serious scientific discussion. "You will remember when we took over the BIOTECH Florida Corporation, that their project for large-scale culture of sponge cells was in its infancy. You will remember that they said it would be possible to harvest the anticancer compounds from sponges in the Bahamas for the early stages of the project."

"Yes, I remember."

"Actually, the cell culture process has proven a little finicky — not as simple as brewing beer in a vat, it would seem. And with our main efforts to position ourselves for a stock offering going swimmingly, despite an adverse market, and with the 'phase one, phase-two' clinical trial going just swell, it would seem necessary to have the assurance of the ability to produce or harvest a good supply of *zagrionic acid* — the *actual anticancer compound*."

His emphasis on these last three words was so visceral that I imagined him parking his broad buttocks on his mahogany desk. I guessed that the fate of his soon-to-be-proffered $200 million stock offering was at risk.

"Yes, I heard that the small-scale clinical trials were very promising."

"Sir Hector Pimentel, an old Cambridge acquaintance, assures me that the Bahamian supply of sponges is substantial . . . and that an agreement for their harvesting could be worked out. In fact, he is enthralled with the idea — from the political standpoint and for increasing employment for his poor island country."

"Is this Sir Hector Pimentel a Bahamian?" I asked.

"Quite so," Dr. Broadmoore said.

I waved to Cal Sumter who was on his way to the showers. The Southern humorist waved back and smiled, too.

"I understand, Dr. Broadmoore."

"The only thing that seems to be missing is *quantitative data* on how many of the correct sponges are in their waters. No one seems to have the foggiest. Of course, the Bahamians' own scientific research is farcical, so there is no turning to *them*. And our discrete inquiries at two leading American marine institutes didn't help much either."

"And you would like me to find out for you."

"Precisely! Since you are in the field, already. You could make some quantitative estimates. And take some underwater photos . . . identify the species of course. And collect some samples that you could send to our Miami facility."

"I would just go out with my inflatable and do this?" I asked, with some irony.

"Quite."

Sure, it would be a fun project. But I wasn't going to let him present it like I was a college student, earning five dollars here and five dollars there. Not when it was really a big piece of work. Not when he had $20 million of his own money riding on it and was gambling on a chance to make $200 million.

Now, to get him to admit to the magnitude of his problem: "The Bahamas is a seven hundred and fifty mile expanse of water. Too much to do from my inflatable. How much of it do you need surveyed?"

"The flat water north of Grand Bahama Island should do. If the sponges prove too sparse, it might be necessary to extend the survey to Eleuthera."

Now to put a frame around the project: "I understand. In short, you want me to make a quantitative survey of the Little Bahama Bank, a sixty-by-forty-mile expanse of water. And you want me to figure out the number of pounds of sponges you can harvest every year without causing ecological concern. And you want me to figure out how many thousands of kilograms of zagrionic acid you could get out of those sponges every year. And you want me to write it all in a report with my name on it, so you can show it to your stockholders and make it part of a Securities and Exchange Commission filing. And it all has to be able to survive an audit so that nobody will get sued or have to go to jail."

"Please rest assured that the company will indemnify you."

"How long do I have for this project?"

"As long as you need. Say one month. One month from today. That is when I would like to have the report, anyway."

"Okay, one month for the sponge count. And another month to produce my final report, which will include your chemical assays of the samples that I will send you."

"Good."

"Working five days a week at one thousand and two hundred dollars a day."

That would come out to $48,800 if we started right away.

"Well . . ."

It was so predictable. Now that he had me pinned down on the number of days, he was dragging his feet, hoping to cut down on my daily rate.

"To get a marine institute to do the job, it would cost you one hundred and fifty thousand dollars, and you'd probably have to wait a year for the report."

"But it would seem . . . when explaining it to my partners . . . to be expensive for the services of just one person."

"Make that two persons, because Rebecca will help. And she's a medical doctor. That will look good on the report."

Cal Sumter came back from the showers, taking his time and probably trying to grab an earful of my conversation.

Broadmoore was taking his time, too. "Well . . ."

How unfortunate, that I had to argue with him, now. "And I won't charge you for the use of our equipment. Hell, a marine institute would probably charge you eighty thousand for use of their research vessel. The only extra expense you will have is the air freight for the samples that I send your Miami lab to analyze."

Cal must have heard most of that. But he was out of earshot, now.

"Yes," Broadmoore said, "your point is well taken. I agree with your terms."

Just in time! He had saved me having to argue that it could be dangerous to survey anything in an area where smugglers are operating.

"Great, Dr. Broadmoore. Just send me a letter, stating the terms we have just agreed to, care of the marina here. I should be able to start next week, after I clear up some odds and ends here." Before we hung up, I gave him my account number for the payments and the marina's address and phone number.

In high spirits, I went back to my original project: the *Second Chance*. After saying good morning to Ivanhoe, who was sitting nearby weaving palm fronds, I went aboard. The motors started up fine and the electric gauges showed that the alternators were still making electricity. Martin and Beth didn't seem to be home on the dive boat next door so I ran the engines for a full ten minutes. I turned on the radar and its screen filled with the same blotchy, overexposed pattern as before. I turned on the VHF marine radio. It kept me company with an occasional announcement on Channel 16: people hailing each other and calling out the numbers of other channels for more extended conversation.

Thinking about radio communication, I looked down on that low-mounted console of radio modules that had gotten so badly sloshed. Maybe Rebecca's fresh water spray bath had done some good. The nervous relay switch wasn't flipping on and off any more. The pilot light said it was permanently on, now. Presumably the radio's electronic modules were getting steady, reliable power. However, I couldn't get the consoles to turn on by pushing buttons. And the LCD displays didn't show a thing. Hopefully they would bake themselves dry and self-resurrect like the relay switch. Once, an FM car radio on the *Diogenes* had self-resurrected for me like that after three months of disuse.

I puttered around the boat for a long time. It was important to remind people of my salvage claim — especially the police. And people did take notice, especially Angie Sumter. She walked up the center dock to the marina office to get a soft drink, then took a wide circle on the way back. We exchanged waves while I was standing on the bow. She walked toward me along the seawall until we were within talking distance. She had such an attractive smile.

"Wow, you had a lot of talking to do on the phone," she said.

I smiled back. "Yes, I had to let a lot of friends and acquaintances know that we're here, and not at the bottom of the Atlantic Ocean."

She held my gaze long after I stopped, as if she were expecting me to volunteer much more. When I didn't, she turned up the smile and said, "Talking about sinking boats — wow! — wasn't that boat full last night? And you and Cal really got that boat rocking!"

"Yeah, we were having a grand ole time doing that thing about Ole Boo, the pickup truck and the Eye-Talian sandwich shop."

Angie gave me a broad wink. "And Cal had a grand ole time looking over Rebecca." She made a gesture like she was swatting a dog that was begging from under the table. "I hope she wasn't insulted."

"That's okay. Rebecca's used to it. She never pays much attention."

"Well, I'm so glad that we all understand each other so well." She put so much music into those words. "Rebecca told me you-all used to live in Miamah. Did she grow up on Miamah Beach?"

She was very good at it — steering the conversation exactly where she wanted it to go. I probably reacted with a shy smile.

"Good guess. Actually, she comes from New York."

"I guess a girl would be used to different customs up there."

"Actually Rebecca is completely omni-cultural. She likes to immerse herself in all kinds of cultures — and in their music, too."

"Really?" Angie batted her blue eyes and didn't give me anywhere to go. "And what about you? Are you omni-cultural, too?"

I took a glance at Ivanhoe, a dozen yards behind her. His smile told me that he'd been following our conversation — our body language, at least.

I couldn't help myself. Just had to have a little fun with Angie. "I really love the Dixie Chicks," I said, swallowing "the."

"Well, I do say!" Angie exclaimed. She combined a shocked tone with twinkling of the eyes. "Maybe I should come over there and slap your face!"

I hammed it up, pleading for her understanding. "No, the Dixie Chicks are the most talented girl band on the music scene. They're not just good-looking. They can all sing, and two of them are real musicians. One plays the guitar and banjo, and I especially like the one who plays the violin and mandolin."

"Why Dr. Candidi, you're such a tease. You sure know how to lead a girl on."

Behind her, Ivanhoe was flashing gold. I looked around, just in time to catch sight of Cal Sumter, coming back from the marina office. I gave him a wave and yelled hello before returning my attention to Angie, who had also noticed Cal.

"Yeah, but I would never get a Dixie chick in trouble with a jealous husband."

"No, Ben, he's not jealous. In fact we decided together to invite you and Rebecca to dinner, tomorrow night, if y'all's free." She looked at me with such vulnerability.

"It sounds great, but can I get back to you after talking to Rebecca? Have to make sure that she doesn't have anything planned."

Angie pursed her lips. "Sure, Ben. Bye!" She turned on a heel and walked towards her husband. I stayed put in case he wanted to come over and talk. But all he did was give me another friendly wave. He linked arms with Angie and she sashayed him back to their boat near the end of the center dock.

I went back to my puttering. This berth was an excellent location for observing most of what went on at the marina. I could see the front of the marina office and most of the boats on the center dock. And I had an unobstructed view up the water lane to the fuel dock. A Waverunner guy pulled in there and pumped a lot of gas. How big were the tanks on those things, anyway?

An hour or so later, my neighbor Wade Daniels appeared on the bow of his *Wholesale Delight*. Standing in the cockpit, we held a conversation across the water lane. I thanked him for the evening, and he said it was his pleasure. I said he had a nice group of friends, and he said that yacht owners are naturally friendly. I asked him if he'd had a good trip into town, and he said it was to stock up on beer and that if we ever needed anything he'd be glad to get it. Then, he asked if the boat was drying out. I said yes, and we'd be putting back the cushions by the end of the day.

After taking a lunch break on the *Diogenes*, I returned to spend the rest of the afternoon on the *Second Chance*. The dive boat was out. The afternoon was uneventful except for a visit from a guy with a Cigarette boat. With its open exhaust and ragged idle, the boat sounded like a couple of oversized Harleys. Ray Vangelden appeared on the top deck of his trawler as the boat came into view by the fuel dock. Tying up for fuel would have been a logical move, but the Cigarette boat guy didn't go there right away. He maneuvered his racing machine down the lane toward me, with a lot of unnecessary stop-and-go action on the throttle that dug in the heavy stern and bobbed the long bow. He was a Bahamian with a heavy, muscular build and skin as dark as his wrap-around sunglasses. And he had a wrap-around attitude to match.

We got a good look at each other when he poked his bow into the diving couple's empty berth. As the guy backed up and started counter-rotating his twin props, Wade Daniels came out with a boat pole like he was ready to lend his weight to push the guy off, if necessary. The two guys seemed to acknowledge each other without waving or saying anything. Ray Vangelden kept watching from the top deck of his trawler, shaking his head. And, next door to him, Angie watched from the flybridge of *Sumter's Forte*. And over the VHF marine radio of the *Second Chance*, I heard an announcement to change to Channel 26.

But the go-fast boat captain gave nobody anything to call the police about. He manipulated his throttles skillfully to lift and swing the bow past the outermost piling of Martin Becker's berth. Next, he showed class, with a fast, gasoline-powered, 70-degree twist. Then he cruised up the lane like a guy in a muscle car who could lay rubber any time he wanted but found it cooler, still, to keep everyone waiting in anticipation.

He pulled up to the fuel dock, threw up a couple of lines, and waited calmly for the attendant to secure them to the dock. Maybe he thought he was cool, but to me he looked out of place. I can't get used to dark, long-sleeved dress shirts and dress pants on the water. But Island standards are different than coastal marinas' standards. Maybe *he* was the one who fit here best — like the name written in creepy-looking red letters on the boat's transom — *Chango*. That's the Santeria god for thunder, among other things.

Too bad that Wade Daniels had disappeared so quickly from his bow. He could have filled me in on this thunder god. But I did flip to Channel 26 in time to hear a scratchy voice say, "Someone oughta tell him to go back to Mulberry Lane."

But since the guy wasn't following standard radio protocol, I had no idea who he was.

As the afternoon wore on, I picked up the rhythm of the marina. I noticed an old Island woman cooking a pot over a wood fire at the edge of the Australian pines by the Customs shed. Probably conch chowder. And I noticed when Edgar the pallet foreman pulled in with a motorboat and tied up along the seawall, not too far from her.

Taking a stroll in Edgar's direction, I learned he was selling conch for two dollars apiece. Placing a shell on the seawall, he would crack the tip of its spiral with a hammer to break the suction and then pry it out of the shell with a knife. I approached and asked if I could watch. He said yes and went back to work. He hummed to himself and threw out occasional words of commentary or explanation, turning up his heavy head to look at me every once in a while. He sure had a big pile of conch in the bottom of that open boat. It was a serviceable boat, painted dark green and outfitted with two 90-horse outboard motors in back. I imagined that he would waste no time, driving it full-throttle and on high plane from one favorite spot on the Bank to another, collecting his daily catch. For two dollars apiece, it was a bargain. I thought about how money comes into the marina and then trickles down when people buy a couple of hundred dollars worth of fuel, a couple of conchs, or a bowl full of conch chowder.

After watching Edgar crack and extract two conchs, I pulled out a five-dollar bill and he packed their meat in a large Ziploc bag for me. I told him to keep the change.

I finished off the afternoon by putting the dried-out cushions back into the *Second Chance*. I locked it down for the night, then went over to say goodbye to Ivanhoe and see what he was making from palm fronds today. It was a cricket. The feelers came out of its folded head as thin strips.

Returning to the *Diogenes*, I sipped a cold beer or two and I tried to keep from worrying about Rebecca. Just before nightfall she trudged back with a big cloth bag filled with groceries under each arm.

I kissed her and asked, "How did the photos come out?"

"Fine. Everything's taken care of. I gave the Sergeant a full set of pictures and we made photocopies of our log and our affidavits. He promised to bring back signed copies, tomorrow." She handed me the pictures. They were very good. "We made the photocopies at the Freeport police station. It wasn't very impressive. Just a little one-storey green building."

"Did you meet Sergeant Townsend's assistant superintendent of police?"

"No, and there weren't too many people working there, either." She studied me for a second. "Ben, why aren't you smiling?"

"Because I still don't trust that guy. He isn't serious about the investigation. He didn't take fingerprints. I think he's putting the stall on us for someone who wants to take the boat."

"Maybe there's a simpler explanation to it. Like he doesn't have any fingerprint dust and is too proud to admit it. Be happy."

"I'll try." I lit the alcohol stove, and Rebecca pulled a tomato and a head of lettuce from the cloth bag, then started chopping with gusto. While returning the log, chart and camera to their places, I told Rebecca about Dr. Broadmoore's proposal. How much fun it would be to explore the Little Bahama Bank while getting paid for it!

"So there!" Rebecca said. "Even if you lose the claim to the boat, you'll have a windfall from Broadmoore."

"Yes, except that I'd like to have both of them."

Rebecca unpacked the rest of the groceries and went to work at the stove. And I showed her the conch I'd bought from Edgar. "Great, we can marinate it and have it tomorrow. No, wait. We are invited for dinner, tomorrow night. Angie and Cal saw me on the way back. They asked me and I said yes. Why are you smiling?"

"I saw it coming. Angie talked me up for a while this afternoon until Cal came by."

"Now, tell me why you are laughing."

"Did you notice last night that Cal was looking you over."

"No. Not especially."

"But Angie did. And she told me so. And not disapprovingly."

"What are you telling me, Ben?"

"There's a lot going on with them below the surface. It might not take more than a couple of cocktails to bring it up."

"And how do you know all that, Ben?"

"From many Swarthmore midnight sophomore bull sessions which infused me with the occult knowledge and ancient wisdom of my old friend Richard Bash."

Rebecca laughed. "Oh, *him* again. Well, I say *bull* to those *sessions*! If Cal or Angie are too forward, we'll just step back onto the dock."

Dinner was soon ready. We took our plates topside, along with a couple of glasses and a bottle of red wine. It was pleasant. Glenn and Stephanie were not at home and neither of our tuna tower neighbors was aloft. Across the lane at the end of the central dock, Ray and Martha's trawler looked cozy with cabin lights shining on polished wood behind the portholes of the lower deck. I could make out Martha's silhouette on the top deck. A transient cabin cruiser blocked any view of Cal and Angie's boat. But farther down the dock, from the cockpit of the next cabin cruiser, I noticed a curious, mostly bluish flicker. It was on Rick Turner's boat, and it took me a while to figure out that he was watching TV.

After a while, we locked up and took a stroll toward the showers. We waved to Chuck who was sitting on the back of his boat, listening to Jay Patten singing about a black hat and a saxophone. I got a glimpse of Bill, lying in the small forward cabin. Farther down the line, Cliff and Ethel were watching satellite TV in the cockpit of the *Engineuity*.

After a visit to the facilities, we took a stroll through the marina. Wade Daniels seemed to have withdrawn to his air-conditioned cabin.

Past the marina office and around the bend in the seawall, the *Second Chance* looked proud and unmolested. I said a good evening to Ivanhoe, who was still sitting in his chair. Martin and Beth's *Rapture of the Reef* was back in its place, and they seemed to be below deck. The shack at the fuel dock was shut down, and so was the customs hut. I threw an arm around Rebecca and we strolled to the west, past a couple of hundred yards of abandoned "commercial harbor." The basin was about the size of the yacht harbor. Apparently, it had been set up to handle small island freighters. We continued until we reached the west shore, which faced the Straits of Florida and Gulf Stream. There the beach was steep, rocky and strewn with patches of seaweed. We could only go hand-in-hand. The high moon glistened the palm trees behind us and sparkled the waves before us. Rebecca stopped. I put my arms around her. We shared a kiss.

Even with the help of the moonlight, it was too rough to stroll the shore, southward. We retraced our steps, passing a still-vigilant Ivanhoe and then the *Diogenes*. From there, we went east along the palm-lined shore that faced the Little Bahama Bank. Here, the shoreline wasn't quite so rough. After going half a mile, I began to make out the shapes of the beached boats. As we walked the second half mile they got bigger, and so did the spotlight on the side of the pre-fab building. It was quite a collection of aquatic toys: Hobie catamarans, sailboards, kayaks and even a couple of sailing prams. A dozen Waverunner machines were secured together with heavy chain.

Off to the right, beyond a ridge of coral ground covered with scrub growth and then pines, we saw a hint of light and heard traces of music.

Rebecca pulled on my arm. "Do you really want to keep going, Ben?"

"No, we can explore the rest of the beach during the day."

When we returned to our dock, Glenn and Stephanie were home. We chatted with them for a while, from boat to boat, until Rebecca yawned and we retired below. In the middle of our second glass of wine, smoke of the pungent weed began wafting in.

8   The Lay of the Land

Our fourth day in Bahamas got off to a brisk start. Dressed in a dark-green blouse and a full-length black skirt, Zelma Mortimer appeared at our dock shortly after nine o'clock. Rhinestones sparkled on her fingernails as she handed me a fax. It was a contract, signed by Dr. Broadmoore with the request that I countersign and return it. I thanked Zelma, saying I would like to fax back an answer in an hour or so. Reading it quickly, I noted that it contained all the terms and conditions we'd agreed to the day before. Broadmoore had even included a page illustrating the sponge's taxonomy. They had thought of everything except for a confidentiality clause. Maybe that was just as well since his decision to fax the contract through the marina office made it impossible for me to keep the project secret.

"What do you think?" Rebecca asked, after I set the papers down.

"The contract's fine. If we start tomorrow, we'll be forty-eight thousand dollars richer two months from now."

"Great. Tell me the plan, Fearless Leader."

"I'll get a couple of tanks full of gas today, and we can go out tomorrow and survey the first quadrant, up to four miles north of here and four miles west of here. Should be able to do that in a day. We'll be under way half the time, and in the water counting sponges the rest of the time. We'll also see a lot of interesting fish, plants and coral."

Rebecca's face clouded over. "Are you going to need me every day, for the whole two months?"

"No, your participation is purely voluntary."

"Good, because I want to see the Islanders, too. What are your plans for today?"

"It will take me only half an hour to get the gas. Then I need to do some calling around."

"You can use your cellphone. Mine's connected. I've checked."

"Great. Then the only thing left is 'matters arising' with Sergeant Townsend."

Rebecca frowned. "He's not here. I've already checked."

"He owes us a signature on our affidavits."

"That's true. But we're not going to ruin our day waiting for him. You know the town of West End from when you were here before, but all I know of it is what I saw through the window of the van to Freeport. Now, I want you to get our bikes out of the V-berth. We're going to explore the town and take a long ride in the countryside."

"Yes, ma'am! I'm clearing the agenda for exploration."

My cellphone did work and Jimmy had some news.

"The post office box listed for the corporation turned out t' be at the Coconut Grove Substation, Ben. Was one of them six-by-four boxes that you open from the lobby with the key they give you. The door on this one was loose enough to get some fiber optic through the bottom. Didn't see nothin' in her. I did a records check with the Florida Department of State. It gave the same post office box, and listed the name of Stephen Maynard as the only officer. A phonebook check didn't show any Stephen Maynard in the Miami area. None in the Keys, neither. There was one in Broward and another in Palm Beach County, but both of them's alive and don't have nothin' to do with no corporation or boat. So what it looks like t' me like the dead man was a druggie who's keeping a low profile."

"Good work."

"Thanks. Of course, I didn't leave 'er at that. I mailed this Stephen Maynard a letter on plain paper saying to get in contact with me concerning an important matter concerning his boat. The number I gave them is to a safe phone that I answer with just a 'hello' so they won't know I'm a detective. Mailed the letter then and there, so the corporation should be getting it in its box today. Want me to swing by and check her?"

"Yes, I'm interested in whether they have someone to pick up the mail."

After finishing the conversation with Jimmy, I signed the contract and took it over to the marina office with a twenty-dollar bill in hand, which I offered Zelma as payment for sending it. Zelma accepted and even opened her Dutch door so I could come in and feed the copies into the machine by myself. But she remained a stickler for correctness, writing out a receipt for the payment. I thanked her and said that a FEDEX letter might be coming in a couple of days.

Ivanhoe was still guarding the *Second Chance*. No, Sgt. Townsend hadn't come. No, he didn't have any idea if or when he would come. Yes, he would tell the Sergeant to see me when he did show up. But something told me that I wasn't going to get any police counter-signature on our affidavits.

I asked Ivanhoe what was the diagonally woven, finger-sized cylinder that he had made. He grinned and said it was for putting your fingers into. It was a Chinese finger puzzle: The harder you try to pull your fingers apart, the tighter they are clamped in the device.

Returning to the *Diogenes*, I found Rebecca making sandwiches. The sailing couple had apparently gone off for a swim. I called the U.S. Embassy and spoke to Ms. Helen Cobb again. She told me that the body had been shipped to the United States and that she was not allowed to give out any more information. I made her take down my cellphone number "in case the victim's relatives want to talk to me." Fat chance of that! And no chance of learning anything from her.

Next, I called my old boss and mentor, Geoffrey A. Westley, M.D. and Chief Medical Examiner for Miami-Dade County. He was glad to hear from me. He would have been glad to help me, too, but there had been no arrangement to ship any body from the Bahamas to his facility. Yes, he would contact me if he happened to learn anything.

I sat in the cockpit for a quarter of an hour, thinking of how to get some more power behind my salvage claim. An idea occurred to me:

I called Daniel Lynch, a lawyer with a one-man practice. I had once done some expert witness work for him.

"Dan, this is Ben. How are you doing?"

"Fine. I don't have any major cases right now. I'm resting up from the last one."

Daniel Lynch was an honest lawyer and that was what I needed.

"I'm calling from the Bahamas. I want to talk to you about doing some work for me."

"You haven't been arrested, have you?"

"No, it's the other way around." I told him about the salvage. "I want you to file a salvage claim against the vessel in Miami."

"Okay."

"I want you to move fast, quick and dirty, just like I did for you in the Saunders case."

"Okay," he said, with less enthusiasm.

"Today, I would like you to send, by certified, return receipt letter to the 'S.C. Corporation,' a formal notification that the yacht was salvaged by me and that I am claiming one hundred thousand dollars or one-half of its fair market value, whichever is greater." I gave Daniel the Coconut Grove post office address and wording to describe the condition of the vessel when I found it.

"Fine," he said. "I will have my paralegal work it up and send it out today. Is there anything else?"

"Yes, I would like you to file a salvage claim in Federal Court."

"Filing a Federal case? Don't you think that would be premature?"

"No. I need it filed tomorrow. I have to keep up the initiative, just like you needed to in the Saunders case."

"Actually, I don't know if I could even file it tomorrow. I will need some research, due to the involvement of Bahamian authority."

"No, they aren't involved in this. Assume that I have control of the boat right now, in International Waters headed for Miami."

"But I can't file a Federal case without doing my homework. I can't take the chance of looking like a jerk in front of a Federal judge."

"Come on! We both know that no Federal judge is going to look at it for months. If it's not perfect as filed, we can always amend it."

"But if I'm up against insurance company lawyers who know better —"

"If there is an insurance company, I'll be very happy. Then there won't be a Federal case and my claim will go to an arbitration board."

"Then why file a Federal case?"

"Because the early warning system in my brain is telling me there won't be any insurance company. There will be a gang of drug smugglers who want to get their boat back and a coven of corrupt Bahamian officials scheming to confiscate it. I need a Federal case filed *now*. You got me?"

"I'm sorry, but I'm not sure if I can do it."

"Then I'll have to find another lawyer and you can —"

"No, wait! Let me think about it."

"Thanks." I really didn't want to tell him to take my card off his Rolodex. "I don't require legal perfection. There will be no blame if it doesn't work out. I need it quick and dirty. Two thousand dollars if you get it filed tomorrow. Or one thousand and five hundred if you get it filed the day after tomorrow. And —"

"Okay, I hear you. Quick and dirty, and no guarantees. I'll send it out tomorrow."

"Great. And I get the papers in my hands the day after tomorrow."

Before hanging up, I gave him the marina's address and telephone number for a FEDEX shipment.

When the conversation heated up, Rebecca moved from the V-berth to the galley to listen in. Now, she was looking at me like I was crazy. "And now we have only forty-six thousand dollars?"

"We're not expensing it to the Broadmoore project. We're expensing it to the one hundred thousand dollar salvage fee. It's only two percent. Think of it as insurance. No, think of it as *immunization* against infection."

"What kind of infection?"

"An exuberant overgrowth of Bahamian bureaucracy. This Sergeant Townsend hasn't done diddly-squat, but he's is still claiming investigative jurisdiction over the *Second Chance*. The best way to fight off officials is with your own official-looking papers. Tomorrow, I'll be able to claim that the yacht is under Federal jurisdiction."

Rebecca gave me a look that said I'd need a stronger argument to convince her.

"Sure, Rebecca, we could give the Sergeant the benefit of the doubt. But tell me, what are the chances that he's going to bring back those affidavits, counter-signed?"

"I don't know."

"I'll bet you he doesn't. I'll bet you in hours of chore duty — twenty to one."

Rebecca responded with a playful smile and threw a dish towel in my face. "Okay. No bet. I'll let you be right if you get those bikes out of the V-berth. I want us to be riding them out of here in five minutes!"

"You've got a deal."

Four minutes later, I had both bikes on the dock and was unfolding them and clamping their frames. Rebecca locked the *Diogenes* and we hit the road. We waved to Cliff and Ethel Grimes. We must have looked like circus clowns on those small-wheeled collapsible bicycles. But it sure beat renting a car, like many of the people in the marina had apparently done. We worked our way between those cars and through the small parking lot and the asphalt circle where the van had picked up Rebecca. I followed Rebecca's lead, out to the asphalt road. This would be Rebecca's day. It was so pleasant seeing her lead the way as she had so many times before, in shorts and Oregon rafting sandals, her loose-fitting blouse flowing in the breeze and her hair bouncing as a ponytail that she'd pulled through the back of her ball cap. A belt-mounted water bottle added to her sporty look. We followed the narrow asphalt road past a smaller one that went off to the left. I remembered it as a road to the defunct hotel. Farther up the road, a broad but disused asphalt lane went off to the right. Bushes grew high on both sides and 50 yards in, it was blocked by a chain-link gate. I remembered it as the road to a defunct airport.

Dragonflies flew around us as we traveled up the main road. We passed the water tower that had guided us in, three days earlier. It stood tall on its four rusty red legs. Paint was flaking from its red-and-white panels. It looked like a sun-bleached circus tent erected on a tall platform. But it was functional: The high aluminum-sided building behind a stand of trees had to be a pumping station over a well. I guessed that the coral rock was an efficient collector of the rain that fell on the island.

The road became wider. A car honked behind us. Rebecca steered to the right and I followed her. An old compact Ford passed us. It was Rick Turner, driving down the center, fast. He passed us before we could wave. The car had left-hand steering but a Bahamian license plate — blue background and yellow letters.

"That wasn't very friendly," Rebecca said to me.

"Rick doesn't like to waste time," I answered. "This reminds me that we should probably be on the left side of the road. They drive on the left, here."

It felt so good to trade the cramped sailboat and the claustrophobic marina for this long strip of sun-bleached asphalt. It took us past a cinder-block house. Then, on the left, came that big expanse of water — the Little Bahama Bank. The road was only three or four feet above sea level. Its crumbled edges gave way to coral rock, which was bare except for the occasional Australian pine or stubby sea grape tree with thick, round leaves. And on the right was a jungle of brush.

A sign informed us that we were on King's Highway.

After a mile came houses on the right. Most were whitewashed clapboards with rickety porches and pitched roofs covered with tar paper. Some were of stuccoed cinder block, painted soft lime green or hard turquoise, and covered with asphalt shingles. The yards were just carved or beaten out of the underbrush. Many had a broken-down car, but a few had one that was roadworthy. Usually, there was a scattering of chickens. Often a long-necked, short-legged mongrel dog would raise its head to bark at us. But there were no playing children. A glance at my watch told me it was Tuesday, a school day.

Sometimes an outboard motorboat was pulled up on shore, sitting on a patch of sand or gravel, or resting on thick pieces of driftwood in places where the shore had only sharp coral.

As we traveled farther, the houses became more frequent. At the town limit of West End, we came upon a small, yellow, concrete building sitting in front of a large microwave and cellphone tower: Batelco, the Bahamas Telecommunications Corporation. It was on a cross street that went off to our right, the southeast. But that street didn't traverse the narrow island to reach the Straits of Florida. It ended after a tenth of a mile in a thicket of undergrowth and connected with a street running parallel to King's Highway.

We continued eastward along King's Highway, exploring the northern side of the island. The next building on our right piqued my interest.

"You don't want to go in there, Ben," Rebecca said, firmly.

It was a two-storey stuccoed concrete block building, painted yellow and sitting 50 yards back from the road on a large lot of mown weeds. Behind it sat a one-storey building of similar construction, but longer and with barred windows. The two-storey yellow building was accessible by a U-shaped driveway of crushed rock. There were no vehicles in front. A large wooden sign announced "Royal Bahamas Police Force, West End."

"No, Rebecca, I have to go in there. Just for a moment to see about the papers." I set my bike against the sign and opened the door that led into a pleasantly cool reception area that ended with a broad wooden counter. To the left was a door marked, "No Entrance." And to the right was another door, marked "Sgt. Leonard Townsend." I knocked on it. I knocked on it again. No answer.

A policeman appeared from a side door behind the counter. He was dressed like Ivanhoe, in a blue jumpsuit. "Can I help you, sir?"

"Yes, please. I am Dr. Candidi. I would like to see Sgt. Townsend. I have been dealing with him in connection with a murder."

"Yes," he said, showing no surprise. "I'm sorry, but Sgt. Townsend is not here."

"Could you get on the radio and let him know that I'm here to see him?"

"I am sorry. That is not possible. He is on leave, today."

"That figures," I said, mostly to myself. The guy's name was over the flap of his breast pocket. "Well, Constable Sutton, I would appreciate it if you could tell him that I stopped by for the papers with his signature."

Rebecca was waiting under the shade of a tree. She read the outcome from my face and from the absence of papers in my hands.

"On leave today," I grumbled. "So, how many hours of chores did you bet me?"

The expression on her face said to not get upset. "I bet you can't guess who I saw driving by," she said.

"No bet, just tell me."

"Wade Daniels."

"In an old, blue, compact Chevy?"

"Yes. And he waved."

"Was he driving by fast, or driving by slowly?"

"Slowly."

I filed that away for future reference.

We mounted up and pedaled down the road. Next came a doctor's office — a long, white concrete block building. And after that came a long, one-storey yellow one that was a lot more interesting: West End Community Clinic. It wasn't too wide where it faced the street, but it seemed to go back a long way. Parked outside was a maroon station wagon with an oval insignia on its door consisting of a caduceus and the letters PHA for Public Hospital Administration. The clinic was open. An Island woman was just walking in. What a stroke of luck — a real working government health clinic for Rebecca to see! After all those months working with paper on a world health fellowship in Washington, DC, bored and frustrated to tears, she now had a chance to see the real thing!

"Rebecca. Look! A clinic. I'll wait here and you go in and introduce yourself. Take as long as you want."

But it was too much for her, all at once. I could tell from the unfocussed look of her eyes behind her aviator sunglasses. "I don't know, Ben. I couldn't just walk in on them."

"Sure, you can. You just say you're in health care and you're here as a tourist, and when you saw what a nice building they have you couldn't resist asking permission to take a look around and —"

"No, that would be too . . . impolite . . . too intrusive."

"No," I said, holding her bike so she could dismount. "They will be *proud* to show you. I bet they're giving their people better basic health care than we are. Go in there and say hi to them. I'll watch your bike."

"No, Ben, I can't do that without an introduction."

She was quite firm so I didn't argue. "Okay," she said, "maybe I can find some way to do that before we sail away."

I took out a piece of paper and wrote down some details — that it belonged to the Grand Bahama Health Service, Public Hospital Authority. Rebecca leaned over, threw an arm over my shoulder and kissed me on the cheek. I mounted up and we continued down the road, which was empty except for half a mile ahead where a blue compact pulled out and drove off slowly in the direction of Freeport.

The next building we looked at was a government administrative complex. It housed their post office, the West End Town Committee, and the "National Insurance Board," whatever that was. Then came a couple of cinder-block houses that had lost their roofs from the last hurricane. Finally, we found a government building that both Rebecca and I could agree on visiting: the Ministry of Education Primary School. The children were outside, in recess, and they flocked to the fence where we were standing. In their plaid-bottomed and white-topped uniforms, they looked well-nourished, healthy and bright. They thought our bicycles looked funny, and they laughed when I loosened the clamp on mine and folded it like a jackknife. They knew all about sailing yachts and where Miami is. Washington, too. Rebecca took the camera from her backpack and took a picture of them.

As we rode off, I said a little prayer for those kids and their island, hoping that when they grew up there would be jobs for them and that the world would continue to give them the love and respect that they had experienced as children in school.

Another couple of hundred yards down the road and on the shore side was an outdoor bar. The "Island Club" consisted of an enormous wooden deck built around a large shack with clap-down sides and a tin roof. Much of the deck was protected from rain and sun by several islands of thatched palm suspended on large poles. It was closed for the day but looked like a good place to visit at night.

The next few tenths of a mile brought us into historical West End. A large two-storey wooden building, named Bethell Robertson & Co., Ltd., seemed to define the center of it. I guessed that it had been West End's general store during its heyday. That would have been back in the Prohibition days when West End was an important port for smuggling in booze to Florida. A couple of gasoline pumps on the lot next to the building seemed the only evidence of present-day commercial activity. And the next wooden commercial building down the road looked like it had been taken over by homeless squatters. Or maybe the guy we saw was just a crazy tenant.

There were no houses between the Highway and the shore, just small docks and occasional boat anchorages with mooring buoys floating in waist-deep water. Over the decades, the inhabitants must have eaten a lot of conch because their shells were piled to form breakwaters that extended dozens of yards into the water. But these weren't breakwaters that you could walk on. They sprouted sharp points and edges. And farther out were wire-framed holding pens for recently harvested conch.

Beyond a couple of swayback buildings with coral columns we came to St. Mary Magdaline Church. Carved in stone over its doors were the words "Consecrated 22 January 1893." It was a tall, roomy edifice, built from quarried coral stones, cemented together, and framing a row of tall, stained-glass windows. We went in and Rebecca photographed the windows from the inside. The shepherd's crook emblem by the altar told me that the church was Anglican. A look in the hymnal and prayer book confirmed this. I memorized details for a future conversation with my old mentor, Dr. Geoffrey A. Westley, who was doing his best to keep anglophilia alive in Miami.

We spent some time looking in the old graveyard behind the church, but we didn't find any headstones older than 1920. But on its edge we found a tall tree that provided a shady place for lunch. And afterward we had no trouble finding a shack where they could sell us a couple of *Kaliks* — "the beer of the Bahamas." As we pedaled on, the houses became fewer and farther between. Finally King's Highway combined with the parallel road and became a high-speed highway.

"That's the way the van took me to Freeport," Rebecca said, gesturing to the left. "Let's go back the other way," she said, gesturing to the parallel road, which was marked as Queen's Highway.

"Fine, you're the leader," I said.

Queen's Highway took us in the direction of West End, but it ran closer to the Straits of Florida side. The island was less than two miles wide around here. The land in the direction of the Straits was covered with small trees, and in the distance there was a hint of elevation, as if the vegetation were growing on dunes. It was impossible to see the Straits. Along the way, we encountered only two paths leading in that direction. I guessed few houses were built there because that side of the island would take one hell of a beating in a hurricane. After a while, Queen's Highway ended. We took a cross-street to King's Highway and rode by the police station and back toward the marina.

We were overtaken by Wade Daniels in his car — his dilapidated Chevy compact with left-side steering. Its blue paint was faded and its interior was a mess, but the engine sounded okay. He slowed to drive alongside of us and asked if we were having a good time. Rebecca said that we'd visited the town, mentioning the church and the waterfront. He agreed that West End was "a nice place to visit." I was about to ask where he'd gone today with his car, but he said it was time to be moving along. He drove off before I had a chance to ask.

As Rebecca and I approached the water tower, I suggested that we take the road that went off to the left and explore the defunct airport. On the entrance road, weeds and scrub bushes pushed through the cracks in the asphalt. The chain link gate bore a no-trespassing sign. A rusty padlock securing a galvanized chain suggested that no car and truck had been through here in ages. But it was no barrier to bicycles. We dismounted and pushed them between the gate posts and the line of bushes that was overgrowing the road.

Rebecca noted that foot traffic had worn a narrow path around the gate. She wondered if it was a lovers' lane, and we noticed a lot of trash along the road and evidence of an occasional bonfire. It was too narrow here for partying. A couple of hundred yards of this and the road opened up to the airport. It had one long runway parallel to the shore. But it would take a lot of work to get it back up to FAA standards. Grass, bushes and even small trees grew between the concrete slabs, buckling them in places.

"Now we know that West End has seen better days," Rebecca said.

"Yes, the runway looks long enough for a medium-size jet."

"Do you think they were landing them here?"

I took a look around. "Maybe, twenty or thirty years ago. That long indentation in the trees is probably the footprint of a strip terminal building. And those pipes on the other side must be the remnants of their refueling system."

"To think of it. Gone and overgrown so quickly! Like instant archeology."

"Mother Nature's revenge. You should see what happened to the Miami Baseball Stadium after they stopped using it as a winter training camp. The whole playing field is overgrown with thirty-foot trees. Nobody planted them. The seeds were delivered in bird droppings."

We pedaled toward the edge of the water and dismounted.

Rebecca looked back at the runway again. "Why did they let it fall into ruin?"

"Multiple reasons. Maybe the place got a reputation for being less glamorous. Maybe the 'in crowd' found another hot spot. There was supposed to be a hotel here, once, but they shut it down. With no big destination, there was no reason for regularly scheduled air service. Same deal for the guys who came in private planes. Maybe there was a big clamp-down and the cocaine smugglers started using other resorts."

Rebecca waded into the water. "And the glamor people left with the smugglers, and the promoters went broke."

I kicked off my boat shoes and waded in after her. "That's the way it goes. Some rich guy gets excited and makes a big investment in a place. The word gets out that it's glamorous and people start coming. The location builds on its own success and it grows — like a pyramid."

Rebecca reached for her water bottle and took a long drink. "And the people stop coming, and it turns into a necropolis." She sank into thought for a minute. "What were they coming for in the first place? Fun in the sun with the opposite sex? Partying? Nose candy? All of this under the emblem of marlin fishing . . . which few of them did, thankfully."

I waded closer. "Yes, that was why they came. And I guess that the fishing wasn't a big enough draw, and they had to go to Freeport where there the casino gambling is."

"Casino. Casino Royale. Bond. James Bond." Rebecca shook her head, sending her ponytail flying. "Oh, phooey to that male fantasy stuff. They ought to design vacations around ecology. Around snorkeling and experiencing nature."

"That might work for families during the vacation season. But it won't work for the singles crowd."

Now it was Rebecca who was going on a rant. "So they either have to be churning the water with their boat motors and seeing who can get the biggest fish, or they have to show how much money they have by throwing it away at a roulette table!" She kicked up a plume of water. "Stupid macho behavior." She tipped her bottle, poured a little water into the palm of her hand, and patted it onto her chest.

"Yes. But unfortunately, Rebecca, that's the type of behavior that females will reward publicly when they're on the make."

"And how do they do that?" she asked, still perturbed.

"By showing them their tits in public." I made my point with an ironic smile.

"Huh!" Rebecca said, with disgust. With deliberation, she opened the lower buttons of her blouse. She waited to make sure I was looking, then flashed me. The little notch in her brow told me she hadn't meant it as a joke. With the same deliberation, she buttoned back up, studying me and waiting for a reaction which I did not give. "Okay, Ben. You've made your point. Now tell me why you're smirking."

"Because women won't reward men for ecology-friendly behavior."

"But they *should*."

"Sure, I can just hear them rewarding a guy." I did an imitation of a sultry Mae West. "Come here, my sporty, right-sized eco-man. I lust for your body and soul. You showed me a cancer-curing *Porifera spongia* today. But all Joe was ever able to show me was a lousy coral head. So why don't you come up and see me, and I'll show you some real symbiosis."

Rebecca cracked up. Then she stepped up and started splashing me with her water bottle.

I continued with my parody, switching back to my own voice.

"No, not with *fresh* water. For the good of the universe, we can't let that go to waste, baby. You think I put on a big eco-display to end up with some water-wasting *loser chick*? I mean, what would that do to my reputation around the marina?"

We joked around on the theme for a long time. Finally, Rebecca cocked her head and said, "Maybe we've been out in the hot sun for too long. Let's go looking for the hotel."

"Great. I think we'll find it on the other side of the road."

We mounted our bikes, pedaled back to the main road, and pointed toward the marina. Soon we were overtaken by a Japanese pickup truck with three guys jammed into the cab. They were body-building types, and I had to laugh when they all turned their heads at the same time to check out Rebecca. In their load bed were a couple of wide, oversized tires like you see on beach vehicles. Several hundred yards ahead of us, they turned off to the right. We turned off onto that road, too, because I remembered that it led to the hotel.

It wasn't a road, actually. It was more like an overgrown asphalt path that was connected to numerous others. It was as if the scrub wilderness was crisscrossed with paths, like a maze. We found the hotel's foundations — poured concrete ridges that ran in a straight line through the bushes. The trees dodged it, but sometimes their roots spilled over it. The size of the grid was about right — about six residential lots. It was fun to interpret the pattern in concrete, like the ruin of a medieval church.

After our archeological study was more or less finished, Rebecca pointed to the north. "If we go this way, we should come to where they had all those Hobie cats and sailboards."

"And Waverunners," I added. "You lead, I'll follow."

It was fun, zigging and zagging from one path to another. And soon, Rebecca was leading us to a community of cottages. It reminded me of a postcard picture of an old-fashioned rustic camp or of a motel scene in a 1930s movie. Little cottages were stuck in the woods. And in front of the third one, we passed a girl who was sitting, smoking a cigarette and reading a magazine — topless. I would have slowed down, but Rebecca was keeping up the pace. We passed a grassy clearing where four girls were playing badminton in bikinis. I waved and said, "Hello."

One of them waved back and said, "*Bon jour*."

The cottages were more closely spaced, now, and we came to an old-fashioned pool where a half-dozen more girls were lounging around with a couple of skinny guys. I slowed down but Rebecca didn't. Past the pool, the water came into view — the Little Bahama Bank.

When we reached the strand, Rebecca came to a halt. Between the palm trees several dozen yards ahead of us they were doing a photo shoot. A line of four girls was squared off to the late-afternoon sun, its yellow rays warming their yellow skirts that were being blown gently by the off-camera fans. They were modeling beachwear ensembles of high-heeled sandals and silky skirts and tops — stuff that would be just right for sipping pina coladas in the pricy restaurant of a fancy hotel, but which could be cast off in an instant to enjoy bikini-clad pleasure in Caribbean water. One model was a rather skinny blond, two were dark-haired with art-movie faces, and the fourth was exotically good looking. She was tall and slim, with jet-black eyes, a beak-like nose, and cinnamon skin.

The photographer behind the camera was blond and long-haired.

A sweater hung over his back, and a cigarette dangled from the corner of his mouth. His face was dominated by wrap-around glasses with thick lenses that were set close to his eyes. He was shooting with a telephoto lens from a long distance, a technique that would keep everything in sharp focus: the staggered line of girls and the hammock strung between the palm trees behind them. He could have used one of those little sportsman's two-way radios to overcome the distance. Maybe they didn't sell them in France. Instead, he used a large repertoire of hand signals to direct his models individually in their poses.

A second string of models was standing to the side, under a palm tree. Also out of camera view were two trucks and a trailer, parked along an asphalt ribbon. One truck was the type of lunch wagon that comes around construction sites. The other was a boxy cargo carrier filled with clothes racks. An ironing board was set up near its tailgate. And the trailer was divided into two dressing rooms which seemed to be air-conditioned, getting their electricity from a large gasoline generator that was humming away at the edge of the bushes.

"I was wrong, Ben. This part of the island does attract glamorous people."

"It looks like a French clothing company doing a shoot for their spring catalogue. Take a good look. That's what you'll see next summer on the beaches around Nice."

"And how can you be so sure about that? ... Oh yes, I remember. You used to hang out at South Beach before you met me." She poked me in the stomach. "But what makes you so sure they're French? Because that one girl said *bon jour*?"

"The team's French. The photog is a dead give-away, and so are the guys with the lights and the fan. Posture's too relaxed to be German, and the gestures wouldn't fit, anyway. The two dark-haired schoolgirl types are French. So is the blond one — I can tell from how she's holding her shoulders. And the really good-looking one with the dark skin is a pick-up that they're using to set a Caribbean tone. Probably an East-Indian from Trinidad. The girls under the palm tree are his second string — all German or Scandinavian. He'll shoot them for a Neckermann catalogue. The Trinidadian will have double duty. I'm quite sure. Wanna bet a few hours of chores, ten to one?"

"No thanks." Rebecca tapped a toe on the asphalt. "Your masculine eye's got it all figured out, huh? Oh, that's right. I forgot. You know all about the business." She paused for a second then resumed, sassily.

"Well, what *did* happen to that fashion model you had been dating before me?"

"The inevitable."

Rebecca answered that with a playful snort. "Sure, of course *that* would have to be inevitable. But what happened after *that*?"

"She left me two weeks older and about eight hundred dollars poorer." I said it with exaggerated remorse.

"Poor Ben." Rebecca said it with fake sympathy, then clicked her tongue.

"No, that's okay. Couldn't have lasted any longer. After I learned all about the fashion model business we ran out of things to talk about."

We mounted up and followed an asphalt strip that ran along the shore, northwest, in the direction of the marina. After a quarter of a mile, we came across the prefab shack and the collection of boat-toys that I had seen before. The Japanese pickup truck was parked near it. Closer to the water, two girls were standing on the trampoline of a beached Hobie cat, each holding onto the mast and hanging a leg out in a different direction.

Rebecca stopped. "And what about these fashion models?"

"They're amateurs. Strictly amateurs. Not getting paid."

"And how do you know that?"

"Because they're having too much fun at it. The guy with the camera looks French. Probably part of the crew but not a photographer. He's probably a rigger who borrowed the camera to go hunting for an evening's entertainment. I wonder if there's any film in the camera."

Rebecca grunted, shook her head and got back on her bicycle. The ribbon of asphalt took us back to the marina. As we skirted its parking lot, I noticed a familiar blue jeep from the Royal Bahama Police Force. My watch said 4:30 p.m. Rebecca headed for the *Diogenes*. I swung by to check on the *Second Chance*. The yellow crime scene tape had sagged but it didn't seem like anything else on the boat had changed. Ivanhoe was still there, looking more vigilant than usual. I waved to him and he didn't volunteer any news.

I got on my bike, rode to the parking lot and found Sgt. Townsend standing next to the jeep. He was out of uniform, wearing dark slacks, a white shirt and black shoes made from woven leather strips. And he was holding a large manila envelope. Great!

I steered towards him and squeezed both brake levers at the last minute. "Thanks, Sergeant, I knew you'd bring us the affidavits." I let go of one of the handlebars and extended my hand for the envelope.

Townsend ignored my hand and answered with an apologetic frown. "I am sorry. I cannot give you them yet. But I do have something I would like you to look at." He thumbed open the flap on the envelope, bent it and looked inside. He extracted its contents gingerly, holding it at the corner. It was a blowup of the photo I'd made of the map, enclosed in a clear plastic protector.

With annoyance, I grabbed it with my left hand. "What about it?"

"Doctor Candidi, I want to ask you to take a good look at that photo."

"Yes," I said, with greater annoyance. I grabbed it with both hands and looked at it carefully. The copying process hadn't fuzzed up any of the detail or distorted the latitude and longitude lines.

Sgt. Townsend looked down at the photo as I held it. "I just need to ask you if that is a true copy of the chart that you made."

"Yes."

"And the upper *X* marks the spot where you found the *Second Chance*?"

"Yes, and the exact longitude and latitude are in my affidavit."

"Thank you." He took back the photo carefully and returned it to the oversized envelope.

"Is that all?"

"One more question. Is it true that Dr. Levis was not on the boat before you brought it in to the marina?"

"Yes, just like I told you before."

"Thank you. That will be all."

"That will be all? What about your signature on our affidavits? What about an official written acknowledgment that you received them from us? And when will you get around to taking fingerprints so I can take the *Second Chance* to Miami?"

"All in due course."

"All in due course, you say, while your crime scene tape sags like crepe paper after an outdoor Halloween party. Look, I've told you before and I'll tell you again. Three days are enough for a crime scene. Tomorrow begins the period when I can move that yacht at my convenience."

"No, we need more time to complete the investigation."

"You need time for the fingerprints that you haven't taken? Let me tell you this — I'm keeping an eye on the weather. It's been dry so far and there hasn't been much dew, either. But after the first good rain, they're all going to be washed away." I hoisted myself onto the seat, preparing to shove off.

"You have no need to concern yourself with the fingerprints," he said.

I shoved off. I'd wait until I had the Federal Court paperwork in my hands.

As I rode up to the *Diogenes*, I noticed that the *Dream Weaver* was gone. I blew off steam, telling Rebecca about my conversation with the Good Sergeant. Then she handed me a beer and I set myself down in the cockpit to cool off. But a visit from the uniformed customs official cut that short. I left the cold beer in the side pocket and climbed to the dock to meet him. Without meeting my eye, he handed me a familiar-looking photocopied sheet: "Fishing Regulations in the Bahamas."

"It is my duty to hand out these regulations to every visitor."

"Thank you. You gave me one when I checked in with you, a few days ago. And I read it. It told me all about how many fish I can take and how big the conch and lobster must be for me to take them." I tapped my temple. "I've got it down."

He still wouldn't meet my eye. "But your permission to fish does not include taking samples of plant life."

"Okay, I can understand that," I said.

He waited, like he was expecting me to put up an argument.

"No. It's okay. I understand." I waved him off. "My permission to fish does not include taking samples of plant life." I stared at him until he left, then returned to my beer.

Rebecca had been listening from the companionway. "What was all that about?" she asked.

"The bureaucratic clam shell drawing shut, trying to catch me by the toe."

9 Bedazzled, Bewitched and *Bewitzled*

Rebecca spread her fingers, pushed them up into her hair and closed her eyes. "And how did the Bahamian bureaucrats learn about your sponge project?"

"That witchy woman who runs the marina must have read the fax from Broadmoore before she delivered it." I chilled out with a sip of cold beer.

"And what are you going to do?" Rebecca asked, with concern.

"I'll record this act of heraldry in the *Diogenes'* log, along with an exact quotation of the official's words. You can witness it."

Rebecca stepped down into the cabin and returned with the log book, a pen, and a beer for herself. It took me only a few minutes to record the details of the visit. Rebecca read it with a little smile, then signed it.

"Okay, Ben, I've witnessed it. Now, why are you acting like it's all taken care of?"

"Because, One, the fact that a plant permission is not *included* in a fish permission does not mean that a plant permission is denied, or even necessary."

"Oh, Ben The Lawyer," she laughed. Apparently the beer was going to her head, too. She latched onto me with a mischievous grin. "And what about your reasons Number Two, Number Three . . . and on to infinity? No, just a minute, let me think."

I gave her a smug grin and then went for a sip of beer while she thought it over.

"Why, of course!" Rebecca said. "Sponges are *animals*, not plants!"

I trumpeted agreement, aerosolizing a lot of beer. We laughed together for a long time. From force of habit, I glanced in the direction of the *Dream Weaver*'s berth. Yes, it was empty. But the next one over was not, and Chuck was watching us. When I waved to him, he pretended not to notice. And none of this was lost on Rebecca.

Oh, to hell with a guy who won't talk to you. I put on a snobbish voice. "Oh, Rebecca *dahling*, I have just had a most horrid thought."

"What," she exclaimed softly, between giggles, "are they up there on their jungle gym, again?"

"No, but I almost forgot our invitation to *dinnah*!" I continued with high decibells. "We must remove with haste."

"Yes, *deah*," she answered loudly. "But please don't ask me to find your studs and cuff links."

"Oh, if I could only lose the *hostess* as easily as I lose *them*," I said with a snobbish nasal. "Her attention is absolutely *withering*."

"*Withering*, you say?" Rebecca exclaimed, with theatrical volume. "Then there should be absolutely no problem."

"But shall I have the strength to protect you from the Bear of Lake Francis Marion?" (We had discussed Cal's connection to Sumter County.)

"A resolute lady is more than a match for any *bear*," she said, in a parody of an English matriarch.

Doing that *shtick* put us both in a light-hearted mood. But if there was really anything funny about it, that must have come from the tension we had experienced in these days around the marina. I couldn't get away from the feeling that we were always under scrutiny, even during the bicycle trip. While locking up and stepping off the *Diogenes*, I wondered if we were now submitting to a second examination by SAWECUSS — the hypothetical Social Auxiliary of the West End Cocaine Smuggling Society. Well, the best defense would be to keep ourselves wrapped in a light-hearted mood.

Walking up the center dock, we made our way to *Sumter's Forte*. Towering behind it was the *Photo Finish* with Ray and Martha lounging on the upper deck. Ray caught my eye and waved. I waved back. But after seeing me carrying a bottle of wine to the Sumters, Martha and Ray moved inside. Standing in the open cockpit at the rear of the boat, Angie welcomed Rebecca aboard, saying she was so glad we could come. And Angie extended her cheek to me for a kiss, which I supplied discretely. I pressed the bottle of wine — a quality Rhine-Hessen Riesling — into her soft hands, saying that I hoped they would enjoy it on some quiet evening. Then I lost no time sidestepping away and shaking hands with Cal who had been slathering butter on an impressive collection of lobster tails sitting on his grill, which hung over his stern on the Vangelden's side. I admired Cal's handiwork and thanked him for his hospitality. Angie slid over to say that she had a blender full of frozen daiquiri. Rebecca and I agreed that a frozen daiquiri would be just right.

We were attentive guests, and the conversation quickly gravitated to Cal and Angie's high lifestyle. His was partially inherited and partially earned. Hers was won through good manners and good looks, if I interpreted her correctly. Their exclusive gatehouse community in Boca Raton became a landmark in our conversation. ("Pete Rose lives there, and boy does he know how to party.") They also knew a rock musician-composer who had been associated with a group that was big in the late 1970s. We all agreed that Boca Raton is a classy place. I resisted the temptation to say that *boca raton* means "mouth of the mouse" in Spanish (the word for rat being *rata*).

We all switched to wine when Angie announced dinner: lobster, Caesar salad and conch salad. It was served on a round table bolted to the floor in the center of the cockpit. Apparently, they had removed their fighting chair to set up the table because I noticed that piece of fish-fighting equipment stowed in a corner of the main salon. The table was about three feet in diameter and was set with folding deck chairs. Rebecca sat across from me, with Angie on my left and Cal on my right. I asked them what they did on their boat.

Angie supplied the answer. "Mostly fishing and a little snorkeling. But not so much because Cal doesn't take to the water like Ben. Isn't that right, Cal?"

I asked a quick question. "What kind of fish do you get, Cal?"

"We get a lot of snapper and dolphin."

"Good eating," I said.

"We don't go out so much anymore for sailfish and blue marlin," he added.

Had he sensed that I don't approve of torturing those big, blue-eyed creatures for sport?

"Not so many of them around, anymore," Cal added with a shake of the head.

"And they accumulate high levels of mercury, so they're not so good to eat, anyway," I said.

"Angie, your conch salad was really good," Rebecca said. "How did you make it?"

"Oh, I start with three pieces of conch from Edgar," she said,

brightly. "I always make sure that he saves the brown *tube* for Cal."
She winked at Rebecca, like that was a good joke between girls.
According to island lore, the brown tube is supposed to increase male
stamina. "I cut the conch in thin slices and pour lemon juice over them
and add chopped onions."

After a leisurely dinner, Rebecca helped Angie collect the plates
and bring them into the kitchen area. Cal collapsed the chairs and set
them to the side. He sat on the starboard rail and I sat on the transom,
the stern rail. There was something likable in that wrinkled face and in
those deep sunken eyes, even when they pulled away mistrustfully. I
guessed that, despite his inheritance, Cal had had to work hard to make
things come out right. Determination by day and two drinks in the
evening had taken their toll on his face. But otherwise, he seemed to
be in pretty good shape for a guy in his fifties. Hoping to bridge the
20-year age gap between Cal and myself, I told him about my
experience with sailing in the Bahamas. When the girls came back,
this evolved into a group conversation.

Cal had some things to say:

Yes, it would be nice to be young again and have all the time in the
world. But when you are in your forties and fifties you need a little
power assist to keep enjoying life to the fullest. And that's where it's
good to have a couple of big engines, even if it does cost you $500 to
get to Boca Raton and back. And even if we don't have a working
schedule, we are on a social schedule — isn't that right, Angie? —
because when there's an important party in a couple of days you're
either going or you aren't. You can't say yes and then depend on the
wind to get you there.

Angie was sitting on the transom close to me to the right. She
faced her husband and was swinging a leg back and forth along the
transom's inside wall. Angie agreed that you can't depend on wind
power to get you back, especially when you have an important party.
She leaned back and her left hand moved closer to mine. I found myself
glancing at her calf which was swinging like a pendulum in front of a
cleat mounted halfway up. What a strange place to mount a cleat for
fastening rope. I glanced up at the flybridge over the cabin roof. No,
there wasn't any canvas awning up there that could be rolled down for
sun protection and would require a cleat down here for a point of
attachment. And that cleat wasn't installed to tie open the transom
door, which was built in as a convenience for pulling in blue marlins

on a gaff. The door had a latch to hold it open. Actually, that cleat was in the way. It was mounted dead center on the transom.

"Yes, I can imagine you attend a lot of elegant social functions in Boca Raton," I said.

Cal nodded and Angie rewarded me with an appreciative smile.

"I can imagine," Rebecca said. She was sitting on the port side, across from Cal. "Tuxedos and evening gowns, and cocktails and dancing on the patio." She said it with such charm. "Are you into ballroom dancing?"

"Oh, old Cal and I have a few steps up our sleeves," Angie said, casting a glance at Cal who answered with crinkling eyes and a sheepish smile.

I leaned backward and looked straight down at the water where the ripples hit the stern. And what I saw, looking down along the stern's center, didn't surprise me: a small pulley wheel mounted several inches below the waterline.

"What about you, Rebecca?" Angie said. "Are you into ballroom dancing?"

"Oh, I learned enough to get by at *bar-* and *bat mitzvahs.*"

Angie and Cal scrunched their faces like this was too exotic for their tastes.

"Come on, Rebecca," I said. "We've danced every step in the book together. Remember that night at Zeekie's Armenian wedding gig."

"Armenian wedding?" Cal said it like he was imagining festivities in Tajikistan.

"They're a Christian ethnic group — Eastern Orthodox. You can find Armenians all over the United States."

Angie wrinkled her forehead. "What kind of dances did you do?"

"You know. The fox trot, the waltz, the cha-cha, rumba and all that stuff. Right, Rebecca?"

Rebecca nodded. She just sat there, looking so lovely. In the long lull in the conversation, I could just make out the sound of the wind moving through the trees. Maybe this wasn't a SAWECUSS interrogation after all.

"I like the quiet nights in the Bahamas," I said. Nobody responded, but what the hell. If our hosts wanted to know what I'm all about, I could tell them. "I like the swish and glide of the hull as it cuts through the water under sail power. And the dolphins must like sailboat hulls. We manage to pick up a pod of them every time we go out. They like my sonar ping and I don't think they like the vibration of a motor. The vibration isn't good for my dopamine levels, either."

"What Ben's trying to say is that noise can affect the chemicals in your brain that are responsible for enjoyment," Rebecca said.

And what I was saying to myself was that cocaine isn't good for your dopamine levels, either. I wondered if Cal and Angie knew that.

"We're into natural things, too," Angie said. "I'm in a yoga class that they have every day at the clubhouse, and Cal — well, I guess he's into the Zen of golf."

This seemed to fluster Cal and I could imagine why. He hadn't struck any sort of resonance with Rebecca, but Angie had been eyeing me all night. And now she was gently making fun of his hobby. Cal's eyelids narrowed for a couple of seconds, then he shot a glance at Angie. "Talking about being spiritual and complaining about engine noise, we ought to be complaining about those damn Waverunners."

"Yes," I said. "Rick was complaining the other night about how they're always running around, making noise and getting in everyone's way. And he said they're tearing up the flats, too."

"Well, he's right," Cal said.

"How shallow can they go?" I asked.

Cal rested his eyes on me, appraisingly, before he answered. "It's supposed to be two feet, but they can run them fast at one foot if they don't slow down. The propeller isn't outside, you know. It's inside and protected. The hull's designed so it sorta scoops the water in. And when the propeller gets through with it, it's thrown out the back a lot faster than the Waverunner is going. When it gets into shallow water the prop doesn't dig in."

Talking about mechanical stuff seemed to take the edge off his irritation.

"What stops it, then?" Rebecca asked, paying more attention to Cal than before.

"The hull starts cutting a groove in the bottom and the prop sucks in a lot of grass and sand and that's what kills it."

"I've always wondered what it would take to foul the prop on one of those things," I added.

"If they go through a big clump of seaweed, that will kill it." His slow, sad eyes seemed to be asking me if I was really serious in asking these questions.

"How long have they had Waverunners here?"

"For just a few months. Seems it's part of their plans to turn this place into a 'high-class resort.'"

He said "high class resort" with such disapproval that I wondered how it differed from his gatehouse community in Boca Raton.

"Oh, that's why I saw surveyors by the cottages, today," Rebecca said.

"What's going on there, anyway?" I asked Cal.

"Oh, they're renting it out to some kind of Eurotrash fashion operation. Shoot their pictures there and put up their photographers and models in those itty-bitty cottages. And there's some kind of a French playboy there. Attracted a lot of groupies that hang out at the reggae place in West End."

"I love reggae and calypso," Angie said. "Maybe we could go dancing!"

"Yes, maybe we should do that some night," Rebecca said.

"You don't like Europeans?" I said to Cal.

"No, the Europeans are okay. Its just the Eurotrash that I can't stand."

"What is it you can't stand about them?"

"A lot of them are loud. And they talk English so bad that they should be ashamed."

"I see," I said neutrally.

Angie chimed in. "And they are always asking for mineral water like the regular water's too bad to drink. But a lot of them don't use deodorant. And the women go topless but don't shave their legs."

"And not even their arm pits," Cal said, with a biting laugh.

I laughed along with him.

"And they smoke like chimneys, even on the dance floor," Angie said.

Then they both paused and looked at us as if worried that we might be offended.

I nodded. "Yes. You're right. They're always lighting up."

"I don't know why they have to come here, anyway," Cal said.

I suppressed a quip about the Europeans coming to see Disney World, the Grand Canyon, Mount Rushmore and maybe even Stone Mountain, Georgia.

"Maybe Mallorca is getting too crowded," I said.

Our hosts looked at me quizzically.

"It's a big European tourist island in the Mediterranean. Belongs to Spain. It's near a smaller island named Menorca. Maybe you guys should take the Grand Tour and see some Europeans in their own countries."

"Grand Tour?"

"Yeah. Down through France to the Mediterranean, then over to Italy, and then over the Alps and come back up thorough Germany."

"Have you done it?" Cal asked, looking at Rebecca.

Rebecca shrugged. "No, we haven't done it yet."

"We haven't gotten the money together yet," I added.

Angie said, "We looked at some package deals, but what we haven't had is *time*. Too busy."

Cal was still eyeing Rebecca, and she was getting fidgety. Angie noticed. Maybe the invitation for this evening *was* socially motivated.

"It looks like a lot of people have run out of time," I said. "Some boats have left the marina."

"Yeah, some go and some come," Cal said. "We'll be going ourselves, in a day or two."

"Are you going back to stay?" Rebecca asked.

"No, just for a while. Things to do and check up on," Cal said.

Angie laughed. "Like the Spanish maid!"

"Yes, I bet she has *mucho trabajo*," I quipped, "keeping everything spick-and-span in your *casa grande*."

A sharp glance from Rebecca told me that I'd crossed the line with that one. And that glance wasn't lost on Cal, who had been watching her with quiet eyes. And Cal's attention wasn't lost on Rebecca, either. She stared back at him for a few seconds, then yawned and covered her mouth.

"Sorry," she said to Cal. "We had an all-day bike ride and I'm afraid I'm all worn out."

"Yeah, riding bikes can do that to you," Cal said. "Especially in the hot sun."

Now was the time for a preemptive release of information.

"And we have a big day ahead of us," I added. "An old Brit that I once did a job for wants us to count sponges for him on the Little Bahama Bank."

Cal's eyes came alive. "You're going to count sponges! So that's . . ."

I waited patiently, but he had decided to not finish that sentence.

"Yes, he has a pharmaceutical company that's done experiments which show that some of these sponges are producing compounds that are good at fighting cancer. He wants me to make a survey and see if there are enough to harvest."

"Interesting!" Angie said.

Cal didn't say anything at first, but he looked me over for a long time. "You getting paid for this?"

"Yes. Handsomely. And the funny thing is that we had no idea that the job was coming. I just called up a . . . friend who told me that the Brit was looking for me."

"Well, I'm impressed. For a guy who works at the patent office, you really get around."

"When opportunity knocks, I come running."

Rebecca got up and moved toward me, slowly. Cal got to his feet like an attentive host. Angie got up too, and we all told each other what a nice evening it had been. And just as Angie was about to present her cheek to me for a kiss, Cal raised his hand and said, "Now wait a minute!"

I might have blinked, but I didn't jump. I just turned slowly to him.

Cal started with a poker face but slowly turned it into a sly grin. "Ben, you're a great guy . . . and you can tell a good story. But I think the other night you got it all wrong."

"Cal!" Angie said. "Shame on you. Ben didn't do anything wrong."

"Yes, he did, Angie," Cal feigned, "and it's important." He turned to me with a good ole boy smile and gave me a pat on the shoulder, and I braced myself for another dollop of Southern humor. "You see, Ben, after that Eye-Talian sandwich guy started yelling 'mondo cane' and waving his broom at Ole Boo, the ole dog didn't move. He stood his ground." We all laughed and Cal's eyes twinkled. "And then Ole Boo pissed on the guy's leg."

I couldn't help laughing. It was so bad it was good.

"Yes, Cal," I sputtered, gasping for air. "But then the old man's son came out of the sandwich shop and told the South Carolinian that he'd have to pay the old man's bill at the Armenian dry-cleaning shop. And he'd better fork the money over now because he was a New York firefighter."

Cal took it all in and answered on the beat. "And then Carolina guy said the Eye-Talian could wash off his pant leg at the fire hydrant that was left running at the end of the street." Cal was on a roll, going faster and faster. "And he climbed down outa the pickup truck and everybody saw that he was Nick Nolte."

The girls were laughing hard.

"Okay, Cal, but then a priest in a starched collar and black cassock came by and punched Nick Nolte in the mouth and told him to behave himself because he was on sacred ground. And Nick Nolte didn't punch back because it was Robert DeNiro who was on his way home from making a movie in the neighborhood."

"Yeah, okay Ben, but then *all of them* saw Woody Allen offering candy to a little girl and they ran off to lynch him, leaving Ole Boo and the Southern boy a chance to get away."

Standing there together holding onto each other, we all laughed so hard that the boat rocked. Angie was leaning into me like she was having trouble standing, and Cal was giving Rebecca a one-armed hug, which she didn't resist.

"Ben," Angie said, "you're funnier than . . ."

"Than Jackie Mason," Rebecca said, showing the flag for Jewish humor.

"And Cal," Angie said, "you're funnier than . . ."

"Than Jerry Clower," I said. He was the first Southern comedian that came to mind.

Angie extracted a kiss on the cheek from me, and Cal was able to give one to Rebecca after he released her from the hug. Out of breath, all of us, we stood there looking at each other. Then Rebecca stepped onto the dock and I followed her, turning several times to wave goodbye.

Rebecca and I were silent until we reached our side of the marina.

"Ben, what really happened back there?"

"A whole lot of things."

"Would you care to elaborate?"

"I could, but it won't be easy. And you might not agree with parts of my interpretation."

We unlocked the *Diogenes* and went below.

Rebecca turned on the cabin light. "But why did you tell them about your sponge job?"

"Cal caught an earful when I was negotiating with Dr. Broadmoore on the phone, and he will probably hear something about it anyway. I decided it would raise less suspicion if I just mentioned it tonight, in passing."

"Well, both Cal and Angie were interested in it. And somewhat incredulous."

"I hope my explanation helped. I don't want people to consider me guilty of spying. In fact, I'm conducting a public relations campaign to proclaim my innocence."

Rebecca laughed in anticipation of some more *shtick*, and I obliged.

"In fact, I've been composing a calypso song that I can sing all day around the marina."

Rebecca egged me on with a wry smile. She picked up a plastic spoon and beat out a calypso rhythm on a coffee cup. I had been messing around with a lyric in my head since getting the sponge job. I sang it to her:

I am the poor young Doctor Candidi,
Fishing for sponges 'cause I'm needy.
And please don't believe what the people say,
I am not D ... E ... A!

Laughing out of control, Rebecca threw her arms around my neck and wept tears on my shoulder. "Oh, Ben. You *witzelmeister*. Now you must compose a verse to protect me." She gasped. "Maybe something about Dr. Levis . . . who drinks Manischewitz."

I was on a roll. I gave it to her:

He loves Doctor Rebecca Levis,
Who's known to drink Manischewitz.
And who even gave cocaine a try,
— instilled in a patient's eye.

Rebecca rewarded my nonsense with an orgasmic laugh, and soon we were quaking in each other's arms. When she threw back her head, I put my teeth into her neck.

"Oh, Ben, you *bewitzel* me. You benumb my every center of resistance. I am putty in your hands. Drag me down and ravish my body."

Which I did.

AS OUR HEADS sank into our pillows for the last time, we agreed that it had been a perfect evening. Well, almost a perfect evening, I thought, while dozing off:

I had forgotten to ask Cal who was the bastard who came into the marina with the Cigarette boat.

Sponges In Paradise   10

Conditions were perfect for the first day of the sponge survey project. The wind was strong enough to cool us but too weak to kick up the open water. Rebecca was packing lunch and assembling our snorkeling gear. I was cranking a winch on the main mast, lifting our Caribe hard-bottomed inflatable. As the jib halyard lifted it by the nose to a vertical position and a couple of feet up the mast, the little rubber boat began to look like a trophy fish on display. But this fish was going back into the water.

"Need any help?" It was Wade Daniels looking on from the dock.

"Not on this one, Wade. But I could use some help with the outboard engine."

While I nudged the Caribe over the side and was lowering it, Wade stepped into the cockpit and waited. After launching and securing the rubber duckie to the side of the *Diogenes*, I opened the hatch in front of the mast and signaled Wade to come forward.

"I have eighty pounds of Yamaha outboard down in the V-berth tied to a rope. You can help me by pulling it straight up." I reached through the hatch, pulled out the rope and tied it to the end of the halyard.

Although Wade's build was a little top-heavy, his legs were good and he moved into position with considerable agility.

Eighty pounds isn't that heavy, unless you are worrying about where to step and about banging things and chipping fiberglass. I cranked the winch and Wade's hands guided the outboard engine up through the hatch, then towards the rail. "Where to, now?" he asked, with first mate's enthusiasm.

"We'll manhandle it over the lifeline. Then you can hold it out while I climb down into the inflatable. Then you can go back to the mast and winch the engine down to me."

Wade said aye-aye to the plan. Under my orders and Rebecca's watchful eye, the captain of the *Wholesale Delight* proved himself a capable deckhand and winch-mate. He let the engine down, inch by inch while I maneuvered its bracket onto the Caribe's transom.

"Thanks," I said. When the maneuver was completed, Rebecca returned to the cockpit.

"You're quite a precision guy," Wade said, looking down at me.

"I don't like accidents — chipped fiberglass, slipped discs or submerged engines."

"Brains over brawn? Looks like you're going out. Snorkeling, I guess, since you said you don't do much fishing."

It was time to turn my face up, lock onto those dark-green eyes, and send out another carefully drafted press release. "No, we're going out to count sponges. Say, could you hand me down those two red neoprene tanks from the cockpit."

It was an easy job, because they were nearly empty. "Counting sponges?" Wade said, while handing them down.

"Yes, we're doing it for an old Brit with a biotech company. He wants to know if there are enough of them to harvest. He's interested in some kind of anticancer compound that he thinks they have. You might say I'm doing him a highly paid favor."

"Interesting." Wade's brow went up, almost touching his Caesar bang. "Is that what you sailed down here for?"

"No, we sailed down here for vacation . . . like I told you. But when we got here, I made one phone call too many . . . and then the guy called us up for a favor."

Wade seemed deep in thought. I wondered if he was hearing this information for the first time.

"So where are you going to be looking?"

"Around here for starters. Today, we should finish off a four-by-four mile quadrant." I was connecting hoses to the tanks but keeping my eyes on Wade.

He frowned. "How many days you going to be doing this?"

"Around here, maybe a week." The frown deepened. "Then," I added, "we'll work our way west to Mangrove Cay, using the *Diogenes* as our base." The frown subsided, slowly.

"Sounds like a big project."

I caught Rebecca's eye. "No, we're just thinking of it as a way to pick up a little extra money while on vacation. I'll be spearing fish and lobster along the way. And we'll collect some conch."

Rebecca came forward and told me that everything was ready. I told her I'd be gassing up at the fuel dock. Wade interpreted this correctly and said it was time for him to leave. The outboard motor cooperated by starting up promptly for the 50-yard trip to the gas pumps. I pulled in at the corner, next to a green, 12-foot, outboard-powered wooden skiff with a funny upright steering station. That boat seemed to be there all the time. The attendant was there, and he did have a couple dozen quart bottles of two-cycle oil. As I was pumping gas and mixing oil, a cabin cruiser came in and tied up in front of me. Small and squat, it looked like the bare minimum you would need to fish the Bahamas. It had no outrigger poles but three antennas.

"Diesel," the captain said to the attendant. He was tall, big-boned and lanky, with a full head of coarse, blond hair. He was hatless but did have eye protection — thick, wire-rimmed sunglasses.

The attendant turned on the pump and asked, "In from the United States?" The boat was flying a U.S. pennant and a yellow flag.

"Yes," the tall guy said.

"You will have to register with Customs." The attendant said it as an order.

But the tall guy took no offense. "Sure."

"They are back there," the attendant said, pointing to the shack.

Apparently in no hurry to pump his diesel, the new guy took a long, slow look at the marina basin. "Thanks. I was going to ask. Mind if I stay tied up here while I'm taking care of it. I also want to make arrangements at the office."

"No problem. You staying here long?"

"For a week or so. My buddy's coming, and we're going to do some fishing," he said with a smile. His skin was too light and untanned to have spent much time on the water. "How is the fishing, anyway?" He asked it loudly, with a look that included me.

I was just stepping back onto the dock and was returning the nozzle to the gasoline pump. "Don't ask me," I replied, "I'm into snorkeling."

"I'm Jay. Jay Sherman." He said it to both of us, but the attendant ignored him.

I stepped forward, offering my hand. "Ben Candidi. We're in the two-master over there."

Jay Sherman looked in the *Diogenes*' direction and waved at Rebecca who was on deck. "Looks like you're set up for a good time in the Bahamas." He said it neutrally, leaving it to me to decide whether he had complimented my boat or my girl or both. His voice was in mid-range and he sounded vaguely Southwestern.

"We're going out snorkeling today," I said.

The attendant wrote down my bill and told me I should pay at the marina office. Jay picked up the diesel nozzle and said he would see me around.

I motored back to the *Diogenes* and spent some time loading the Caribe with the bare essentials for the expedition: a little picnic cooler to keep our sandwiches and drinks cool, a collapsible grappling anchor, life jackets, our snorkeling gear, and some extra rope. The Caribe has an aluminum cross member that spans the port and starboard inflation chambers and serves as a bench for a passenger to sit. Attached to its underside is a vinyl pocket in which I stowed several Ziploc bags, containing my hand-held GPS satellite navigation unit, my hand-held compass, and folded copies of my charts and survey forms.

The only thing left was to pay the bill at the marina office. When I walked up to the Dutch door, Zelma was not there but Jay was. He was hanging around inside her office.

It was time to tell him about the house rules: "I don't know where the marina manager is, Jay, but she usually doesn't like —" I stopped, hearing Zelma's approaching footsteps.

"Excuse me," Zelma said, as she whisked by me and into the office. "Business is conducted at the counter," she announced to Jay, dropping her voice on the last word.

Jay made no move to get out. Zelma sidestepped past him to her place behind her desk and closed a ledger journal that was lying on top. She fixed a witchy stare on him, converting her statement into an order. Jay ambled out, closing the Dutch door behind him with care, but otherwise seeming heedless of Zelma's disapproval.

"You can take Ben first," Jay said. "He's just paying for gas, and I want to rent a slip."

"That is okay, Dr. Candidi," Zelma said. "I have already booked the gasoline and oil to your account." She must have had an intercom connection to the fuel dock.

"Great." I lost no time getting back to Rebecca and the Caribe.

THE MOTOR RAN as smooth as a cat's purr and the water in the channel was as flat as a billiard table. And with nothing to do but enjoy our hard-earned vacation, my spirits rose. How useless it would be to worry right now about when Sgt. Townsend would let go of the *Second Chance*. My lawyer was probably filing my salvage suit in Federal Court this very minute. Tomorrow, I would have documents that would prevail over that miserable excuse for a police sergeant. And we should not have to worry about the people berthed at the marina. Surely we had passed muster after those two social evenings.

Rebecca sat on the bow chamber of the eight-foot inflatable, looking at me through her aviator shades and enjoying herself. She was wearing her blue bikini, a ball cap, and a white blouse to keep the sun off her shoulders. I was dressed according to the same strategy: Speedo swimsuit for hydrodynamic efficiency and a khaki shirt with lots of pockets. And what could feel better, I asked myself, than having the subtropical November sun on our backs, a mild breeze in our faces, and 12 gallons of 25:1 mix at our feet? That was enough go-juice to zip us around on plane, all day.

After we cleared the channel, I steered to the right. Minimal waves, none higher than four inches. Great conditions for high-speed exploring. I told Rebecca to hold on with two hands. Then I twisted the throttle to up the revs, and the engine responded with willingness. Unfortunately, with the second tank plus Rebecca on board, I wasn't able to get the boat up on plane.

However, it wasn't bad, moving along at only six knots, even if we were wasting a lot of gasoline and making a big ugly bow wave. Rebecca looked lovely, sitting balanced on the front chamber, smiling at me from behind her aviator shades. Her unbuttoned blouse fluttered in the wind, her right-sized breasts pushed against her tightly spanned bikini top, and her flat stomach performed a subtle belly dance as muscles flexed and relaxed to maintain balance against the pitching of the boat.

And how delightful to contemplate the seascape! It was painted with a full repertoire of colors from mossy dark brown, to brownish green, to light green, to sandy light green, to pale blue. And to an experienced eye, this palate of colors tells a story of water depth and bottom cover. The water we were moving through was four feet deep and appeared brownish green, due to the textured bottom. I aimed in a direction parallel to the ledge. With the Straits of Florida on our left, we made our way past the sunken sailboat and the mangrove island named Indian Cay. Then we bore down on the remnant of Indian Cay Light and adjusted course 10 degrees to the right to head for Marker

#2. At that point, we abandoned the ledge and steered northeast, moving back onto the Little Bahama Bank and following the markers between the shoals and sand flats.

What a pleasure it was to navigate so effortlessly. Coming through here on the *Diogenes* would have required extreme care against running aground. But in a hard-bottomed inflatable with a one-foot draft, there was nothing to worry about. It took us only half an hour to run the length of that three mile channel. From there, a big sweep of six-to-eight foot water was open to us in all directions between north and southeast.

I chose due east. As we proceeded with that course, the Grand Bahama Island fell away from us to the south. Under the surface, patches of yellow sand alternated with patches of green. No other boats seemed to be out. After a couple of miles of travel, Rebecca and I agreed that it was time to stake out a little patch of paradise. Circling back on a big patch of green, I powered down and threw out the grappling anchor.

How easy it is to enter the water from a rubber boat! You just put on your fins, mask and snorkel, then you just lay yourself on one of the side inflation chambers and roll off. A second later, you're in with the fish. Sure, the November water wasn't as warm as in August, but it wasn't unpleasant, either. With breath whistling in my snorkel, I scanned the bottom, looking for interesting things. This was a mixed patch with lots of turtle grass, numerous sponges and sea fans, and occasional brain corals ranging from two to six feet in diameter.

I felt an implosion of water to my left side when Rebecca rolled in. She looked so beautifully streamlined in that blue bikini. What graceful angles and curves! During her first couple of dives, I loitered to admire her lean, athletic body: the angularity of her thin arms held out straight before her and locked together at the thumbs; the dither of her ponytail over the ridge of her shoulders; the graceful arch of her back and the interesting groove following the spine; her thin waist and the flange of her hips; the tightness of her small buttocks; enticing movement of the crevasses around them; and the fluttering movement of her long, shapely, widely spaced legs as they propelled her downward to examine the coral heads.

As a further postponement of work, I amused myself diving down to the brain coral heads and looking at the sea anemones that grew in their crevasses like tiny colored Christmas trees. Those delicate filter feeders have a primitive nervous system that is sensitive and responsive. At the first touch, these lacy cones would pop back into the coral crevasse, like a jack-in-the-box in reverse. I swam around a big brain coral, touching them and playing a game of "putting out the lights." My fascination with the sea anemones seemed to amuse Rebecca, who had been following me down.

Now it was time to face the big question: Did the Little Bahama Bank have the sponge Dr. Broadmoore was looking for? According to his information sheet, the sponge I was looking for had a light, rusty red color and a conical shape. It was supposed to range in size from a couple of centimeters to three feet. What would differentiate this species from others was the presence of deep pocks or even holes on the side. And the reason I had been putting off the hunt was because I had seen plenty of brown sponges, and some yellow ones, but no red ones. I snorkled around on the surface until I found a candidate. I hyperventilated and dove to it. It was conical, about six inches tall and rusty red, and had a lot of indentations and . . . yes . . . a couple of holes in the side.

Good news! The Little Bahama Bank had at least one. Now I could get to work and determine how many per square mile. Now to perform a quantitative survey!

I flutter kicked back to the boat and pulled at the end of a 25-yard line that I had tethered to it. I swam due north until the line was completely stretched. Then, with line in hand, I made a complete circle around the boat, counting all the sponges I found within a 25-foot swath. Then, I shortened the line by 25 feet and made another complete circle. After repeating the procedure once more and adding a couple of sponges that were directly under the boat, the survey for this patch was completed. I pulled myself back onto the boat, removed my data forms and GPS unit from under the aluminum bench, and recorded latitude and longitude plus the fact that 21 sponges were found within an 87½-foot radius.

Great! This project would just be ordinary work — nothing that would require me to deal with paradoxes or to hope against hope. Now, to get myself back into an enjoyment mode.

I helped Rebecca aboard. She dried herself off and pulled up the anchor. The motor started right up, and we took off due east for about 20 minutes until the GPS showed that we'd gone two miles.

"Ben, do we really have to stop so soon?" Rebecca asked, as I powered down.

"To earn my pay from Broadmoore, I've got to make these measurements at regular intervals."

"It's starting to sound like work."

"I won't make it all work. I'll tickle some more sea anemones while I'm down there."

The search went a lot faster, this time, because I had thrown the anchor out blindly. Half of my underwater circle was an expanse of sand. But blindly means unbiased, and although my sponge count was only nine, it was more representative of the overall bottom. I'd improved my methodology. By the end of the day I would have it standardized. When I climbed back onto the boat, Rebecca was already eating lunch. She handed me a sandwich. I ate it underway to the next spot, two miles eastward, where we repeated the process.

After having repeated the process seven times and having moved ourselves about 14 miles eastward, Rebecca showed less enthusiasm for the water and more for lazy sunbathing. When I returned from my seventh survey, I found her in a vacation mood — sipping beer and draped luxuriously along the length of the starboard inflation chamber, and naked except for her sunglasses. There was no problem of privacy here. Except for the glint of a tuna tower miles to the east of us, there was no evidence of another boat.

Rebecca looked down and spoke to me with the voice she uses for impersonating a bored princess. "Please tell me, dear Sprite of Neptune, is Dr. Broadmoore going to rake countless treasures from the sea?"

I formed my dripping hand into a cone-shaped mouthpiece and trumpeted a misty fanfare, wetting her down in the process. "King Neptune announces that Dr. Broadmoore will have innumerable riches."

Rebecca tossed her head and laughed. "Then Neptune's Sprite could lay down the search and pick up with me. I'm in need of a kiss."

"Yes, my little sea anemone." And I gave her a kiss. A very special one. A very long one.

I can't say how long my fantasy on depleting dopamine from the pleasure centers of the brain actually lasted, but when we brought it to an end Rebecca looked down on me with concern.

"Ben, your lips are blue. You are hypothermic! Come out of the water immediately."

Rebecca's treatment for hypothermia consisted of sunning me on the other inflation chamber . . . and other ministrations. These revitalized me quickly, and soon we were rearranging ourselves in the rubber duckie to enjoy Nature's miracles at their resonant best. These pleasures promised to be even more delicious than those of the last two sessions. But our pleasures were interrupted when Rebecca turned her head and looked up.

"Ben, do you hear a whine?"

I turned my face upwards, scanning horizon and sky. And there it was, with the sun sparkling on sleek wings tipped in our direction. The executive-type jet was orbiting us like a model airplane on a two thousand foot line, its two rear-mounted turbofan engines broadcasting a suppressed scream. It was a FalconJet, 56 feet long with low, swept-back wings, a needle nose, and completely white except for the diagonal red line on the side of its fuselage and the red highlighting on its large stabilizer. And it had three viewing ports on the side.

"U.S. Coast Guard," I said, grabbing an offshore life jacket to cover my posterior but not abandoning my wild abandon.

"What are they doing here?" Rebecca asked, pulling the other life jacket over her upper body.

I strapped the life jacket around my waist. "Let's talk about it later."

We persevered while they orbited us a dozen times before flying off. After recovering our resonances and bringing things to a natural conclusion, we relaxed in each other's arms.

"The U.S. Coast Guard," Rebecca said. "What they doing here?"

"Photographing us."

"What?"

"Don't worry, we're probably not going to be recorded in any official archive. All they'll record officially is our registration number." I patted the two-foot-wide patch on the bow on which I'd stenciled the *Diogenes'* name and Coast Guard documentation number.

"Burr! Then they photographed our faces . . . and everything."

"Our faces probably weren't identifiable with sunglasses. And the life jackets did a pretty good job with the everything else."

"Why were they here in the first place?"

"They patrol the Straits of Florida for safety and drug interdiction. But the Bahamian Government doesn't mind if they swing in here. At their speed, it takes only three or four minutes."

"They sweep in here and photograph the boats?"

"Sometimes, if there's one they are interested in. And I wouldn't be surprised if they have a radar plane. They had one the last time I was here."

That was on one of the Bahama cruises I'd made before meeting Rebecca.

"You mean they fly one of those big airborne radar jets that they use to keep track of air battles?"

"Yes, but the one I saw was a P-3 Orion — a four-engine turboprop that the Navy uses as sub-chasers. They have a radar antenna that hangs out the back like a pole. My guess is that they were using Orions to keep track of boats crossing the Gulf Stream to the coast of Florida."

Rebecca nodded. "Then they tell the Coast Guard people to go out in their Cigarette boats and intercept them off the Florida coast."

"Yes, that's the Bahama-side part of the drug interdiction program. Informants at the docks and electronic spies in the sky."

"Then they might have a radar record of what happened to the *Second Chance*."

"Good point, girl. But there's no chance of getting the information. Anti-drug operations are very hush-hush."

Rebecca smiled. "What now, Cherub of Neptune?"

"Demoting me from sprite to cherub, are you? Hell, I thought today's performance would earn me a promotion to archangel. Well, to angel, anyway."

"Okay, you are an archangel. I was just wondering if we should be going back."

"I agree, but we'll do some surveying on the way back."

We motored two miles south, then worked our way westward, stopping every two miles for a survey. On the way we saw another glint in the sky towards the shore of Grand Bahama Island. Watching carefully, I identified it as a two-engine seaplane. It descended until I lost sight of it between the water horizon and the thin tree line marking the shore of the island. From this, I deduced that the plane had landed. We stopped to do another sponge count. Afterward, I caught sight of the plane taking off and flying eastward. Curious about where it was operating, I pulled out my hand-held compass and took a bearing.

On the return trip we worked our way in closer to the island. A couple of miles from the marina we came onto a pair of yellow Waverunners — or I should say they came onto us. A muscular guy was in the lead, making all sorts of unnecessary turns. A bikini girl was following and imitating his moves, but not as radically. He straightened out while approaching, then laid in a big arcing turn in front of us. Through his shades he took in an eyeful of Rebecca, but he didn't wave back to me. His black hair was crew-cut and a big tatoo sat on his left shoulder. The bikini girl did wave back when she zipped by.

"Why do they shoot that stream of water so high out the back?" Rebecca asked.

"It's cooling water from the engine," I said. "They shoot it high so that it increases the Waverunner's visibility. They're so small and fast that it's easy for them to get mixed up and run into each other."

We passed the Waverunners' base of operations — the shack and collection of boat-toys on the shore east of the marina. We got back about an hour before sunset. I tied the Caribe to the *Diogenes*' side. Rebecca climbed aboard to prepare dinner, and I went to check out the *Second Chance*. On the way, I stopped at the marina office. There, Zelma handed me a large FEDEX box. I thanked her and carried it off to the *Second Chance*.

Constable Ivanhoe was still on duty. He said that Sgt. Townsend had not visited and that nobody else had, either. The crime scene tape was indeed sagging and the no-trespassing notice had fallen to the cockpit floor. I opened the door and checked inside. Everything looked okay. It felt a lot drier inside. And the console of radio equipment must have been drying out some because its speakers were making intermittent noises, like it was trying to amplify static.

For good measure, I started the engines and ran them for a while. Standing in the cockpit listening to them run, I waved to Edgar the conch man as he pulled into the marina with his dark-green work boat. He tied up between the end pilings of Angie and Cal's slip and announced that he had a load of two-dollar conchs. Angie was his first customer, and there were a lot more. He was a good salesman, keeping up his line of chatter and putting on a show as he busted them open and loaded them into plastic bags.

When doing business with Edgar before, I hadn't had much of a chance to look at him. But I could do that now. Standing there, bare-chested and wearing only a pair of dark blue boxer trunks, he reminded me of a boxer — a semi-pro, middle-weight who picks up fifty bucks every once in a while making an appearance here and there. He didn't have the bulging biceps and tight stomach of a real contender. His biceps were tough and wiry — like the attitude he reverted to between lines of carnival gab. While standing in his boat, turning his big head looking for customers, he held his stomach loose but his chest high. When a new customer came, he assembled a package of conch quickly, moving his heavy frame around the boat with great agility. Did he go around all day shirtless and hatless? Wouldn't the sun damage his skin when he exposed it this way, day after day? It was black, but with a reddish cast. His curly black hair receded on his head. I wondered about his age and guessed an athletic 40.

When I shut down the motors, Wade Daniels appeared on his deck and waved. After locking up the *Second Chance*, I chatted with him at the base of his dock.

"Find any sponges out there?" Wade asked.

"A whole bunch of them," I said. "The Brit's going to be happy when I report back to him."

"Great. And how's the salvage project going?"

"Hell, I'm through with that. Just waiting for the police to get done. They still have authority over the boat," I said.

Wade winked an eye and took a step forward. "If I were you, I'd just drive it back to Miami." He said it with a soft voice and an attitude of concern. "I've been here most of the day. It's clear that they haven't done anything with it. They're probably just drawing things out and looking for an excuse to confiscate it."

"Yes, that's what I'm beginning to think, too, Wade."

He looked both ways, then moved still closer. "Take my advice," he said in a half whisper. "Just wait 'til that guy in the blue suit goes home. Then hop in it and drive it to Miami."

"That's probably good advice, Wade, but I have to think about it. I don't want to make things complicated."

Wade stared at me with sleepy eyes. "Possession is ninety percent of the law."

11   Of Pirates in Paradise

Back at the *Diogenes*, Rebecca told me that Martha Vangelden had invited us for drinks after dinner and that she had said yes. We figured it would be a relaxed evening because neither of them would be members of the hypothetical SAWECUSS. Before dinner, I unpacked the FEDEX box from Dr. Broadmoore's company. It contained a lot of test tubes and solvents, plus a good set of instructions on how to extract zagrionic acid from the sponges. The procedures were simple enough to perform on the Caribe inflatable, where the Bahamian authorities couldn't hassle me for disturbing any living materials.

After dinner we headed off for Ray and Martha's trawler. With its high, nautically shaped bow, gracefully curving lines and three levels, it was the largest and most expensive yacht in the marina — and Ray didn't mind saying so while showing us around. The lower level housed the staterooms forward and the engines aft. The uppermost level had a semi-enclosed piloting station and a railing-protected aft deck, which seemed to go on forever. It covered the aft portion of the middle deck that was open to that side.

Martha met us at the doors of the middle deck. She was wearing the same type of jeans-skirt as the other evening, but with a semi-silky purple blouse under a light-weight black-and-gilt shawl. She looked stylishly thin. She led us into the air-conditioned main salon. "We use the air conditioning in the summer and for privacy," she said.

"I understand. Marinas put you at closer quarters than in a trailer park."

Martha answered my remark by arching an eyebrow — the one on my side. They were thin and penciled a shade darker than the auburn hair which framed her broad, wrinkle-free forehead.

Blinds were drawn before the window on the Sumter's side. On the other side, a large expanse of smoked glass afforded a broad view of the Little Bahama Bank. And behind the clear glass of the hooded windshield, the sun was setting over the Straits of Florida.

I did a quick survey of the interior: on the starboard side, a full piloting station up front, chart table behind, wet bar and kitchen behind that; on the port side, a large table and booth that would do justice to an elegant restaurant.

Ray said, "We don't mean that the people at marinas are trailer trash, but sometimes we do have to shut up the boat to get away from the smell of their barbecues."

"What can I get you?" Martha interjected. "We have pina colada, daiquiri, rum and coke. Or we can offer gin and tonic, vodka tonic, Tom Collins or whiskey sour." She recited it like an inventory with no twinkle in her brown eyes. She had a far-sighted look that seemed to always focus beyond us and sometimes straight through us.

"Martha knows how to keep me happy," Ray quipped, aiming a big grin at me. With his ears standing out a half inch from his head and with the space between his eyes punctuated by that bulbous nose, the grin really did seem aimed at me. But the grin was warm-spirited and was modulated by twinkles of the eye.

I laughed. "A gin and tonic would make me happy." I turned to Martha. "That was a most impressive recitation."

Martha raised an eyebrow, then showed me a hint of a thin-lipped smile. Her red lipstick was applied quite precisely. She turned her face to Rebecca. "We also have wine — an Italian red or a Chablis, and we also have beer."

Rebecca said, "I'll just have what you are having."

"Then you'll have water," Ray said with a laugh that creased his nose, which I now noticed was crazed with a network of small red arteries.

"I drink Perrier," Martha explained, evenly. "Are you staying with gin and tonic, Ben?"

"I'd like one of what Ray's drinking," I said. "I like Ray's mood, and I envy his success."

That candid comment earned me two raised eyebrows then a full smile.

Then came a slap on the back from Ray. "Make that two Tom Collins, sweetie."

"And I'll have a Chablis," Rebecca added.

Ray ushered us into the booth and Martha went to the bar corner to get the drinks. And we all talked about the excellent features of his yacht, including his bow thruster for turning in tight places and his gyroscopically driven fin stabilizers which keep it from rolling in beam seas.

Rebecca said that they must be able to cruise any ocean with such a yacht. Ray answered that he could cruise the Caribbean, but he wouldn't cruise the southern Caribbean.

"Why not?" I asked.

"Too many hijackers down there, and this is just the type of boat that they want. And they can kill the owner and throw him overboard."

"What about around here?" Rebecca asked.

"No hijackers around here," he said. "Around here it's smugglers."

While passing out the drinks, Martha added her view on the subject. "If you stay away from them, they will stay away from you." She looked around, as if considering what to say next. I had noticed the other evening that she used few words, but that everything she said was well thought out. She lifted her Perrier bottle, ready to pour it into her glass, but then she put it back down. "Hijacking, piracy and smuggling has been the history of the Bahamas. One might say that those activities are the Bahamas' claim to fame."

"Yeah," Ray said, "that's what they need for a tourist attraction in Freeport — a Pirate's Hall of Fame."

Three of us laughed and Martha eventually joined in. She wrinkled her brow, ever so slightly. "They could do it as a wax museum, I guess. They could start with Captain Bartholomew Roberts who was known as Black Bart." She was talking like a volunteer docent in an art museum. "And then would come Captain Charles Vane and Captain Jack Rackam. And with him came Anne Bonny and Mary Reed."

"Women pirates?" Rebecca said.

"Yes. Victims of circumstance, one could say. They were as ruthless as many pirates, but they fought more valiantly than their men on the day they were captured." She poured half of the contents of her bottle of Perrier into a glass.

"What about Black Beard?" I asked.

"Yes, Edward Teach was the most colorful. Before going into battle, he would braid his beard and soak the tips to make fuses for firing his pistols. He was a fearsome sight with his face smouldering." She took a small sip.

We talked about piracy for quite a while. Martha said that many pirates started out as privateers. In time of war, the King of England handed out letters of permission to plunder Spanish ships. When peace was established, the privateers found it difficult to change their habits, and they continued to plunder anything that came their way — as pirates. But it wasn't always like Robert Louis Stevenson's *Treasure Island*, fighting to the death or walking the plank. Sometimes an act of piracy was a simple coercion, when the aggressor appeared quickly with superior force. And sometimes the surrender was more of a collusion between captains at the expense of the insurer of the cargo. Often it was not easy to draw the line between the good guys and the bad guys. Sometimes, reformed pirates were sent out to capture the ones who were still active. Sometimes a pirate would even be appointed to government office.

With all that said, Martha allowed herself a parsimonious sip of Perrier.

Rebecca wondered why things had been so chaotic in the Bahamas.

Martha answered that the "Carolina Proprietors," granted the Bahamas in 1668, were more interested in exploiting the islands than in controlling them. But Ray said that you couldn't expect anything different because if you're running something, it's got to be run as a business because nobody goes into business for his health. Martha didn't take offense at that, but she pointed out that the Bahamian soil was too poor to create much wealth and that it could only support the buccaneers.

Martha went on to explain that the original buccaneers were the settlers who came after Christopher Columbus' Spanish successors had depopulated the Bahamas of its native population. They had enslaved all the Lucayan Indians and shipped them out to Hispaniola (present-day Haiti and the Dominican Republic) to die in the mines and on the plantations. She explained that the buccaneers got their name from *bucan*, barbecued pork. Numerous Spanish shipwrecks had seeded the islands with herds of wild pig, and the buccaneers had made a good living by supplying vessels with cured meat. They also salvaged goods from wrecked vessels and often caused the vessels to wreck by putting out false lights. As their society evolved, they began performing other acts of mischief that came to be associated with the term "buccaneer."

"They're keeping their barbecuing traditions alive here," Ray said, pointing a finger in the direction Angie and Cal's boat. "And smuggling, too."

I tried to get Ray's attention and raise an eyebrow to ask if he really meant to say that Angie and Cal were smuggling. But Martha beat me to the punch.

"Perhaps one cannot *expect* better from the Bahamas," Martha said quickly. "So much is determined by geography."

Martha took another parsimonious sip from her glass of Perrier. If she kept going at that rate, she could recap the bottle for the next evening.

"What do you mean?" Rebecca asked.

"When the Americans adopted Prohibition, smuggling of liquor from the Bahamas to the coast of Florida was inevitable. The Florida coast is only forty miles from Bimini and sixty miles from here. Smuggling during the Prohibition was an economic boon to West End."

Rebecca said that was very interesting and Martha continued. "Geography has always controlled the fate of the Bahamas. When the

Spanish were staging their treasure galleons in Havana, they had only three ways to start their sail towards Spain and each one involved the Bahamas. If they went up the Straits of Florida with the Gulf Stream, pirates would be waiting for them around here on the western shore of the Bahamas. If they chose to cut through the New Providence Channel to the south of here, they had the Bahamas on all sides. Or if they tried to sail west along the coast of Cuba, Hispaniola and Puerto Rico, they had to fight wind and current, and they were still exposed to Bahamian pirates from the north. The Bahamas has always been the perfect area for scoundrels to lurk. It is a simple fact of geography."

Ray had been replenishing our drinks with great friendliness and generosity. I tried to think of a way to learn about present-day scoundrels lurking around West End. I said, "Barbecuing, wrecking, hijacking, piracy and smuggling — West End has had it all." When nobody said anything, I pressed on. "Do you have any idea what the murder victim, 'Steve,' was doing here?"

"No, we do not," Martha said, throwing a quick glance to Ray.

"He didn't seem to do that much fishing," Ray said. "Sometimes, I'd see him walking around, but usually he kept to himself in his boat. A lot of the time he was away. He took the van to Freeport."

"How long was he here?"

"Came a few days after we did. About a week before you came."

"I guess that Cal and Angie and Wade are old hands around here."

"That could be," Ray said. "We've seen them here every time we've come through for the last couple of years."

"Are they into fishing?"

"That's what they say, and they are always grilling fish in their cockpit."

The main salon went silent. It would have been nice for Ray and Martha to tell us if any of the people around the marina could be dangerous to us. But I couldn't come right out and ask: There was still a small chance that the Vangeldens might be indirectly involved in illegal activities. It was a tricky thing, like groping in a dark hole to retrieve a mousetrap. Maybe a big show of enthusiasm for the fish fryers would make our hosts shed some light on the subject.

"But you have to admit, Ray, that Wade showed us a grand old time at his fish fry last week. Cal and Wade were a barrel of laughs when they got going with their stories."

"About the man on his porch with the shotgun?" Martha said,

warily. "I suppose that could be called *regional* humor." She punctuated the expression with a wave of a thin arm.

"No, that wouldn't be funny in New York," Ray said, with a wide-eared frown.

"Nor in Boston," Martha said, wrinkling her seamless forehead for the second time that evening. "Actually, they were more boisterous than droll."

To me, that sounded too much like a put-down. "Their stuff was funny if you think of where they are coming from. I've been told it's Gaelic humor with a strong streak of individualism. People in the South didn't get squeezed together like people did the northeastern cities."

"Be that as it may," Martha said. "A pickup truck is a *farm* vehicle."

"Except that in the Southeast where the weather's mild, people keep finding more and more uses for them. Not that I'm for driving around with a big, gas-guzzling engine or anything. But down here a lot of those pickups are used for pulling boat trailers." Neither of the Vangeldens gave me any encouragement. "I guess you could say that I'm slowly developing Southern sensibilities."

Martha was observing me with unblinking concentration. "I thought you were from the Northeast."

"Newark," I said.

"But you don't sound Newark," she said, scrutinizing me like this was the second time she'd gotten to look at me. "I would have thought Connecticut."

"And he doesn't sound like any kind of New York, neither," Ray added.

"It was a hobby as a kid, fighting off the regional accent. But when I had to, I could bring it out to communicate on the street."

"I see," Ray and Martha said, simultaneously.

Martha was an active listener. "And Rebecca mentioned that you are involved in a sponge survey, here?"

I told them all about it.

"That is interesting," Martha said. "You follow your opportunities . . . like Ray did."

It was time for another public relations announcement, although I doubted that the Vangeldens had the connections to broadcast it. "Yes. I'm just waiting for my luck to change and the Royal Bahamas Police Force to release the boat I salvaged, then I'll take it to Miami and get on with my sponge survey. We'll be working our way east."

"Yes, we both wish you the best of luck with that," Martha said. "Bahamian bureaucracy can be tricky."

"Yeah, we wish you lots of luck," Ray said. "You came into a tricky situation, and you've been handling it right."

We all looked at each other in silence for quite a while. Martha was the last to blink but the first to speak. "We should be going to the Abacos soon. Green Turtle Cay."

Turning to me, Rebecca said, "Martha knows a whole lot about the island. The other night she was telling me about the old families of British Loyalists there, and the inn, and the famous artist who painted the two women looking at the land and the sea."

For the next few minutes, Martha gave us a lot of information on Green Turtle Cay, emphasizing that we really had to visit it. And all the while, Ray was yawning. Rebecca thanked them both and said we had to be going, and I affirmed it saying that we had to get up early for tomorrow's sponge survey. I promised that we would migrate eastward with them.

Martha showed us to the door. "In the Bahamas, people are always coming and going. It's strange that they come and go like migratory birds."

"Snowbirds," Ray said.

Martha looked down on the two rows of boats tied to the center dock. "And it looks like we are going to have another migration," she said wistfully.

Her prediction proved true. And the arch of her eyebrows told me that she knew a lot more than she was telling us.

High-Class Hospitality   12

Our next morning got off to a slow start. While topping off my Caribe's tanks at the fuel dock, I exchanged some small talk with Rick Turner, who was fueling up his *Completed Circuit*. It had a big cockpit dominated by a fighting chair, a couple of long outrigger poles, and a high tuna tower. I wondered how much longer he would be waiting for his partner. But not wishing to pry, I didn't ask. I also wondered what had happened to Chuck and Bill. Their boat was still there but I hadn't seen them climbing their tuna tower recently. Another person I hadn't seen recently was Sgt. Townsend. At the *Second Chance*, Constable Ivanhoe was still doing guard duty and was stripping palm fronds to go into hat production, it seemed. He didn't know where his sergeant was.

After motoring the Caribe back to the *Diogenes*, I put in a cellphone call to the Good Sergeant, leaving a message that the *Second Chance*'s usefulness as a crime scene had now come to an end and could he call me at his earliest possible convenience. It was important for me to keep up the offensive. To deny him any possible excuse, I decided to take the cellphone along. I inserted the teak boards into the slots in the companionway, finagled the sliding hatch into place, and inserted the lock into the hasp to secure the *Diogenes*. Then, remembering that I'd forgotten to take the binoculars, I undid and redid that work, cursing the sticky hatch.

The weather for our trip was as good as the day before. Wanting to keep Rebecca's interest up, this time I selected a route that took us north, ten miles along the shelf's edge. There, we saw lots of sea fans and coral. And there were plenty of brain coral heads, studded with sea anemones to provide the type of artistic inspiration I had experienced the day before. But here along the ledge we encountered frequent boat traffic and jostling waves from the Florida Strait. Not only did the waves disrupt my note taking, they also interfered with the chemical extractions of the sponge samples I collected. And the smell of organic solvents made me feel queasy much of the time.

We followed the shelf doing surveys for a couple of miles past Sandy Cay. The tides coming off the flats were strong — between two and three knots. It wasn't easy to swim against them, even when beating my fins with full power. I decided to start making notes on the strength of the tide throughout its cycle. This information might be useful for backing up the drift calculations that I'd made for the *Second Chance*.

Later in the day, we turned east and went several miles onto the Bank before turning south. This put us on the other side of the Barracuda Shoal. On the way back, I counted and sampled a lot of sponges. And I didn't see any boats or glinting tuna towers on the southward leg of the journey.

When we returned, around five o'clock in the afternoon, there were fewer boats in the marina. I noticed that Rick Turner's *Completed Circuit* was gone. As we made our way to the showers, we noticed that

Cliff Grimes had his engine compartment open. He was working on his engine with all his "engineuity," judging from the big heat exchanger that he had taken out and from the oversized wrenches that were sitting next to it.

And as we approached the showers, we noticed a Jaguar with right-side steering parked by the office. It was a recent S-Type in British racing green. A uniformed chauffeur stepped out and approached us. In his face, I noticed a resemblance to Edgar, the enterprising conch man.

He greeted us formally in a resonant baritone. "Doctor Candidi and Doctor Levis, I presume."

"Yes," I said.

"My name is Kevin, in the service of Sir Hector Pimentel."

Rebecca looked at me with surprise.

"Yes," I said, half to her and half to Kevin. "Doctor Broadmoore mentioned him to me. They were once friends at Cambridge."

Dressed in his gray chauffeur uniform, cut to specifications from hat to shoes, and speaking his part so properly, Kevin made me feel like we were outside a hotel in London. He extended a gloved hand to give me an envelope. "Sir Hector requests the pleasure of your company for dinner at his house this evening at eight o'clock. No formal attire will be necessary."

"Yes. Thank you. We would be most delighted."

We had to hurry to get everything done. First, I raced over to the *Second Chance* where I learned from Ivanhoe that Sgt. Townsend had not visited. But he said that Sgt. Townsend had told him to remind me that the *Second Chance* was not to be moved.

Checking in with the marina office, I was given a FEDEX letter which contained a copy of my salvage claim, filed in Federal court. That was good news. I was getting my ducks in a row. The envelope also contained a bill for $2,000.

I hurried to the shower and returned to the *Diogenes* for better clothes.

The Jaguar had a sand leather interior, and it was well air-conditioned. We sat in back, I in a dark-colored, long-sleeved shirt and dress slacks, and Rebecca in her little black dress with gold chain and flats. Rebecca asked Kevin a couple of simple questions and received short formal answers. I surrendered my body to the contoured seat, relaxed my head against the headrest, and enjoyed the ride.

It was a short ride, past the overgrown entrance to the defunct airport, the water tower, and the clapboard houses. The town limit came quickly, as did the now-familiar string of landmarks: the Batelco tower, the police station, the health clinic, the administration building and school, the "Island Club," the church, and the historical downtown. Soon we were out of town and were traveling toward Freeport on the highway where Kevin showed us some six-cylinder acceleration. A mile or so farther, he slowed for a left turn onto a gravel road named Royal Lane. There were no houses along this narrow road, just pine and underbrush.

After two miles travel, the road dead-ended at Sir Hector's gate. It was black iron in a picket design with a royal crest in the center. From either side of the gate extended a concrete wall that was embellished with coral rock, inlaid conch shells and bas relief sculpture on the theme of the kingdom of the sea — Neptune and mermaids. After 50 yards the wall gave way to a hedge.

Kevin pushed a button on the dashboard, the gates swung open and he drove into a large oval covered with gravel and lined with flowers in wooden boxes. In the center stood a fountain of cut coral. Kevin followed the perimeter, driving in the clockwise direction. Beyond the flower boxes was a vast lawn that gave way to undergrowth and then to indigenous pines. The house stood at the end of the oval. It was built with quarried stone and was two-storey, with a peaked roof covered with gray slate. Its most remarkable feature was how it sat on an elevation, a grassy mound that must have been built to protect it from hurricane flooding. A V-shaped flight of two dozen steps led from the gravel oval to a modest front door.

Kevin stopped the car in front of the stairs. Observing protocol, we waited until he got out and opened the door for Rebecca. I got out behind her.

At the top of the stairs, the door opened and a dark-skinned, gray-haired man in a black suit came out and stood to the side. He just stood there, with a slight slouch, gazing off in the distance. I had a hard time figuring out who he was. The black suit was a regular cut with no tails. His tie seemed to be of silk, with subdued color and design. I couldn't see his shoes.

"Sir Hector Pimentel," Kevin said softly. He gestured for us to go up the stairs.

The next several seconds were strange. As we walked up the stairs,

Sir Hector smiled down in our direction without really looking at us. Following one step behind Rebecca, I suppressed the urge to speak out to him, wave a hand, or even smile up at him. Apparently, these two dozen steps were meant as a barrier to more than hurricane-driven flood waters. Rebecca took my arm, and we climbed the steps toward him as a couple.

As we neared, Sir Hector seemed to come to life. His big head turned to greet us, and his mouth turned up in an effusive smile. "Doctor . . . Candidi and . . . Doctor . . ." He lingered on that last word.

"Rebecca Levis," my fiancée added quickly. She greeted him with a prim smile and extended her hand.

Sir Hector clasped it with two broad hands, encircling it with stubby fingers. "Yes. Quite. I am *so* glad to meet you."

His cheeks rose toward his heavy eyebrows and the skin around his dark eyes crinkled into a grandfatherly smile. He was an inch or so taller than us, with a large-boned frame that carried more muscle than fat. His broad shoulders were slightly rounded. I guessed he was in his middle sixties, judging from the prominent gray in his short curly hair, which showed a few traces of the original black. Similarly, his skin seemed a lighter shade of black than he was born with. In several places it was freckled in white.

"And we are thrilled by your invitation," Rebecca said.

Sir Hector's warm eyes lingered on Rebecca for several seconds before his hand released hers and extended to me. "When Brian . . . Dr. Broadmoore, that is . . . told me that you were . . . in our area, we decided that I *must* make your acquaintance." He shook my hand with vigor and spoke while looking past me. "It was such good news to hear of his interest and of your work. It is not often that the Commonwealth receives such good news."

Sir Hector said all this with Ox-Bridge cadence and enunciation. But he didn't use the sharp inflection which is common to that university-derived style. He seemed like a nice guy who was a bit shy of eye contact.

"I am glad to be back in the Bahamas," I said. "And although I am not far along in my work, I am fairly certain that I will not be bringing bad news."

"Good. Yes, very good," he said, moving toward the open door, which was fitted with an old-fashioned thumb button and latch mechanism that harked back to colonial Williamsburg, Virginia. "We will certainly have much to talk about. But first, could I show you the house?"

Sir Hector led us into a large room with a high ceiling. It was configured as a grand entrance, with a red carpeted stairway leading upward, with an electric chandelier, and with a mezzanine level organized around it, two rooms on each side. To the right of the stairway stood a long table, set for three. Kevin closed the door behind us. Sir Hector led us past the ascending stairway and through a door to the left along the wall.

Sir Hector's study was a veritable four-walled bookcase. By the south window that faced the road stood an elegant brass floor lamp with an interesting shade: high-reflective white on the inside and dark black on the outside. On either side sat an oversize leather chair. To the side of one chair was a small reading table. On it stood a silver-framed, black-and-white portrait photograph of an attractive, dark-skinned, middle-aged woman with a warm smile.

The sun's low rays came in through the bookcase-framed windows and illuminated an antique globe and models of sailing ships. These shared the top of an oak table with an oversize dictionary that was opened to the center. The volumes on the shelves along the outer wall were mostly leather-bound. The works of Shakespeare and Milton caught my eye, but all of the classic English authors seemed to be represented. Judging from the other leather-bound titles on his shelves, Sir Hector was heavily into turn-of-the-19th-century disputations on empire and economics.

The interior wall was a red, blue and green matrix of cloth-bound books. I moved closer to read a few black- or gold-printed titles. Most were works of modern, mainstream literature. Apparently, the books' dust jackets had been sacrificed for aesthetic unity with the rest of the room. Rebecca expressed her appreciation of Sir Hector's literary interest, and I complimented the nautical display.

"This room feels like it is oozing with history," I said.

One of the bookcases was a cabinet with a lockable wooden door. One of the leather chairs faced it. I guessed that this contained a TV and a video player.

Sir Hector led us to an adjoining room toward the rear. "This one is dedicated to my other pursuits."

The back room was done in white Formica. On one side was a

counter, holding a desktop computer and a fax machine. On the other side was a large built-in glass case containing shotguns.

"When I'm not shooting off e-mails and faxes, I am often shooting pigeons," he said, with a mischievous smile.

"Real pigeons?" Rebecca asked.

"Mostly clay pigeons . . . when Kevin is around to pull for me, anyway. You will see the trap apparatus when we go outside." He turned to me. "But I have also hunted real pigeons, too. They are quite plentiful, here."

I asked, "Do you mean the kind with the small head and noisy wings that always seem to take their time flying away from cars?"

"Yes. Quite. No bother about *them* going extinct, here," he said, looking at Rebecca and then to me. His English cadence was on a roll, but he seemed to be talking to the floor. "Of course, it's but a poor semblance of the grouse hunting that we did in England. But when one bags two dozen pigeons, one can put on a good dinner party."

Rebecca jumped in with a couple of quick questions, which Sir Hector was glad to answer. When he noticed me peering through the glass at the shotguns, he drifted toward me.

"How long were you in England?" I asked.

"From boarding school until graduating from Cambridge," he said, with a flourish. He produced a key, unlocked the case, and pulled out one of the shotguns, handing it to me. It smelled of gun oil and wood polish. With a schoolboyish grin, he pointed to a lockable drawer under the case. "I have several boxes of ammunition if you would like to have a go at it."

"Uh, no thanks. Maybe . . . some time when there's . . . more light left in the day."

"Do you shoot?" He posed the question like a challenge.

"Not as an active hobby. But I have had the chance to take a few shots from a lot of different kinds of guns. I guess you could say I have some familiarity." I handed back the shotgun.

"And you?" he asked Rebecca.

"No, guns and I don't get along. And I'm afraid firing one would knock me down."

"One must brace oneself," he said. He demonstrated the stance, pointing to the ceiling and leaning a big shoulder into the wooden stock. After receiving a nod from Rebecca, he let the gun down and shrugged his shoulders. He returned the shotgun to the case, locked it and put the key in the drawer under the computer. "I should like to show you the grounds," he said to us both, with a soft laugh.

He ushered Rebecca through the back door and led us out onto a large patio area that was on the same level as the house, about 16 feet above ground.

"The house is constructed on a mound of boulders with concrete fill." Sir Hector explained it like a tour guide. "A hurricane might wash away the lawn and leave us looking like a lighthouse, but we would be otherwise untouched."

Parked along the wall of the house at the edge of the patio was a sporty-looking motorcycle. I pointed to it and said, "Are you into hill climbing, too?"

"Oh, no, that belongs to Kevin. Rather more exciting than driving the Jaguar, is it not?" Turning his head, he noticed that Kevin was not with us. "Oh, yes, I forgot that he is seeing to the evening's meal."

A path with occasional steps led from the patio down the grassy hill to the shore of the Little Bahama Bank. A white-painted, wooden dock extended about 25 yards. A small fiberglass boat was tied to the end. A dozen miles beyond that had to be the area where Rebecca and I had done the first sponge survey. To the left, the sun was getting ready to set over West End, which lay somewhere beyond the horizon along that curving, uninhabited shore. And off to the right was wooded shoreline, with no houses to be seen.

Sir Hector had moved to the side of the patio and was lifting a tarp from a desk-sized contraption. "Here is the trap apparatus."

I must have smiled as he proudly displayed this last accoutrement of an English country gentleman. Such anglophilia! Emulating the idealized manners of a country in which he was not born — of a country that had enslaved his ancestors.

"So you stand here and tell Kevin to pull, and the clay pigeon comes arching over your backyard, and you shoot it."

"Yes! Quite. Indeed, my dear chap." He said it with sporting enthusiasm. "And now, Dr. Candidi, could I suggest a spot of Campari?"

In the middle of the patio sat a table already decked out with glasses and a bottle of that marvelous red liquid. We sat down to enjoy a cloudy sunset and a meandering conversation about the island. Eventually, Sir Hector asked about my relationship to Dr. Broadmoore.

"I once did a consulting job for him. It was on short notice, and I uncovered a lot of important things for him."

Sir Hector pulled at a sleeve. "On what topic were you consulting?"

"On whether a company's claims about the anticancer activity of zagrionic acid compounds from sponges were supported by their data."

"Are these the same sponges as you will be surveying here?"

"Yes. And you were friends with Dr. Broadmoore at Cambridge?"

Sir Hector looked out on the water. "We knew each other. But we were in different colleges and separated by a couple of years."

Since that answer sounded pretty much no, I didn't follow up on it. We talked about English universities instead.

The sun was down and it was becoming dark. The patio lights went on, and Kevin came to tell us that dinner was served. He was now dressed in a white waiter's jacket. Under the lights, I once again noticed a facial resemblance to Edgar, the conch man. The bodies were similar, too, the difference being that Kevin's looked softer. In-door versus outdoor work could account for the difference. Of course, it would have been a faux pas to ask Kevin about a brother.

We returned to the air-conditioned house and took our places in the dining room. Sir Hector sat at the end of the long table and Rebecca and I sat to either side of him. The first course was soup. With Continental grace, Kevin filled our glasses with red wine. Sir Hector proposed a toast to Dr. Broadmoore's endeavor, and we drank to that.

Sir Hector said, "We are always in need of a leg-up, in the economic sense, that is. We are a poor country, seven hundred and fifty miles of far-flung islands. We feed ourselves by subsistence fishing and what we can grow in our gardens. Anything that we do to further ourselves comes from tourism, banking and other forms of money from the outside. We rely on partnerships between the government and private capital to make improvements that will bring money in."

"Are you a member of Parliament?" I asked.

"Yes. I am a Senator." Anticipating my question, he added, "The Senate is our upper house. The lower house is called the House of Assembly."

"And what is your constituency?"

"They are as far-flung as the islands, I should say. I do keep in touch with my electorate."

It was interesting how he usually looked to Rebecca while answering my questions. She always nodded in encouragement and agreement.

"How do you cover seven hundred and fifty miles?"

"By aeroplane and boat. Aeroplane, mostly. A seaplane takes me. It is a commercial venture, but the government supports it for the common good."

"That's interesting, Sir Hector. From the water, I saw a seaplane descending to land in an area that must have been close to here. It was just yesterday. The plane was a two-engine Grumman Mallard like Chalks Airline flies out of Miami."

"Yes, that was the type aeroplane and I was aboard. But it belongs to a Bahamian company that has nothing to do with Chalks. They collected me from Spanish Wells and brought me to my dock."

"That is interesting. As I understand, there is no regularly scheduled amphibious airplane service to the Grand Bahama Island."

Sir Hector looked at the ceiling. "That is correct. The airport at Freeport provides too much competition. But unscheduled or not, amphibious aircraft are an important transportation link for us."

"I can imagine. You have a lot of water, and thus a lot of landing places."

Rebecca asked, "Do you use the seaplanes for transportation of public health workers?"

"Yes, transportation of medical personnel and evacuating critically ill patients is one of their major uses," Sir Hector said.

"Rebecca's specialty is medicine in developing countries," I said. "She just finished a World Health Organization fellowship in Washington."

Sir Hector's eyes twinkled as he turned to Rebecca. "I should hope that you would find us quite advanced in this area. We strive for universal coverage, using clinics for islands which have towns, and using itinerate nurse-practitioners for the islands that do not."

"We passed by your West End clinic when we visited the town on bicycle," Rebecca said, hesitantly.

Sir Hector didn't pick up on this.

I chimed in. "Yes, I was asking Rebecca what medical conditions your health workers are treating there, and she could only guess."

Sir Hector turned to Rebecca. "Would you like to visit the clinic? I am sure that they would be delighted to have you."

"Well, yes," Rebecca said, wrinkling her brow. "But I don't feel like I could just drop in."

"Not to worry. I shall arrange it tomorrow. For tomorrow morning, if that suits you."

Rebecca's face lit up. "Yes. Thank you. That would be wonderful."

I pulled out a pen and folded sheet of paper and wrote down our cellphone numbers for Sir Hector.

"Capital!" he said to Rebecca. He inserted the paper into the inside pocket of his jacket. "They will come to collect you tomorrow morning."

Kevin had been removing the soup bowls and now was bringing plates with the main course — thinly sliced and delicately braised beef steak, small potatoes, peas and a mixed salad.

"This looks great," I said. "My compliments to the chef!"

'Thank you," Kevin said. He disappeared quickly into the kitchen.

"Kevin studied culinary arts in Switzerland," Sir Hector. "He is quite a talented individual."

Sir Hector seemed more at ease with us after receiving the compliment for Kevin and after having done something for Rebecca. I was still wondering if he had any other reason for inviting us, besides getting the scoop on the Broadmoore project. Of course, I couldn't ask him directly. I told Sir Hector that having sailed the Bahamian waters, I was becoming more and more interested in its recent history and economics.

Sir Hector responded to this with a disjointed mini-lecture:

"Wallace Groves can really be seen as a founder of Freeport. There was not much in the way of employment before him. In the nineteen forties, he started a lumber company. We have done well in planting and harvesting. The Hawksbill Creek Agreement of nineteen fifty-four and investment by Sir Charles Hayward — there's a library named after him in Freeport — strengthened this. He invested much of his own money. Sir Charles was a major partner and was much responsible for Freeport's commercial success. Thus he earned his knighthood."

"That's interesting," I said. "Economic contributions as a basis for knighthood."

"That, you will find, Dr. Candidi, is a pattern which goes back to Sir Walter Raleigh, or farther." Sir Hector smiled at me and I smiled back. "My own contributions were more in a *political* direction. At a time when such were quite necessary. We first became independent in nineteen seventy-three, you know."

"You have a very interesting political system," Rebecca said. "I understand that your Governor-General is appointed by the Queen of England."

"Yes," Sir Hector said. "And with veto power over the actions of Parliament. It was a wise decision which has spared us the sort of chaos experienced by our brethren in Jamaica."

"Which political party do you belong to?"

"To the PLP — our liberal party. We have just returned to power after ten years of rule by the less liberal FNM."

We talked about the Bahamian political system for quite a while. Thunder rolled in the distance and, finally, rain came down.

"We wish you luck," Rebecca said, as talk of politics began to dwindle.

Sir Hector shifted in his chair so that he was facing Rebecca.

"Thank you. Economic development is a slow process. With limestone quarrying — you must surely have noticed it on the way to Freeport — we have the wherewithal to build our own houses without having to import foreign materials in bulk. And the Lucayan Harbor has become a major port. We now have a dry dock capable of handling the largest ships. These are proving to be a major source of employment and foreign revenues. As you can imagine, that is an urgent consideration for our poor country."

Rain splashed on the window.

"And you have the tourist industry," I said.

Sir Hector gave me a sideways glance. "Yes, but the tourist industry is seasonal, with ups and downs. And it does not create that many high-paying jobs. And often, as we have seen, it is the slave to the whims of big investors," he looked in the direction of West End, "who cannot sustain their improvements, or who die and leave them to less interested heirs. Yes, the tourist industry is so hostage to vicissitude and whim." He shook his head, sadly, and so did Rebecca.

Sir Hector fingered the small bell standing next to his place at the table. He frowned. "And we are also hostage to a massive illegal immigration of Haitians. Or we are at least bearing the burden of it, that is to say."

Sir Hector rang the bell, and Kevin came and collected our plates. Then Kevin brought a dessert course, consisting of coffee in delicate cups and chocolate mousse in elegant, faceted crystal.

I asked Sir Hector a leading question about foreign investment. I was really hoping he would tell us what was going to happen to West End.

"Yes, Dr. Candidi, North American and European investment in timeshare properties should raise our economic base slowly. As often as not, a partnership between the government and monied foreign interests is necessary to get large building projects underway. The more outsiders who have a *legitimate* stake in our country, the better." He smiled slyly and turned in his chair to be facing me directly. "Which brings me to your activities for Dr. Broadmoore. We are looking forward to sponge harvesting as a source of foreign exchange."

I took a couple of seconds to think over my answer. Outside, it was raining hard. The *Second Chance* was being washed clean. The uncollected fingerprints and blood spatter evidence were gone. So much for Sgt. Townsend's claim on the boat as a crime scene. And so much for Sgt. Townsend's unnamed superiors, Bahamian bureaucracy, and whoever else was giving me problems. And I wondered whether Sir Hector had anything to do with this.

I shifted into a business-consultant attitude.

"Yes, Sir Hector, it would be great if the Little Bahama Bank could be shown to have enough of the right sponges to be sustainably harvestable. It would create a large number of jobs for harvesting. And I would guess that an extraction plant would be set up here. That would create a number of high-paying technical jobs for measuring the concentrations of zagrionic acid — the active compound — in the extract, and for doing the first steps in the purification."

Sir Hector was leaning forward. I laid in a pause and raised a hand to my mouth to cover a deliberate yawn before resuming.

"Of course, I'm just talking to you about the realm of possibility. I'm not making any predictions. And I cannot make any promises for Dr. Broadmoore." I looked down at my chocolate delight and frowned.

"But you did say that you do not have bad news about the survey."

"I have been able to find a few sponges around here. But I must find a lot more of them around here and on the rest of the Little Bahama Bank. And we have not yet demonstrated that your sponges are producing zagrionic acid, the active ingredient. And, to make things more complicated, there are three variants of its chemical structure — the alpha, beta and gamma compounds."

"When will you know?" Sir Hector asked, trying hard to play down his curiosity.

"I cannot say. Actually, I have been experiencing difficulty doing my work here. You could help to relieve one of these difficulties."

"How?"

I set my gaze on Sir Hector and held it. "Did you know that just before sailing into your waters we discovered a sinking yacht with a dead man aboard?"

"Yes, it made the *Nassau Guardian*, actually."

I had a question about that, but I kept it to myself. If he had known about the incident, then why hadn't he brought it up in conversation?

"I'm surprised that it made the newspaper. No reporter interviewed us."

"The reporter probably got his information from the police after they talked with you."

"Would you happen to have the article? I could put it in my scrapbook."

"No, I am afraid not."

I waited a long time for him to volunteer further information, which he didn't. He turned his palms up and looked confused.

"Anyway, we found and salvaged the boat outside your territorial limit. But we brought it to West End because it was the nearest police authority. I have filed a salvage claim for the vessel in the U.S. District Court of the Southern District of Florida where the yacht is home ported. I can show you papers to prove this."

"Yes." Sir Hector wiped his cheek with a napkin.

"From the time I brought in the ill-fated yacht — it is named the *Second Chance* — I cooperated with the head of your local police. Sergeant Leonard Townsend is his name. And, properly, he took police custody over the yacht to protect it as a crime scene. And I, in fact, gave him bullets and casings that I found and showed him where to photograph blood spatter evidence and collect fingerprints."

"Yes," Sir Hector said, cautiously.

"My problem is this — Sergeant Townsend is continuing to assert jurisdiction over the yacht past the point where any more evidence could be collected. In fact, the rainstorm outside is washing away any remaining blood spatter and fingerprints as we speak."

"I see."

"My point is that Sergeant Townsend must relinquish police jurisdiction over the yacht immediately. Otherwise, that will constitute interference with my salvage claim which is being pursued properly under United States and International Law."

Sir Hector wiped his cheek again. I waited and said nothing more. Finally, he straightened in his chair and cleared his throat.

"Yes, I see." Sir Hector said this with a magisterial tone, like he'd just heard a good argument from a petitioning lawyer but, for the sake of decorum, couldn't grant instant approval. He frowned down at his crystal goblet of mostly eaten chocolate mousse and rearranged his tie with two hands. Then he raised his eyes to me. "But how would this involve me?"

"You could pursue the matter from the other end. Tomorrow morning I will be giving Sergeant Townsend notice of my intention to motor the *Second Chance* back to Miami at the first available opportunity. I hope that he doesn't answer, as he has before, that some unidentifiable ASP in Freeport has put a hold on the boat. A word from you could keep that from happening."

"Yes, if there were to be a problem, I could look into it."

That was too tentative. Time to push him harder. "And you don't foresee any problem with my plans, as I have told you."

He touched his forehead. "Err. No. There shouldn't be."

"Great. I will leave with the yacht in a couple of days."

Sir Hector looked at me incredulously and wordlessly. And under the table, Rebecca's toe touched my shin.

I pressed on. "That should leave me free to do my scientific survey. And that would leave me safe in the presumption that property rights in this country are protected by law and are not impeded by mid-level bureaucracy."

Sir Hector shot me a glance. I caught and held it. He looked away and fumbled with his napkin again. His face clouded over. "Jolly good," he said, with no enthusiasm.

And Rebecca's toe hit my shin, hard this time. She leaned forward towards Sir Hector. "Thank you so much, Sir Hector, for the splendid dinner and conversation. And thank you for the introduction to the clinic."

"No, it is my pleasure." His hand moved to the bell.

"We should be going," Rebecca said.

Sir Hector rang the bell, then reached into his jacket and pulled out two cards, giving one to each of us. "If there is anything I can do, please call." Then he looked toward Kevin, who had just opened the kitchen door. "Please bring out the car to take Doctors Levis and Candidi back to the marina."

We rose and started saying our goodbyes. As we moved toward the door, a portrait photograph on the wall caught Rebecca's eye.

"Is this your son?" she asked.

"Yes, my son Reginald." His left hand clasped his right forearm.

"He looks so handsome," Rebecca said. "Does he live here with you?"

"No, he has his own house . . . on Mulberry Lane . . . on this side of the island."

"Is he in government, too?"

"No, he is concerned with the business, not with the politics, of our country."

I was glancing at the picture, noting the similarities in the faces of father and son, when memory of an incident at the marina popped up. "Does he have a boat?" I asked.

"Yes."

"Yes, I think I saw him fueling at the marina. He has a motorboat, doesn't he?"

"Yes," Sir Hector said, putting his hands together at chest level.

"A fast motorboat named the *Chango*?"

"Yes." Sir Hector said, bringing his hands to rest over his stomach.

"I understand that Chango means thunder — which is what it seems to be doing outside right now, along with the rain."

"Yes. Quite." He put fingers and thumbs together to form a triangle.

We made our way to the door. Sir Hector moved ahead of us and lifted the old-fashioned latch and opened the door.

We stood together under the overhang by the open door, watching the rain until the round-mouthed Jaguar pulled up to the base of the stairs. We said our last goodbyes as Kevin came up with a golf umbrella to ferry us to the car.

On the trip home, Rebecca and I talked about how impressed we were with meeting a knight of the British Empire, with what we had learned about the Commonwealth of the Bahamas, and with the good food. Rebecca had a lot to say on that last point. She didn't give up until she got Kevin to say a word or two about having studied cooking in Switzerland. He answered crisply in a well-enunciated baritone, but he passed up all opportunities to tell us more about himself.

I asked Kevin if the picture on the reading table in the study was of Sir Hector's wife.

"Yes," Kevin said, with formality. He peered through the windshield. The rain was coming down heavily.

"The picture is not recent."

Kevin did not respond at once. "Lady Pimentel died twenty-five years ago. There was a long illness."

"I'm sorry to hear that. I suspected it might be something like that because Sir Hector did not say anything about Reginald's mother. It must have been hard for him and for his son."

"Yes, I believe it was, sir." Kevin leaned closer to the windshield. It was a simple syllogism:

He'd called me "sir." That increased the formality between us. And that put a lot of questions off limits.

"Have you been in Sir Hector's service long?"

"For twenty-two years, sir." He intoned the word this time.

"I extend my congratulations," I said.

"Thank you, sir. I do my best to carry on the traditions."

The parking lot was full of puddles. Kevin pulled out the golf umbrella and accompanied us to our boat. I climbed aboard and opened the combination lock with my small pocket flashlight. We waved goodbye to Kevin. Finally, when we were inside with the companionway slats and roof hatch back in place, Rebecca had something to say:

"I played along with you, Ben, and I think I know what you are doing. But don't you think it was a little brash telling Sir Hector that you'd turn in a bad sponge report if you don't get the *Second Chance* back?"

"No. He had to hear that."

"And you practically accused him of conspiracy to confiscate the boat."

"If he's on the level, he should be concerned that we're being treated unfairly. And if he's not on the level, I have warned him that I'm not going to be an easy cookie to crumble."

"But you talked to him like he was already connected."

"And I strongly suspect that he is. I found it suspicious that he didn't bring up the salvage, himself. And I also wonder if there really was a newspaper article."

"Okay, but you didn't give him the benefit of the doubt."

"I can't afford to give it. *We* can't afford to give it. He's the biggest honcho on this side of the island. A two hundred thousand dollar boat comes up for grabs. And the only thing that's keeping him from grabbing it up is a couple of little twits in a thirty thousand dollar sailboat."

We argued through another round. We agreed to disagree. But we both did agree that chauffeur Kevin looked a lot like conch man Edgar and that they were probably brothers. And Rebecca didn't disagree when I proposed to take a look around the marina before turning in.

Ivanhoe's car was not there. Had the rain driven him away, or had he given up covering the *Second Chance* on evenings? Anyway, he wasn't there, and that was useful information. And Rick Turner's boat was still gone. Now that was really interesting information.

13   Poison in Paradise

The next morning brought no more rain and plenty of sunshine. The day started with a call to Rebecca's cellphone from a nurse practitioner with the Grand Bahama Health Authority. She had learned from Sir Hector of Rebecca's interest and was calling to invite her to spend the day observing at the West End clinic. The nurse offered to send a station wagon to pick her up. Rebecca lost no time accepting.

"Fine," I told Rebecca. "I'm glad for you. I'll go off for a day of sponging by myself." I told her what area I'd be surveying. And I gave her a kiss goodbye and left to check out the *Second Chance*.

Constable Ivanhoe Walker was back on guard duty. Next door, Martin and Beth were up and about. She was doing a lot of errands topside, but there was no reason she shouldn't hear what I had to say to Ivanhoe. I told the Good Constable that it had poured the night before and that the yacht had been washed clean and could he please pass that on to Sgt. Townsend. Ivanhoe shrugged and suggested I do that myself.

"Okay." Standing right there, I pulled out my cellphone and got Sgt. Townsend at his police station. Our polite preliminaries lasted no longer than eight seconds. "Sergeant, there are three things that I would like to bring to your attention. First, is the fact that there was a vigorous rainstorm last night that washed any remaining fingerprints off the *Second Chance*."

"Yes," he said frostily. "And what is the second thing?"

"That the *Second Chance* is now under the jurisdiction of the government of the United States of America. I have the Federal court papers to prove it.

"Yes," and what is the third thing?"

"Last night we were dinner guests of Sir Hector Pimentel. He is a member of your parliament."

"I am aware that he is a member of Parliament."

"As a courtesy to you, I would like to inform you that I discussed the matter of the detention of the *Second Chance*. We discussed it while it was raining last night, and he is aware of the Federal jurisdiction. Sir Hector agreed that he could see no reason why the yacht should be detained much longer. I thought you would like to know that, against the probable case of inquiries from higher quarters."

"Yes. Thank you. Will that be all?"

"Yes, except to say that I would expect to move the yacht in a day or two."

"Then thank you very much." (Click)

Just as I finished the conversation, Martin and Beth started the engine of their *Rapture of the Deep* and began maneuvering the boat out of the berth. They were not the only ones leaving. On my way back to the *Diogenes*, Cliff Grimes was pulling out, too. He waved to me, saying he was going back to Florida for a few days. I returned to find the *Diogenes* locked and Rebecca gone. I loaded the Caribe inflatable with the regular stuff, plus some fishing line and my Hawaiian sling.

It wasn't bad having the Caribe to myself. Once outside the marina, I twisted the throttle all the way and found that with the lighter load the boat went right up on plane. Boy, did that outboard motor hum! What more could I ask for than high speed and low fuel consumption?

I zipped along at high speed the length of the channel below the Barracuda Shoal. And as I zipped past Marker Number 8, I noticed the *Rapture of the Deep* off to the north. It was at anchor with one man in the water and one woman on deck. My first thought was that they might have mechanical trouble, so I veered toward them. That was my first thought because they were anchored over uninteresting ground. They were directly up-wind, and while approaching I noticed a familiar smell — resin for fiberglass repairs. As I neared, Beth didn't return my wave like she was happy to see me. That was when a second thought crossed my mind. I waved once more, then veered back to my original course and left them alone. From 300 yards, it was clear to see that Martin was involved in a serious underwater project at the *Rapture*'s bow. And the less I seemed to know about it the better.

I headed straight east at planing speed. The Grand Bahama Island fell away quickly to the southeast. The curvature of its north shore makes a large bay on the western side of the Island. When I reached half way to Cormorant Point, I picked up on the survey where we'd left off two days before. I didn't shoot any fish with the Hawaiian sling, but I did count a lot of sponges and make a lot of chemical extractions. Working efficiently at each site and running fast to the next one, I was able to finish the large area of the bay.

While working that area, I did see the Navy P-3 Orion. It was flying far off to the east, but its form was recognizable: a rounded nose, four long turboprop engines mounted on the low wing, propellers spinning in the sunlight, and an elongated tail with the long, pole-like radar antenna coming out the back. It was flying back and forth, north and south, at a position that must have been in line with Mangrove Cay. It was just like I'd told Rebecca. They were flying electronic picket duty over the western side of the Little Bahama Bank. I guessed that the tail had a fancy phase-array radar that could pick up every boat from here to Palm Beach. Anything as big as a Boston Whaler would carry enough metal to give a good reflection. That would be drug interdiction, Federal style: informants on the shore to track the comings and goings, and an electronic picket line to track the boats' movements across the Gulf Stream.

I was sitting on the floor of the Caribe, using the aluminum bench as a desk to make some notes when my cellphone rang. I retrieved it from the pocket under the bench and pulled the phone from its Ziploc sandwich bag to answer it.

"Ben Candidi."

"Ben. So them cellphones do work in the Bahamas." It was Jimmy.

"Yes, even several miles out, sitting in a rubber boat."

"Oh, some people got all the fun. I guess that's why I didn't hear from you. I'm callin' to tell you someone picked up the letter I sent that S.C. Corporation two days ago. Morning after I sent it, I saw it in the box. And the next morning I swung by and it was gone."

"Good. Your fiber optic gizmo let you see it clear enough to be sure it was your letter."

"Sure, I'm sure," he said, sounding insulted. "I marked it on the edges with yellow Magic Marker stripes to make dang sure I'd be able to see it."

"Okay, okay. And nobody called you like you requested in the letter."

"That's right. And it ain't because they're getting too much mail to answer, 'cause mine was the only letter in the box that day and the next day all that was there was one of them 'attempted delivery' slips they use for return receipt mail."

"That would be the notice my lawyer sent to notify them that he has filed a salvage claim."

"They picked up that slip some time between yesterday and today. Of course, I can't tell whether they went in and signed for the letter. Seems like you're the only one they're getting mail from. Now, if you really want to find out who they are, I could mail another letter and stake out the mailbox."

"No thanks. Your work has told me enough. The Corporation has someone taking care of its business, and they are shy about talking to me."

"Sounds like good thinkin' to me. Anything else I can do for you?"

"Not right now, thanks."

After we hung up, I called up my lawyer and thanked him for the Federal filing. He told me that he had not received a delivery verification on the return receipt letter. After finishing that call, I pulled a sheet of paper from under the aluminum bench and wrote down what I knew about the S.C. Corporation:

One: They know that I have the *Second Chance* and that I want to do business with them.

Two: But they don't want to do business with me.

Three: They don't want to talk to anybody, not even Jimmy posing as a private citizen.

Then I wrote down my situation with the Sgt. Townsend:

A: He refused to give me any information on "Steve."

B: He is insistently holding onto the *Second Chance* for a false reason.

C: He has stopped guarding the *Second Chance* at night.

Then I wrote down a description of my overall situation:

YOU ARE A SITTING DUCK.

I would have to keep a close eye on the *Second Chance*. And I would tell Rebecca that we would have to watch our backs.

Time to move on. I squeezed the rubber bulb and pulled the cord on the outboard. It wouldn't start. I took off its housing to sniff the carburetor and check the spark plug connections. The plugs were okay, but I noticed a line of salt buildup on the cylinder head. I scratched if off and found a hairline crack. This was bad news: a cooling water leak. The cylinder head's days were numbered. I'd have to keep a close eye on it or I might find myself broken down miles from shore.

I put the housing back on and kept pulling the rope and playing with the choke until the motor came to life. I headed back toward the marina, putting on enough revs to keep the boat up on plane but not enough to tax the engine.

I returned to the marina a couple of hours before sunset. Rebecca was not there. Cliff Grimes' *Engineuity* wasn't there either. By now he must be safely tied up to a dock in Florida, taking apart his heat exchanger and reaping the benefit of yesterday's ingenuity. The *Rapture of the Deep* was gone. That didn't surprise me in the least. I hoped that their sled made good time gliding on the cocaine-filled fiberglass runners that they had bolted on.

I looked around for Constable Walker and couldn't find him. Had they now given up guarding the *Second Chance* during the day? I boarded the yacht and took a look around. Inside, everything looked fine but outside it was not: Sgt. Townsend had taped on a note. It said that he was retaining authority over the yacht and that I was not to move it until receiving written permission from him. Okay, if they could play games with me, then I could play games with them. I locked the door, then whisked the note off with the back of my hand. Unfortunately, it fell into the cockpit and not into the water. I placed the note on the rail where it would have a 50-percent chance of blowing overboard.

As an afterthought I looked around, wondering if anyone had seen me. Angie was sitting on her flybridge. I waved to her and she didn't wave back.

As a more important afterthought, I reopened the *Second Chance*, crawled into its engine compartment, disconnected the throttles and hid the link pins.

After locking up the yacht, I hiked over to the Waverunner rental shack, hoping they might be able to get me a new cylinder head. I knew they were open because a couple of girls were running Waverunners just off shore, bouncing around in the light waves and shooting mouse tails of cooling water a dozen feet in the air.

The shack itself seemed deserted, but 100 yards down the beach a girl and a couple of guys were hanging out around a picnic cooler. The beach crowd gave the Waverunner girls the high sign every time they did something mildly spectacular. Farther down the beach, the fashion crew was making use of the yellow rays of the low sun to bring out attractive features of human skin and colorful fabric. But at the Waverunner shack, nobody seemed to be around.

Viewed up close, the building looked like a cross between a house trailer and a utility shed. Its sides and roof were made of white-coated, corrugated sheet metal, and it was built on a wooden platform that rested on skids. Maybe they winched it farther inland before a big storm. In front of the building were a couple of Waverunners, sitting on metal trailers with oversized, extra-wide tires.

Since nobody came out to greet me, I spent a minute studying the features of the two machines: approximately eight feet long, scooter nose, small windscreen, motorcycle-type hand grips, and engine completely covered by the cowling which went down the center and fused with the elongated Yamaha-style seat. Yes, there might be some sport in jumping these things over waves. Straddling the thing like a motorcycle with your feet in the trough on either side, you'd half sit and half stand. I'd heard that those things would go 55 miles an hour in smooth water. Of course, in six-inch waves you'd have to slow it down some. In three-foot waves it would be a real art to keep the machine up on plane, jumping from one wave to another without going over nose first.

Remembering the conversation with Cal three nights ago, I took a look at the backside. I inspected the tube where the propulsion water came out. It was linked to the hand grips to provide steering. And I peered up the induction slit in the center of the hull and looked for the enclosed propeller. And I read the instruction plate under the steering grips. It said that the craft was not designed to carry more than 400 pounds. How far, I wondered, would it go on a tank of gas?

I yelled hello and went inside the building. A sign on the wall said that Waverunner rental cost $50 per hour. Renting a catamaran cost about as much, and the Windsurfers were less expensive still. They did business from a counter, but the counter gate was up. A door behind it led to a back room. I yelled a second hello and stuck my head in. Nobody answered. The room was set up like a mechanic's workshop, and it housed three more Waverunners that looked like hotrod versions of the yellow ones outside. They were clad in a coat of black rubber, and they were fitted with stirrup bands in the trough for a secure foothold. This was obviously a competition version of the Waverunner, built for special jumping and acrobatics. And the rubber would soften the blow when you wiped out.

"Can I help you?" demanded a voice from behind. It was the muscular, black-haired guy with a crew cut that Rebecca and I had seen on the first day of the sponge survey. He was wearing jeans and a T-shirt with the arms cut short and ragged, all the better to see the U.S. Navy emblem tattooed on his left shoulder. From his age — mid-thirties — and from his military bearing, I guessed that he had spent some time in the Navy and had risen in rank to senior enlisted. He had a hard stare.

"Yes, thank you," I said, standing my ground. "I need a mechanic to replace a cylinder head on my outboard motor that's developed a slow —"

"We don't work on outboards, even if we know what's wrong with them."

"Well, that takes care of that, I guess. Thank you."

He took his time stepping to the side as I moved to the door. I held my next question until I was in customer territory — the outer room.

"I was looking at your Waverunners outside and thinking. You see, I'm getting paid by a guy to do a marine survey of the Bank, north of the island and way out east of here."

"Okay."

I threw a glance at the $50-an-hour sign. "I was wondering if you could rent me a Waverunner at a weekly rate."

"We don't do weekly rentals. It's fifty dollars an hour, or three hundred dollars a day — ten in the morning to four in the afternoon." He said it like he had a line of customers waiting.

"Yes, but I was thinking that if I rented it for a whole week, that would save you having to launch it and take it back in at night. And with a week's worth of business in one transaction you could afford to —"

"Have to be back way before sundown. Insurance regulations. And we don't give discounts."

I wondered about this guy. A brusque style might be appropriate in the U.S. Navy, but it certainly wasn't in retail business. I mean, he would have been intimidating enough, even if he delivered the information gently, with a smile. He had a weight lifter's body, a thick neck and an oversized head.

I stepped backward until I was outside. "Okay. Thanks for the information . . ." I smiled and paused like I wanted to say his name. "My name's Ben. Ben Candidi. I'm at the marina."

"Harold Pearce." He reached into his shirt pocket and handed me a card.

The card said "Fun In The Sun Rentals." It gave the shack's location and phone number, and it listed all his aquatic toys. I thanked him, stuffed the card in my pocket, and walked away.

"Sorry," he called after me, softening just a bit. "The insurance says we've got to have the Waverunners back and locked up by sundown. And we take regulations seriously."

I acknowledged his recitation with a shrug, suppressing a comment on his expertise on insurance regulations versus customer relations.

I hadn't walked more than a couple of hundred yards back along the beach when I saw Angie Sumter coming my way. She didn't respond to my wave from far off. She just kept coming. When we came within speaking distance, it was clear that she wasn't happy to see me.

"Hey, Angie, I thought you were leaving today. What's the matter?"

Her eyes were full of anger and resentment. "Don't pretend you don't know."

"No, I don't. Was there something wrong with the bottle of wine?"

"Very funny!" She spat the words at me.

"Look, I am not in the mood to play games. You either tell me or you don't. Now, what is it?"

"You know already, but I'll tell you anyway." She looked away.

"Tell me about what?"

She looked back and her eyes flashed. "About what happened to Glenn and Stephanie."

"That couple in the little sailboat?"

"Yes." She took a step closer.

"No, I don't know. What happened?"

The rims of her eyes were red and so were the whites. "They were busted."

"Busted like busted on a coral reef, or busted like by the police?"

"Don't try playing dumb with me, Ben Candidi! They were *busted*." Her hand was up at face level, shaking.

I stared back at her, taking care not to blink. "I'm sorry to hear that."

"They are *nice people*. Real nice people. They were locked up in jail. Both of them."

"Here in the Bahamas?"

She took a deep breath. "Not *here* . . . in Miami." It seemed to disconcert her when I let my eyes ask the questions. "Stephanie just got out on bail. She called me up . . . on my cellphone."

"I'm sorry to hear that, but I really don't know them. And I don't know anything about it."

She stared at me like her willpower could force a confession out of me. "No, you don't know anything, do you?"

"No, I don't. All I know is that they were horribly uncool. They smoked pot on their boat every night. That's pretty uncool if they were hauling it."

"And you didn't have anything to do with anyone finding out about it, either, did you?"

"Nothing." I held her gaze until she looked away.

But when she did look back at me, she took another step forward. "And how do you expect me to believe that? You come in here carrying on like you're 'Mister CSI-Miami' on TV, telling the police how to do their investigation and making all your phone calls and then patrolling the flats pretending you're doing something scientific with sponges, and you expect me to believe that you didn't turn Stephanie and Glenn in?"

She said it so fast — hardly pausing for breath — that I had to laugh. "Listen, Angie, I don't —"

I grabbed her hand as it came across to slap my face. I grabbed the other one when she tried again. I didn't let go. I spoke to her slowly and seriously.

"Angie, I swear. I'm a not DEA officer. I'm not a DEA informant. I'm not working for the Coast Guard, Customs or any other agency. I *am* surveying for sponges along the Bank. That work is legitimate. If you don't believe me, look up the Broadmoore Capital Company's website. I'm working for its president, Dr. Brian Broadmoore."

"Sure you are!" Her defiance was solid but her fury was subsiding.

"And if you don't believe Dr. Broadmoore, you can verify that with Sir Hector Pimentel who invited us to dinner last night."

Angie's arms relaxed. She looked down and sighed.

I threw her arms away, pushing her back. I whipped out my cellphone. "You don't believe me? Then let's call them up and ask them." I shouted the words. "We came here on a sailboat for a vacation. We didn't come looking for any sinking yachts or murder victims. But since we went to the trouble to salvage the *Second Chance*, we deserve to be paid for it. And when that police sergeant says he's done with the boat, we're outa here. *Basta!* And the *Diogenes* and the sponge survey, they're going way east of here."

Angie listened, watching me through teary eyes and nodding like she wanted to believe me.

"Look, Angie, I don't give a damn who's doing it with who in front of whom or who's partying with nose candy. I don't give a damn who's hauling the stuff into Florida. It's none of my business."

She drew herself up. "Well, you'd just better keep your mouth shut, because you can make a lot of trouble for people with loose talk."

"Hey, girl, I *do* keep my mouth shut. I didn't grow up in Beaufort where they teach girls good manners and not to gossip because it isn't polite. I grew up in Newark where you learn to keep your mouth shut or the guys on the street will smash your face."

"Well, you'd better keep your mouth shut or that's what's going to happen. And tell that to your New York doctor girlfriend, too."

"Fiancée," I corrected. "She does what I say." It was a necessary lie.

"Well, she'd better. And you two just watch it, or a lot of innocent people are going to get hurt. It shouldn't have happened. It isn't supposed to happen. I told him and he — she's okay. Stephanie deserves a good life. She doesn't deserve to go to prison."

Angie's voice cracked, and she slumped forward and threw her arms around my shoulders and buried her face in my chest. I hugged her for a second, then partially disengaged, holding her by the shoulders at arm's length. She had told me too much already, and I didn't want to learn any more. Not from her. I didn't want her to tell me who was giving them protection, even if she told it as a secret. It was better — safer — for me to guess.

"Look, Angie, you're a very attractive lady, but Rebecca's a jealous girl and I'm sure that Cal would be jealous, too. Now, I want you to wipe away those tears and go straight back to your boat, without talking to anybody. I'm going to do the same. But you're getting a ten-minute head start. And we're going to pretend this conversation didn't take place, except that you told me that Glenn and Stephanie got busted. Got it?"

"All right." She presented her cheek for a kiss.

I kissed her on the cheek, then let go of her shoulders. "And when you and Cal get back from Boca Raton, we can have drinks together on the *Diogenes*."

She stiffened. "How'd you know that we're leaving for Boca?"

"Because you both *told me*, the other night, damn it." I turned her on her arm and swatted her rear, almost hard enough to hurt. "Now get going."

She did, but not before searching my face. Personal relations, not the rules of logic, were the major forces in this woman's universe. According to her logic, nothing bad would come from my side of the universe after she had charmed me. She would expect me to protect her, just like her husband.

I thought about this while standing there on the shore, waiting for Angie to reach the marina. And I thought about this when I walked back. As I passed the marina office, I saw Angie on the dock talking to Wade Daniels, a few steps from his boat. They were conversing at close quarters, and Angie wasn't putting on airs like a Southern belle this time.

I returned to the *Diogenes* to find Rebecca home and almost finished with cooking dinner. "How was your day?" I asked her.

"Let's forget about mine right now, and you tell me about yours. You look worried, Ben."

First I told Rebecca that the S.C. Corporation was ignoring messages from my lawyer and from Jimmy. Next I told her about the hairline crack in the outboard's cylinder head and my encounter with Harold Pearce at his Waverunner emporium. Finally, I told her about Angie's accusations, recounting every detail of that soap opera scene except for the embrace.

Rebecca was incredulous. "How could she think that you would turn in Glenn and Stephanie?"

"Someone must have suggested it to her. She doesn't do abstract thinking on her own. Someone is worried that we are spies. And maybe someone sent her to find out."

"But you convinced her that we aren't spies."

"Yes, but she may be still be worried that we won't keep our mouths shut."

Rebecca frowned. "A big heap of danger brewed up by that Newark Yankee and his loudmouthed Jewish doctor girlfriend from New York."

"She didn't say 'Jewish' and she didn't call you a loudmouth."

"Okay, we just survived another challenge from — what did you call it? — SAWECUSS."

"Yes, the Social Auxiliary of the West End Cocaine Smuggling Society."

"And who do you think is in it?"

"Most of the people at the fish fry, plus many others that we don't know."

"Do you think that Angie and Cal are smuggling cocaine?"

"Most definitely. I can even give you a good guess as to how they're doing it. When we were on their boat, I noticed a pulley mounted on the stern, just below the waterline. On the inside of the transom there was a matching cleat. My guess is that they tow their cocaine in a heavily weighted, watertight container. They probably give it about twenty-five yards of line so that it won't be visible through their prop churn, even from the air."

"And when the Coast Guard stops them?"

"Baby Doll unties the line from the cleat and the dangerous evidence goes slithering down one thousand feet where nobody can get it."

"What makes you so sure of your theory?"

"Can you give me some other reason for having that pulley?"

"Okay, Ben. But they're not big-time smugglers."

'No, they just sell and barter in a small circle of friends. It's a boost to their lifestyle . . . ten thousand dollars brings fifty thousand dollars every time they do a run. Four runs a year, and they've covered all their boat expenses plus the mortgage on their starter castle inside their 'gatehouse community.' This little business is propelling them from a basic upper-middle-class lifestyle into the air-headed heights of the *nouveau riche* – the *faux* upper class."

Rebecca smiled at my *faux* eloquence. "And I guess that Martin and Beth are doing it, too."

I told her about discovering the four bolts sticking out from the bottom of their hull when I was working with the pallets. And I told her about smelling the batch of fiberglass resin they'd cooked up at the edge of the channel.

"Wait! Don't tell me," Rebecca said, with a sly smile. "You think they have put their cocaine into some kind of hollow runner that they seal with fiberglass resin and bolt onto their hull."

"You've got it. They didn't return to their berth. They made their run today."

"What about Rick Turner?"

"He's the first one that I noticed was gone. I don't think he uses any tricks. Too impulsive. He just gets the stuff and runs with it."

"What about Cliff Grimes?"

"You mean 'Mr. Enginuity' who was always talking about working on his engine, and who was working yesterday with those big wrenches on his big water jacket and heat exchanger. Mr. Enginuity also made his run to Florida today."

"I remember him talking about problems with his engine overheating," Rebecca said.

"Yeah, his heat exchanger's clogged up with red herrings. Methinks he doth protest too much."

Rebecca laughed. Then she thought for a minute. "But Ray and Martha aren't smuggling."

"No, I think the Society keeps them around for window dressing. Ray and Martha are taking a 'see no evil, hear no evil' approach to the matter."

"What about poor Glenn and Stephanie?"

"That's what I find interesting. They weren't connected to the Society when they first came. Maybe Angie had plans to put them under the Society's protection. I don't think that they were smuggling coke. I think they were smuggling grass, and they made their score back on Abaco Island."

"And Angie thinks that they have a certain *entitlement* for smuggling."

"Yes. I think that the Society is organized to pay for protection."

"Paying the Bahamian police?"

"Yes, and people in the Coast Guard or Customs Service who are responsible for interdiction."

Rebecca frowned. "Who do you think is the head of SAWECUSS?"

"I'm wondering if it isn't Wade Daniels."

I looked at the stove top.

"Yes, dinner is ready," Rebecca said.

I helped set dinner on the table and we sat down to eat. "How was *your* day?" I asked.

"Oh, it was fine. They do a lot of good in that yellow building."

"Did you have any interesting patients?"

"Yes, I did. We had some skin infections and one gynecological problem. But I came two days late to see a really interesting case. Ciguatera! The nurse told me all about it. It happens when they eat old barracuda or large grouper — big reef fish. The fish concentrate a toxin from algae, you know." Rebecca got into a groove, describing it like she was making a presentation on rounds. "The patient was awfully sick. They evaluated him at the clinic and evacuated him to the Rand Hospital that night. It was a full-blown case, with full neurological symptoms — cold felt like hot and hot felt like cold. A lot of internal pain, shifting to different parts of the body. And it was the third day of the poisoning. The symptoms got worse and worse. And do you want to guess who it was?"

I put down my fork. "Who?"

"Bill! You know, one-half of the Bill and Chuck couple."

"Damn," I exclaimed. "Now let me get this right. Bill was in the clinic with symptoms two days ago."

"Yes."

"And he had had the symptoms for three days before coming in."

"Yes."

"That means he ate the bad fish on the day of Wade Daniels' fish fry!"

"Yes, but it's not probable that he got it there because nobody . . . else at the party got fish poisoning." Rebecca began the statement fluently but ended it indecisively. "I mean, we were all eating the same . . ."

"Wade handed me a plate with two fillets. I passed it on to Bill."

Rebecca pushed her plate away. "Yes, of course! Wade could have kept a piece of barracuda with the other fish and singled it out for you. He was trying to poison you. But, why?"

I was as shocked as Rebecca, but I had an answer. "Because he's the chairman of SAWECUSS."

We stared at each other for a long time, thinking the same thoughts — apparently. I'm not sure who said it first:

"We have to get out of here. We are sitting ducks."

We discussed how to do it. What I would have liked best would have been to sail the *Diogenes* to Abaco Island, far away from here. But that would have meant abandoning the *Second Chance* and my $100,000 claim.

"Rebecca, I've got to take the *Second Chance* to Miami. Got to leave at the crack of dawn."

"What about Sgt. Townsend's orders?"

"I will defy them. His investigation is a sham. The S.C. Corporation might even be paying him to hold me back until they can make off with the yacht. Constable Ivanhoe doesn't seem to be guarding it anymore."

"What about Sir Hector? You haven't given him a enough time to help you."

"I don't think that he has been completely honest with us. And I'm not sure he isn't trying to get the yacht for himself. Right now the use of his name is more valuable to me than the man himself. No, I've got to get the *Second Chance* out of here before someone else does. I'd better do it tomorrow before Constable Ivanhoe shows up. Don't worry, I can do it single-handed."

"Is that legal?"

"Depends on who's doing the interpreting. Once I get the boat past the Twelve Mile Limit, it's under International Law and my Federal papers are stronger than anything that Sergeant Townsend has produced. Here's my plan. I leave just before dawn — early enough that I won't have to deal with Constable Walker but not so early that it looks like I'm doing anything underhanded. Around ten o'clock, you give my immigration and 'permission to cruise' cards to the customs people. I'll be well past the Twelve Mile Limit by then. If anyone cross-examines you, tell them I had to leave early because I couldn't trust the engines."

"What will you do in Miami?"

"I'll clear U.S. Customs on the Miami River and then take it all the way up the River to the Bojean boatyard by the airport. Scott Smith is a good guy. I'll have him haul it and put it in storage. When that's done, I fly back to Freeport and hop a van back here."

"What if they decide to take it out on me, Ben?"

"Sergeant Townsend or the Customs officials?"

"Either of them."

"Just act innocent. Tell them that we split up. We aren't married, so they don't have any way to pressure you so they can control me. Actually, you came in here as the captain of the *Diogenes*. That's your status with them. In fact, they might not even be sure who the boat belongs to. But I'll give you a power of attorney anyway. If they really start making a stink, just cast off the lines on the *Diogenes* and motor to Palm Beach."

"What about the marina bill?"

"Good for one more day. That works out just right."

We talked about the escape for the better part of an hour. I drank two beers to make me sleepy, set the alarm on my watch, and turned in early.

Running with the Dawn, Dancing at Dusk   14

Working as much by feel as by sight, I put back the link pin and inserted the cotter pin to hold it in place. I flanged the cotter pin, using a small pair of pliers and repeated the process for the second throttle cable. I switched off the flashlight and climbed out of the black darkness into the gray darkness. It was half an hour before sunrise and the *Second Chance* was ready to go.

I had stowed everything needed for this run: an offshore life jacket, a flare gun, a hand-held VHF marine radio, a hand-held GPS unit, a pair of binoculars, a yellow quarantine flag, and a small cooler with sandwiches and beer. My cellphone was in my pocket, and my passport and Federal court papers were aboard.

I checked once more to be sure nobody was up and about. I pulled down all the sagging crime scene tape and rolled it up in the corner of the cockpit. Sgt. Townsend's pasted-on notice had already succumbed to the forces of nature.

Now was the time. I removed and stowed the bow lines. Slowly the cabin cruiser's bow drifted to the piling on the south side facing the marina office. I took off the portside stern line and threw it onto the floor of the cockpit. Then I scrambled to the flybridge and started the two big motors. Thank God, they sounded healthy. I rushed down to the cockpit and took off the dock line at the stern. The *Second Chance* was free.

Ever so cautiously, I threw the idling motors into reverse. Playing the throttle levers in and out, I inched the behemoth backward until its nose was clear and my transom was under the anchor jutting from Wade Daniels' bow. Oh, so cautiously, I counter-rotated the twin props to turn the *Second Chance* on its axis. The bow made it okay, but Wade's piling made a crackling sound as my stern drifted into it. I corrected that quickly with some carefully balanced forward thrust and headed the yacht up the lane at crawl speed.

The light was really too weak to judge. Luckily, nobody seemed to be on deck. At the end of the lane by Ray Vangelden's trawler, I threw the wheel hard to starboard for the necessary right turn. No, a lumbering powerboat doesn't respond to rudder like a sailboat: I had to use some reverse on the starboard prop to keep the bow from going up on the coral wall. With patience, I brought it around so that the yacht was facing the *Diogenes* where Rebecca stood, waving goodbye. I crawled forward another 20 yards and executed a left turn at the fuel dock.

I was well centered in the tree-lined exit channel and was just passing the fuel dock at a good rate when he came running up — Ivanhoe.

"Stop," he shouted. "Stop right now, man. You are not to move the boat."

I inched the throttles forward and turned my body to wave to Ivanhoe, acting like I couldn't hear him over the engines.

He had to jog to keep up with me. He was a lot more athletic than I had imagined. "I tell you now — stop! The boat is not to be moved."

I waved again, then cupped my ear like I couldn't hear him. He pulled out his gun. I turned my face forward, acting like I didn't see him. I pretended to be concentrating on the controls and the clearance in the narrow channel. My wake was giving its banks one hell of a wash. Ivanhoe fell back out of the field of my peripheral vision. It took lots of concentration to negotiate that sharp left where the channel turned to the west. I narrowly missed running aground on the north side. I straightened out and upped the revs to go as fast as I dared. To the left, the commercial harbor was zipping by and Ivanhoe was not on the seawall. Ahead, the channel entrance marker grew before my eyes. Surface patterns on my right told me I was dealing with a strong incoming tide. The light improved as I got away from the trees.

At about 25 yards from the mouth of the channel, I pulled out my GPS and laid in a waypoint. Twelve miles to freedom. Then I looked back and said, "Damn!"

A skiff was coming around the corner on plane. It straightened out and headed straight at me. Ivanhoe was hunched over the wheel looking like he meant business.

My hand went for the throttle levers. And almost as quickly I took the hand away. Speeding up would just make me look guilty. I was doing six knots already, and that was taking me away fast enough for around here. I could keep going for an hour, arguing with him, and be six miles away from this place. And when we got out in the big waves I could outrun him, or maybe he'd turn chicken and go home.

Just as I passed the channel entrance marker, Ivanhoe pulled up along side me and powered down. It was the green skiff that was tied up by the fuel dock, the one with the funny pulpit that served as a steering station. After the boat came off plane, Ivanhoe stood up, holding on by the steering wheel. He reached into the pulpit, pulled out a gun, and waved it at me.

I steered jerkily so that he wouldn't get any ideas about pulling up aside and jumping aboard.

"Stop right now, or I shoot," he yelled.

I cupped my hands and hollered, "I'm taking this yacht to Miami under Federal court mandate."

That terminology ought to have stopped him.

But it didn't. He pointed the gun in my direction and fired. It was a short pistol because the blast was noisy. He must have aimed high because I didn't hear the bullet hit the yacht or whiz past me. It was time for Plan B.

I gave him a wait-a-minute sign and turned on the VHF marine radio, flipping the switch that converted it into a PA system. I grabbed the mike and squeezed down.

"Why the hell did you do that?" my voice boomed.

"Police order," he yelled. "You turn around and go back."

It seemed that he could speak intelligible English if he had to. We were 50 yards out, now, and his little boat was pitching in the growing waves. He was having trouble standing, and he was waving his pistol around wildly.

I inched up the throttles and squeezed down on the mike again. "I am moving this boat, pursuant to an official salvage action which has been filed in Federal Court — a court of the Government of the United States. I have papers aboard to prove it."

He answered with another shot. This one was closer. I heard it whiz by.

That was good for another 200 yards. The sun was rising from behind the marina. Time for Plan C.

"Okay, okay," I boomed down on him. I set the autopilot for the course I was heading — due west. And I surprised him abandoning the wheel and climbing down to the cockpit.

Plan C: Hell, I was a reasonable guy. Sure, I'd come down and talk with him. Hell, we could have a big pow-wow for the next two hours. And if he fired another shot, maybe I would drop to the floor because he scared me. And if he used his gun after that, maybe I'd crawl to the protected steering station in the main salon and push those throttle levers all the way. ("I'm sorry, officer, but when he started shooting at me, I took cover. And I didn't put my head back up until I saw the high rises of West Palm Beach.")

From the cockpit I yelled over to Ivanhoe: "You aren't allowed to use deadly force to deal with a technicality."

I stopped talking when I saw our Caribe inflatable planing towards us. Rebecca was driving it like a hydroplane racer. Ivanhoe was standing there, yelling unintelligible things at me and waving his gun. He aimed in my direction and shot again.

"Put that gun down and we'll call your sergeant," I yelled to him.

Luckily, he did put the gun down. He couldn't see it, but Rebecca was on a mission. She made a shallow turn to the south, then reversed it to come at him broadside. I kept talking to keep Ivanhoe distracted. Rebecca didn't let up until the last minute. She came off plane a few yards from him, generating a large bow wave which rocked Ivanhoe's skiff. She stopped her motor an instant before she rammed his port side. She used her forward momentum to spring into Ivanhoe's boat and knock him overboard.

"Oh, excuse me," she yelled down to him while he splashed in the water. She was acting out a monologue. "Watch out for the propeller. I'll have to stop the engine. What, you can't swim? Then grab this." She threw the metal gas tank overboard. "Use it as a float. No, watch out. The gas cap's off. Stay away from it and don't get gas in your lungs."

Rebecca signaled me to get the hell out of there. Then she dangled the fuel hose over Ivanhoe.

And as I scrambled up to the flybridge I heard her saying, "Here, grab this. Oh, so you *can* swim." I upped the throttles, then looked down from the steering station. Rebecca dove in the water and Australian-crawled toward the inflatable. Being lighter than the skiff, it had drifted a good 20 yards away. Ivanhoe was dragging himself back into the skiff. With the incoming tide, I wouldn't have to worry about either of them being swept out to sea.

I pushed the throttle levers all the way to get full revs.

The *Second Chance* crawled over its bow wave and went up on plane. I squeezed down on the mike. "Don't worry, Ivanhoe, Rebecca will take care of you. And I'm calling your boss on my cellphone. We'll get things worked out."

Fifty, 100 and then 150 yards they dropped away from me as the *Second Chance* plowed ahead at full speed. And as soon as Rebecca pulled herself onto the inflatable, I knew things would be okay. She'd done a great job. And if she stuck with her story, she should be able to brass it out with the Sgt. Townsend.

It felt good to have the *Second Chance* throbbing under my feet and plowing through the two-foot waves at 20 knots. I'd pushed the throttles all the way and it wouldn't go faster. Well, that was fast enough to get me out of the Bahamas in 36 minutes.

Four minutes and about one and one-half miles later, I felt secure enough to pick up the binoculars to see what Rebecca and Ivanhoe were doing. With the distance and looking into the rising sun, it was hard to see. The two boats looked close together, but they would anyway, despite the magnification. When I looked again, after having traveled another half mile, it seemed like the boats were on top of each other. And the longer I watched, the less I liked what I saw. The bow of the skiff was pointed at me. It was up on plane, and growing larger in relation to the inflatable. Damn! Somehow Ivanhoe had gotten his fuel system back together. I turned on the GPS and took a reading. Only two miles out — 10 to go to the 12-mile limit.

Holding my breath, I followed the scene in my binoculars. Ivanhoe was gaining on me. He must have been doing 30 knots. But he hadn't come to the rough water yet, and maybe that would slow down his planing.

Then I noticed that the inflatable's bow was pointed at me, too.

Rebecca was pursuing my pursuer. Damn. She should have stayed there. Twelve miles is too far to go out with an inflatable powered by a defective outboard motor. A few minutes later, Ivanhoe was bouncing heavily in the rough water. But he wasn't letting up.

Plan D: Lock myself in the main salon. Drive the boat erratically when he approaches so he wouldn't try to board. Use the loudspeaker to tell him that I wouldn't stop to rescue him if he capsizes. Use it to tell Rebecca to turn around and go back. Keep on going even if he fires shots into the hull. He'd used three shots already and probably didn't have more than eight left.

My cellphone rang. Of course! Why hadn't I thought of using it to call Rebecca? I pulled the cellphone from my pocket and said, "Rebecca, you did good. But fall back now. I can brass it out with this guy myself."

"I advise you not to *brass it out* with us, Dr. Candidi." The voice was baritone and it belonged to Sgt. Townsend. "I have given Constable Walker orders to shoot holes in your hull at waterline as soon as he overtakes you. And he will."

I thought of hanging up, but I couldn't.

"He has enough rounds to incapacitate your boat. And we can have the U.S. Coast Guard on top of you in ten minutes."

"It would be better to put the boat in their custody than in yours. I trust you as far as I can throw you."

"If the Coast Guard gets the boat, they will send it back to us."

"Based on your lies."

"I resent that. I have never lied to you."

"You lied that you still need the boat for CSI investigation. That's a damn lie."

"No, that was under orders from my superiors."

"From superiors who cannot be reached, who cannot be named, and who will not put their orders in writing. What do you call that? I call it lying by proxy."

"And I call it an unfortunate situation, mate."

"So you have directed your subordinate to sink me on the high seas to enforce unwritten edicts by officials who cannot be named."

"That is my unfortunate situation, mate. You have put me in a jam."

"Do you have three-way calling on your phone?"

"Yes," he said, after some hesitation.

"Then please call the Coast Guard, and we will discuss it together. I will tell them that the boat is subject to my salvage claim filed in a Federal court."

Ivanhoe was getting a lot closer.

Sgt. Townsend took his time answering. "I cannot make that three-way call, mate. It will have to be two-way."

"If you call them without stating my case to them, you will be guilty lying to a Federal agency — lying by omission. And if Ivanhoe starts shooting at my boat, I won't be responsible if he gets capsized and sunk. He is armed and dangerous."

"That would be very serious, mate."

"You leave me no other choice."

"Then you would leave me no other choice but to arrest Dr. Rebecca Levis for obstruction of justice."

We were both silent for a long time. Ivanhoe was riding the skiff like a cowboy and was gaining on me. It wouldn't take more than three minutes.

Sgt. Townsend was the next to speak. "Doctor Candidi, if you return the boat and refrain from taking it for the next seven days, you have my personal promise to not interfere with your effort to take it after that."

"Does that promise go for the Royal Bahamas Police Force?"

"It goes for the West End station and everyone under my command. Furthermore, I will place the yacht under guard to ensure that nobody else takes it. *Nobody else*."

"Will you put that in writing?"

"No mate, I cannot put it in writing. You have put me in enough of a jam already."

"But I have your word."

"You have my word. But we have to decide this quickly, mate. Constable Walker says he has only three hundred yards to go."

I looked back and could see Ivanhoe's face, partially obscured by what had to be a hand-held radio. "And you will hold Rebecca and me harmless for everything that occurred today?"

"Yes, as you will hold Constable Walker harmless for his actions."

"And what do I tell all the busybodies and drug smugglers at the marina?"

"You will tell them the same thing that I will tell my superiors — that you took the boat out to test the engines and the Constable overreacted."

"You have a deal." I turned the wheel to execute a 180-degree turn.

RAYS OF THE HIGH SUN illuminated the engine compartment. I straightened the cotter pins and pulled them out. I removed the link pins to the throttles and hid them in a corner. I returned topside to rehang the yellow crime scene tape. Everything else was put in its place. Ivanhoe had returned the red neoprene fuel container that he had taken from Rebecca. He had been able to find the skiff's metal fuel container grounded on the edge of the channel. And the green skiff was tied up at its spot by the fuel dock. It turned out to be the marina's work boat.

We had all returned separately. I had spoken to Rebecca on her cellphone but had not yet had a chance to give her the hugs and kisses she deserved.

"I'm sorry, Ben," she had said on the cellphone, "but he was close enough to shoot me when he started threatening."

"You did great, darling. I loved the way you pushed him overboard and kept talking while you sabotaged his fuel system." I told her about the agreement with the Sergeant and what all of us would use as a cover story.

Ivanhoe wasn't on the dock when I finished with the link pins and went topside to take took a look around. I guessed he'd gone off to get a dry uniform. I busied myself inside the yacht for a while.

Wade Daniels came aboard, ever so quietly, just like he did the first time.

"You took the boat out this morning." He said this blandly and his face was as expressive as an owl's.

I gave Wade the same slow-eyed wink that he'd given me three days earlier when he'd advised me to ignore the police and drive the boat to Florida. "Yeah, I switched out the transmission oil, but you really can't get rid of all the salt water without turning the shafts at high speed."

Wade didn't say a thing. I wondered if he had heard the shots and my announcements to Ivanhoe on the PA loudspeaker.

I rattled on. "I guess you can call it a shake-down cruise . . . which might be the right term for it because conditions are a little rough out there today."

When Wade raised his eyebrows as if to ask what that meant, I added, "You know, the Gulf Stream against an opposing wind."

Wade nodded. "An opposing something, anyway."

"Talking about opposition, you know that Sgt. Townsend is still treating the boat as a crime scene. I got off the phone with him less than an hour ago. His Constable Ivanhoe, that guy in the blue jumpsuit, is going back to guarding the boat twenty-four seven. And what I told you about not leaving fingerprints on the boat still goes."

Wade pulled his hand back, in a delayed reaction. "Didn't they dust for fingerprints already?"

"No, Sgt. Townsend hasn't done diddley-squat, as far as I can tell. But that doesn't mean he couldn't come here with a CSI crew this afternoon."

Wade took out a handkerchief and wiped where he'd touched the door frame. "Thanks for the tip. I bet you'll be glad to be able to get things done with this boat so you can pick up on your vacation."

Although it was clear that we were both acting, I kept playing the part I had chosen. The show must go on.

"Yes, we want to pick up with the vacation and move eastward. I'm doing a sponge survey for a venture capitalist out of Boston. He called to offer me the job after he learned that we were here."

"Yes, Angie told me some about it."

And I'd told him directly when he'd helped me lower the outboard motor on the *Diogenes*.

I asked, "How's Angie, anyway?"

"She and Cal have just left for Boca Raton."

"Yes, they told us the were planning to leave soon. Charming gal, that Angie. And Cal's a real gas, once he gets going. We'll be getting together again for cocktails if I'm still here when she gets back."

"When do you think the Sergeant will let you go?"

"It's hard to say, Wade. But at least I don't have to worry about anybody stealing the *Second Chance* while Constable Ivanhoe is guarding it."

"He takes his job real serious, does he?"

"Yes."

Wade winked at me. "You remember the tip I gave you a few days ago."

"Yes, Wade, I do remember it. I thought about it and can't say anything about it — yes or no, or when or why. Like you were saying, Wade, it's a sticky environment around here. I'm usually a pretty gregarious guy, but certain things a guy's just got to keep to himself."

Turning serious, I took a step forward to move him farther back in the cockpit. It felt like a replay of our first encounter. "No, Constable Ivanhoe might be gone for a little while to change into a fresh jumpsuit, but I'm sure that when he gets back he's going to be taking his duties twice as serious as before."

"I understand. Time to get off."

I waited in the companionway until Mr. Poison Fish Vendor stepped off the boat. I noticed that *Sumter's Forte* was indeed gone. And I went back to puttering around on the *Second Chance*, just to show everyone that I was still in control of it. Ivanhoe didn't return, but maybe it was just as well that I didn't see him.

I returned to the *Diogenes* and gave Rebecca a week's worth of hugs in one hour. I told her she was the luckiest thing that ever happened to me. Told her she was a woman for all seasons. Told her a whole lot of things, and she said a lot of nice things back.

Afterward, I made an important phone call.

Sir Hector's phone was answered by his chauffeur-butler-cook, Kevin. Yes, Sir Hector was available. Not wanting to spoil our polite relations, I worked up to my point slowly, thanking Sir Hector again for dinner the other evening and extending Rebecca's thanks for putting her in contact with the people at the clinic. When he started moving the conversation toward an end, that's when I slipped it in:

"Another reason I had for calling was to ask if you have spoken yet to Sgt. Leonard Townsend — the one in charge of the West End station."

"No, I did not speak to him, but I have taken . . . err . . . some action in that regard. I have made a polite inquiry to headquarters in Nassau asking if something could be done to speed up the process."

"Thank you! And . . ."

"And no one has gotten back to me, yet. I sense your impatience, old boy, but one must go through channels, you know."

"I understand. And it is just as well that you didn't talk to Sgt. Townsend directly, because it appears, now, that the delay is not due to him. It appears that someone higher up has his foot on the brakes."

Sir Hector cleared his throat. "What appears to be an unnecessary delay may actually be dictated by proper police procedure."

He could deliver his words with conviction, now that he didn't have to look me in the eye.

"Sir Hector, if one makes the inquiries with that attitude, my case is lost already." I repeated my arguments with emphasis.

"You are expressing yourself in very strong words, Doctor Candidi." He was back in his magisterial mode.

"I would prefer the term 'succinct.'"

"You are a young chap, but you *must* have some idea of how difficult it can be to deal with bureaucracy."

"I have had plenty of experience with bureaucracy. I maintain that they have no authority unless they can *prove* they have authority. I demand that when they disagree with me, they must *put it in writing*, citing chapter and verse."

"I see." Sir Hector dropped his voice as if those two words were an effective argument against me.

"I am glad. Then you will also understand the implications this has for my report on the economics of harvesting sponges for medicinal purposes."

"No, not exactly."

"In the report, it will come under the heading of 'political and economic environment.' International businessmen are aware that many developing countries are top-heavy with bureaucracy. Sometimes the countries squeeze money from foreign investors by using one bureaucracy to put a hold on the project to satisfy the needs of another bureaucracy. Crassly stated, it is conspiracy between bureaucracies to hold projects and property for ransom. Worse still is when bureaucrats withhold permissions in order to receive bribes. If Dr. Broadmoore's company were to commit to harvesting sponges here, it would have to make a big investment in physical and real property. Their property rights would have to be respected. To the extent that my present experience is indicative of the way business is done in Bahamas, that would be reflected in my report."

"I can only promise to continue to look into it. Cheers."

"Thank you."

We hung up and I let out a big sigh.

With a sad smile, Rebecca handed me a beer. "You don't have to make your case again to me, Ben. I understand and I agree. You have to be demanding — tough — to find out who's telling lies."

I put down the beer. Rebecca moved to my side and hugged me for a long time, like I was a big Teddy bear. And that's probably how I looked to Rick Turner as he pulled in and tied up to the fuel dock. Two days ago he had left for a run to Florida. Now he was back again. Had things changed for him in Delray Beach, and the electrical contracting business didn't require that much supervision after all?

Rick spent a few minutes in the Customs building, then returned to gas up his boat and move it to the same berth as before. But he didn't stay there long. He walked to the lot and drove off in his car.

I spent the rest of the day with a book I'd been reading. At sunset we enjoyed dinner. Afterward, I plugged a small lamp into the 12-volt socket and went back to reading in the cockpit. But somehow, William H. Prescott and I weren't connecting.

"What's the matter, Ben, is the Montezuma getting the best of Cortés?" Rebecca asked. "You're frowning and pulling out hair."

"No, Cortés did it elegantly. Now I'm on the *History of the Conquest of Peru*. Pizarro and his clan were a bunch of bunglers. Got themselves into a lot of stupid situations. It reminds me too much of our present situation."

"Then let's find something to take your mind off it. No, not in the cabin! Outdoors. What about a bicycle ride in the romantic moonlight?"

"Good idea!" I looked at my watch.

"No, it doesn't have to be according to a schedule."

"Rebecca, dear, I was looking at the *day*, not the time. It's Saturday. Saturday night! And I have a case of Saturday night fever. You can help me burn it off at the Island Club. I want to get out on that dance floor and show off my princess — Xena the Warrior Princess."

Rebecca laughed, reached back, and acted out a side-armed shot with a sharp metal Frisbee aimed at my neck. "Okay, but you've got to treat me like the other type of princess and pay me a lot of loving attention."

"A deal!"

"And one more thing, *dahling*," she added, slipping into her imitation of a bored socialite.

"Yes, *deah*," I answered.

"If you cannot find our ear protectors, I shall not go."

"And we will have to make sure that Ivanhoe has come to watch the baby," I added.

IVANHOE DID ARRIVE to babysit the *Second Chance*, and the Island Club didn't disappoint us, either. Cars were parked all along darkened King's Highway, and the outdoor bar was like an island of light. And it was packed.

Rebecca looked like an island princess in those loose-fitting white shorts and an Hawaiian print blouse, which was held closed by the two center buttons. The open space was charmed by an elaborate sea shell necklace that she had assembled with monofilament line and artful use of my cordless drill. I matched her wardrobe with my usual khaki shorts, a Florida Keys shirt, and a simpler necklace.

The Island Club's three-man electric group was doing a funk number when we arrived. Those guitars made plenty of sound — enough noise to drown out the recorded rap music coming from the two-storey wooden building across the street. That place was dark and mostly empty, with a few people silhouetted in the light of its neon beer sign.

The funk number was a good one for making our entrance to the dance area between the bar and tables. Rebecca can be disjointed when she wants to, and she has lots of funky moves. It was fun to play off of them, repeating her steps with a four-beat delay to produce counterpoint, or mirroring her arm and leg action in real time for close-in harmony.

The guys in the band stretched the number when they saw us having fun with their stuff. Dancing was good for our bodies, and after the day's frustration, it felt good to be making some kind of a statement. The crowd had only a handful of locals, and I wondered where all tourists were from.

When the band switched to a reggae number, Rebecca and I bumped along with it and the dance area started to fill up. The bartender eyed me like he thought I was having too good a time for a guy who hadn't bought a drink yet. I flashed him two fingers and yelled an order for two daiquiris.

I fell into a mindless reggae vamp, pushed the autopilot button, and relaxed into the milieu. The bar stools were occupied by couples that matched us in age. Their friends were crowded into the spaces between. It was a typical scene, with an excess of girlfriends' girlfriends close to the bar and with a lot of guys milling around farther away, trying to think up some way to do something about it. I wasn't completely surprised to see Rick Turner. I gave him a nod, bumped butts with Rebecca, and spun around for a look at the tables.

Their lighting scheme was indirect, with a spotlight shining up into each of the thatch roofs over the individual tables. And that broad deck had plenty of tables — thickly varnished cable spools surrounded by semi-circular benches that would accommodate four to six people. Every table was occupied, and most of them were full.

The most interesting group was halfway back. The leader had long, dark-blond hair and wore a loose, European-cut white suit. Three of his table mates were models from the fashion shoot. I saw lots of close-in conversation between the girls. When it seemed to lull, an occasional monosyllable from him would get one or more of them tittering, and it would start all over again. It wasn't possible to learn what they were saying by watching their lips, but I guessed they were all speaking French. The girls were quite visually aware, but the guy moved his head hardly at all and kept his eyes hidden behind his heavy-framed, wrap-around glasses. Along with his earlobe-length hair, those glasses just had to be a fashion statement. I mean, a guy in his low forties should be able to wear contact lenses, shouldn't he?

Rebecca bumped butts with me. I answered her frown with a smile and shifted my attention to another table.

A couple of tables back, tattooed and muscular Waverunner entrepreneur Harold Pearce was talking with two friends. With them were sitting a couple of all-American cheerleader types who just had to be into Waverunners. Harold was wearing a loosely fitting black shirt with a large orchid print like you can see around Key West. His friends were dressed like Parrot-Heads but looked like they worked out.

Way off to the left side of the deck, Reggie Pimentel had a table with five Island ladies all to himself. They weren't stunningly beautiful, but they weren't Bahama mamas either. They were dressed like the gals in rap videos, and their projected attitudes fit the part. And in a designer T-shirt under an unstructured white jacket, Reggie looked like he was trying to recreate the Disco '70s.

Rebecca was getting into some interesting hip action, and I was sorry when the song came to an end. I suggested that we go for the bar and Rebecca agreed. We went for the least crowded spot. The couple there was nice enough to let us in to make an order. They had come over on a Royal Caribbean liner and were staying in Freeport. They had rented a car to get around the island and had been told this was a good place for a drink on Saturday night. While talking to them, I kept an eye on Harold, Reggie, and the fashion guy.

When the bartender finally asked what we wanted, I said, "Two frozen daiquiris just like I ordered before." I plunked down three fives and told him to keep the change, which would have been one dollar.

Over the noise of the band, the four of us talked about what a visitor could do on the water around here. After a while, two girls standing next to us — Vicki and Kathy — joined in the conversation to recommend Harold Pearce's "Fun In The Sun" rental concession. I recognized Vicki as the girl who had been following Harold on a Waverunner when we were out on the inflatable. I told her so and she remembered.

Vicki explained that she was taking a semester off from Stetson University and that she just loved West End for all the excitement. When she asked if I knew about Stetson, I correctly identified its founder as the guy who'd invented the hat. I was also able to name a couple of brick buildings and locate them with respect to the gazebos and walkways. The campus blends so perfectly into De Land's central neighborhood of old Victorian houses that it is hard to say which houses belong to the campus and which belong to the gentry. It is hard to imagine how something so genteel could survive 40 miles inland from that motorcycle magnet called Daytona Beach.

"How do you know so much about Stetson?" Vicki asked.

"I used to date a Stetson girl," I replied.

Vicki told me that she was staying in the cottage complex. "It's so international, with French designers, fashion models and photographers, and all."

When I asked about the guy in the white suit, she told me he was Jacques d'Alembert, a French clothing designer who had a big condominium in Freeport. She confirmed most of what I had guessed when Rebecca and I had watched the fashion shoot.

Vicki and I were leaning into each other to be able to converse over the band, but that seemed to be okay with Rebecca.

"Do you know that guy over there?" I asked, pointing to Reggie.

"Oh, that's Reggie. He's supposed to be a big shot on the island, but the girls and I stay away from him. He's too much of a party animal."

The whole time I'd been watching Reggie, he hadn't moved from his table. He had been talking to his women in a much less democratic manner than the Frenchman. From the movement of his lips, his sentences were short. I guessed he wasn't as articulate as his father. His women responded with all sorts of facial expressions. It was what Rebecca would definitely call "a male dominance thing."

I asked Vicki, "Does Reggie party long and hard?"

"Some of the girls told me that he parties rough."

"What does he do for a living?"

"He's supposed to be some kind of English nobleman because of his father. And they say he's into real estate development."

I had another question, but I couldn't ask it directly.

"When I saw you riding the Waverunner the other day, you were handling it like a pro. You must be really into that stuff."

"Oh, I could do it all day."

"Pretty expensive, at fifty dollars an hour."

"It's not so bad. Harry gives me a break. He'll do it if you're a regular around here."

"Is Kathy into Waverunners, too?" I asked, glancing towards Vicki's friend.

"Not so much."

"Is she from Stetson, too?"

"No, she's from Gainsville — the University of Florida."

I was about to ask Vicki more about Harold when we were interrupted by Rick Turner. The go-go electrician from Delray Beach had been watching us for the longest time from the far side of the bar. Finally, he'd decided to make his move. He walked up and slapped me on the shoulder like we were good buddies.

"Ben! How you been? Man, I saw you and Rebecca dancing a while ago. You guys cut a mean rug."

"Yeah, it's Saturday night, and we've got disco fever."

Rick eyed Vicki and Kathy, receiving no encouragement from either of them. And I wasn't ready to offer him any help just yet. It would be interesting to see him work for it.

"Rick, I saw you pulling into the marina this morning, but you didn't wave back. Then you took off in your car. I hope you got everything done you wanted to."

"Yeah, I had a little business in Freeport." He puffed up his chest and looked at me like it was my cue to say something about his cabin cruiser.

"Oh, the lifestyles of the rich and famous," I said.

Vicki didn't act impressed. Kathy was half listening. Rebecca glanced our way.

"Vicki's into Waverunners but Kathy isn't," I said.

"Great," Rick said. "Maybe we can take you out on a real boat sometime."

Vicki turned her head to look across the dance floor. I looked in the same direction in time to notice a "come here" gesture from Harold Pearce. And I caught the second gesture that he made to Kathy.

"Nice to meet you," Vicki said to Rick, "but we have to meet someone."

Vicki and Kathy moved out, waving to the band as they made their way around the dance area. A minute later they were seated with Harold Pearce and his friends. I turned my attention to Rebecca, giving her an occasional kiss on the cheek while we talked into each other's ears over the loud music. I told her that I'd learned a few things about Harold Pearce and Reggie Pimentel.

"It looks like Harold and Reggie know each other but don't socialize," Rebecca said.

"Yes, maybe each one wants to keep his girls to himself."

"It looks like all three groups keep to themselves. The fashion people, the Waverunners, and Reggie — each one with his harem."

"Except that the Waverunner girls practice their French on the fashion girls. Poor Rick Turner! Three types of girl and he can't get started with any of them. And Reggie is sitting over there acting like he owns the place."

"Maybe he does," Rebecca said. "The waitress is giving him and his girls good service."

"Talking about service, Harold is giving Vicki a reduced rate on his Waverunners. Even so, I wonder if her riding habit is more expensive than a cocaine habit."

"Talking about habits," Rebecca said, "do you think they are selling drugs in the building across the street? Did you see those two guys by the door?"

Yes, I had. Two Islanders with loose-fitting, urban-style clothes.

"While you were talking to Vicki, I've been watching. They've been standing around, acting like they were carrying on a conversation. But any time someone goes by, they try to bring him into it. Sometimes one of them follows a guy in and comes out a short time later. I bet they're selling cocaine to the boaters and Ecstacy to the college students."

"Okay, the building is a retail drugstore. What else did you notice?"

"Well, Ben, I'd say that it's a hangout for the locals, and they get their drinks for half price. And I'd say they are making their money from the yachting people like Rick Turner who come here looking for girls. And I guess that the women at Reggie's table are available for about sixty dollars a night."

"You're street wise." I nibbled on her ear.

She pulled away, laughed and came back and tickled mine. "No more than your average female ER physician."

"What about those two guys standing behind you? Do you think they are here on a fox hunt?"

Rebecca laughed. "That square-looking one with the glasses? He made a point of telling the barmaid that he flew in with his Cessna to the airport at Freeport. He sounds like Al Gore, and I think he comes from Tennessee. I don't think he's a smuggler. I think he just likes to have interesting places to fly his plane."

"I agree."

"Anything else you want to know from Xena the Warrior Princess?"

"What's your take on the Waverunner girls?"

"Maybe you should be telling *me*," Rebecca said, dropping her street-wise attitude. "You and Vicki seemed to be getting along very well." She said it with a mock frown.

Rebecca jerked back in surprise when I French-kissed her ear.

"Well, she didn't offer me her body," I said. "She is doing a pretty good job of taking care of that body, though. I forgot to ask her if Stetson has a swim team. Corn fed, healthy and likes to party. And her friend Kathy seemed a little prim. My guess is that those two belong to the fortunate upper five percent who get big allowances. I wouldn't guess that either girl is a cocaine whore."

"Yes, if they don't get hooked in another month. You wouldn't believe some of the cases I have seen at *Dade County General*."

The healer-nurturer spirit in Rebecca is irrepressible. When I feel it coming out, it is hard to resist a smile.

Rebecca noticed. "Okay, my smirky-faced, unpaid private eye. What else do you want to do?"

"Why don't you watch while I go over there to use the facilities." I leaned across the bar and asked the barman, "Do you have restrooms here?"

"Over there at the General Store."

"Great. I wouldn't feel right about using them if they weren't under the same management."

"They are," he said.

I crossed King's Highway and the gravel parking lot to the wobbly building and waved at the two guys as I approached the door. "Been drinking across the street. They told me I can use the facilities here."

"No problem," said the shorter one.

Inside, it felt like an oats and feed store, except that the floor felt too creaky to support stacks of bags. Two monster speakers were filling the wooden cavern with a rap that was strong enough to kill termites. The only light was from the neon beer sign that stood over an improvised bar. The guy behind it paid no attention to me, and the guy in front of it looked ready to mobilize at the first sign that I was looking to score. I gave no sign and headed straight to the gents'.

The men's room was set up well for drug dispensing. Between the two stalls, a big hole was knocked out of the beaverboard partition to allow transactions to be made while sitting. I used and flushed the urinal and turned the rickety faucets to get water to wash my hands and splash my face, using the mirror to keep an eye on the door behind. Nobody came and I left.

Back at the bar, Rebecca kissed my cheek, then lined up on my ear to deliver a message. "When you took off, the bartender gave a signal to the two guys at the door. He shook his head."

"Warning them that I wasn't a customer. Thanks. I've seen enough here. What about you?"

"No, you have to dance with me again."

"Sure. Too bad that Angie and Cal aren't here to see us."

"Oh *dahling*, you slay me." Rebecca grabbed my face with both hands and planted a deep kiss in my mouth.

Maybe it was the influence of the music, because the band had just started an old Sade song — "Smooth Operator." The rhythm guitarist knew all the words and sang them well using a muted falsetto. We fell into the groove as fast as we stepped into the dance area. I pulled Rebecca close and said, "You slay me, too. It takes two to tango."

Rebecca cocked her head like an exotic bird and draped her long fingers over my shoulders. After a few slithery steps we came to a consensus. Then Rebecca started throwing in tango moves. The dance floor thinned out, leaving us lots of room to move around and strike poses. At the end of the number we actually got a sprinkling of applause. I threw a wave to Rick Turner at the far end of the bar and we left.

On the way out, we passed Jay Sherman, the new guy in the marina. Great! Now Rick Turner would have someone to talk to.

We walked along King's Highway. I started to thank Rebecca for being a good princess, both warrior and trophy variety, but I cut it short when we came across Wade Daniels moving toward us at stroll speed.

"Hey, Wade," I said when he came within range, "you ought to go over there. Rick's there and the band is excellent."

He smiled. "Then I'll drop in for a drink."

We all kept walking. Shortly before we reached our bicycles, I noticed a man loitering along the shoulder, on the far side of the cars. It was Sgt. Townsend, out of uniform. In the faint light I noticed he was wearing a loose shirt with a guayabera cut and dark slacks.

"Lovely evening, isn't it, Sergeant?" His answer to my remark was nothing more than a nod, so I tried again. "Are you off duty tonight?"

"A police sergeant in West End is always on duty," he said.

15   Farewell in Freeport

The dancing must have been good for me because I slept deeply and long past sunup. What awakened me, actually, was Rebecca talking on her cellphone. The conversation sounded overly formal for a Sunday morning. When she noticed me stirring, she moved from the cockpit to the dock. Not wishing to distract or inhibit her, I made a bee line for the restroom and took my time under the shower.

I returned to find Rebecca in a strange mood, looking off in the distance with a frown, curling her hair around a finger, pursing her lips, and avoiding my eyes.

"Rebecca, something's bothering you. What is it?"

"Oh, Ben, I don't know what to say or what to do. Barbara had talked to me about the possibility a couple of days ago. But the professor was out of the country. And he called me, just now. But, I don't know. It's so complicated when we have so many things up in the air."

"Don't worry about complications. Just tell me who *he* is and what's the *possibility*."

Rebecca pouted. "Actually, it's very good luck. But it's just coming too soon." She still hadn't met my eyes.

"Good luck, *schmoodluck*," I said in loose parody of an old Jewish wise man, "at least it isn't *bad* luck."

Rebecca laughed as if hearing a joke told by a child. Then she smiled, grabbed her knee, and swung her leg over the cockpit floor.

That leg was so attractive I could have kissed it. She glanced at me cautiously. "Well, you know that Barbara was going to put out feelers for an ER job for me."

"Right. Are you being offered one?"

"No, but she told Professor David Thompson about me and he's interested. He's in charge of tropical medicine at Bryan Medical School. He goes down to Brazil and Central America several times a year."

"Yes."

"He wants to build me a position."

"Great! A position in tropical medicine. That's what you've been wanting, all along."

"But it involves writing an NIH grant. He will be my mentor."

"Sounds great. When will the position start?"

"Actually, the NIH grant would kick in nine months from now, but he has six months worth of bridging money, so I could start in three months."

"Wonderful. That leaves us plenty of time to complete our cruise."

"Yes. But there's one real problem."

"What?"

"The deadline for the grant application is the end of this week. I'd have to rush back to Miami and leave you alone."

"Go for it," I said in a burst of bravado.

"But I feel bad about leaving you here with so many enemies lurking around."

"Forget it. Maybe they will feel less threatened when they see two spies reduced to one."

"You think so?"

"Most definitely."

"But I worry that my leaving would make it more likely that they'd snatch the *Second Chance* away from you. I should be here to help you defend it."

"That damn Ivanhoe is supposed to be guarding it for us. And if he fades into the shadows and lets a bunch of bad guys come here to take it, I wouldn't want to risk either of our lives trying to stop them. What would we do? Threaten them with flare guns?"

"Oh, I just don't know."

"When does Professor Thompson want you there?"

"Tomorrow, actually." Her voice quavered. "You see, we'd have only five working days, and we haven't even defined the project." Her eyes moistened and she was speeding up. "And I might have to digest a lot of scientific literature before I could *even* —"

I moved over and wrapped an arm around her before it was too late. "Go! Opportunity demands it. Call him up right now and tell him you'll be there tomorrow morning."

"But —"

"Stop protesting and grab that duffel bag with your regular clothes in it. And throw in all your professional papers. Hurry. The van arrives at ten-thirty. Make sure everything's packed. You can call Professor Thompson with the good news while we're underway."

"You're ready to send me off, just like that?"

"No, I'm going along with you as far as Freeport. I need to drop off a FEDEX package to Broadmoore, anyway."

OUR CELLPHONES WORKED fine in that little white Toyota passenger van, just like they had on the marina's parking lot. We had a reservation on a Miami-bound plane for Rebecca by the time we were passing the Island Club. It felt good to wave goodbye to that now-empty place. It felt good to leave West End behind, along with Wade Daniels, Rick Turner, Sgt. Townsend and his tenacious Ivanhoe, who actually was guarding the *Second Chance* when we left.

The driver made frequent stops to pick up formally dressed Islanders and deliver them to roadside churches, but he assured us that Rebecca would get to the airport on time. The grandmothers looked so proud, and the little girls looked so cute in their frilly dresses. The boys looked less comfortable in their white shirts and black pants, but one of them had a fine repertoire of hymns.

And I learned a lot about the island while looking through the van's window. We passed Sir Hector's Royal road, then rolled past two clapboard historical settlements: Holmes Rock and Eight Mile Rock. Then King's Highway took a sharp left, conforming to the shape of the island. We crossed an expanse of scrub land. This led to an industrial area that Sir Hector had mentioned — a big quarrying operation and a cement factory. Behind it, we could see the gantry cranes, container ships in the Lucayan Harbor, and cruise ships anchored beyond. In the distance, we could make out an enormous dry dock. The industrial area gave way to pine forest. Then it turned low-rent residential which transitioned to light commercial. We passed a radio station, "Cool 96." Then the van took us into an unimpressive looking "downtown" and stopped at a Winn-Dixie supermarket lot which Rebecca told me was Freeport's transportation hub. We got off and caught a taxi that took us about 10 miles north to the Grand Bahama International Airport. It wasn't as big as its name implied.

As we pulled up to the terminal, Rebecca turned serious. "Ben, promise me that you won't take any chances."

"Promise. I'll do my best."

"Keep a real low profile. Don't start any investigations, no matter how interesting it seems at the time."

"I promise. Curiosity won't get the best of this cat."

I paid the taxi driver.

"And stay away from that Island Club."

"Yes, I'll stay away from the fashion models, the Waverunner girls, and the fashion mogul with the funny glasses. What else do you want me to do?"

She smiled with pursed lips. "If you have any extra time, could you *please* sand the top edge of the top board for the companionway. It makes the hatch so hard to slide shut. Every time I lock up, I'm afraid I'm going to break something."

"Boy Scout's honor, I promise to fix it. That should be worth fifteen merit points. And while we're on the subject of Boy Scout things, if I'm talking with you on my cellphone about something important, we might have to do it in code."

After checking in at the counter, we agreed on code words for various disagreeable situations. Rebecca promised to return as soon as possible. I kissed her goodbye at the security checkpoint.

I caught a cab — the same one we had taken. The driver was glad to see me again because I'd given him a good tip. "Where to, Captain?"

"Freeport."

"Transportation center? No problem. And I'll take you to a place where there's a box to drop off your FEDEX package. It's on the way."

"Thanks. Good thinking. I'm also interested in a place where they rent motorcycles."

"You want to go scooting around town?"

"No, I want a real motorcycle that will take me the length of the island."

"Yes, I know what you're talking about, Captain, an' I can take you there, right after I take you to FEDEX."

It worked out fine on both counts. The motorcycle shop was enough off the tourist track to have real cycles, and they took plastic. They offered me a good weekly rental rate on a dirt bike that met my requirements — big wheels for going fast on the highway, a springy suspension and high clearance for the back roads, and a solid carrier platform behind, on which I could tie the Caribe's gasoline tanks. They even supplied a heavy chain and a lock. I thanked the taxi man, paying off his meter and adding a generous tip.

I wasn't doing this rental thing on a whim. I'd been thinking about it for a while. As my survey grounds shifted further to the east, I would lose a lot of time on commuting with the inflatable. It would be more efficient to chain it to a tree by someone's house every night and return to the marina on motorcycle. And the motorcycle could be used to deliver gas to the inflatable far from the marina.

What an empowering feeling to have horsepower between my legs! The throttle seemed to have only two positions: rough idle and flat out. The chunky treads on those big tires made for a bouncy ride on the pavement. The machine just seemed to be screaming for me to drive onto the shoulder where it could really kick up some dirt. For my getting-acquainted session with the bronco, I took it northward through residential and undeveloped sections. I found a number of places where the shore was accessible and my Caribe could be stored overnight. With that out of the way and with the machine under control, I returned to town.

Freeport is not what you would imagine for a Caribbean-style town. Think of the suburban developments they are carving out of North Carolina pinewoods around Durham and Raleigh, North Carolina. Lay them out on a grid with wide streets, keep it low-rise, and avoid the tacky strip-mall approach, favoring grass or a pine needle carpet. And give the buildings Bahamian shutters and paint with pastel colors, and you have Freeport.

I decided to spend the remainder of my daylight hours seeing for myself what made Freeport tick.

I paid attention to the signs along the boulevard and followed streams of tourists to the International Mall. It was designed like one of these modern Florida shopping centers, where grassy embankments break up the monotony of the parking lot surrounding clusters of shops connected by walkways. This one was a bazaar of winding passageways and shops with pirate or seafaring names. Their wares included swim- and beachwear, African costumes and drums, and various woven goods,

some of them handmade on the island. But the really authentic stuff —
handmade straw hats, shell jewelry and hammocks — was offered at
the stalls of a dusty, fenced-in compound on the other side of the street.
While the cycle was parked, I walked over to the main casino attached
to a high-rise hotel. I just had to see it.

Walking up to the door, informally dressed as I was, a part of me
was bracing against challenges from white-gloved doormen. But the
doors opened automatically, and the scene that I walked into wasn't
the least bit James Bond. No gentlemen in tuxedos or ladies in plunging
evening gowns. No roulette wheel or croupier's paddle in play over
green felt. No tight clusters of glitterati saying *cart, banc* or naming
colors in Italian. Hell, the patrons weren't dressed much better than
me!

Actually, it was almost as bad as Saturday night bingo at the
Miccosukee Indian Reservation at the edge of the Everglades. Walking
through a hundred-yard expanse of video slot, bingo and poker
machines that accepted any denomination of bill between one and 100
dollars, I remembered a sad fact learned in Psychology 102 —
diminishing the rewards will actually reinforce a conditioned behavior.
Maybe it's a survival mechanism to keep the poor animal foraging for
a hard winter. But it's a sad thing to view your fellow human beings as
rats in a Skinner Box. And it's sad to think that we are pre-programmed
to be exploited by machines.

At least the blackjack game at the end of the hall was run by a
human being. A card near the table gave the following information:

"$3 min., $5 max., dealer must stand on 17, draw on 16,
Blackjack Pays 3/2."

The neighboring crap and the poker tables had no dealers nor
players. It was probably too early in the day. The card next to the
poker table announced "Caribbean Stud" and gave a listing of payouts:

"Royal Flush jackpot, Straight Flush $103, 4 of Kind $500,
Full House $100, Flush $50."

I stood there for a while, trying to calculate how much the odds
favored the house and how much skill you would need to break even.

Back at the blackjack table, the house dealer was doing his work professionally and efficiently, offering a minimum of polite conversation with four players who seemed to be friends. Maybe gambling is like cigarettes: a habit that you pick up from your friends.

Then I looked upward. The hall overseer was watching me, disapprovingly, from the parapet attached to the high wall near these tables. I looked higher, still. Inside their smoked-glass ceiling turrets, the video cameras were probably registering disapproval, too.

Returning to my motorcycle, I set off for a quick glimpse of the other part of the Bahamian economy — banking services and tax havens. I followed the winding road a few blocks north to the "downtown." It was about four blocks by four blocks square and was easy to take in with a motorcycle. On the west side was the Winn-Dixie grocery store parking lot and the transportation center where we'd already been. To the east were many bank buildings. The CIBC Banking Centre was a typical architectural example: a three-storey concrete block building painted light yellow, with white columns, three-foot-wide and going all the way up but without any Ionian or Corinthian capitals. Green storm shutters framed the windows. There was a whole colony of banks like this. And the nearby Bahamian Government Office Complex didn't look any different from the banks.

Yes, the banks seemed to be pleasant and harmless enough places to stash a fortune. If they hadn't been closed for Sunday, I would have gone in. Their doorways displayed no information about the spectrum of financial services offered inside. But elements of their names — Canadian, Nova Scotia, Barbados, Caribbean islands, etc. — suggested freedom from U.S. regulation and the ability to move money to other countries.

I checked the telephone directory at a pay phone by the Winn-Dixie and found plenty of listings for financial advisors and lawyers specialized in creating Bahamian corporations to the client's specifications. Many of them had offices nearby.

To the east of the downtown was a boulevard with a broad median planted with rubber trees. On the far side was the Rand Hospital, a relatively narrow, one-storey, white-tiled, pitched-roofed structure that sprawled eastward for a city block. The parking lot held a motley collection of cars. There were also a couple of white-and-orange ambulances like the one that had taken away murder victim "Steve." They were Ford vans with left-side steering, outfitted just like ambulances in Miami. For Rebecca's information, I copied what was written on its side: Ministry of Health, Commonwealth of the Bahamas, Emergency Medical Services.

And for Rebecca's sake I paid the hospital a visit. The one and only entrance opened to a 50-by-50-foot lobby, at the end of which was a small door. A triage nurse sat to the left of it and a security man sat to the right. I loitered for a while, trying to figure out the medical cases and the personnel that were treating them. Nurses in blue or white pantsuits came and went.

While dismounted, I visited the Sir Charles Hayward Public Lending Library that stood on an adjacent lot. The librarians inside told me that it had been set up as a subscription library but that I was welcome to browse. They had a great collection of books on Bahama history which I didn't dare look at for fear of being lured away from my major objective of the day.

The Freeport headquarters of the Royal Bahamas Police Force was on Pioneers Way, a street that formed the southern boundary of the downtown section. Its one-storey building was obviously constructed before the banking boom. What a strange combination of concrete and wood! Poured concrete formed its foundation, floors and walls up to chest height. From there up to its flat roof, it was built of lumber and sheet plywood that gave way to numerous awning windows. The whole thing was painted lime green. Beside the building rose the type of antenna that you see around highway patrol stations. In the gravel parking lot was only one vehicle, a white van with the Police Force's insignia.

Peeking through the side windows, I saw enough wooden desks and paper clutter to believe that the place was a headquarters. I went in the narrow front entrance. The wooden counter had several decades worth of scratches and gouges. I told the corporal behind it that I was Dr. Benjamin Candidi and that I wanted to talk to the ASP who was in charge of the investigation of the murder that I had reported in West End eight days earlier. The corporal reminded me that it was Sunday and said that the ASP was not in.

I pulled a sheet of blank paper from my back pocket, unfolded it, and composed a letter to "The Superior Officer Sgt. Leonard Townsend" on the subject of "Homicide Investigation Involving the U.S. Registered Vessel, the *Second Chance*." My bottom line was that the Superior Office must contact me immediately on my cellphone if they had any intention of maintaining any sort of jurisdiction over the vessel. Reluctantly the corporal made a photocopy for me in the back office.

With a copy of the letter in my pocket, I hopped back onto my motorcycle and roared off, throwing up some gravel in the process. Near the International Mall, I found an Internet café that offered connectivity for $10 an hour. I used the time to go to the NOAA website and hunt down graphics on the Gulf Stream and tidal currents on the Little Bahama Bank. The ocean current vectors were very close to the ones I'd used when calculating the trajectory of the *Second Chance*. For a couple of extra dollars, they let me hit the print button and make copies.

I also looked up the Internet version of the *Nassau Guardian*. It was too abbreviated for me to expect to find any news story on the murder of "Steve" and our salvage of the boat.

It was getting late in the afternoon. I got back on the cycle and took off. Half a block down the street, I noticed Wade Daniels' car. The fade-and-flake pattern in its blue paint made the car easy to identify. It was just parked there. Wade wasn't in it, and I didn't see him around. I waited awhile, wondering if this was a coincidence, before going on to my next project — checking out the real estate.

I worked my way eastward on Pioneers Way, and then southward, looking back often to be sure that I wasn't being followed by a blue car. I wasn't.

Eventually, I found the inlet of the Lucayan Waterway, a broad canal carved out of coral rock and mangrove swamp. It bisects the island and allows yachts to go from the south to the north side. Its numerous inlets led to marina basins and countless water-front mansions. At the mouth of the Waterway and along the south shore of the island is a collection of high rise hotels and condominiums that are as closely packed and regulated as on Miami Beach. Wanting to sample the lifestyle of the rich and famous, I found a parking spot for my motorcycle far enough away from their security and valet parking people, but close enough to go in on foot.

I reached for my collar and verified that I was wearing a polo shirt and not a T-shirt. An I-belong-here-and-can-afford-anything attitude got me through the front door of the hotel that I picked. It had a charming terrace restaurant overlooking the Waterway. Being in greater need of glucose than alcohol, I opted for a "Caribbean Sundae." The waiter was nice and didn't hassle me to order more.

My old mentor Dr. Westley would probably have felt compelled to remind me that the Bahamas are not technically part of the Caribbean system because they are north of Cuba. But misnamed or not, my

Caribbean Sundae was a triple treat: It came with edification and entertainment — a sales presentation for Bahamas-style financial services. At the table next to me, a wily looking Brit was making a pitch to an American couple:

"You see, sir, 'ere is how it works. After the initial payments to our trust fund account — set up under bond with a highly reputable bank, and the payments can be cash or even transfer from an American bank, if you prefer — the funds are transferred under *banking secrecy* to the account of your Bahamas-chartered corporation, which will be an International Business Corporation or I . . . B . . . C, actually. Under your directions, we, as agents for your corporation, can invest these funds in stocks or bonds from *any country*, the dividends, capital gains and proceeds of which will be received by you. The proceeds are subject to only *minimal taxation* (ha, ha, ha!), allowing your money to *grow*. The stocks and bonds can be converted into money at any time, and can be used for *any purpose* that you designate!

"And as for using your money in the good old U . . . S . . . of A, if you wish? That is really not a problem. Our most convenient method is to 'ave the corporation issue you a credit card — easy-to-remember variations on one's *own* name are most popular (ha, ha, ha!) — so that when you are buying your gasoline or your restaurant meals, all you 'ave to do is *scrawl* (ha, ha, ha!) your signature on the slip and the matter of payment will be taken care of 'ere as fast as the wire can carry it to us (ha, ha, ha!)."

The moustachioed huckster's presentation was rendered all the more picturesque by a variety of British accent in which payments were "pye-ments" and agents were "eye-gents," and where the gains were "gynes" — for everybody except for Uncle Sam in the good old U . . . S of A. (Ha, ha, ha!)

All of that played pretty well to the prospective client, a gray-haired American with the heavy-framed glasses who looked like he belonged to a half-dozen civic organizations, served as an usher in a Presbyterian church, and owned a Cadillac dealership in a second-rung Midwestern city.

The huckster's visual awareness was every bit as sharp as his presentation. When he noticed that I was listening, he caught my eye and said, "Oh, yes, you were the gentleman I met on the *plyne*, and I didn't have a card. Well here 'tis. My receptionist will be glad to schedule you an appointment."

I accepted his card graciously and promised to ring him up in the morning.

A couple of hours before dark, I was rolling out of Freeport and past the cement works and the container ship port. Between the Eight Mile Rock and Holmes Rock settlements, I came across an outdoor bar and restaurant. It was a thatch pavilion with a bar around the perimeter and a grill in the center. A cold beer seemed in order. After several sips of beer, the red snapper that they were grilling and the conch fritters that they were deep frying seemed infinitely better than a warmed-up can of beef stew back at the *Diogenes*.

Some kids came up from a house that sat at the end of the side road pointing toward the Straits of Florida shore. They were the owner's kids, and the guy appreciated my playing with them while waiting for dinner. His name was Jethro, he was middle-aged, and he had a weary smile and a worldly wise manner that suggested he'd worked some hard, far-away jobs before settling down here. When I told him about my sponge survey, he told me that there were a lot of sponges off their shore. He said I could store my inflatable in his yard when my survey brought me this way. After a great meal and a delightful conversation, I fired up the motorcycle and headed home.

At the crossroads of King's Highway and Mulberry Lane, I was treated to an interesting sight — the underside of a Grumman Mallard shining in the low sun. It was descending over me, left to right, for an amphibious landing at some not-so-distant point on the north side of the Island. Since I was looking for access points on the island's north shore, I turned north on Mulberry Lane to follow it. Along the Lane were a few shacks but mostly trees and undergrowth. I stopped for a few minutes to watch some children playing front yard soccer. Farther down the road were more shacks. Then the road dead-ended at a large property behind a chain link fence. There would be no water access for me from that road unless I wanted to make arrangements with Reggie Pimentel.

As I rode back toward West End, I began to feel an allergic reaction. It was a multiple allergic reaction: to the police sergeant who was adamant about holding the salvaged yacht but was soft on the investigation; to the part-time smugglers at the marina; to the witchy marina mistress who wouldn't give me any information on "Steve"; and to Sir Hector who was so comfortably ensconced in his shrine to anglophilia that he wouldn't raise a finger to help me.

In the Cards   16

It had just turned dark when I chained the motorcycle to a tree by the marina office. Wade Daniels' car was in the parking lot. The *Second Chance* was still in its berth. Constable Ivanhoe was still guarding it, lying in a hammock strung between two palm trees. The *Rapture of the Reef* had returned to its berth.

I decided to pay a visit to Zelma Mortimer's office. She needed to know that the motorcycle was mine and that I would be staying for another week. In the reception area, the noisy television was off and so was the noisy air conditioner. At the end of the room, the top half of the Dutch door was open. I walked up to it and looked in. Zelma was sitting behind her desk, which was illuminated by candlelight. She looked up at me with the softest attitude that I had seen yet.

"Are you still open for business?"

"Yes, please come in." She gestured for me to open the Dutch door. "Please come in and sit down."

Was the wall of formality starting to crumble?

I pulled a chair to the side of her desk. On the opposite side, the candle was burning inside a glass chimney. Next to it stood a bottle of wine. In the center was a deck of cards and a glass of white wine, half full. A stick of incense was burning inside a conch shell at the front of the desk, and some sort of world music was playing softly.

I concentrated on the business at hand. "Doctor Levis has returned to Miami for a few days. I will be taking care of the *Diogenes* while she's gone." My statements evoked a little smile. "We want to keep the *Diogenes* here for another week."

"That will be fine," Zelma said. "We will simply add it to your bill. We have your credit card number. Would you like a glass of wine?"

Why was she so pleasant this time?

"Yes. Thank you. That would be very nice." I relaxed in my chair.

"The cups are there," she said, waving a manicured hand toward a stack of clear plastic cups.

They were within easy reach. Zelma watched with amusement while I selected a cup from the center of the stack. I smiled back and set it on the table, next to her cards. She poured generously and replenished her own glass. I brought my glass to chest level, holding it there in case she wanted to propose a toast. She didn't. As a face-saving gesture, I swirled the wine in the glass a few inches under my nose.

"Nice bouquet." I took a sip and showed appreciation.

The label on the bottle identified it as a California chardonnay.

Zelma regarded me calmly and said nothing. The music was African percussion, coming from a small CD player. Well, if she expected me to supply the conversation, I would be glad to oblige.

"I also need to tell you that I have rented a motorcycle. It's chained to a tree outside the building. I'll be using it to haul gasoline for the inflatable. My idea's to increase the inflatable's working range on the sponge survey I'm doing."

She smiled without explanation, leaving me no alternative but to continue.

"I can take in the sights a lot better on a motorcycle than in a car. I had a great time motorcycling through Jamaica. Lot of nice hills there. Have you been there?"

"Yes, once."

"Did you like it?"

"Not as much as the Bahamas."

"Well, I agree with you there. The Jamaican landscape is more interesting, with the hills, but the water is more interesting in the Bahamas." I wondered if she could swim. There was much that I wondered about her. "Did you grow up on the Grand Bahama Island?"

"Yes."

"Here?"

"No, in Freeport." She regarded me for a minute. "You just went there. Did you like it?"

"I liked their island crafts. I was impressed with the quarry and the port that I saw on the way. I was impressed with the your banking section, and I hope you have continued success selling residential real estate. But I didn't think much of the casino."

She answered that by picking up the deck of cards and shuffling them. Pretty good, how she could do that without her fingernails getting in the way.

"I once made my living from cards," she said, looking down at them.

"I didn't mean to disparage a job that you had, it's just that I . . ."

"I wasn't a dealer in the casino. I did readings for Madame la Dauphine."

I must have smiled at that. It came as a triple whammy: Zelma doing readings for a fortune-teller . . . with a French name that meant "wife of a prince" . . . which could honestly be confused with "dolphin." And add to that Sir Hector's complaint about there being too many Haitians in the Bahamas!

"You worked in a fortune-teller's . . . parlor?"

"Yes, after an apprenticeship."

I must have smiled at the thought of that, too. "Did you read tarot cards?"

"I did, if the client insisted on them," she answered, matter-of-factly. "But the predictions are much stronger with regular playing cards." She said that with enthusiasm.

"How does it work?" I asked. "Does the king stand for the king, and the joker for the fool, and the number cards stand for different characters?"

"The numbers stand for beginnings, connections, communication, foundations and awareness," she said, dreamily. "The suits stand for life's expressions — mental, material, intuitive or emotional. Their true meanings are revealed by how they fall into the *Houses*." Her eyes softened.

"The *Houses*?"

"Yes, the Houses of *Eye* and *Wee*," she said, with a far-off look.

I worked hard to suppress a smile. "What are the 'Eye' and the 'Wee?'"

She studied me for a long time before answering. "The House of *I*, as in 'I am.' And the House of *We*, as in 'We are.'"

"Oh, I see! Sorry. Can you tell me more about the Houses of I and We?"

"The Houses of the I and We are where the numbers and suits come to life."

"I don't understand."

She shook her head, almost sadly. "No, you would not be able to understand unless a reading were done for you."

I slipped into the role of an interested student. "Is there a fixed set of rules? Can a person use them to make his own reading."

"There are rules but a person cannot make her own reading. The cards you draw will hold your future. But your future can be seen only through the prism of another person."

There would be no arguing with her on this. If I was going to learn any more about this gobbledygook, I would have to meet her halfway.

"I understand. People can't read their own futures, even when it's handwriting on the wall. They are blind to the parts they don't want to see. The fortune-teller is very intuitive and can pick up — well, you'd say 'read' — things that others can't see. Some fortune-tellers are better than others. And I guess that you can't have one reading after another because that would be like shopping around for the best deal. And I also guess that your future is best revealed only when you are really open to it."

Zelma smiled in encouragement. "You have had readings before."

"Once by a palm reader, a long time ago. She told me that I would become a successful academic."

"Lifelong fate can be read from a palm. But to read short-term fate, the cards are better."

"Yes, that stands to reason. The cards can change faster than the lines on your hand." I probably said it glibly, but the wine was rising to my head. I was enjoying the interplay with this mysterious woman. "Can you tell me more about your *system* for reading the cards."

Zelma inhaled deeply. Her jade necklace moved up on her black silk blouse. "It would be easier to show you."

It was the second time she'd said that.

"Okay," I said.

"But for it to have meaning, you will have to *wish* to see your future."

I laughed. "Please rest assured that I have a most *fervent* wish to see my future. The suspense about when the Bahamian constabulary is going to release the *Second Chance* is just killing me. And although I find this corner of the island utterly charming, we really want to move on and explore eastward. And although everyone in the marina is delightful, it is hard to ignore the fact that that guy 'Steve' was shot to death on his boat for some damn reason that I don't know and don't want to learn."

Zelma listened unresponsively through to my self-serving

proclamation, then shook her head at the end. "The cards will not tell who shot the man, and they will not predict the future of the boat. But they can tell about the forces around you."

"The forces? Great! I'd give anything to know about the forces around me."

Zelma shuffled the deck and handed it to me. "Pick, without looking at the bottom, fourteen cards from this deck. Lay them facedown, left to right."

I did what she said, paying some attention to withdrawing cards from different levels of the deck.

"Now, you have picked the cards that hold your future. I will interpret them through my prism."

One by one, left to right, she began picking them up and laying them face up on the desk. They were

3♠ A♣ K♠ 8♠ Joker 2♦ 6♠ 3♥ 2♠ 4♠ J♠ K♦ J♦

She kept the last card face down.

One thing was for sure: It was an improbable draw of cards. There were eight black cards and only four red cards. I did a quick-and-dirty statistical analysis, comparing the difference between eight and four with the square roots of those numbers. I estimated a one-in-seven chance of getting so many black cards. The cards seemed to be saying my luck was black.

Also, the distributions within the suits were also improbably skewed: seven spades versus one club, and three diamonds versus one heart. Also improbable was the joker. I had beaten one-to-four odds to pick up that clown.

I managed to suppress a quip that I was a joker and that my future was black.

With great solemnity, Zelma put the first card in the center. Slowly she built around it four rows of three. Each row went out in a separate direction, like the four directions of the compass.

Zelma offered no explanation until she was done. "The card in the center position speaks for your focus at this time. Each of the other cards has gone into a separate House, where it bears witness. We will start in the center, then go through the Twelve Houses."

"Okay."

She announced the cards softly and interpreted them with a farway voice. "The center card is the three of spades. This is a strong card. The three stands for communication and the spade stands for a lack of it."

'Okay," I said, without enthusiasm.

"Negative communication surrounds you." She said this matter-of-factly. "We will move on to the First House. The First House is the realm of your focus — the attitude you show to the world. It contains the ace of clubs which signifies power of intellect."

"Okay," I said, with some satisfaction.

"But keep in mind that the First House signifies only the *attitude* you show to the world."

"Okay," I said, with less satisfaction.

Zelma was making it impossible for me to interpret her eyes. When they were not looking at the cards, they looked past me with no apparent focus. She continued in a low, unmodulated voice.

"The Second House is the realm of your resources. In it is the king of spades. The king stands for authority. When combined with the spades, it stands for an encounter with authority."

"Okay. What does that say about my resources in my encounter with authority?"

"It usually means that they are inadequate."

"I see." My enthusiasm for this parlor game was dwindling.

Zelma continued as if in a trance. "The Third House is the realm of communication." She ignored my premature groan. "The eight of spades signifies a lack of fulfillment or a drain on resources."

"With respect to communication," I said, "is the drain inevitable, or is there something that I can do to stop it?"

"It is not inevitable. But it signals a need to look below the surface." She concluded with a sigh.

"I'm all for that! Do you have any suggestions?"

Zelma's eyes flared for an instant. "I can only interpret the cards through my prism. I cannot tell people exactly what they must change."

"Okay, I accept that. Now, what about the Fourth House? Is it full of bad luck, too?"

Her eyes sank to the cards but her voice rose with emphasis. "The Fourth House tells of your foundation — your sense of security and belonging — your home. A joker here indicates the presence of a *trickster*, here. The joker here is a warning to expect the unexpected."

Okay, I was ready for dirty tricks. I'd been ready for them since learning about Wade Daniel's poisonous fish fillets. I must have clenched my fists or have done something to blow off steam. Zelma waited, silently.

I looked to the next House. "Okay, what about the Fifth House? It has a two of diamonds."

"The Fifth House is the House of Risk. The two of diamonds says that you may find a profitable interaction or collaboration if you are willing to take risks for it." This time she lowered her voice. For the first time, she met my eyes. Now, she was sounding less like a distant oracle and more like an advisor.

I nodded in agreement. "Good. I'll keep looking for helpers and collaborators."

"The Sixth House is of mastery of life skills. The six of spades indicates stress and anxiety. Sometimes, it indicates the lack of skill to deal with certain situations."

I suppressed a groan and said nothing.

"The Seventh House is the House of We Consciousness. The three of hearts means you are very close to someone, that this person is helping you, and that there is a flow of positive energy between you."

"All right!"

"But the two of spades in the Eighth House says that this resource is being weakened."

"What's the name of the Eighth House?"

"The Power of We," she said.

"And what is the name of the Ninth House?" I asked, noting the four of spades in it.

"It is the House of Wisdom and Broadened Experience."

"And the four of spades probably means I don't have enough wisdom or experience," I said, with irritation.

"It means that there are problems with the foundation of your thinking and planning. Increased understanding and awareness are needed to keep your foundation from being undermined."

"I see. Well, what else do the cards advise to make up for this *deficit*?"

"Their advice would be to look for an ally. The diamond in the House of Risk says this strongly. The jack of spades in the House of Community Status, the Tenth House, delivers this message strongly. The jack is the card of intense friendship and life-changing encounter."

"But it is a jack of *spades*."

"Which means that gaining friendship will have certain risks. Such a tight constellation means that the cards are saying this strongly."

"And the king of diamonds in the Eleventh House?"

"It means an opportunity to take charge of groups and organizations."

Now the reading was looking better. "And what about the jack of diamonds in the Twelfth House?"

"It is especially significant because the jack indicates friendship and change. And it comes at the Seed Point for the future." Zelma noticed when I wrinkled my nose. "The Seed Point is of things to come — things that we are not aware of. The jack of diamonds suggests that a clarifying encounter with an unexpected ally may be in your future."

"Okay, I hear the cards speaking through your prism. I will keep looking for a friend or ally from an unexpected quarter."

Zelma responded to my comment with the tiniest of smiles. She turned over fourteenth card which had been lying on the table untouched and facedown. It was a five of spades. She placed it over the three of spades which lay in the center. She looked deeply into my face.

It occurred to me that I was becoming emotionally involved in this game. "Okay, my 'focus' went from a three of spades to five of spades. Does that mean I'm going to have any improvement in my communication skills?"

"No. The only signs on communication were from the other cards. The five of spades signifies a venture into the unknown." Her lips seemed fuller than before.

"Does it say whether the venture will be successful?"

"It says neither yes nor no. The signs for success depend on how well you handle the forces moving around you as revealed by the other cards."

Zelma's face seemed more relaxed, now. It felt like I was talking to a friend.

"What do you think was the strongest message from the cards?"

"The appearance of the joker is most troubling. He can be very destructive, especially close to home. After dealing with him, look out for the jacks. They may be able to neutralize the negative power of the spades." She made it sound like chess strategy.

Watch your back around "home" and look for an ally. That was Zelma's message.

I took a moment to think it over. It was good advice, but maybe only general advice. Did she know of specific dangers around the marina and was she reading them into the cards? If so, she was pretty good at making up her card-reading rules as she went along. But could she remember them?

"Zelma, could we go over your interpretation of the cards again?" She nodded.

I played all the reading back to her, naming the Houses and the significance of the cards. As a test, I put some minor mistakes into the interpretation. I misnamed some of the Houses and swapped meanings between a couple of numbered spades.

Zelma corrected every mistake I made. She always corrected me with a smile. If she was making things up as she went along, she was a wizard at remembering them. She smiled while I took a minute to think.

It was either a smart message delivered by a smart lady, or it was a dumb message delivered by a very improbable combination of cards. My belief in science and logic wouldn't allow any interpretations outside of these two "limiting cases." *Basta!* I certainly wasn't going to contaminate my brain with supernaturalism.

The wine glasses were empty, now. At the end of my thoughts and with nothing left to say, I felt drained. And with so few facts around me, I felt naked.

"Thanks for the reading, Zelma. You are a great prism for spiritual energy. I will be on the lookout for tricks from the joker and help from the jacks."

Zelma's facade had softened, now, and so had her eyes. I waited patiently to see if she had anything to add. She looked down and spoke with a full voice. "Yes, be on the lookout. The cards showed jacks in a strong constellation. They are your major asset for overcoming the forces of the spades. And although one of the jacks was a spade, it came down in an important House."

A question was burning in my throat but I couldn't ask it directly. "Should I look for the jacks near or far?"

"When in such a tight constellation, I feel that they must be near."

"Could my ally be really near? In this room?"

Zelma's eyes flashed and her lips tightened. "A reader of cards is the prism for seeing the cards. The reader is not one of the cards." In one swift movement, she raked the cards together and picked them up. "The reader cannot be a force behind the cards." With a quick snap, she shuffled the 14 cards into the deck. She slid the deck into a small velvet purse and pulled the draw string. She returned the wine bottle to the shelf. End of session.

"I understand. Thank you so much for the reading. You gave me many things to think about."

"You're welcome." She dropped both wine glasses into the wastebasket beside her desk.

I got up. "Sorry, Zelma, but I *do* need help. Beyond the reading, is there anything else you can tell me about my situation here?"

"No."

She regarded me with the same hard, jet-black eyes as in our first encounter. She held her face proud, like a statue carved from ironwood. I thanked her again and left.

Leaving the office in a state of heightened vigilance, I noticed that Cal and Angie Sumter's boat had returned. Could Angie and her cocaine-smuggling husband Cal be my allies? Or was that purveyor of Southern humor the joker — a trickster, just like his poisonous-fish-grilling buddy Wade?

Walking back to the *Diogenes*, I rapidly descended into low spirits thinking of Zelma's predictions — of my dwindling resources, of adversity and bad luck dealt out in spades, and of my conflict with authority. Luckily my thoughts returned to the joker at the right time — as I boarded the *Diogenes*.

While thumbing the combination wheels on the lock, I noticed that the tension in the hasp seemed different. On inspection, the sliding hatch was in a slightly different position than I usually left it. Yes, I had been the one to lock it, not Rebecca. I paused for a minute, wondering if Zelma's card reading had made me suspicious or if all of this could be just a coincidence.

It was just today at the airport that Rebecca had told me to sand down that sticking board. And now the hatch cover was giving me a warning. Questioning whether my mind was playing tricks on me, I shut my eyes and played back our departure. The playback returned a clear image of Rebecca standing impatiently on the dock while I put the teak boards into the companionway slots and locked the *Diogenes*. After that, we had gone directly to the van.

I shut my eyes again to retrieve kinesthetic memory of how I'd locked up the boat. No, I had not varied from my routine. No, I had not left the lock and hasp like this.

Someone had been aboard the *Diogenes*.

Open House 17

I turned on the interior lights and carefully searched the cabin. I found it behind the refrigerator — a Ziploc sandwich bag full of white powder, about 250 grams of it. Using a wetted finger, I sampled it. Sweet. Confectioner's sugar that they use for cutting cocaine. It didn't numb my lips, not even after a minute. It was not cocaine. But fishing around in the bag with a spoon, I found a smaller packet inside. It was made from a small piece of twisted stretch wrap and it contained about one gram of white powder. Using kitchen knives as forceps, I pulled it out and extracted a small sample. It tasted bitter and made my lips numb.

One gram of pure cocaine nested in one-quarter kilo of confectioner's sugar. The Joker had paid my house a visit and his purpose was clear:

"Yes, sir, we found a quarter kilogram of white powder behind the refrigerator of Defendant Benjamin Candidi's yacht. Yes, sir, we tested a portion of it, and it was cocaine."

And my blood boiled at the thought of those drug smugglers putting me in prison with one hundred dollars worth of cocaine. Or was it a low-budget operation carried out by Sgt. Townsend to deliver $200,000 worth of boat into the hands of a corrupt bureaucracy? These were the questions I stewed over while searching the boat for more planted evidence. I didn't find any.

Carefully, I put the package back together, bagged it and carried it down the dock to the soda machine outside the marina office where I laid in some quarters. The soda tasted good and did wonders for my dry mouth. For any unseen eyes, I made a big deal out of enjoying the soda. I strolled around the marina office until I was on the blind side where I couldn't be seen from the docks. I walked into the Australian pine woods until I was out of sight and jogged for a couple of minutes before searching for a rotting tree. I pulled out the incriminating sandwich bag and stuffed it in the rot hole. Then I retraced my steps on the pine needle strewn floor, eradicating one footprint and being careful to leave no more. I deposited the soda can in the trash can outside the marina office and went back to the *Diogenes*.

To be 100-percent sure, I spent the next couple of hours searching again every drawer, hold, nook and cranny on the boat. I didn't find anything else. Then I took a motorcycle ride up the road and found a pay phone near West End. Reaching my lawyer's answering machine, I dictated a two-minute description of planted cocaine and what I'd done about it, requesting that his secretary transcribe it.

Back on the *Diogenes*, I rewarded myself with a cold beer. Sitting in the cockpit, I thought a lot about spades and kings. And I scripted a plan for my upcoming encounter with the king of spades.

WHAT A BEAUTIFUL morning it would have been for a sponge survey! I stayed at the marina instead, sticking close to my boats. First, I located the little hexagonal rod that came with the locks and changed the combination on every one of them on the *Diogenes*. Then I went to the *Second Chance* and said a pleasant good morning to Ivanhoe, who had gone back to weaving crickets from his palm leaves. After changing the lock's combination, I gave the boat a thorough search, which I interrupted every once in a while to climb the tuna tower to make sure that nobody was anywhere near the *Diogenes*.

I struck up a conversation with Wade Daniels on the way back. I trusted that poison fish chef about half as far as I could throw him. However, Zelma's cards had told me that it was necessary to keep up communication.

"I took Rebecca to the airport, yesterday. She will be gone for a few days. You didn't see anyone looking for me around my boat yesterday, did you?"

"No, it's been real quiet around here."

"What about Constable Ivanhoe over there?"

"He's kept pretty much to himself."

I thanked Wade and said I had to get back to the *Diogenes*. On the way back I noticed Chuck lounging on the fighting chair on the back of his boat. I asked him the same questions I'd asked Wade and got the same answers. Funny how neither of us mentioned his friend Bill. I trusted Chuck about as far as I could throw him in his fighting chair.

Back on the *Diogenes*, I sat in the cockpit reading the *Scientific American* and keeping an eye on the comings and goings around the marina. Around one o'clock in the afternoon, Angie Sumter came over, saying that she wanted to talk with Rebecca. She seemed just as happy to talk to me. We hadn't gotten very far along with the conversation when two visitors came. It was good to have Angie there, standing on the dock. She would be useful to have as a witness — along with the hand-held tape recorder that I had just turned on.

Sgt. Townsend was dressed in his salt-and-pepper uniform and wearing sunglasses. The other sergeant was dressed similarly, but didn't wear shades. I was very disappointed to see Sgt. Townsend coming on this mission, even if he wasn't leading the way. We had a deal and now he was breaking it, in spirit at least. But I couldn't complain about his breaking our deal in front of Angie. She stepped back as the pair approached, but she quickly noticed my raised finger and correctly interpreted it as a signal to please stay. That woman is a social genius.

The new sergeant walked to a spot on my dock where he could look down on me. "Are you Mister Benjamin Candidi?"

No reason to make a big deal about my academic title. "Yes, I'm Ben Candidi."

"And is Miss Rebecca Levis living on board this vessel."

"No, *Doctor* Levis is in Miami. And who are you?"

He pointed to his badge and said, "Detective Sergeant Gregory Toomey." He took a step toward the edge, ready to step down.

I rose to my feet, showed him two flattened palms and shouted, "Permission to come aboard is denied." He was skinny enough for me to throw him overboard.

"I have come to conduct a search of your vessel."

"Do you have a warrant?"

"No, but we can take you to the station while I get one."

I grabbed the tape recorder from the bench and held it up to him. "When you come marching up to a guy and interrupt his dictation, it's your own fault when our oral threats get recorded on tape. I invite you to state a formal reason for searching my vessel. And I *demand* that you turn your pockets inside out before coming aboard."

Sgt. Townsend didn't react to my statement, but Sgt. Toomey's chin began to quiver with indignation. "I am an officer of the Royal Bahamas Police Force, Drug Enforcement Unit, Freeport."

"And I trust you about as far as I can throw you — which I hope won't be necessary. Anyone who comes aboard my vessel has to convince me and my witness that he isn't carrying any throw-down narcotics."

I punctuated the statement with a glance to Angie who was watching with interest from the base of my dock. She didn't seem upset to be named a witness.

Sgt. Townsend nudged his colleague. "Do it so you can get on with it," he said, as if discussing latrine duty.

The Freeport sergeant shot the West End sergeant a look of disgust. Then he turned his pockets inside out to reveal a wrinkled handkerchief, keys, pocket change and a compact mirror. I snickered and held out my hand to receive the compact for inspection. He opened it to show that it contained no powder.

"You carrying a wallet? Please open it up so I can confirm that there are no suspicious packets."

Sgt. Toomey didn't like me talking to him in cop language, but he did what I said.

"Okay, you have had your fun. Now we are going aboard," he said.

Toomey took a step forward, and so did I.

"I disagree with your grammar. Only you will come aboard. Sergeant Townsend obviously does not intend to come aboard or he would have submitted to inspection. And you will not receive permission to come aboard until you kick off those leather-soled shoes."

Sgt. Townsend gave me a bemused look and stayed put on the dock. This surprised Sgt. Toomey, who took off his shoes, grudgingly.

"And turn down the tops of your socks."

Sgt. Toomey ignored this, stepped aboard, and made his way around me.

I called after him, "And if I see you reaching into your pants or if you come back with your shirt untucked, your search is invalidated."

Sgt. Toomey did his best to ignore that while making his way to the cabin. I watched him carefully from the cockpit. And Sgt. Townsend watched me from the dock, with veiled curiosity. And Angie watched us all like it was a soap opera working toward a climax. Martha Vangelden would have made a better witness, but this seemed to be the morning that she and Ray chose to stay buttoned up in their trawler.

First, Sgt. Toomey took a cursory look in several places around the cabin. Then he took out his compact and twiddled around with it in the shadows behind the refrigerator. "Ah!" he exclaimed for my benefit. Then he reached in around the coils. But he didn't find anything to grab.

I laughed and said, "Yeah, I'd say 'ah,' too. Those coils get hot when the refrigerator's going."

Sgt. Toomey groped all the harder.

"And the coils have sharp edges. Careful you don't scratch yourself."

He leaned a few inches more over the refrigerator. I grabbed a flashlight from the side compartment and shined it down on him. "Here, maybe this will help you find whatever you're looking for."

Sgt. Toomey grunted curses under his breath.

"I mean, it just has to be there," I added. "Right? Here, take my flashlight." I set it next to him.

Sgt. Townsend was hanging 10 at the edge of the dock. It was time for me to ask him a question. "Say, Sergeant Townsend, while your colleague is breathlessly groping around my yacht, looking for narcotics, maybe you could tell me how he got the complaint in the first place."

Sgt. Townsend took off his sunglasses and looked me in the eye, earnestly. "I do not know, mate. The action came from the Drug Enforcement Unit, not Homicide and Special Crimes."

"Then why did you come along for the bust?"

"I was asked to."

Sgt. Townsend put his sunglasses back on. "Gregory," he yelled. "I think you have spent enough time searching Dr. Candidi's yacht."

Sgt. Toomey appeared in the companionway and climbed the steps to the cockpit. The stretching and reaching must have been considerable exertion for him because he had broken into a sweat. Without thanking me or meeting my eye, he handed back the flashlight and stepped onto the dock.

"Thanks for the flashlight?" I boomed it out for Angie to hear. "No, think nothing of it, Sergeant. Now, for your official report? Did you find any narcotics or illicit substances?"

"No," he said under his breath.

"Please speak up, Sergeant, so my witness can hear."

"The search didn't find anything."

"Thank you. Now could you tell me who gave you false information that I had illicit substances on board."

"I am not required to tell you."

Now, Sgt. Townsend was looking almost as uncomfortable as Sgt. Toomey.

"Very well," I said to Toomey. "But you have written this person's name and statement down and will keep it on file so that my lawyer can subpoena it, if that becomes necessary."

Sgt. Toomey turned away, muttering to himself.

Sgt. Townsend didn't move. "And why would that be necessary?"

"Because the person who told the Good Sergeant there were illegal substances on board was also the one who planted it."

As if to escape my words, Sgt. Toomey walked away. But Sgt. Townsend stood his ground. "What are you saying?"

"I'm going to make a short statement that I want you to note. Someone thought he was going to blow me off by stuffing a one hundred dollar packet of cocaine in a sandwich bag full of sugar and planting on my boat in the exact spot where the good sergeant came searching. I don't know who did this or why. But if it was done to frustrate my salvage claim on the *Second Chance*, I'm telling you that getting rid of me won't get rid of the claim because Doctor Levis is a co-claimant. And the Royal Bahamas Police Force isn't going to bust her because she is in Miami, now."

Sgt. Townsend started to say something, then took a deep breath. He looked at my tape recorder and to Angie, then said nothing. He turned on his heel and walked off to catch up with Sgt. Toomey. I let both of them get halfway to the marina office before speaking to Angie, who was still watching in awe.

"Thanks, girl. You were a big help, keeping them honest."

"They searched your boat for drugs?" She was wide-eyed and sounded like a 12-year-old girl.

"Yes, and they thought they were going to haul me off to jail."

Angie nodded like she was convinced of that. "And they didn't find anything?"

"Correct. Someone planted an incriminating package on my boat yesterday. I discovered it last night when I came home. I got rid of it. And you heard the rest. Did you see anyone around my boat yesterday?"

"No, Ben. But we didn't get back till late yesterday afternoon. But I will keep an eye on your boat, now. Boy, that was something how you handled them. You're just like . . . I mean you really know how to handle yourself. And you really told them where to go."

Anxious to know what the detectives would do next, I ambled with Angie in their direction, as far as the marina office. They drove off in separate jeeps. I left Angie and returned to the *Diogenes* where

I grabbed my cellphone and placed what was intended to be a friendly call to Zelma.

"Zelma, this is Ben."

"Good morning." She sounded more formal than ever.

"Thanks again for the reading."

Zelma took her time answering. "You are welcome. I see that you received a visit."

"Yes, from the king of spades in the Second House. Luckily I didn't lose any resources." I gave her a long time to reply in kind, which she didn't. "It happened because the Joker was in the Fourth House — my house, yesterday while I was gone."

During the long time I gave her to respond, she remained absolutely silent. It was impossible to push any harder on this without knowing how much of last night's message had come from the lay of the cards and how much had come from her "prism." And if the message had a product of her mind, there was no way of knowing whether she was working with hard information or intuitive impressions. In any case, there was no way for me to force answers from her.

I continued in friendly tone. "What I really need to say involves our landlord-tenant relationship. Please be informed that cocaine was planted on my boat yesterday and that the police came to find it and arrest me today. But they couldn't find anything because I'd already gotten rid of it. Whoever planted it, did it with a knowledge of the combination on my lock. We didn't give anybody the combination. Whoever got the lock combination did it by sneaking behind our backs."

Again, Zelma took a long time to respond. "All I can suggest is to change the combination."

"I've done that. And I want to tell you as marina manager that from now on we don't want *anybody* on our boat."

"Very well. We will keep an eye on your boat. But the marina cannot bear *responsibility* for it."

My next call was to Rebecca. It had to be private, and I was afraid that a cellphone call might be intercepted, especially if Batelco was still working on the old analog system. I hopped on my motorcycle and headed up the road for the pay phone at the edge of West End.

It took three calls to the pathologically decentralized Bryan Medical School to get Prof. David Thompson's number. But when I finally reached him, he proved glad to put Rebecca on.

"Rebecca, how are you doing? Can you talk?"

"Yes, Ben! Professor Thompson's a great guy and we have all kinds of common interests! My fellowship proposal will be built on one of his existing programs, so I won't have to write the grant from the ground up. I should be done by Friday. We'll be using a lot of his language and his citations of scientific literature. The things that I picked up during my fellowship at George Washington University will fit right in. And some of Professor Thompson's work is with the Yanomama Indians! Their health status is — well, you remember our talks about the recent controversies."

"You're in heaven!"

"Yes, actually!"

I was so glad for her.

"And how are you?" she asked.

"I'm fine but the situation isn't. But I don't want to bum you out and sap inspiration you need for your grant proposal."

"Are you calling by cellphone?" Her voice darkened.

"No, I'm at a phone booth, far from the madding crowd. It should be secure."

"Then tell me what happened."

I told her about the warning implied in Zelma's card reading, the change in the position of the hatch, and about the planted cocaine and what I did with it. And I told her about the visit from the two sergeants, going into considerable detail but playing down the macho aspects of the confrontation and Angie's wide-eyed enthusiasm.

"Do you think the police planted it?"

"No, they would have looked too out of place going on the boat, yesterday."

"What about Ivanhoe?"

"Yes, he could have planted it — if someone had given him the combination to the lock. That's what I wanted to talk to you about — who could have come by and read the combination off our locks when they were open. Wade Daniels might have, the first time he came aboard the *Second Chance*. But after that, I erased the combination right after opening it. I did it every time, religiously. So Ivanhoe and Martin and Beth couldn't have gotten our number from the *Second Chance*. Did any of them come aboard the *Diogenes*?"

"No, none of them did. Wade didn't come aboard when he invited me to the fish fry. But do you remember when he helped you lift the outboard from the hold. The padlock was dangling on the hasp right in front of him when he came on board for that. He had a good chance to see the combination."

"Right." I must have said it with a groan.

"We can't blame ourselves. We just didn't think to erase the combination when we were aboard our own boat. Around hospitals, we're thinking about it all the time. That's why hospital combination locks are the kind with buttons that don't show the combination after they've been opened."

"Yes, a hospital can be a hostile environment. Can you think of anyone else who could have sneaked aboard the *Diogenes* to read our combination when we were around but not looking?"

"The only people close enough for that were that poor sailing couple that got busted — and that other couple, Chuck and Bill."

"Yes, one of them might have climbed down from their jungle gym."

Our shared a laugh was all too brief.

"Did you hear anything about Bill?"

"Chuck's still here at the marina, Bill hasn't returned, and nobody's talking about what happened to him."

"Convalescence for ciguatera can take a long time. So, Ben, what's the bottom line?"

"The suspects for stealing our combination are Wade, Chuck and Bill. And the suspects for planting the cocaine are anyone connected with them. This includes Wade, Cal, Angie, Chuck, Martin and Beth, Rick Turner and all the dock hands and people who hang around here. And if we want to entertain ideas of police conspiracy, we can include Ivanhoe."

"I'm wondering if it isn't a SAWECUSS conspiracy. That fits with Angie coming to watch the bust."

"Yes, except I got the feeling she was on my side. And she seemed surprised when the cops came. I don't think she's enough of an actress to manufacture so much surprise."

"Oh, she's an actress all right."

"She hams it up when things go along with her feelings. But I don't think she can play a part that goes against her feelings. She's too self-centered."

"Maybe Cal told her you were going to be busted," Rebecca said. "Maybe she came along, hoping against hope that it wouldn't happen."

"Yes, it could have been something like that. Cal might keep a few things from Angie, and Angie probably keeps quite a few things from Cal."

"Yes, like accusing you of informing on Glen and Stephanie."

"Yes, I don't think that Cal would have approved of Angie accusing me directly."

"Do you think that SAWECUSS wanted you arrested to see if you were a DEA informant?"

"Yes. If I were with the DEA, the cops would let me off the hook and SAWECUSS would know to worry about me. If I weren't an informant, I would go to jail and SAWECUSS wouldn't worry about me, anyway."

"Or maybe you were framed because of your claim to the *Second Chance*."

"Yes, maybe one of our suspects is helping the S.C. Corporation to get the yacht back for free. Or maybe our suspects are aiding a coven of corrupt Bahamian officials who want the boat and are using the police to get it. The trouble is, we have so many hypotheses and no way to test them."

"What are you going to do?"

"I'll call up Sir Hector and force his hand. And around here, I'll act righteously indignant. Let everybody know that by the grace of God, I discovered the plant and foiled the bust. Tell everyone I'm a live-and-let-live kind of guy, except that I'm not giving up the *Second Chance* until I get paid for it. And tell everybody that as soon as I get things straightened out here, we're moving the *Diogenes* and the sponge survey eastward."

"If things work out, where are we going with the survey?"

"To Sale Cay with the *Diogenes*. But first I need to finish a wide swath of flats on the north side of the island." I told her about the rented motorcycle.

"But promise me you're not going to do anything major until I get back."

"I promise. I'm going to sit tight on the *Diogenes* and the *Second Chance* to keep those people from pulling another fast one."

"You shouldn't have to sit tight too long. I should be back by Saturday. Then there'll be two of us. If you can't get control of the *Second Chance*, I'll help you abscond with it again. We'll start earlier, next time."

"Great. And we'll leave for Florida with both boats, this time. I can always fly back and rent a small boat out of Freeport to complete the survey. We've got to get out from under these people at West End."

"Like 'Out of sight, out of mind?'"

"Yes."

We said "I love you" a lot of times before deciding to hang up. Then I remembered to ask Rebecca to get me a new cylinder head if she had time. She agreed and took down the information. We finished with another round of "I love you."

I motorcycled into West End and bought two six packs of beer from a family who sold supplies from their living room. Back at the marina, I strolled around the docks with the six packs under my arm as an unspoken explanation for my motorcycle trip. Wade Daniels, sitting in his cockpit, lost no time in asking for my version of the story. I told it to him with special vehemence:

To think about it, if that pot lid hadn't fallen behind the refrigerator, I wouldn't have found the packet and I would be in a Bahamian jail right now.

Of course, I said nothing about the combination lock.

Wade listened with owlish patience and made comforting grunts every once in a while.

Finally I set my eyes on him and asked, "Who the hell would do that kind of thing, Wade?"

Wade shook his big head like a guy who'd seen it all and wasn't surprised by anything. "My guess is that it's the bad guys who are behind the boat. They probably don't mind losing it to the sea as much as they mind having someone making money off of them. They probably want to get rid of you so they can come in and snatch it some time."

I thanked Wade again and went over to thank Angie. She was home and so was Cal — she in the cockpit and Cal in the main cabin, behind an open door. From the dock, I thanked her again for her support. She accepted it graciously, but with less enthusiasm than before. From the doorway, Cal said that it makes his blood boil when people do things like that. It wasn't a long conversation.

Back on the *Diogenes*, I sat down with pen and paper and drafted a script for my conversation with Sir Hector. I decided to call him on my cellphone. If our conversation was intercepted by the bad guys, so much the better.

At first, chauffeur-cook-butler Kevin said he'd have to check to see if Sir Hector was available. I quickly answered that it was a timely matter of great importance. Maybe Sir Hector wanted to script his end of the conversation, too, because he took five whole minutes to come to the phone.

He answered cordially. "Doctor Candidi! How are you? I trust that you are doing well on all fronts."

"No, I'm sorry to say that I'm not. And that's the reason for my call."

"I can understand your impatience to speed up the release of the yacht you salvaged but . . ."

"Then let's talk about my new problem. This morning, I received a visit from a Sergeant Toomey of the Drug Enforcement Unit, Freeport. He brought along our local Sergeant Townsend. They demanded to search my boat for illegal substances."

Sir Hector went into magisterial mode. "Doctor Candidi, cocaine smuggling is a persistent problem in our islands, and the only way to combat it is through frequent, routine inspections. I would hope you would not take this personally. And it would be wrong to use our connection to complain about a harmless, routine inspection."

"It wasn't routine. Sergeant Toomey came in and started looking in a specific place."

"I do not know what you mean by that. Any place is *specific*."

"He went to a *specific* place and was upset when he didn't find anything there."

"That could just be a matter of your interpretation." His voice sharpened, with high inflection.

"No, because the day before, someone planted a packet of cocaine in the same specific place. I learned that after searching my yacht. And I searched my yacht when I noticed that it had been secretly entered."

"I see." Sir Hector offered nothing more.

"Planting cocaine on my vessel and then sending in the police for a bust is harassment."

"I hope that you are not implying that our police planted cocaine aboard your vessel."

"I can't rule it out. Sergeant Toomey wouldn't tell me what prompted him to demand to search my boat. When I asked if it was a tipster and demanded to know the person's name, he said he wasn't required to tell me."

"Please forgive my unfamiliarity with police procedure, but perhaps he was not, indeed, required to tell you."

"But he would be required to investigate the tipster, which he has tacitly refused to do."

"But perhaps there would be some alternative explanation."

"Yes. The *alternative* to there being no tipster is that the police cooked up the whole thing themselves. I have already suffered harassment from Sergeant Townsend. He is holding my salvaged yacht without justification."

"What do you expect me to do?"

"Just tell whoever is in charge of the police on this island to release jurisdiction of the *Second Chance*. And tell him to have Sergeant Toomey and his ilk stay away from me."

"I am, myself, becoming impatient with the matter of the yacht. I will look into it and see what I can do. But I can make no promises."

Now, to get something that would make me unstoppable on Saturday:

"Perhaps you could agree that if the police do not respond to you by Friday evening, our present conversation will become a *supersedeas* over previously expressed police prerogatives."

"Well . . . yes . . . I suppose."

"Thanks. I'll take that as affirmative. Thank you very much."

After hanging up, I went below and recorded in the *Diogenes'* log a transcript of my conversation with Sir Hector, paying special attention to accurate transcription of my *supersedeas* language, to which he had just agreed. Hell, of course his tacit agreement with me must *supersede* — replace or force out — a half-baked opinion of a police sergeant this coming Friday. Hell, Sir Hector was a Member of Parliament!

To celebrate my paper victory, I treated myself to a beer — two beers, actually.

I locked the *Diogenes* and went to visit the *Second Chance*. On the way, I crossed paths with Jay Sherman, the new guy at the marina. His greeting in passing was an incongruous mixture of smiles and nonverbal protestations that seemed to say, "Have to hurry, I'm late." That seemed to be true. He hurried to his car — a black Ford Focus rental — and drove off.

I waved hello to Ivanhoe and checked out the *Second Chance* to make sure it hadn't synthesized cocaine in the last few hours. And since the *Rapture of the Reef* was back in its berth and Martin and Beth seemed to be aboard, I spent some time puttering around, hoping to engage them in conversation. But my only conversation was with the water-damaged radio which gave off a static signal every once in a while. Neither Martin nor Beth appeared topside while I was there.

And, as hard as I tried, I couldn't think up a pretext to hail them and tell my story. Actually, I had the feeling that they were the ones who most wanted me gone.

18   The Eleventh Day

Sleeping late is no sin when you have nothing to look forward to. A cellphone call woke me up.

"Dr. Candidi, this is Dan Lynch. I got your message and transcribed it as you requested."

"Thanks," I yawned.

"And I have some excellent news."

"Thanks, Dan. My phone's acting up. I'll call you back. Don't call me."

And in very few seconds I had locked down the *Diogenes* and was approaching the restrooms like I was having reactive bladder problems. I spent 30 seconds acting out the ruse in the men's room. And 30 seconds later I was on the motorcycle traveling at 30 miles per hour toward the roadside pay phone. And several minutes later, I was pulling up to it like a cowboy.

"Sorry, Dan, but I couldn't take any *excellent news* on the cellphone. Can't take a chance of the conversation being intercepted. I'm on a land line now. We can talk freely."

"We've received an offer of fifty thousand dollars for a quitclaim on the salvage."

"Great! Who's it from?"

"The offer was tendered by Jackson and Reichart — a prestigious Miami law firm. They take care of a lot of money from up north. They also do a lot of corporate shell and off-shore work."

"Did they tell you the name of their client?"

"No, but it would be on behalf of the S.C. Corporation."

Dan Lynch read me the complete text of the agreement. It was very short and simple. I would be paid for dropping my salvage claim, and I would have no responsibilities. That was it, except for a blank, which was to be filled in with my bank account number.

"So I will never learn who wants to give me the money."

"No, only if they would ask you to sign another salvage affidavit at a later date."

"Understood."

"So what do you think, Ben?"

"I like it. But first I want to try a counter-offer of sixty thousand. I want you to handle the negotiation. Call them up and tell them that I have spent a lot of money on the salvage and for making the salvage claim, itself. If they try to probe you on that, act like there is a whole lot but that it would be onerous and counterproductive for you to go into the specifics. If they feel like they aren't getting their extra ten thousand dollars worth, tell them that we can add language to the agreement specifying that I will hold confidential all information about the yacht and the results of all inquiries that I have made."

Dan Lynch agreed to that. I gave him my account number. I authorized him to say yes to $60,000. Told him if it was a yes, he should make sure the money was received in escrow right away. Once it was received, his secretary should call me on my cellphone, and I would return his call by land line.

I took a couple of minutes to give Dan full details of the attempted cocaine bust that took place the previous morning. He told me that the call from the other law firm came late that afternoon.

After hanging up, I did two things: First, I let out a big whoop. Second, I called Rebecca with the good news. "Ben, that's great. What are you going to do if they refuse your counter-offer?"

"I'll accept the fifty thousand. We're going to take the money and run."

"I agree. Why do you think they caved in?"

"Because I toughed it out and convinced them that I could make more than fifty thousand dollars worth of trouble."

"Do *they* include Sir Hector?"

"Could be. They caved in not long after I read Sir Hector the riot act."

"What are your plans?"

"To keep my head low until my lawyer gets the money."

"Good. Just wait for the papers and stay out of trouble. We're mostly done with the grant proposal. Maybe I could come back a day early. What are you going to do after the deal is done?"

"Prepare to get us out of Dodge City so we never have to come back. I'll give up the motorcycle, and we can survey the north side with the Caribe. It will be fine once I get the new cylinder head. In the mean time, I'll take the Caribe around the tip of the island to survey the south side over to Eight Mile Rock. There's different flow and maybe even different water quality on the south side, so I should really survey it for Broadmoore."

After we exchanged our love and kisses and hung up, I let out another tremendous whoop. And I did a lot of hopping and skipping around. Boy, it was great to get the weight of this thing off my shoulders. Riding back to the marina, I worked on suppressing my joy. It might be dangerous to let it show before the money was in the bank.

As I was chaining the motorcycle to the tree by the showers, Rick Turner came out and caught me with a wry smile. "You get up in the morning and have yourself a little motorcycle ride?" He said it half as a joke and half as a query.

I returned the smile and used it to gain time. What should I say to a guy who was out on the water the night "Steve" was killed?

"Sure. I'm paying extra for a dirt bike. That entitles me to kick the shit out of it every morning. Boy, you should have seen those Australian pine needles flying! Did you hear me out there?"

Rick was walking along beside me, his blue jeans swishing. "No. You had breakfast yet?"

"You offering me some?"

"No, I was goin' to offer you a beer. But I didn't want to do that if you haven't had breakfast yet." He turned to examine me more closely. "You're looking pretty scratchy this morning."

"Rebecca's back in Miami for a while so there's no reason to shave. And I drink beer any time I want to."

I tagged along behind him to the central dock and past Wade Daniels' cabin cruiser. Rick Turner's sport fisherman yacht was in the next slip on the right. He jumped aboard and went into the cabin. I followed him in. "Only one stipulation on the beer," I said.

"What's that?"

"The stipulation is that *I'll* be the one who grabs it out of the refrigerator. Also, I'll drink the beer outside."

Rick laughed, then made a gesture that said to reach in and do my own grabbing. I pulled out two cans of Budweiser and handed him one. As we moved back to the cockpit, his face settled into a frown.

"And why are you stipulating all that?" he asked.

I saluted him with my can. "Because I've been getting paranoid, recently. Did you hear about how somebody planted cocaine on my boat and then called the cops on me?"

"Yeah, Wade told me," he said, offhandedly without a lot of sympathy. He parked his butt on the starboard rail.

"Did you see anybody messing around my boat the day before yesterday?"

"No, I didn't or I woulda come told you," he said.

"Because if I ever find out who that bastard is, I'm going to beat the living you-know-what out of him. Say, maybe it would be better if we sat up on your flybridge. I could keep a better eye on things."

"Sure, we could perch on top of the tuna tower if you want to," he said with a grin.

The flybridge was good enough for me. I sat in the first mate's chair. Apparently, the captain's chair was too close for comfort because Rick sat on the rim of the flybridge, a couple of feet farther away. The flybridge afforded an excellent view of the *Second Chance*. And in the other direction, there was even a damn good view of the *Diogenes*. I wiped off the top of my Bud with my slept-in T-shirt and popped the tab.

Rick already had his open, and he had drunk it down quite a ways. He leaned back and said, "I hear that when they came to search your boat, you really kicked ass." He ended the statement with high enthusiasm.

"Who told you about that?"

"Angie told me. She said you put them through the wringer, making up a lot of legal crap."

"I made up a lot of bureaucratic crap, too. You can learn a lot of that working at the patent office."

Rick leaned forward and waved a hand like he was throwing me a towel. "Hell, from the looks of them when they pulled out of here, you *really* kicked butt. They walked out of here like a couple of hangdogs."

I slapped the back of the captain's chair. "Well, if you want to see me kick someone's large intestine up into his throat, you just tell me who it was that planted that cocaine on my boat."

Rick reached through the side of his cut-away T-shirt and scratched an armpit. "Yeah, that was pretty mean, huh? Well, I wouldn't worry about anybody doing that again. Well not anybody around here. Everyone knows that you're a stand-up kind of guy."

— Which sounded to me like SAWECUSS wouldn't do it again

because everyone in SAWECUSS knows that I'm a stand-up kind of guy.

"Thanks, Rick. Maybe that sorry excuse for a police sergeant will learn that, too, and will take down his police notices so I can take the *Second Chance* to Miami and get my money for it."

Rick stared down on me for a couple of seconds. "Look, Ben, you've just got to stop partying so late and start getting up earlier. If youda driven that boat outa here at five in the morning, you wouldnta had any trouble with that conch coon in the blue jumpsuit."

"Yeah, that's what Wade was telling me, too. Say! Talking about partying, how'd you do at the reggae bar the other night, after we left? Did you get any?"

Rick's eyes rolled into his forehead. He shook his head. "Those damn college girls are more interested in trying to talk French than going fishing."

"Yeah, but guys can be a lot less intimidating when they go hunting in pairs. When's your partner going to show up, anyway?"

"The guys say they're going to fly over but then they always crap out with some damn excuse at the last minute."

It was time to mix it up a little. "Say, that guy with the Cigarette boat is a real chick magnet. Did you see the girls he had at his table the other night?"

Rick almost popped a vein in his forehead. "What t' hell you talking about, Ben? He didn't pick them up. He *brought* them there. That frigging Reggie! Someone ought to do something about him. He's the most obnoxious guy on this side of the island."

"Well, what else does he do that's obnoxious besides bringing his own chicks and making fancy moves with his Cigarette boat in the marina?"

Rick's brows narrowed. "That spoiled brat's messing up the place."

I gave Rick a look that asked for further explanation.

Rick shook his head like we were talking about a bad wiring job. "Him and his frog friend and their plans to tear down the whole place an make some kinda Club Med, Mondo Condo, Eurotrash haven outa it. Hell, the marina will get so expensive that an ordinary guy won't be able to stay here no more."

"Is that what's going to happen?"

"That's what they say's gonna happen."

I wanted to pursue this further, but another opportunity presented itself. Jay Sherman stepped off his boat. I waved to him, but he was too far away to see us. His boat was tied up at the far end of the western dock, almost at the fuel dock.

"What do you know about *that* guy, Rick?"

"He's an asshole." Rick said it with disappointment.

"But he's always seemed friendly to me. Always waves when he walks by."

"Okay, then he's an asshole trying to look friendly."

"You might have something there, Rick. He always seems to be in too big a hurry to stop and talk."

"That figures."

Rick grew thoughtful after that exchange. It would have been a mistake to ask him to explain his last comment. He had been telling me so many things without knowing it.

Sensing that Rick was dying on me, I threw out something to liven him up. "I hear that this Reggie is upper class and has lots of political connections. But that's hard to believe because he doesn't seem to be getting a lot of respect around the marina."

Rick shook his head and smirked. "Well, those frog fashion people think he's hot stuff."

"Yeah, but that doesn't mean anything, Rick. Someone told me that the *frogs* think that Jerry Lewis is hot stuff."

We laughed long and hard on that one. But then Rick seemed to snap out of it, all at once. For a second his light-green irises dilated. Then he locked eyes with me. "Hey, Ben, are you shitting me?"

"Shitting you? What? What are you talking about?"

Bleached eyebrows knotted into a penetrating frown. Rick brought both feet on the deck and leaned forward.

"You *know* that Reggie is Sir Hector Pimentel's son." His pitch went high and whiny. "And you've been to Sir Hector's house. Kev— uh, the old man's chauffeur picked you up and took you there for dinner."

"Oh! Was that the one whose picture we saw on the *mantle*? Yes, of course." I laid in a pause, hoping that Rick would lean back again. He didn't. I frowned back at him. "Well, I hate to disappoint you, Rick, but the old man didn't want to talk about his son at all. It seemed almost as painful a subject as his dead wife. And the punk sure as hell doesn't live there, either. Where does he live, anyway? You got any idea?"

Rick straightened up, took a sip, and didn't say anything for a while. As he sat balanced on the rail, he seemed to dissolve in thought. He looked over the side.

"We were all wondering at how you two got invited to dinner."

"Are you telling me," I asked jokingly, "that Rebecca and I aren't classy enough for Sir Hector?"

"No," he said earnestly, "but it happened so all of a sudden."

"Listen pal, it happened right after I got the *sponge survey job*. The old Brit who's running the company I'm contracting for was friends with Sir Hector at Cambridge University . . . back in England. When the Brit told Sir Hector I was here and working for him, Sir Hector invited me to dinner. He wanted to pump me about how much money sponge harvesting would make for his country. Nice dinner, but otherwise a big disappointment. Sir Hector hasn't helped a bit to get that piss-poor excuse for a police sergeant off my back."

"Maybe the old fart's losing it," Rick said. "Want another beer?"

On an empty stomach, that was the last thing I wanted. "Sure, just as long as you bring it up here unopened. Bud regular, not Light."

"Still paranoid, huh?"

"Sorry to say. I'm not going to breathe an easy breath until we move out to Mangrove Cay. Then we're moving to Sale Cay and beyond. There's just too much crap going on here that I don't want to get involved in."

While Rick was down in the cabin, I took a good look at the *Second Chance*. It was easy to see down on the cockpit but I couldn't see in through the window. That was good. And beyond the *Second Chance*, Ivanhoe was guarding the boat from his hammock. Rick reappeared with his engineer's cap on and with two types of Bud, both unopened. I chose the regular and wiped it's top with my shirt, again, before clicking the tab. In salutation I said, "Here's polishing the top in front of you, kid."

"Yeah, here's looking at you," Rick said with a grin.

We chugged down a good quantity and burped together.

"And you were over at Sir Hector's house for dinner. What's the place like?"

"Set up like an English country house. Real out of place in the Bahama sun. He's trying to be more English than the English, talking about cricket and pigeon hunting. He's got shotguns and a trap shooting setup in his backyard patio, if you can call it that. Actually, there's lots of room behind the house — he has no neighbors — with a dock for shallow-draft boats."

Rick sneaked a sideways glance at me. "Yeah, I hear that's where the private seaplane docks, when it flies him around."

"Yeah, but it wasn't there when I visited. I once saw it coming down for a landing near his place," I said.

"Wouldn't you like to own a seaplane?" Rick said, wistfully.

"It's not Sir Hector's. He told me that he just gets rides on it."

"No, he's probably just saying that so it doesn't look like he's too rich. The man's loaded."

"But I've seen that seaplane landing at another place around here."

Under the hat brim, light-blond eyebrows went high. "Where?"

"It was several miles east of Sir Hector's. No, there was no chance it was landing at Sir Hector's. It was landing at the end of Mulberry Lane. I noticed it when I was coming back from dropping Rebecca off at Freeport. It was two nights ago. I remember it well because it was the next morning when the police tried to bust me."

Rick drew a bead on me with his hat brim. "You're pretty sure it was the same plane as Sir Hector's?"

"Sure. Looking at planes is my hobby. Especially the amphibious ones. I've always loved to see those Grumman Mallards take off and land on Government Cut in Miami."

"The seaplane was landing at the end of Mulberry Lane?"

"Yes. On the Little Bahama Bank side. It was before sundown. I was coming back from Freeport on the motorcycle. You know that I'm going to use it to pre-position gasoline tanks so I don't have to go back and forth so much with the inflatable."

"Okay. And you're sure it was landing."

"Of course. I can tell when a plane is landing."

I laid in a pause and did a weak parody of Rick's "are you shitting me?" stare. Then I went argumentative:

"I was on Kings Highway. The plane was flying northward, going down at a steep angle. The motor went into low revs after I lost it in the trees. And then I didn't hear it. And then, quite a few minutes later, I hear it coming at me. And this time it was at high revs and climbing. Now don't you think that means that it landed north of there?"

"Yeah, it sure does."

I quickly changed the subject to my sponge survey, explaining how I had to go over the side to identify them and count them, and telling him how I had to lay down grids and search the whole Bank. "You know, Rick, one of those Waverunners would be the perfect way to get around on my survey because they go so fast. But when I talked to Harry Pearce about renting one on a weekly basis, he turned me down flat."

Rick dug his fingers into his forearm and scratched hard. "That damn Harry's a worthless piece of shit."

"Yeah, I'll say. And it seems that everybody I talk to has a grudge against him. What's yours?"

"That worthless piece of shit's messing up the island." Rick mumbled the words, took a big pull on his brew, and took a good look at me while it was going down.

"Yeah, he's a worthless piece of crap, all right," I said.

Retreating from Rick's scrutiny, I turned to look back at the *Second Chance*. So Harold Pearce was the same as Reggie — "a worthless piece of shit messing up the island." The jack of spades had spoken. So what about "Steve"? From this vantage point, Rick should have seen a lot of him. I searched for a good lead-in for "Steve" but didn't find one. And my next reading of Rick's eyes said that this jack would speak no more in this session. I looked down at my brew, swirled it, and realized that it was empty. I swirled it again and feigned one last chug.

"Thanks for the brews, Rick. Gotta be going."

"No problem, man. You gonna count them as breakfast?"

"Liquid bread!"

Rick laughed. "Don't worry about the cans. I'll throw them away later. Gonna sit here and listen to weather radio for awhile."

He flipped on the radio as I climbed down to the cockpit.

I crossed paths with Angie Sumter just as she was coming from the showers. She rummaged in her bag during most of the approach, then greeted me with a smile but didn't slow down for our passing.

"Hey, Angie, thanks again for your support, yesterday."

"I was glad to help." She repeated the smile but didn't break stride.

Conscious that Rick was probably watching from his flybridge, I didn't break stride either. While unlocking the companionway of the *Diogenes*, I noticed the *Photo Finish* pulling away from its dock. And as it approached and negotiated the sharp left turn that would take it out the channel, I noticed that Ray and Martha were waving to me. He was piloting, and she was standing behind him, wearing shorts this time.

I cupped my hands around my mouth and yelled to them, "Are you leaving?"

"Yes," Martha yelled back. "Channel Twenty." She fortified the message by showing me 10 fingers, twice.

I went below and turned on my VHF radio. "*Diogenes* to *Photo Finish*," I said into the mike.

"*Photo Finish*, here." It was Martha. "Yes, Ben, we're leaving. Going to Green Turtle Cay."

"On Abaco Island?"

"Yes. We know a lot of people at the Club there, and it's *really* time for a change of scene."

"Well, Rebecca and I are going to be working our way in that direction in a few days. We might be there in a couple of weeks."

"If you do, look for us in the north anchorage. In three weeks, you'll be just in time to see a performance of one of Dr. Sandra Riley's plays on the Alton Lowe estate. You really must see them. They're *so* historically accurate."

"Yes. We'll make a real effort."

"Thanks. And if we don't see each other again, it was *so* nice meeting you. We wish you both the best of luck."

They had rounded the L-turn in the channel, and I was losing sight of them behind a veil of Australian pines.

"I feel the same way, too. And I'll pass it on to Rebecca."

"Here's Ray."

Over the radio, Ray's New York voice sounded twice as throaty. "Just wanted to say it was a pleasure meeting you. Now you kids take care. Take real good care."

And his message wasn't lost on me. After we signed off, I ate a lot of bread and jam. The bread sopped up the beer, and the jam saved my blood sugar from a losing battle with my blood alcohol. The best way to fight off the alcohol was with physical activity. It would have been stupid to spend the day sitting around waiting for news or for my enemies to make their next move.

I decided to use the day surveying the south side of the island. Since this could only be done from West End, it made good sense to get it done now so that we could get out of here soon after Rebecca's return. I gave some thought to logistics, then packed the Caribe inflatable with my snorkeling gear and sponge survey kit, plus a day's worth of sandwiches, my VHF radio, my GPS unit, my cellphone, and a collapsible bicycle. Then I thought a little more and loaded the Caribe with anchor chain from the *Diogenes*. I removed the combination locks from the fender and the life jacket compartments.

After locking up the *Diogenes*, I motored over to the *Second Chance* and spent a few minutes on an underwater project — locking one end of the anchor chain around the propeller shaft pylon. I locked the other end of the chain around a dock piling, well below the surface.

Feeling bodily and mentally refreshed from the dip, I motored out the channel. Off to the northeast, a couple of bikini girls were putting on a good show with their Waverunners, sending up rooster tails and bouncing their eye candy in the sun. I headed in the opposite direction, traveling south along the westward side of the island. The breeze was fresh. I stayed in close where the water was shallow and free of waves, running along happily on plane at an estimated 25 miles per hour.

I let my mind wander over the morning's events:

It had been nice to learn that Rick Turner thought I was a "stand-up kind of guy" and that he and his SAWECUSS friends approved of how I had handled the two sergeants. I guessed that SAWECUSS had stopped worrying that I was a spy. It was no surprise that Rick had kept an eye on me that day. But it was worrisome that Angie didn't feel comfortable talking with me now.

As the defunct airport came abreast, I cut the motor and threw out the anchor. I counted plenty of sponges within the 25-yard radius and cut up and extracted some, too. After filling out the forms, I pulled up anchor, got up on plane, and did ten minutes of thinking on the way to my next station.

Rick had told me a lot about lines of communication in SAWECUSS and their attitude toward me. First he'd said that *Wade* had told him about the police visit. Then he quoted from Angie's account of it. But when we got to my actual confrontation with the those two sergeants — a matter dear to the heart of a stand-up kind of guy — then Rick essentially told me that he had witnessed the whole thing with his own eyes.

Two miles down the coast, I powered down, threw out the anchor for the next survey. There, too, the sponges were plentiful. Strong and efficient leg action got my heart-lung machine cranking and told my liver to stop worrying about the alcohol versus glucose conflict because my muscles would be demanding fatty acids from now on.

The next spot, two miles down the coast, proved to be unlucky. Try as hard as I could, there were no sponges to be found.

Funny how emotions can betray you. Here I was, a presumably dispassionate scientist performing a survey according to protocol, and yet my emotions came out when one site turned out "empty."

Of course, emotions betrayed Rick Turner a lot worse. He flared up at the mention of profligate son Reggie, and he flared up exactly the same way at the mention of Waverunner concessionaire Harold Pearce. And it had to be more than sexual jealousy, because he hadn't flared up at the mention of the French fashion mogul. We'd both had a good laugh at that guy's expense. What was the explanation for Rick's hatred of Reggie and Harry? Obviously, they were doing something more serious than hogging all the girls.

I broke out my sandwiches. I ate and pondered how differently Rick had reacted to the newcomer, Jay Sherman. There, Rick's reaction had been dismissive: "just an asshole," albeit a smiling one. Sure, the newcomer was a loner, but was that enough for Rick to write him off as an "asshole"? I wondered if "Steve" had been a loner, too. And I wondered if that might be significant.

After pulling up the anchor, I pondered Rick's interest in the fact that the seaplane didn't always land at Sir Hector's place. I motored for ten minutes and then splashed down at my next sampling point. While paying out the anchor line, I recalled the interesting slip of tongue that Rick had made when mentioning that Sir Hector's chauffeur had picked us up for dinner. Rick had actually started to call the chauffeur by his first name: Kevin. But he'd quickly corrected himself in mid-syllable, changing it to "chauffeur."

Yes, it had been an interesting conversation with the least social member of the Social Auxiliary of the West End Cocaine Smugglers Society. And this SAWECUSS member had been out on the water the night that "Steve" was killed. Rick Turner didn't need much provocation to shoot off his mouth. Did he need much more to shoot off a gun?

As the day wore on, I did less thinking and more snorkeling. I finished 10 miles of linear survey. My cellphone didn't ring and there were no messages on my voice mail. Shortly before sundown I was near my destination: Eight Mile Rock. Cruising the shoreline, I found a notch in the dune. Behind it, a narrow road that led to the open-air roadside grill operated by my new friend. I pulled the Caribe inflatable up the steep beach, walked up to the house, and announced myself.

Jethro came out to greet me. He helped carry the Caribe up to his house, which was several dozen yards behind the dune. While I chained the boat to a nearby tree, he instructed his children to keep away from it. I gave him a generous payment, telling him I'd be back the next day. But before I could say another word, Jethro was tugging me by the arm toward the grill where he told his wife to feed me, "on the house."

The food was good, the sunset was spectacular, and the conversation with the other guests was comfortable. We talked about their island — the settlements, the churches, and the schools. The conversation acted as a salve to the irritating experiences I'd had in the last days. I would have liked to have stayed longer, but that was impossible with 13 miles to ride in the dark on a small-wheeled bicycle.

It was a weary ride under the faint light of that sliver moon. I passed the Holmes Rock Settlement and pedaled for a long stretch of nothing. My only landmarks were Mulberry Lane and a bend in the road several miles later. When I reached the crossroads of Royal Lane, which led to Sir Hector's house, I felt more at home for some reason. West End greeted me as a series of bare light bulbs shining on bare interior walls. Sometimes people waved to me from the shadows of their porches and sometimes dogs ran out to bark and chase me. The Island Club was open for business but wasn't getting much. The police station was well lit. The water tower blinked its red aircraft warning light. Off to the left, all was dark and quiet around the defunct airport. Approaching the marina's parking lot, I noted that it had taken 90 minutes to get home. While pedaling through the parking lot, I noticed that Rick Turner's car was not there.

After I passed the marina office, it was gratifying to see that the *Second Chance* was still in its berth.

And it was interesting to see that Constable Ivanhoe wasn't there.

Triangulation and Convergence   19

I was in the middle of breakfast when the cellphone rang. It was my lawyer's secretary. I told her that I would call back in ten minutes. Four minutes later I was on my motorcycle, and in another four I was at the phone booth, dialing David Lynch's number. My heart was thumping hard in my chest.

"Good morning, Ben. I take it you have a secure line, now."

"Yes."

"Well . . ." He couldn't resist a dramatic pause. "You are a lucky guy. They have accepted. On my desk in front of me I have a cashiers check for sixty thousand dollars."

I let out a whoop.

"I have a contract for you to sign. Could you receive it by fax at your marina office in ten minutes, sign it, and turn it right around to me?"

"Yes."

"Good. Then I will have an assistant take the check to your bank. Of course, you will have to mail me the copy with your actual signature."

"Sure." I was having trouble keeping up with all this good news. "What about the boat? I have a lock on it. What do I do about that?"

"Take it off and walk away from it. The contract is just a quitclaim. From the moment you sign, you will have no further responsibility towards the boat."

This seemed too good to be true. "But what if other people go aboard and take things?"

"That will not be your problem. You will have no further responsibility to the boat."

"Are you sure?"

"Yes, I specifically discussed that with the lawyer from the other side. And, from the moment of signing, you will have no authority over the boat, either."

"But . . ."

"Of course, I put in a clause that holds you harmless for any damage that occurred as the result of your salvage action and while the boat was in your custody."

"Okay, but . . ."

"What's the matter, Ben? You don't sound too happy."

"No, I am. It's just that when the pressure lets up this quick, it feels like I'm going to explode."

"Then I'll turn the pressure back on. Get your butt over to the marina office, get that fax, sign it without asking me a lot of questions, and send it right back to me. Then I'll withdraw Federal lawsuit, turn off the clock for you, and turn it on for my next client. Okay?"

"Okay. All right. And thanks for the job well done."

I raced back to the marina office and presented myself at Zelma's Dutch door. A twenty-dollar bill bought me renewed access to her fax machine, and in a couple of minutes it was feeding the quitclaim document into my hands. It was a simple document that stated exactly what David Lynch had said. In less than two minutes I had signed it, transmitted it back, and made a copy.

Back at the *Diogenes*, I finished my breakfast and called Rebecca over a cup of coffee. "Rebecca, this is Ben on the cellphone."

"Your cellphone seems to be working fine today," she answered, confirming that it would be a guarded conversation.

"We had a glorious sunrise this morning."

"Great. What's it shining on?"

"The *Second Chance*. And I won't be taking care of it anymore."

"Great, you'll be able to spend more time with me. Some more sensuous moments on the inflatable."

"Careful what you say, girl. You're having a strong effect on me already."

'Save all your love for me because I'm coming home tonight."

"Great. You really were able to get it done with a day to spare?"

"I just signed the face page of the grant application. Professor Thompson's secretary is going to walk it through all the University offices that need to sign approval. She will send it off tomorrow." Rebecca gave me the number and arrival time of her flight, and I told her I'd meet it.

"But Ben, you have to promise me when I come back that we're going to leave that unlucky place."

"I promise you. Love you, Rebecca."

"Love you, too, Ben." (Click)

I grabbed Rebecca's diving mask and a couple of tools, locked up the *Diogenes*, and walked over to the *Second Chance*. Ivanhoe was not there and there was no sign of his hammock, his beach chair or his car. I put on the diving mask, let myself down in the water, undid the combination locks, and released the anchor chain from the propeller shaft and dock piling. I set the stuff on the dock and gave it a good hosing down.

Next, I stepped over the sagging crime scene tape and opened the boat up. I crawled into the engine compartment and reconnected the throttle cables. That was the least I could do for the S.C. Corporation. But I resisted the urge to start up the engines. No reason: The batteries were topped off and the engines had started right up several times before. No reason why they shouldn't start right up, any time. I let my eyes sweep around the main salon again. Everything was shipshape. The cushions looked fine. No indication that a man had died here and that water had come up to waist height. There was nothing at all out of the ordinary except for that old radio direction finder. It was still sitting at the side of the table. Now there was nothing left to do but take off my lock and my hasp and walk away from this jinx ship. Let someone else come and give the *Second Chance* its fourth chance.

The van would be pulling into the parking lot at 10:30 a.m., and I could be on it. I could get off at the outdoor grill and motor the Caribe back here well before it would be time to pick up Rebecca. And tomorrow morning we would be out of here.

That was when I noticed the radio noises. They were coming from the radio console that Rebecca had given the fine mist treatment. After several days on steady power, it was resurrecting itself! The noise was coming out in tiny bursts, one after another. It was amplifying static. A closer look told me that the indicators were also resurrected. And the LCD display was working now, proclaiming "Electrocom Spectrum All-Band Radio Receiver/Scanner." And the display said that the station it was set to pick up was 462 Megahertz. If I remembered right, that was the working frequency for personal two-way radios — those inexpensive, pocket-size walkie-talkies that they are selling and building into cellphones. I wrote down the frequency.

I pushed the radio's buttons and got the main menu. It seemed to be a very capable device, able to receive a wide spectrum of signals: from the low-frequency long-wave, middle-wave and short-wave AM range; through the very-high frequency (VHF) FM range; and through the ultra high frequency range and up to the Gigahertz microwave range. The thing probably cost a couple of thousand dollars. I highlighted and selected "VHF-Marine." It went automatically to Channel 16 and the speaker put out the familiar background hiss that you hear on marine radio, between transmissions. After a few seconds, the noise was quenched and I heard, "Marlin Spinner to Dollfan."

Then came the answer, "Dollfan to Marlin Spinner, switch to twenty-five."

"Marlin Spinner to twenty-five."

Okay, this $2,000 radio could do the same as a $150 VHF marine radio. Now, what kinds of special things could it do? I went back to the main menu and selected "Scan Display." It gave me a so-called power histogram, the type of thing you get on the screen when you play music on your computer. But the peaks and valleys on this one didn't jump, dive and shimmy like they did to DJ music. It was a power output spectrum as a function of *radio frequency*. The low-frequency AM was on the left and the high Gigahertz frequency was on the right.

When I punched "scan," the display asked me to choose a radio frequency range and to "set thresholds." I chose the VHF-to-Gigahertz frequency range and selected a threshold that would let though only the 12 strongest peaks. The displayed numbers whirled after I hit the go button. They stopped momentarily at several frequencies that were carrying the type of white-noise signal you hear from a fax or computer modem. The scanner dwelt on the signal for a few seconds, then went on. Finally, it stopped on a strong signal and locked onto it.

And the cabin was filled with the warm, cordial tones of Angie Sumter!

Angie was carrying on a cellphone conversation, apparently with a friend at Boca Raton. Was Batelco still using analog transmission for cellphones? I turned the volume down so nobody outside could hear. It was strange to hear Angie talking, just like she was sitting next to me. Of course, I could hear only her side of the conversation because her friend's answers were coming back on a different frequency. But I could understand the conversation like she was standing next to me with the phone to her ear.

It was gossipy girl-talk stuff, not deep secrets. Boy, I was glad that I'd used that far-away pay phone for my serious conversations. This radio was an eavesdropper's delight.

Eavesdropping — that was what "Steve" had been doing here. He'd been eavesdropping with electronic ears — an expensive radio with built-in and external antennas and smart electronics to switch between them.

My eyes rested on the old RDF dish, the radio direction finder, lying on the table. On a hunch, I went back to the menu and found "input selector." Right now, it was on "A1." I switched it to "A2." Angie stopped talking. The radio went silent.

Slowly I remembered the coaxial cable that had been dangling over the top of the unit for the first two days. I located it on the back panel, plugged into a socket labeled "A2." I pulled at the free end.

It was no act of genius, actually. The caged monkey grabs the stick and uses it to pull in the banana. The radio direction finder had long black dangling coaxial cable and so did the high-tech radio. And easier still, one plug was male and the other was female. I plugged them together and Angie's voice returned, but with a lot of distortion. But the distortion went away when I picked up the RDF dish and pointed it at *Sumter's Forte*. And when I pointed the RDF dish in the opposite direction, I lost Angie completely.

Now, to put the RDF through its paces. I pushed buttons to expand the power histogram and display the bar corresponding to the strength of Angie's carrier signal. When I pointed the RDF dish at Angie's boat, the bar grew tall. As I turned the dish away, the bar grew smaller. By turning the RDF dish back and forth and taking readings from its built-in compass, I located Angie at a bearing of 055 degrees.

Eavesdropping and tracking people down — that was what "Steve" had been doing. And that would be a dangerous activity around here.

That got me thinking: Could my backyard neighbor Wade Daniels have seen my experiment through the open door? Outside the sun was bright. Inside it was relatively dark. Hopefully, he couldn't see in, just like I couldn't see in through his front window. But just to be safe, I closed the cabin door most of the way.

I spent a quarter of an hour proving that "Steve" could locate ships at sea up to 20 miles out from their VHF radio transmissions. And I was just starting to look for signals around 462 Megahertz when I saw movement in the side window and heard footsteps.

I quickly put the RDF down and jerked out its coaxial cable. It went silent immediately. I felt the boat sway as he stepped aboard. I walked toward the door. "Hello," came a voice from the cockpit. Before I could respond, the door started opening — slowly. It was Jay Sherman. He stuck his big blond head in, leaning with one hand on each side of the doorframe.

"Sorry, Ben. Wasn't sure if you were here or not. Thought I saw you on deck a while back."

I didn't answer. I just stared and let him dangle.

He was wearing a crazy smile. "You never told me that you were a hero — that you rescued this boat from sinking. The guy at the fuel dock told me yesterday. I just had to come and see this guy myself."

Quickly, I decided to handle Jay the same way as I'd handled Wade and Martin.

"Sure. I don't mind. But the cops are still treating the boat as a crime scene." That was true, even if Ivanhoe had given up watching the boat. "You'd better wipe your prints off the doorframe."

Jay Sherman produced a handkerchief and wiped the spots he'd touched. And like Wade, he took his time, looking in at the cabin. But with those sunglasses, he would not be able to make out any detail. "I hear you found the boat so low in the water it was a couple of inches from sinking."

Thank goodness the radio was staying silent. Of course! I'd yanked out the cable.

I stepped forward to block Jay's view. "Yes, I was lucky to be able to jam a piece of foam into the hole and get it here. But, look, I promised the police I wasn't going to let people aboard. Not until tomorrow, anyway." I took two more steps towards Jay to keep him from coming in. He didn't take that as a signal to leave.

"I guess it was lucky," he said. "If they'd made a bigger hole, it would have gone down all at once. Did you see any other boats around?"

"No, I didn't. And sorry, Jay, but after I made a full statement to the police, they told me not to talk to anybody about it. And I've been trying to forget about it. It was such a gory mess. If you're interested in the hole, take a look at the patch. It's on the port side. The best place to see it is from the seawall."

I inched forward, putting us at close enough quarters for me to get a good look at his sunglasses. They were prescription; one lens was thicker than the other. Okay, he was myopic. But was he also totally obtuse?

"Jay, I've got to insist that you get off. I have to keep my promise to the policeman. Otherwise it was going to be his padlock on the boat instead of mine."

"Okay, I read you," Jay said, hardly looking at me. Showing no offense, he turned and stepped off.

I returned to the main salon and turned off the radio and tucked its length of coaxial cable behind it. And I stowed the RDF unit with its dangling cable in a corner. Through the front window, I saw no evidence of Ivanhoe. Let it be. Now for my last act on the *Second Chance*: I pulled out my Swiss Army pocketknife, unscrewed the hasp, and pocketed it, together with the lock. I shut the door and stepped off the yacht for the last time. I draped the anchor chain from the *Diogenes* over my shoulder.

Jay Sherman was standing on the seawall looking at my fiberglass job with a professional eye. I walked past, determined to ignore him.

"Yes," Jay said, "that's a pretty big hole. Hard to imagine the bilge pump keeping up with it. What size pump does the boat come with?"

"Can't tell you, Jay." Okay, I'd see if he could carry his end of the conversation. "You into boats? You do a lot of your own work?"

"All the time."

It was impossible to make out his eyes behind those sunglasses.

"What kind of business are you in, anyway?" I made no effort to hide my irritation. "You've always looked so busy, running off to your car every time I've seen you on the dock."

"Travel business," Jay said. "I do a lot of consulting and some writing."

Good cover for a drug smuggler, or for a smuggler's hit man. Or maybe Rick was right about him being a "friendly asshole," whatever that was.

"Sounds interesting, Jay. Maybe you're involved in the big renovation around here that everyone's talking about."

"No, but I consult for some operators in Freeport."

"But I bet you know what they're going to do here. I hear that the marina rates will be going through the roof. And Rick Turner — he's the guy over there with the second-tallest tuna tower in the marina — he was complaining that the place is going to fill up with 'Eurotrash.' That was his term, not mine. He's talking about the French fashion crew that's set up in those cottages." I stared at Jay, wide-eyed, like I couldn't wait to get the scoop from him, and it had better be good because the chain was weighing heavily on my shoulder.

A slight pull-back of the head was the only indication that Jay gave that I was having any effect on him. "No, I didn't hear anything about marketing to Europeans. I heard it will be an upscale timeshare and hotel operation with a family emphasis, catering to Americans." He moved a little closer.

"Great. Rick will be glad to hear that. He was also wondering whether the Waverunner concession is going to be part of the scene. He was complaining all to hell about how they're tearing up the flats."

"Can't help you there, Ben," he said with a twang. "Haven't looked into it."

"Thanks. But it's not like I have any professional interest in the travel business here in the Bahamas. Rebecca and I are just interested in exploring the waters. Hell, if I hadn't found this tub and hadn't gotten all this bureaucratic hassle, we would have been gone ten days ago." I laid in a pause, inviting a response — which was not forthcoming. "We should be working our way to Little Abaco in a day or two. See you later. Now's time for a lunch break."

"Hey, come over to my boat. I make a pretty good deli sandwich." He delivered the invitation with a wooden smile and with a low voice, now that he was much closer.

No, I would not let this curious stranger pump me for information.

"Thanks. But what I really need is a *siesta*. And I've got a real bad headache."

"Good luck with it."

"Thanks."

I walked towards the *Diogenes* and Jay Sherman ambled towards his berth at the end of that row, near the fuel dock.

It was noon — much too late to retrieve the Caribe inflatable. On the *Diogenes*, I made myself a sandwich. While eating it, I thought about what sort of Megahertz communications "Steve" had been monitoring and vectoring in on that night in the Gulf Stream. And I thought about some experiments I could do in the safety of the cabin of the *Diogenes*. After lunch I took a motorcycle ride down to my favorite phone booth and called Rebecca to ask if she could swing by Radio Shack for me.

"Okay, Ben, but exactly what kind of 'personal two-way radio' do you want me to get you?"

"The type that has the most channels and has at least two watts and is supposed to work for five miles. And if it has a 'scan' button, that would be better."

"And how much should I be willing to pay for it?"

"Up to one hundred and fifty dollars for a pair. They usually sell them off the wall in pairs. But if you can get a single one, that's fine."

"Then I guess that you don't want them to talk with me."

"They might come in handy for us when we're separated a mile or two. Their signals go out that far."

"Ben!" She said my name with irritation and impatience.

"They work in the four hundred Megahertz range."

"Ben, are you thinking up a new experiment."

"Yes, but the kind that can be performed at home."

"Is it necessary?"

"Yes. Just trust me."

"Then I'll see what I can do, darling." (Click)

On the way back, I took a dive in the marina's dumpster and retrieved a large tin can. Put it in a plastic bag and carried it back to the *Diogenes* for a science experiment to be performed below deck. After washing the can thoroughly, I punched one hole in its bottom and another in its side. I played around, sticking the short antenna of my hand-held VHF marine radio through the holes, listening to transmissions, and taking measurements with my hand-held compass. My science project wouldn't be good enough to win a Westinghouse science scholarship or anything, but I could vector in on yacht VHF transmissions with an accuracy of plus-or-minus 15 degrees.

Late in the afternoon, I went off on the motorcycle to get Rebecca. What a relief to get away from that confining marina and all the problems it had brought us. For the first time on this trip, I was starting to enjoy things. Behind me, the low sun flashed on and off my back as I sped along that asphalt strip lined with Australian pines. I looked to the left as the site of the hotel ruin sped by. A Japanese pickup truck with a couple of guys was stopped at the side of the road. While speeding by, it occurred to me that it was the same one that Rebecca and I had seen on our bicycle trip. Seconds later I looked to the right, catching a glimpse of the overgrown entrance to the airstrip. I sped past the water tower. How wonderful to feel all sensations amplified and speeded up by the motorcycle — the cool wind on my face and chest, the infrared rays that penetrated my shirt and warmed my back intermittently, the smell of the crabs and rotting seaweed as the road aligned with the coast, the hot silica dust of West End as I roared through it, and the aromatic smell of the thicket that lined most of the highway.

After a few more miles, while I was slowing and leaning into a turn, the smell of a dead animal fouled my nose. But when I got back to speed, the stream of pure air washed away all but the memory of it. I passed Royal Lane, the road that led to Sir Hector's house. Several minutes later, I was speeding through the crossroads of Mulberry Lane, the road that led to Reggie Pimentel's house. Boy, it would be good to be able to forget that guy.

Several minutes later, I was passing the conch fritter and fish grill. I slowed to wave to Jethro and resolved to stop there for a beer on the way back. The rest of the trip was a kaleidoscope to the sights and smells of settlements, of pine forest, of rock quarry, of urban streets, of sprinkled lawns, and finally, of jet fuel near the airport.

Rebecca's plane arrived half an hour after dark. It was such a joy to see her slender form walking up the corridor. It was good to receive a $60,000 hug from her and to return it with a congratulatory kiss for her new job.

Rebecca's enthusiasm was palpable. "The grant application's sent off, we're together again, and you can carry my bag."

I shouldered her duffel bag and we walked to the parking lot.

"Don't grimace, Ben. It has the replacement cylinder head you asked me to get."

"Thanks."

"And it has the radios you told me to get."

I rested the duffel bag on the motorcycle's handlebars.

"Are we riding home on *that* tonight?"

"Yes. I told you I've rented it." She frowned and I smiled. "Where's your sense of adventure?"

Her frown changed to a cautious smile. "Okay, if you want adventure, let me drive it."

"Well, I don't know."

Her smile broadened. "You know that I rode a motorcycle all over Jamaica . . . even if it was a little Honda."

"You've got a deal. Why should I have all the fun?"

I started wrapping a rope around the duffel bag to tie it to the handlebars, but Rebecca stopped me.

"Just a minute, Ben." She opened the bag. "Here are your radios. I know they must be important."

She handed me an off-the-wall package of cardboard and clear plastic, containing two units. I read the product description on the back and nodded my approval.

Rebecca handed me a pack of batteries to go with them. "Now, tell me what you are going to use them for."

"Do you remember spraying the fine mist to desalt the radio console that was drowned on the *Second Chance*?"

"Yes."

"Congratulations. Your resuscitation efforts paid off. Your patient came out of the coma this morning, babbling in the four-hundred Megahertz range and smiling its last frequency on its LCD display. Apparently, its internal lithium battery didn't short out and the unit saved its previous setting."

"And?"

"That is the frequency for the personal two-way radios like the ones you just bought me. *Ergo* . . ."

"You think that the victim was monitoring that kind of radio conversations before he died."

"Right. And not only monitoring them, but zeroing in on them. He was using that RDF dish to take bearings."

"And when he zeroed in on them, they killed him? And you think you can find out who are the killers by listening with these little two-way radios?" Rebecca frowned.

"Or the two-way radios will at least help us to stay away from them," I said weakly.

I went back to tying the duffel bag to the handlebars, positioning it sideways and resting it partially on the headlight.

The frown lines on Rebecca's face deepened. "Ben, the victim's company has paid you to walk away from the *Second Chance*. You did walk away from it, didn't you?"

"Yes, I turned the radio off, tidied up a little, took off our lock and hasp, and walked away from it."

Rebecca was staring at me, intently. "And?"

"It's not an *and*. It's a *but*. But I had a close call when that new guy, Jay Sherman, came aboard right before I unplugged the RDF dish."

"He came aboard?"

I tore open the package and started inserting the batteries.

"It seems that Ivanhoe is no longer on guard duty. Probably on instructions from higher-ups who are in collusion with the S.C. Corporation. Anyway, I didn't invite Jay Sherman aboard, and he didn't see me experimenting with the RDF, either. He came aboard like he'd just heard the news of our big adventure and he wanted to hear more from me."

"Which sounds pretty naive. Do you believe him?"

"It's hard to say. Maybe he's a jerk with a social IQ of about eighty. Or maybe he has something to do with the murder. I can't say. He was interested in the fiberglass patch today, but that might be just a ruse. He's had days to look at it. Anyway, I got rid of him when I was on board. And if he's crawling all over the *Second Chance* right now, it's none of my business and I don't care."

"That's okay as long as none of the bad guys think we know too much. And did anything else happen at the marina?"

"Nothing, unless you count Ray and Martha Vangelden moving out."

"Our only friends!"

"Don't worry. We'll catch up with them in the Abacos."

While talking to Rebecca, I had turned on one of the radios, had disabled its so-called interference-elimination codes and had put it into scan mode. While half listening for the last minute, I heard quite a few transmissions. Well, that made sense because we were close to Freeport. West End would be another story.

I handed the other radio to Rebecca.

Rebecca frowned. "What am I supposed to do with this?"

"We can turn them on when we're alone on the *Diogenes*. We might find out who's using them within a two-mile radius of the marina." I set my radio in the so-called scan-and-lock mode. Then I jammed it into my shirt pocket, next to my address book.

"I hope you aren't planning for us to sit around the marina, day after day, listening to that thing squawking in your pocket."

"No. And it should quiet down once we get away from Freeport."

"Well, what is your plan, anyway?"

"We're done with the marina, and we're done with the sponge survey on the south side of the island, out to Eight Mile Rock. My plan is to get us out of here by the day after tomorrow. Tonight, we go straight to the *Diogenes*. Tomorrow morning I use the motorcycle to provision the *Diogenes*. Then, you drop me off with the motorcycle at a guy's house where I stashed the Caribe. It's thirteen miles up the road from West End. It shouldn't take me more than an hour to motor the Caribe back to the *Diogenes*. Then I take the motorcycle back to Freeport and come back with the van with more supplies. And the morning after that, we unhook our dock lines and sail the *Diogenes* eastward towards Mangrove Cay."

"So it looks like I really do have to drive that thing."

"No, I can do everything with the van if you feel it's too much for you."

Rebecca gave me a funny smile that was at least 30-percent frown. "No, I want to drive it, too."

"You'll get the hang of it by watching me. The hardest part is remembering to drive on the left. Let's go."

I fired up the motorcycle and Rebecca got on behind. As we worked our way past Freeport, I showed Rebecca how to work the clutch, the gearshift, and the brakes. After we got past the town and there was little traffic, we switched places and I coached her from behind as she piloted the heavy machine into the ever-increasing darkness. Rebecca was naturally skilled. It was fun to see her building up her skills, anticipating the curves and leaning into them. We passed the quarry and the settlements lining the road.

And after we were five miles past Freeport, the radio did go silent for lack of nearby signals.

After those few miles, Rebecca had no need for my advice. There was little for me to do except to hang on and enjoy the wrap-around speed. The headlight pierced the darkness and cast shadows past distant objects, which seemed to come up quickly. With Rebecca, I was in good hands. We were safe. Like in that old Barry Manilow song, we'd made it through the night. The pressure was off. We could enjoy life again. I had a good partner — a partner I could trust with my eyes closed. I remembered a so-called couples-therapy game that she'd explained to me and we'd once played — closing your eyes and letting your partner guide you on a walk.

On the back of the motorcycle I played that game of closed eyes, my hands holding Rebecca's flat stomach, my cheeks tickled by wisps of her hair, and my spine soaking up the vibration of the motor and wheels rolling under me. I felt the gentle deceleration as she rolled through a small settlement or readied the cycle for a banking turn. Feeling secure, I graduated to a new game: registering differences in temperature, humidity and smell, and deciphering them into probable landscape. Could I differentiate between bare coral, grass, and wooded areas? I opened my eyes only to verify my guesses. I was good but not perfect. I didn't pick up the smell of Jethro's conch fritter and fish grill until we were riding past it.

Next came the salty smell of the sea air with an occasional twist of dying seaweed — the road was following the coast. Then came the terpene smell of Australian pines. It alternated with a dry, dusty smell — swaths of underbrush and patches of high, exposed coral ground.

Rebecca slowed and I opened my eyes to verify that it was a crossroad. It was Mulberry Lane where I'd last seen the seaplane landing, its underside reflecting the setting sun. I opened my eyes again several minutes later, when Rebecca slowed for the junction with Royal Lane which went to Sir Hector's house. West End would be coming up soon. And after rolling along for another couple of miles, my nose caught the smell of the rotting animal that I had noticed before. It grew stronger over the next half mile. A large dog, at least. I opened my eyes just before Rebecca slowed for a right-hand curve — just in time to catch the glint of a shiny object deep in the underbrush, reflected from our headlight.

"Rebecca, could you stop right here?"

"What is it, Ben?" she asked, coming slowly to a halt.

I put my feet down to help her stabilize the cycle. "I thought it was a dead animal back there. But I saw a car back there, too. I need to check that it isn't a dead man. Wait here and keep the motor running."

"And what am I supposed to do if someone comes by and slows down?"

"Good point. Hop off and I'll hide the cycle off the road." I did it and we walked about 50 yards back along the curving road to the spot where I saw the glint. I found it again, using a penlight. It was about 35 yards in, mostly obscured by rough bushes. Rougher still were the agave plants whose long stake-like leaves came to sharp points right at calf level. The ground consisted of a couple of inches of sand over coral rock. Rebecca followed me, closely. The stench became intolerable as we came close enough to make out the form of the car. It was an old compact Ford, parked at the end of a narrow path. The closer we got, the louder was the buzzing. I laid down a palm frond to stand on for a closer inspection. The driver's side window was smashed in. The man in the driver's seat had suffered numerous shots to the chest and at least one shot to the head, which was thrown back over the top of the seat. Flies swarmed inside the car like bees around a hive. They buzzed around his face and his opened shirt. Maggots were crawling in his open mouth, in his nostrils, and around his thin blond moustache. And the thin blond hair on his head and the engineer's cap on the seat beside him left no doubt: It was Rick Turner.

I moved to the side so that Rebecca could come closer, then I swept the penlight over him slowly.

"It looks like at least one, maybe two days since death," Rebecca said. "The maggots are small and there's no liquification."

"That checks out, because I talked to him yesterday morning." I swept the light over the window ledge, down the side of the door, and on the sand underneath. "It looks like he was ambushed in his car, but not here — somewhere else. There's no broken glass on the outside. There's a lot of blood pooled on the floor of the passenger's side. They pushed him over and drove the car here to dump it. I bet the killer is a local. An outsider wouldn't know about this path."

I shined the light along the driver's side of the car, working backward. By the rear bumper, I caught a well-defined footprint that pointed back toward the road. I knelt to illuminate it horizontally and enhance the shadows. It was a boat shoe, size 9½ or 10, and the detail was remarkable.

"Rebecca did you pack a camera?"

"Oh, no you don't, Ben! We've had enough trouble."

"You're right. Let's get the hell out of here — the way we came. Try to step in your old tracks and I'll try to eradicate them.

Rebecca took the lead and I followed behind, dragging my right foot sideways behind. Foot dragging! That's all that Bahamian law enforcement had done; now it was my turn. And I dragged a palm frond behind. After we reached the middle of the road, we walked down its center, to where I stashed the motorcycle. I fired it up and guided it out to the road. Rebecca used the frond to destroy its tracks, then jumped on. For a minute, I stood there on the asphalt, revving the engine and thinking what to do. When it became clear, I peeked under the duffel bag to get an odometer reading. Then I let out the clutch and started us off with a careful turn — toward Freeport.

"Ben, what are you doing? The marina's in the other direction. We're going the wrong way."

"Just trust me," I said. "There's no other way."

I went through the gears like a demon and breathed deeply to rid my lungs of the lingering stench.

We roared past Sir Hector's Royal Lane. But as we came up on Mulberry Lane, I slowed to see if our headlight would pick up any sparkles of broken window glass. Finding none, I twisted the throttle to hell and we roared on. Several miles down the road came what I remembered — a bus stop, a clump of houses, and a pay phone. I killed the engine and coasted, coming to a stop about 100 yards short of the phone and the single street light.

"Okay, Ben, I understand. You're going to call the police. And you're going to use one of your *voices* to keep us uninvolved. But what, then?"

"We're sailing the *Diogenes* out of the marina tomorrow morning."

"What are you going to do with the motorcycle?"

"We can call the motorcycle rental place in Freeport and tell them to pick it up at the marina. They can bill my card for the extra service. We don't have to be there when they pick it up. A more important thing is to get the inflatable back tonight. It's chained to a tree by a guy's house, on the Gulf Stream side, near the roadside grill that we passed. It's only a few miles up the road. If you drop me off to get the inflatable, would you be able to ride the motorcycle back to the marina by yourself?"

"Yes."

"Good. Then we'll do that right after we make the call. You should be back at the marina before the police come out to investigate. And I should be able to make it back in less than two hours."

"You be careful. It will be very hard to see."

"I know. But there will be plenty of lights to home in on, once I get within sight of the marina."

"And you have to watch out for other boats. You don't have any navigation lights."

"If I see anybody, I'll signal them with my penlight."

"Ben, I don't like it."

"I don't see any other way. We have to notify the police. But if we identify ourselves, they'll pin us down at the marina. Then we'll be sitting ducks, just like before with the *Second Chance*. We have to get out of the marina before they come and start interviewing people."

"You're right. And we can't tell them we know a thing."

Walking up to the pay phone, I practiced a nondescript Southern accent. After making sure nobody was around, I picked up the handset and deposited two Bahamian quarters. The operator connected me with the Royal Bahamas Police Force in Freeport.

"This is a good citizen call . . . well I'm not a citizen, really . . . and I'm reporting a dead body in a car in the brush off of King's Highway. Now listen good 'cause I'm only going to say this once. The car's in the brush some thirty-five yards to the south of King's Highway. It's about three-point-two miles west of Royal Lane, right where the road takes a bend. I noticed a bad smell and got out of my car to investigate."

"Sir, can you tell me exactly where the car is on King's Highway."

"I just tol' yuh. It's about three-point-two miles west of Royal Lane, right where the road takes a bend. Just get yourself out there, roll down your window and follow your nose. When you reach the bend, your headlights will catch a reflector on it. That's how I came across it and stopped to check it out. I walked in sideways to the car and did my best to keep from making tracks. And on the way out, I mushed them up so you wouldn't go barking up the wrong tree."

"Could you give us your name, sir?"

"Can't help you, there. My vacation's over, and my plane takes off from Freeport tomorrow, and I've gotta be on it."

I hung up and wiped off the handset.

I fired up the motorcycle, and we headed back to Jethro's conch fritter and fish grill. I stopped a couple of hundred yards short of it and turned the cycle around. It would be simpler if Jethro didn't see Rebecca. I got off and held the machine upright while Rebecca wiggled forward.

"When you get there, lock it to a tree by the marina office. Don't talk to anyone. If they ask about me, tell them I'm on the boat or in the men's room — any old lie that explains why they didn't see me. Don't worry, even if it takes me four or five hours. If the motor acts up, I have the oars, and the water's so shallow close to shore that I could never drown. Whatever you do, don't involve anyone else. Like you said, we don't have any friends at the marina. Everyone is a possible enemy."

"How will we communicate?"

"By cellphone, using code. Don't use the two-way radio."

I could see her frustration, not being able to let go of the handlebars for a goodbye hug. I hugged her and kissed her. "Now go like hell. And don't stop that thing until you've reached the marina."

The transmission clicked as she threw it in gear. "I love you, Ben."
"Love you, too."

I stepped to the side and steadied the cycle by the back of the seat as she revved the motor and let out the clutch. And as I stood there watching that red taillight recede in the distance, I knew that nothing would stop her.

When I walked up to his stand, Jethro was glad to see me and didn't ask for any explanations. I told him that I'd come to take the inflatable and might be coming back in a few weeks. He said the boat was fine, and he accepted my 20-dollar bill for looking after it an extra day. But he insisted on my drinking a *Kalik* with him. At first I declined, saying beer would affect my navigational skills, but I quickly relented. It would be unfriendly to leave him no way to reciprocate. I paced my side of the drinking and conversation, aiming for ten minutes.

When I said it was time to leave, Jethro abandoned his stand to walk me down to his house. He hushed his family's scrappy little dog and helped me carry the inflatable over the notch in the dune and down to the water. It was damn heavy with the engine on back and I was grateful for his help. Before taking off my shoes to wade into the water, I remembered to jam my cellphone in my shirt pocket, next to the personal two-way radio and my address book. Before shaking Jethro's hand, I pushed the glow button on my watch. It was ten minutes after ten.

I tossed my shoes into the boat and guided it away from the steep beach until I was up to my thighs in six-inch waves. After squeezing the rubber bulb, manipulating the choke and pulling the cord a dozen times, the motor sputtered and showed signs of life. Dancing around on tiptoes, I kept two hands busy finding the right combination of throttle and choke to coax that sputter into a roar. It put out a lot of oily smoke. Jethro waded in to help steady the boat, wetting the legs of his long pants in the process. We said goodbye. I threw myself into the boat, while twisting the steering lever/throttle and turning it to a sharp angle to get the boat moving away from the steep shore.

For the first 10 minutes, I kept a course perpendicular to the coastline. When I was half a mile out, estimated from the narrow angle of tree line between water and dark sky, I turned parallel to the coast and put the boat up on plane. And as I sat there bouncing through the waves on my soggy bottom — soaked-through underpants and cargo shorts — zipping along at about 20 miles per hour and peering ahead over water that was poorly lit by the quarter moon, I settled into a mental game called "Who Killed Rick Turner and Why?"

Start with the observed fact that Rick was a member in good standing of the SABWECUS — the Social Auxiliary of the West End Cocaine Smuggling Society. Rick was, after all, the "cuss" in SAWECUSS. And why was Rick in SAWECUSS? Probably because it was a cocaine-buying cooperative. I doubted that a stand-up kind of guy like him would need a Society for protection. But he probably did benefit from the Society's occasional guidance. He was a lot better at kicking butts than thinking on his own. Our two-beer breakfast had shown me that.

What got Rick killed? A general answer was quite easy. It was his fast mouth and his proclivity for jumping in with two feet:

"That frigging Reggie. Someone ought to do something about him."

Rick had great animosity for Reggie, the guy who pulled into the marina with his thundering Cigarette boat and acted like he owned the place. It went beyond sexual jealousy.

Since Rick seemed to have gotten along with everyone in SAWECUSS, it seemed unlikely that any of them had killed him.

Okay, let's say that SAWECUSS was Rick's ally and Reggie was his enemy. What other clues had Rick given me? I replayed my conversation with him — the one where he'd wanted to know about my morning motorcycle ride. — The same conversation where he'd offered me beer and hadn't been insulted when I joked that he wanted to poison me. — The same conversation where he'd practically admitted to spying on me from his flybridge to see how I would handle the police after the cocaine plant. — The same conversation where he'd unwittingly told me that he knew Sir Hector's chauffeur-butler by his first name, Kevin. — The same conversation where he'd been so interested when I'd told him about the seaplane's alternate landing site.

I was thinking too deeply about Rick and my course was running too close to shore. It wouldn't do to hit a grassy flat at 20 miles per hour and get tossed head over heels. I corrected course by steering more to the left.

Why had Rick been so interested in the seaplane? It was easy enough to postulate an answer for that question: Maybe it was Santa's sleigh. Maybe it brought lots of toys and goodies. And why would the seaplane owners choose Sir Hector's dock as an unloading site? Because nobody would pull a raid on Sir Hector. Maybe Sir Hector's chauffeur Kevin unloaded the cocaine. Maybe that was why Rick so quickly stopped himself before mentioning Kevin to me by name.

So the seaplane brings the cocaine to Sir Hector's, and Kevin brings the cocaine to SAWECUSS, and Rick gets his share and is the first one to head for the Florida coast. So, what got Rick killed? It had to be something new that got him killed.

I remembered how interested Rick was, when I had told him that the seaplane had landed at the end of Mulberry Lane. And who lived at the end of Mulberry Lane? Reggie lived there.

"That frigging Reggie! Someone ought to do something about him."

So Rick got mad when he learned that the seaplane was delivering cocaine to Reggie, too. And Rick drove down to Mulberry Lane to do something about it — and got himself shot. It all fit. The timing fit, from the time Rick drove off to the incubation time of the maggots. And the personalities fit with the action.

I wondered how Reggie got his cocaine across the Florida Straits without being stopped by the Coast Guard. His boat practically had the word "smuggler" written all over it. Approaching Palm Beach, he would stick out like a sore thumb.

To make sure that everything fit, I went down the roster of SAWECUSS. Mr. "Enginuity" and his mousey wife were members in good standing. They paid their dues, bought their cocaine and paid for their protection, and didn't hurt anyone. Same deal for Cal and Angie Sumter. And she was the one who showed me that they were paying for protection and getting it. I learned that when she accused me of tipping off the Coast Guard that the daysailer couple was on a smuggling run. Martin and Beth were members, but they kept to themselves and probably didn't hurt anyone. What about Chuck and Bill? Now they were interesting. And more interesting still was Wade Daniels. He organized the fish fry, so he had to be the chairman of the Society.

Wade Daniels, Chairman of SAWECUSS. Head of the cocaine buying cooperative. Pay him and he will make sure that the drug interdiction people don't mess up your drug run. Pay him and bad things don't happen to you. That's what Angie had said: "Things like that aren't supposed to happen."

I imagined their fear and curiosity of us when we came in with the dead man and the salvaged boat:

"Mister Chairman, is this Ben Candidi a threat to us?"

"I don't know, folks. Let's invite him to a fish fry and see."

And Mr. Chairman had tried to take care of the problem by handing
me a plate full of poison fish. Too bad he hadn't told everyone to keep
an eye on what I did with it.

I imagined SAWECUSS deliberating a few days ago:

Member: "Mr. Chairman, we once again request assurance
that this Ben Candidi isn't some kind of an informant.
After all, we're paying protection. If you don't know, then
we respectfully suggest that you do something to find out.
Or get rid of him."

Chairman: "Okay, this time I will put him to a cocaine test.
Plant stuff on his boat, tip off the Bahamian police, and
see what happens? If they don't throw him in jail, then
we'll know he's a government informant. If they do throw
him in jail, too bad for him."

Yes, that was probably how their deliberation went. And I imagined
SAWECUSS convening after the visit by the two sergeants:

Rick Turner: "Boy, that was a knee-slapper! You should have
seen his face when they walked up that dock. Looked ready
to tear them out a couple of new assholes!"

Angie: "He looked hurt and angry at the same time."

Chairman: "Okay, he isn't an informant because nobody could
act that part. Okay, the kid's straight. But he isn't stupid."

Member: "It would be a lot better if he'd just go away. Why is
that sergeant holding onto that boat, anyway?"

Yes, it was a lot of speculation, but a lot of things were falling into
place.

I began to make out lights from the West End marina. Pretty soon,
I would be coming abreast of the airport. For an instant, I saw a flicker
of light on the shore.

I dropped the "Who Killed Rick?" game and started playing "Who
Was Steve?"

What did I know about "Steve," anyway? I knew that he stayed in a slip across from Wade Daniels. I knew that he was not a friend of Wade Daniels or any other member of SAWECUSS. They all said they hardly knew him. And they weren't lying because Ray Vangelden, useful fool that he was, would have contradicted them.

Yes, they hardly knew "Steve," and they didn't know what he was doing. They didn't know that he had been listening to their cellphone conversations and vectoring in on their VHF marine communications. So who was this "Steve" who got himself killed, waiting 15 miles west of West End in the middle of the night wearing his night vision goggles and with his radio direction finder plugged into a high-tech radio scanning around 462 Megahertz?

And who had killed him with a shot from below and finished the job by climbing aboard for an executioner's shot? What person had almost succeeded in erasing the story with several well-placed shots just below the waterline?

A sound went off in my shirt pocket. The personal two-way radio had found a signal and locked onto it. "Launch number two," came the voice, loud enough to hear over the noise of the outboard and so clear that it felt like the speaker was standing right next me. The bottom fell out of my stomach.

In that instant *everything* became clear. I knew who "Steve" was, what he'd been doing, why he was killed, by whom, and what sort of watercraft the murderers were using.

But now *I* was "Steve." And the killers couldn't be more than two miles away. For all I knew, they might be coming directly at me.

20   Apocalypse, Now

I twisted the throttle as far as it would go, increasing my speed to about 25 miles per hour. They were probably launching a cocaine run from the shore along the deserted airport. Another mile and I'd be past it. I peered into the darkness in the direction of the shore, looking for him so I could avoid him. But he came up on me faster than I expected. He was going due west at a good 40 miles per hour, sliding into me on a collision course at a relative bearing of 45 degrees. I steered hard to the right four seconds before the crash point. He didn't respond to me until the last minute, either. He veered sharply to his right and we passed each other with maybe 20 feet to spare.

I saw it all in an instant, and it was a ghostly sight: a man straddling a black Waverunner like a rider on a galloping horse. Stalks of night vision goggles bulged from his eyes. His black wetsuit glistened in the weak moonlight. His bare arms were encrusted with strapped-on equipment, probably a GPS as well as the personal two-way radio. Strapped on his waist was a gun holster and strapped on his leg was a diving knife. And strapped on the side of his steed were glistening black packages — obviously a payload of cocaine.

The image seared in my brain — Horseman of the Apocalypse.

And in an instant he was gone, lost in a trail of mist. There was no roar. The motor must have been fitted out with an extra-long muffler. There was no rooster-tail stream of cooling water shooting up 12 feet behind him. They must have mixed that water with the exhaust to suppress the heat signature. It was a stealth Waverunner: minimal visible signature, no heat signature, minimal radar signature, and delivering 200 pounds of cocaine from the Grand Bahama Island to Palm Beach in a little over an hour.

The radio crackled. "Outboard-powered inflatable heading north at twenty," the voice said, with suppressed motor sounds in the background.

"Number Two, you copy that? Caution." This one had no motor in the background.

"I copy that, Number Three." It was a different voice, with a motor in the background.

They were talking over personal two-way radios, with the anti-eavesdropping feature turned off.

"Number One, does the vessel have eyes?" asked Number Three.

It sounded almost like military communications, which was impossible because they were smuggling. I recognized Number Three's voice, now. It was Harry Pearce, the guy with the Navy tattoo who ran me out of his Waverunner shack. And he was asking if I had night vision goggles.

"Negative," said Number One.

"Did he sight you?"

"Affirmative," answered Number One.

So deadly clever: Talking with low-power personal radios so the drug surveillance planes would have little chance of hearing them. Not using the radios' anti-eavesdropper features to avoid suspicion in case their transmissions *were* intercepted.

I started a turn that would take me back where I came from. I had to get out of these guys' way.

"Damn, I told you that you've got to keep a lookout. Number Two, intercept at stand-off distance."

"Vectoring in. Got him in sight," reported Number Two.

I did it all at once: Killed the engine and jammed the radio and cellphone into a cargo pocket of my shorts. I braced myself as the inflatable came off plane and set itself down in the water. I had to look harmless.

"What's he doing, Number Two?"

"Looks like his engine quit on him. He's shaking his tank and pumping his line. Pulling the starter. Looks like he's having trouble." His background whirl slowed down and became silent.

I threw up my hands, then shook my fist in the direction of the first Waverunner, trying to imagine myself as an old grandpa on a fishing expedition who got all flustered by the near miss and got his engine screwed up royally. I couldn't see Number Two but I tried to keep my face away from where he probably was, to shore.

"Describe assets," said Number Three.

"No binocs, no radio, no offensive capability. Nothing. Having a lot of trouble. Taking off his engine cowling. Pulling out his oars."

I continued acting it out for a silent, unseen audience of one.

"Any identification?"

"Affirmative. Bow's marked with Delta, India, Oscar, Golf, Echo, November, Echo, Sierra."

Damn! He had just spelled out *Diogenes* in military nomenclature. The radios were silent for a while.

"Shit!" said Number Three. "Number One, is that you keying down? Cut it out."

"Negative. Not me."

"Number Two?" he asked.

"Not me," Number Two answered.

"Then where the hell's it coming from?"

Damn, it was coming from me! When I bent my leg it was squeezing the transmitter button, sending out a carrier signal and erasing the background static they normally heard between transmissions.

"What's he doing now?" asked Number Three.

"He's put the lid on the engine. Looks like he's given up on it. He's trying to row to shore."

"Number Two, return to mission," said Number Three. "I'll take care of him. Tell them I'll be delayed fifteen minutes."

No question about it, now. Number Three was Harold Pearce. And he was coming after me.

"Roger," said Number Two, his engine accelerating in the background.

I listened hard between strokes of the oar. I could barely make it out — the swish through the water and the high frequency whirl. It felt like he went far north to clear me before turning west for the Florida coast. Against the chance that he might look back, I made myself do 30 more strokes before abandoning the oars.

How do you escape a hunter who can see you in the dark and who can run almost twice as fast as you? You run silently. I took off my life jacket and tied it around the cowling of the motor. And you run unexpectedly — not toward the marina but in the opposite direction. My brain whirled, calculating the odds. One mile to shore would take me three minutes. Doing it 45 degrees to the shore would make that 4.2 minutes.

I got the motor going. I ran it full speed and crouched in the back of the boat.

Could I make it? It would take him 1.5 minutes to go one mile out. I pushed my legs under the aluminum bench and sat deeply on the floor, at the back of the boat. Sitting low, I would deny him the familiar profile of a man sitting on a boat. I'd make him spend those 1.5 minutes coming out to where his buddies had seen me. I'd make this sausage-shaped boat blend with the waves. Deny him any sharp feature in the green after-image-blurred picture that his night vision goggles delivered.

But the deeper I lay, the slower the inflatable moved on plane. With my feet, I pushed the tanks forward to balance it out. Taking a quick fix on the moon, I performed an unnatural act. I lay down on my back and inched my way forward, feet first until my chest was under the bench. I had to stretch my arms back to maintain a grip on the control rod. As my weight shifted forward, the boat went into flatter plane and the motor went into higher revs. It felt like an Olympic Alpine Sled competition as I hurled forward, feet first. I would go all the way with the engine on full revs until the Caribe threw me up on the shore. Then I would jump out and run for my life.

It took a lot of patience to count out 180 seconds — the three minutes that it would take to bring me close to shore. After counting to 100, I started thinking of abandoning the 45-degree angle and heading directly for the beach. But a thud at my feet told me that I wasn't going to luck out. The smell and feel of gasoline told me that his bullet had hit one of the neoprene containers. He had to be shooting from close range. A second's hesitation could cost me my life. Straining my arms, I pushed the control rod to the side, putting my craft into a bouncing skid. Then I threw it the other way and headed straight for the beach.

The next shot went through the transom, spraying my ear with shattered fiberglass. I threw the control rod left and right for more evasive maneuvers. Then, the motor slowed. No, I hadn't lost my twist on the throttle. The motor was plowing through a sandbar or shoal flat. Gritting my teeth against his next shot, I reached up and used all my strength to pull the engine into the tilt position. The propeller came out of the sand and whined, cutting and throwing up water faster than gravity could replace it.

Sitting duck that I was, why wasn't I dead?

My boat picked up speed and the motor got a better bite in the water. I had made it over a sandbar. In a couple of seconds I was back on plane. A chunk of fiberglass slammed into my right leg. The right chamber deflated and started fluttering like loose tarp on a semitrailer. I shifted my weight toward the left inflation chamber. Saw a line of palm trees — small, but growing quickly.

No more shocks or splinters. Maybe I'd lost him at the sandbar. No time to look back. The sand line of the steep shore was coming up fast. The engine slowed, the hull bumped and I felt myself thrown up like in a carnival ride. The engine faltered. I hit the stop button as the boat came to a halt.

I pulled the aluminum bench out of its rubber socket loops and ran off with it, using it as a shield for my head and upper spine. It was the wildest run of my life — hands behind my head, zig-zagging back and forth as I climbed the beach and slalomed between the palmetto pines and agave plants, impaling my legs twice before making it past the brush line and into sight of the airport's runway.

I stopped and listened. Couldn't hear him following. I listened carefully in the direction of the shore. After a while I was able to hear it over the crickets and frogs: a high-frequency whine, modulated as you might expect by rocking. I crept back to the brush line and scanned the water. There he was, 100 yards out, using brute force and high revs to drag his craft off the sandbar and out to open water.

I didn't stay around to see if he got off. I ran due east, across the airport, toward the road that would take me to the marina.

I was in the middle of the runway when his voice came over the radio. "Candidi, you tell anybody about this and I'll kill you. And I'll slice your scraggly girlfriend to bits. I promise you."

When I got across the runway, I stopped and reached in my pocket for the cellphone to warn Rebecca. Couldn't find it. Must have fallen out of the pocket when I was squirming on the floor of the inflatable. Using the two-way radio to warn Rebecca would be too dangerous. But maybe it could warn me of the next attack. I searched the pocket attached to the aluminum bench seat and pulled out a loaded flare gun and two rounds. I stuffed it in my waistband. I abandoned the bench and set out for the path to the marina.

By alternating between running and a fast walk, I made it back to the marina in a short time. I kept out of sight, slinking through the Australian pines that lined the northeastern shore. I worked my way parallel to our row until coming to the level of the *Diogenes*. The lights were on; Rebecca must have been below deck. But the lights were also on at the boats belonging to Chuck, Cal and Angie and Wade Daniels. And I didn't want to see any of them, especially Wade.

I worked my way parallel to the channel that led out of the marina, then crossed through the line of Australian pines. I remembered to set down the two-way radio and flare pistol before letting myself into the canal. Taking care to not make ripples, I waded and swam along the seawall, back to the marina. I came up to the *Diogenes* amidships and used a knuckle to beat out Beethoven's Fifth on the hull. Rebecca came out.

"Rebecca!" I said it with a stage whisper.

"Ben?" she said, tentatively.

"Over here on the port side. But don't look down. They may be watching."

She moved to my side. "Ben, what happened?" she asked with a low voice.

"It's Harold Pearce and his Waverunner crew that killed Rick Turner. And they're the ones who killed 'Steve,' too. And he just tried to kill me. We crossed paths while he was starting a big smuggling run. They're using Waverunners to smuggle cocaine to the Florida coast. He chased me up onto the beach, firing all the way."

"What are we going to do?"

"We're going to get on that motorcycle and run for Freeport. I'll meet you at the motorcycle. Listen, here's what I want you to bring — the motorcycle key, our money, our passports, a flashlight, our diving knives, and your cellphone. Put it all in a wash bag and take along a towel, like you are going for a shower. Turn on some music before you leave, but don't lock up. Look behind you before you go into the showers. Come out three minutes later, and walk directly to the motorcycle, ready to roll."

"Okay."

"See you there."

I retraced my strokes and steps, remembering to retrieve the two-way radio and flare gun. I was halfway to the cycle when Rebecca made her move. From between the Australian pines, I tracked her progress and watched to see if anybody was following her. After she popped into the shower room, I made a wide sweep of the immediate area to make sure nobody was lurking. She came out of the shower room on schedule, with the motorcycle keys in hand. We unchained it, inserted the key and pushed it a long way up the street. Then I started it and we ran like hell.

We flew past the fashion colony, past the airport, and past the water tower. When the road straightened out, I really gunned it. The wind evaporated water from my damp clothes, chilling me. I guess that was why my teeth were chattering.

Rebecca was holding me tight, molding her body to mine. "What are we going to do?" she yelled in my ear.

"Haul ass for Freeport." I hollered against the wind. "Check into a hotel there — one with good security. Then tomorrow morning . . . I don't know exactly what we are going to do. All I know is that back there we were sitting ducks."

I drove along that rough asphalt lane as fast as my headlight could guide me. Bushes and trees were flying by.

"What happened with the Waverunners?"

"They had night vision goggles and I didn't. Lead man wasn't watching. Almost ran into me. Big mistake for their operation."

"You said they were smuggling?"

"Three of them, loaded to the gills with black packages — probably two hundred pounds each. I should have figured that out before. The perfect smuggling machine. Can go fifty-five in flat water and probably goes thirty in waves. Those guys know how to jump waves. They'll make Palm Beach in a little over an hour."

"Go-fast boats. I understand. But why did they pick Waverunners?"

"They're so small the Coast Guard can't see them. No radar reflection. The only metal is the engine. And they've modified them into 'stealth versions.' Should have thought of that when I saw one in Harold Pearce's shack. That's why he was so mad at me. They've coated them with rubberized plastic to absorb radar waves. Probably gives less reflection than a tin can."

We were coming up on the town limit.

"Should we tell the police? I could call them on my cellphone."

"Not until we're safe in Freeport. I don't trust them."

We were coming up on the police station, all lit up but with no jeep parked in front. I slowed and took a sharp right onto the connecting road that went past it.

"What are you doing?" Rebecca asked.

"We're taking Queen's Highway to bypass downtown."

It wasn't much of a bypass since Queen's was only 100 yards from King's, running parallel to it. But at least we wouldn't be seen by the people at the Island Club.

I slid on a patch of gravel in a left-hand turn onto Queen's.

Rebecca tightened her grip. "Maybe I could call the Coast Guard," she said.

"Good idea, but not from around here. The bad guys might intercept our conversation."

Queen's Highway was a lot narrower, and it took a lot of concentration to avoid encroaching shrubs and parked cars.

"You mean they could intercept us like 'Steve' with his fancy radio?"

"Yes, except that 'Steve' was a good guy," I said.

"What was he doing?"

"Monitoring SAWECUSS until he got suspicious of the Waverunners."

"And they killed him?"

"Yes, when he was tracking them down using the RDF dish — fifteen miles west of West End." The road widened and I sped up. We went through the Y-junction onto King's Highway. I twisted the throttle as far as it would go.

"Do you think 'Steve' was working for the DEA?"

"Yes." We were moving so fast that I had to go back to shouting. The wind was trying to blow the words back into my mouth.

"Then why didn't the DEA come and interview you?"

"I don't know. That doesn't seem to fit."

"It was hard to drive down that road at 50 miles per hour and keep track of the rearview mirror and think, all at the same time. But we were making great progress. The town of West End was far behind.

Rebecca said, "Someone took away the *Second Chance*. It wasn't in its berth when I came back."

"Those people work fast."

"Do you mean the DEA? The DEA works fast? After all the trouble they gave you?"

I didn't answer. There was a lot to think about. It was time to slow for the bend where we found Rick Turner. My nose told me he was still there. And flashing red and green lights told me that the police were there, too. I tried to show no attention to the Royal Bahamas Police Force jeep parked at the side of the road with its headlights shining into the crime scene. I accelerated moderately coming out of the turn and then twisted the throttle all the way.

As the bike climbed toward maximum speed, its chunky tires vibro-levitated over the asphalt. Wind streamed over my squinted face like a high-velocity shower.

"Ben, you don't have to be so reckless."

"There are two cars behind us. They fell in behind us after West End. They may be harmless, but it's too risky to find out."

As our speed maxed out, chunky rubber and rough asphalt conspired to make steering difficult. Keeping the cycle in the center of the road demanded my full attention. I didn't dare look down at the speedometer to see how fast we were actually going. It was dangerous enough to look in the rearview mirror to check on the two pairs of headlights.

The headlights did not get any smaller. The cars must have speeded up as radically as I had.

"Rebecca, they are chasing us!"

And they had all the advantages — four wheels to keep them on the road and knowledge of its every turn. Here on the straight, the brush was flying by at what seemed to be 80 miles per hour. And they were gaining on us. And in the beam of my headlight, I saw that a right-hand bend was coming up. The only way to get rid of them would be to ditch.

"Rebecca, this is going to be hairy. I'm turning off the lights. We're going to ditch in the bushes. Got to shake them off."

"Won't they see your brake light?"

"Good thinking."

I took a good look at the asphalt ribbon in front of me then turned off the lights. Counted the seconds for the turn to come up and leaned into it. After the engine braked us down to 50, I switched off the ignition and crash braked down to about 25 before leaving the road on the inside.

"Cover your face!"

I turned more to the right and the bushes came up in a flash. I managed to steer between the first four of them. Sideswiped the next one. Lost a lot of momentum rolling over another one. Came to a halt just as the first car roared past.

I set the motorcycle down on its side and stood up. We were deep in the bushes — so deep that I couldn't see the car's taillights as it roared out of the bend. All I could see was the aura of its headlights reflected from the asphalt strip that ran through this jungle of bush. And, strangely, the second car didn't come by.

We waited a long time. A very long time. It still didn't come. I pulled out the two-way radio and set it on scan. No transmissions. I handed it to Rebecca.

"I'm going to reconnoiter. Listen for transmissions and stay with the motorcycle. Cover the reflectors. If they come here, work your way to the east and listen for my whistle."

I inched my way to the road. Looked down both ways and didn't see anything. Not satisfied with that, I went back into the cover of the brush and worked my way westward to where I could see around the bend in the road. Nothing there, either, as far as the eye could see in the weak light. I jogged 100 yards farther to make sure, then jogged back to Rebecca.

"The coast is clear, at least for a quarter of a mile. They shouldn't hear us start up if I keep the revs low."

"Are you sure we were really being chased?"

"Yes. Two cars close together at high speed. Then after we turn off our lights, the first keeps racing on and the second one stops or turns around. Sure, they were chasing us. And they have radio communication."

"What's your plan?"

"I don't know. If we stay here until dawn, that will make it all the easier to find us. Doubling back would make no sense. There's no protection for us at West End. Going forward makes sense. It's almost certain the first car is waiting for us somewhere ahead. But if we go fast enough, we might get past them before they can pull out to block the road."

"No, they'll hear us coming."

"Then I'll alternate between running the engine and coasting. That should confuse them even if they do hear us in the distance."

"And what will you do if they're blocking the road up ahead?"

"Pull off again. We have less than twenty miles to go. We could go deep in the brush where they can't find us and then hike toward Freeport."

Rebecca agreed. And she had an excellent idea — wrapping the towel around the muffler to extend the exhaust channel and dampen the noise. Together, we pushed the motorcycle to the edge of the road. The coast was still clear. We push-started the cycle in second gear, and I kept the revs low for the first mile. Then I lost no time getting it up to 50, the highest speed for safe running without lights. The towel cut down the exhaust noise by one-third and my coasting strategy worked better than expected. After about a mile of coasting, we were down to 25 and were in need of another spurt. Again, I accelerated to 50.

Rebecca shouted into my ear, "They're talking on the radio, now, but it sounds garbled."

We were coming up on the Mulberry Lane crossroads, our speed was dropping to 20. It was time for another spurt. And I didn't like what I saw in the shadows, on the far side of the intersection. To confirm it, I turned on the headlight for a split second.

It was a compact car, parked on the side of the road at a right angle and poised to drive onto the road to block or ram us.

No time to think. I squashed the brakes and turned the cycle around. Twisted the accelerator as far as it would go and went through the gears like a demon.

"What will we do?" Rebecca screamed in my ear.

"Get far enough away from him, ditch the cycle, and walk," I said.

It was a good enough plan, but circumstances didn't cooperate. The car was amazingly fast in getting back on the road and getting up to 70. His headlights were on upper beam and I was sure that our reflector was giving us away. He was too close behind for us to get away with the ditching trick in the bend. We roared through it and he roared after us. I turned on the headlights so that we could run at top speed. Our headlights wouldn't make any difference if we couldn't pull away from that first car. They had radio communication. Where was that second car, anyway? For several long minutes, the first car inched up on us until it was only 50 yards behind.

The crossroads for Royal Lane were coming up and the second car stood on the far side. It stood ready to make a roadblock, just like the first car had.

Rebecca saw it, too. "What are we going to do?"

"Either try to get around it, or head for Sir Hector's."

"But he's —"

"He's got to protect us. And he has shotguns."

I put on as much speed as the cycle could give me. The car ahead moved to block the center of the road, facing left.

I shifted to the right side of the road like I would squeeze behind him. The shoulder was too rough to do it at 70, but we might keep our wheels under us at 30.

He moved backward a few feet. Would he stay in reverse gear?

I kept my speed up. I turned off my light. The car behind was furnishing plenty of light.

The car behind me fell back. It was getting damn crowded.

I dropped speed to keep it crowded and shifted to the left to go in front of the second car. He didn't go for it.

I braked hard. The left shoulder was too rough to go for. I kept on the brake, weaving like a fishing lure.

The second car turned off his lights to keep his buddy from being blinded.

I feigned to the left and the second car moved to the left. No way. No way to make it past him.

I threw the motorcycle into a right tilt and power slid around the intersection, sliding onto Royal Lane, then off it, and then onto it again, kicking up gravel.

Then came a tremendous bang. They'd tried to take the intersection at the same time. As we accelerated toward Sir Hector's, crossed headlights receded in my mirror.

I shouted my plan to Rebecca as fast as I could think it up.

"We'll hide the cycle behind Sir Hector's house. When he opens up, we'll tell him that we've called Broadmoore on your cell phone and that he has to protect us. If he's not there, we'll smash in a window. We'll take his shotguns. That should even the odds."

"And wait for them to come after us?"

"No. We can ride the cycle along the shore. They can't drive their cars there."

Headlight glow on the tops of the Australian pines told me that at least one of the cars had survived and was following us. The entrance of Sir Hector's estate was coming up fast. The lights were on. Good. The front gate was closed, probably locked. Good. The Jaguar was parked inside the gate. Good. And I saw where I could go.

"Rebecca, keep your legs in and your face down. Hug me."

I steered past the ornamental wall, selected the thinnest spot in the chest-high hedge, and plowed us through. We roared around the house and found no other cars. I went into low gear and took the steep embankment at an angle and rolled onto the back patio. No sign of Kevin's motorcycle. Good. We could go in. I set the dirt bike in Kevin's spot and we ran to the front door. I pounded on it while Rebecca rang the bell. A light went on in the living room. I pulled the flare gun from my waistband and kept pounding. If Kevin came to the door, I was prepared to use it on him.

"Please, please, please. What is the meaning of all this clamor?" It was Sir Hector. He sounded so irritable but ineffectual.

Behind me, the headlights were still only a glow, but there was no time to spare.

"It's Ben Candidi and this is an emergency. Please let us in."

I tucked the flare gun back in my waistband. Rebecca motioned to the bag with the diving knives, flashlight and cellphone under her arm. "He keeps the key to the gun case in the center drawer of his desk," she whispered to me.

"Yes, yes, yes," came Sir Hector's voice through the thick door. "Please be patient. What happened?"

The headlights were getting closer. I banged the door again. "Please open, right now! It's a matter of life or death."

The deadbolt slid inside the door. The Williamsburg-era thumb button depressed, indicating that he'd raised the latch inside. And the door opened a couple of inches to reveal Sir Hector in a white shirt, black pants, socks and no shoes. I put my shoulder into the door and forced my way in. Rebecca followed, closed the door and locked it behind us, turning the deadbolt.

Sir Hector's face was hard to decipher. It was putting on a randomized display of surprise, embarrassment and suspicion that alternated with strong indignation. "A matter of life and death? You look very much alive."

"We're being chased by two carloads of gangsters. Is Kevin here?"

"I have given him the night off."

"Good. Are all the doors locked?"

"Yes."

"Good." I nodded to Rebecca and said, "Go to it."

To Sir Hector's consternation, Rebecca walked off to the next room with the cloth bag under her arm.

"She's just checking and shutting the curtains," I said. "For our safety, you must not open that door for anyone. Not even Kevin. Not even Reggie."

"A 'carload of gangsters'? I cannot let in my own son? Are you not imagining things?" Sir Hector was congealing into an attitude of shocked gentility.

"I have approximately two minutes to tell you what's happening. Then I'm going to call Brian Broadmoore and tell him that it is you who guarantees my safety."

Sir Hector's eyes flashed, then he stuttered, seemingly unable to form words — like he was choking.

"No, I'm not imagining things. Harold Pearce who owns the Fun In The Sun Waverunner rental place chased me tonight, shooting to kill. We crossed paths when he was starting up a cocaine run for the Florida coast using Waverunners. He shot my inflatable boat out from under me. I was lucky to get away. I made it back to the marina and collected Rebecca on the motorcycle. Then two cars chased us at breakneck speed."

"Maybe the motorcars were just a coincidence."

"No way. They pursued us and set up roadblocks. We were lucky to make it here. And they are on their way here, right now."

"Then, perhaps, we should call the police."

"After we've called Dr. Broadmoore. I don't know who the hell I can trust."

Sir Hector jutted his jaw and stood there, looking like I'd delivered an insult.

I peeked through the drapes. It was too late to switch off the lights, now. Two cars had pulled up to the gate. Two cars with three headlights between them and a cloud of steam. "Rebecca," I called out, "careful around the windows. They're at the gate."

Was she too busy to answer or too far away to hear? I turned to Sir Hector. "Pretend there's nobody home. If they knock or the phone rings, don't answer."

Sir Hector hadn't moved a step from the door. I wished that I'd remembered to ask Rebecca for her cellphone before she went off to get the guns.

Sir Hector's attitude shifted from insulted to imperious. "All this mystery and suspense, yet you refuse to call the police?"

"Maybe in Freeport, but not here. The ones I've seen around here seem to be marching to the wrong drummer."

"*Indeed?*"

"Yes, *indeed*. And please keep your voice down." I grabbed him by the elbow, trying to pull him away from the door but he resisted. "No, I don't trust police who were unwilling to investigate the dead man on my salvaged yacht but who are quite willing to plant cocaine on my personal yacht."

He glared at me. "Is the matter of the *Second Chance* still a bee in your bonnet? You accepted my promise to take a look at that situation — to make some inquiries and get the wheels turning, so to speak — and I understand that the situation is now satisfactorily resolved."

"Yes, but only after my attorney forced the fictitious S.C. Corporation to close a quitclaim deal with me. For all I know, the police are in on Waverunner Pearce's stealth smuggling operation. An operation that big has to be paying protection to someone."

I really could have used that cellphone right then.

"Maybe they are so stealthy that their activities are undiscovered," Sir Hector coaxed.

"Let's get real. If they weren't paying protection to DEA informants working on this island, they wouldn't last a month."

Sounds of a jarred table and breaking glass came from the other room. Hopefully, Rebecca would come any minute with two shotguns.

The doorbell rang. I put a finger to my lips, grabbed Sir Hector by the elbow and pulled him from the door.

"Unhand me," Sir Hector shouted, struggling against my grip. "I won't be manhandled in my own house."

Damn him! I dug my thumb deeper into his arm and pulled him farther back. I pulled the flare gun from my belt, cocked it, and pointed it at Sir Hector's face.

The doorbell continued to ring, impatiently. Where was Rebecca?

A fist pounded on the door. "Sir Hector, open up. I know you're in there."

"Make one peep and I'll shoot off your face," I growled under my breath.

"It's important." It was Wade Daniels. "If we don't talk now, it will be ruined. *Everything.*"

That word had a galvanizing effect on Sir Hector. His arm muscles hardened under my thumb. His face froze in an electric chair grimace. He turned from me and pulled toward the door. And before I could brace in the other direction, he had already fallen onto the door and was turning the thumb knob. As I jerked him back, the door opened and Wade Daniels forced his way in.

Why didn't I kick Wade's head off, then and there? Instead, I aimed the flare gun at his big face — 10 feet away.

"Make one hostile move, Wade, and I'll blow you away. It shoots a shotgun shell."

For some reason, Wade didn't seem concerned. He closed the door behind him like he was part owner of the house and full master of the situation. He let his arms dangle loosely at his sides. His T-shirt hung over his oversize belly.

"Yes, you'll blow me away just like you did to Rick Turner," Wade said smoothly. He turned his attention to Sir Hector who was clearing his throat. "He's wanted for questioning about the death of one of our marina patrons. The body was just discovered."

"Just discovered but two days old," I interjected. "But your lying mouth makes it sound like you're a good citizen responding to an all points bulletin. Come on, Wade, tell it to him like it is. Your Waverunner buddy called you up and said everything would be ruined if you didn't stop Ben Candidi dead in his tracks. So you and your buddies tried to kill me at the crossroads of your old smuggling route — King's Highway and Royal Lane." With that, I sensed Sir Hector going limp. I pressed harder. "And just before that, you and your buddies tried to kill me at the crossroads of your *new* smuggling route — King's Highway and Mulberry Lane."

Sir Hector groaned. Wade tried to play it cool. He wrinkled his long nose in disgust and shook his head. But that didn't slow me down.

"And that's the place where your buddies killed the marina patron, Rick Turner. You killed him because he was snooping around Mulberry Lane."

Sir Hector gasped. I shouldn't have told him that so soon.

"Come on, Wade. Don't tell Sir Hector that you bashed up your car chasing me on police business. Take a peep through the drapes, Sir Hector. You'll see two bashed up cars, three headlights and one steaming radiator."

"Sir Hector," Wade Daniels said, with amazing smoothness. "He *is* wanted by the police."

"No, Sir Hector, I'm wanted *dead* by Harold Pearce, Wade's client." Sir Hector gasped.

"Yes," I added, "Wade is doing big business on the side. It's not just with a few people at the marina anymore."

Wade took a deep breath. "Just let me do what we have to do, Sir Hector. You know that I am legally authorized to take him into custody. Just let me do my job."

Those words delivered the final proof.

I said, "Just like I expected — a DEA agent turned bad. Hired to stop drug trafficking but actually promoting it. Some people might find that tolerable. But can you let him go around killing people?"

"Gentlemen, be reasonable," Sir Hector exclaimed. "There is no evidence of any wrongdoing." He stopped as quickly as he started.

"No, Sir Hector, there's plenty of evidence of Wade's wrongdoing. A big long list of methods and smugglers who are paying him protection. And the list is in safe hands," I fibbed. "To be opened in the event of my death."

Wade eyed me and the flare gun, then turned his attention to Sir Hector. "He's just talking chicken shit — nickel-and-dime stuff. He won't get away with accusing highly respectable people, Sir Hector. None of it would stick."

"No Wade, it's going to stick this time. Because your protection client Harold Pearce killed an *honest* DEA agent — internal affairs variety — who was sent to check whether Wade Daniels was doing his job."

Sir Hector stuttered in confusion. "Was this Rick Turner a DEA agent? I thought . . ."

"No, Rick was one of Wade's protection clients who was upset that the Waverunners were getting the big bags and that he got only little bitty bags. The murdered DEA agent's name was Steve and his boat was the *Second Chance*. It was fitted out as a spy ship and sent to check up on Wade. It picked up every electronic conversation around here."

I pressed my momentary advantage, focusing all my willpower on Wade's dark-green eyes. "Wade, why don't you just cut your losses. Just go out that door, tell your partners to clear out and lay all the karma at the door of the Waverunner shack and —"

Wade turned his head away and took one step sideways, extending his left hand like he was reaching for the door latch. But his other hand reached for the small of his back. His .38 came up at my stomach faster than I could decide what to do. Squinting his eyes, he half-turned his face toward me and raised his left hand to protect it. He did it slowly, as if afraid of provoking me to shoot.

"Wade, that's not going to change anything. I can still blow out your brains with one shot. And there's still the letter that will be opened after my death. Once we get blood all over Sir Hector's carpet and walls, he won't be able to play innocent any longer. Then the case against Reginald will be sealed with Super Glue."

Sir Hector slumped. Wade's confidence seemed to fade.

And I raised my bluff one notch. "Yes, I'm sorry, Sir Hector, but I had to put out an SOS signal before I got on that motorcycle. A case against Reginald has been stated. It may be deniable now, but it won't be after Wade pulls the trigger. If Wade shoots, all three of you are going to prison."

Sir Hector stiffened and addressed Wade. "Put that gun away. Disappear from here. Clean up your filthy mess, and never come here again."

Wade peeked in my direction once and registered surprise. Then his free hand came down, revealing a smirk on his face. His body relaxed.

"Rebecca won't be shooting any shotgun," announced a voice from behind me in resonant baritone. It had to be Kevin. High-pitched breathing from that direction told me Rebecca was alive. "Ben, I have a shotgun aimed at you. Behave accordingly. I'm sorry, Sir Hector, but you will have to take back your decision. I'm a small man caught in the middle. I'm in it too deep. But I will not be the goat who is sacrificed."

Preserving my only option, I held my aim on Wade Daniels' face.

"You did what?" Sir Hector asked incredulously.

"The plane is also delivering to the Waverunners," Kevin said. "Hundreds of pounds a week. Under your protection."

"How *could* you do that?" Sir Hector exclaimed. "How could you use my name for such quantities!"

"It wasn't me, sir. It was Reginald."

In my peripheral vision, Sir Hector seemed to have crumpled.

Wade said, "Sir Hector, just let us do what we have to do. If we hang together, it will turn out alright."

There was pounding on the front door. Standing beside it, Wade answered in a loud voice. "Let yourself in when you're ready, Reggie. But be careful. Candidi has a flare gun pointed at me."

Wade had relaxed his aim while giving directions to Reggie. Now his gun was pointed at my crotch.

I thought quickly: As soon as the door opened behind him, I'd jump to the side and fire into Wade's face and then go for his gun. Maybe Rebecca would be able to spoil Kevin's aim.

The latch lifted. I tensed as it opened. The hair was blond, the face was light, with steel-rimmed glasses. And the gun came in through the half-opened door and went right into Wade's neck, directly under his jaw.

"One false move and you're dead," the blond-headed man said, from behind the cover of the door. "Same for you, Kevin. I'm Special Agent Sherwin James, cover name Jay Sherman. Your DEA days are over, Wade. Now point that gun to the floor, take a deep knee bend and set it down."

I didn't wait for Wade to do it. In agony, I turned to see what happened to Rebecca. Her blouse was covered with blood — Kevin's blood, still trickling from the arm that was around her neck in a strangle hold. With his other hand he held the shotgun, butt into his shoulder, aimed at me but wobbly. Then, suddenly, Kevin released his arm from around Rebecca's neck. I jumped as she dropped and rolled. I tried to point the flare gun at him. But it all happened so fast — Kevin's lurch for the connecting door, the two shots fired in rapid sequence, and the third that jerked Kevin's shoulder.

The shotgun fell to the floor. Kevin went down in pain. Wade Daniels lay on the floor, dead or dying. And Jay Sherman was making his way to Kevin, his pistol trained on him.

Kevin sat on the floor, writhing in pain. "You did not have to do that to me, man! Why you do that?"

"Because you were pointing a shotgun at my friend Ben," said Sherwin James, alias Jay Sherman.

I grabbed Kevin's shotgun.

Sir Hector was crumpled on the floor, babbling protestations that he didn't know, that he had no idea, and that this shouldn't have happened.

Rebecca got to her feet and threw her arms around me, speaking in a ragged whisper. "He sneaked up from behind. He smothered me with a napkin. He strangled me. I couldn't breathe."

"You did good," I said, hugging her back. "Where are the others?" I asked Sherwin James.

"There's only one — Reggie," Sherwin James said. "His arms are handcuffed around a tree, and he's experiencing vivid dreams." He winked at Rebecca and pushed two fingers against his thumb to suggest squeezing a syringe.

"You injected with ketamine IM to sedate him?" Rebecca said.

"Yes, I couldn't have him screaming out warnings. I was a little shorthanded."

"You did great," I said.

"Compliment accepted," Sherwin James said. "But it would have been easier if you'd accepted my invitation to lunch and we'd gotten to know each other a little bit more."

"Yes, I was worried about food poisoning when I should have been worrying about lead poisoning."

I delivered that quip with a nervous laugh. The laugh stopped abruptly with my second look at Wade, dead on the floor. At head level on the wall, a fan-shaped pattern of blood spatter memorialized the event.

I was shaking all over. My left hand grabbed my right to get it under control. I looked at my watch — 40 minutes since my encounter with the Waverunners.

I took a deep breath. "We have to make a phone call. In less than thirty minutes, three Waverunners and a big load of cocaine will be hitting the Florida coast."

Sherwin James nodded. "We noted their time of departure from their transmissions when they tangled with you. Our helos are looking for three watercraft. But it would help if you could add some description." He pulled out a cellphone, punched in some numbers, and handed it to me. "After I intercepted Harold Pearce's call to Wade concerning you, I had my hands full keeping track of him and Reggie."

In my ear, a military-sounding voice answered on the other side of the Florida Straits: "Duty Officer."

I told him how to intercept three stealth Waverunners and 600 pounds of cocaine.

21 Under the Radar Picket

A cool, brisk north wind propelled the *Diogenes* on a beam reach toward Mangrove Cay at a gratifying seven knots. The tops of the small island's trees were just beginning to roll up from below the horizon. Far above that horizon I could make out the moving shape and occasional glint of the Navy P-3 Orion turboprop flying back and forth on radar picket duty.

The *Diogenes'* hull cut through the water with splendid hydrodynamic efficiency, the only telltale of any wasted energy being a steady whisper and occasional gurgle from our hull and the two parallel tracks of foam, one from the starboard side and one from the port side. Normally, these would stretch far behind us like a railroad track on the prairie.

But blemishing the picture was our Caribe inflatable. At the end of a 30-yard line, the Caribe inflatable, our rubber duckie, was making an enormous bow wave and leaving an ugly V-shaped wake, just like a smudge-pot cabin cruiser. Well, that's the difference between a planing hull and a displacement hull. If I'd really wanted hydrodynamic efficiency, I should have carried the rubber duckie on the *Diogenes'* bow.

We were lucky that the Caribe was still with us. Luckily, it was a steep sand beach where I'd run it up on that hair-raising night. It had come to a halt well above the high tide line. The next morning I found it were I'd abandoned it. There was nobody at the Waverunner shop to object to my borrowing their thick-tired trailer to bring the injured rubber duckie home. And when I rolled into the marina pulling the trailer behind my motorcycle, there was hardly anyone to cheer or boo me. All the members of SAWECUSS were gone, headed for the Florida coast, as fast as diesel and gasoline power could carry them.

The Caribe got the same care that I had given to the *Second Chance*. I routed out the shattered fiberglass on its transom and glassed it over. And I patched the inflatable chamber from both outside and inside.

The patches were holding up well. And with the new cylinder head installed, the engine would give us lots of good service.

Harold Pearce and his gang were in jail. A police helicopter's searchlights caught Harold's two buddies as they were pulling up to a boat house on the canal leading into West Palm Beach. They ditched their guns and cocaine, then headed up the canal at high speed. But they couldn't lose the helicopter, and they chose the wrong backyard to make their landing — a backyard guarded by a pair of rottweilers. Jay Sherman told me that it was all recorded and played on TV news. Palm Beach Sheriff deputies retrieved the cocaine, and police divers retrieved the guns.

Harold Pearce's attempt to kill me had delayed him considerably. A Coast Guard helicopter intercepted him a mile off Palm Beach. Jay told me it was a real James Bond chase, with Harold Pearce running his Waverunner up the beach and taking off on foot and trying to blend in among the seaside mansions. Unfortunately for him, the social season had begun and a lot of pool-and-patio parties were underway — with security. Running through the properties in his black wet suit and with a big knife strapped to his leg and various electronics strapped to his forearms, he didn't blend in too well. If only he had thought to wear his tuxedo underneath!

The police recovered a gun from him. Hopefully, a test firing of the guns would generate a match for the bullet that killed "Steve." Then justice would be served.

Steve was his first name, actually. He was an internal affairs agent for DEA, just like I'd guessed. The Agency had assigned him to find out if their agent Wade Daniels might be missing a lot of cocaine smuggling activity out of West End — missing it on purpose. Steve was doing picket duty off of West End on the night that he was murdered. Everything fit. He was tracking them by the low-power signals from their personal two-way radios. When they saw him with their night vision goggles, they put two and two together. A chest shot felled him from his flybridge. One came aboard to give him an executioner's shot to the head. And back on their Waverunners, it occurred to them to scuttle the boat by shooting holes at the waterline. As I had been trying to tell the Sergeant, you can shoot a tight pattern of holes with a pistol if you are at short range.

Wade Daniels had sealed his own fate when he tried to shoot Jay Sherman. People make their own choices, and one bad choice can bring on another. First he was only a DEA agent gone bad, accepting protection money from the smugglers that he was supposed to watch. His first step was easy to rationalize — protecting social climbers who used smuggling as a way to pay for those extras that belong to an upper-class lifestyle. But rationalization brings on more rationalizations.

When Wade protected Cal, Angie, Rick, Martin, Beth, the tuna tower guys and Mr. Enginuity, that was "just nickel-and-dime stuff." Kevin had off-loaded the cocaine from the seaplane and had given it to his brother, Edgar the Conch Man, to distribute. Sir Hector had received payments for protection under his good name. He was too big a political honcho for the DEA to take on, even if they had learned what was going on. But when Reggie decided to make use of his father's assets and hooked up with the Waverunners to convert the seaplane into a larger and more efficient operation, Wade accepted bribes from them, too. I guessed that he didn't agonize over it. He just rationalized. It turned out to be a murderous decision.

I wondered if Wade Daniels knew that Steve was a special agent sent to check up on him. After Harold Pearce caught Steve snooping and sent him to Davy Jones' Locker, he must have told Wade. What a surprise it must have been for Wade when I came in with the salvaged boat. How unnerving it must have been for him to watch me working on the boat. How worrisome, not knowing what I had found out. First, he tried to get rid of me with the poisoned fish. Then he must have wondered how much information I would give the police and whether the DEA might be using me as an informant. It had to be him who planted the cocaine on my boat.

Kevin was arrested for attacking Rebecca and threatening me. The Government was building a case that he was the one responsible for unloading the seaplane and that his brother Edgar had been using his conch boat to supply members of SAWECUSS.

Sir Hector's son Reggie was arrested, too, but unfortunately he was released. I couldn't truthfully identify him as one of our pursuers. And Jay Sherman's description of Reggie's actions prior to receiving the ketamine shot were not incriminating enough to warrant any sort of criminal prosecution. Well, that was what the assistant superintendent of police — the ASP — handling the case had decided. I was pleased to have ruined Reggie's stream of income. I was told that he was dumped by the consortium that was buying up the marina and the fashion colony.

Maybe there is a "Disneyfication process" going on in Grand Bahama Island. Maybe it was good.

I hoped that the new resort would offer a job to Zelma Mortimer where she could put her considerable skills to better use. I was thankful for the warning received in her card reading, although it was still not clear how much came from the lay of the cards and how much she had read into them. All I know is that her system of interpretation was still unchanged when I questioned her a third time, a couple of hours before setting sail. Of course, I couldn't press her any harder. I understood the kind of jam she had been in, not being able to tell me directly what she knew. Well, as I had been joking with Rebecca, that's how the tradition of calypso songs got started. It was a way to say things without really saying them.

Unfortunately, the ASP had not found sufficient incriminating evidence to charge Sir Hector with anything. Truthfully and objectively, all I could complain about was his unlocking the door for Wade Daniels and his dithering during the stand-off. Being ineffectual is not a criminal charge. But we hit him in his pocketbook. His silver bird had flown away. It would no longer be flying white powder under the protection of his name and bringing him supplemental income. I guessed that he would retreat deeper into his shrine of anglophilia.

It seemed that Sir Hector had no idea that Reggie had been using his silver bird and the protection of his good name. Sir Hector's fervent wish had been to spare his son the entanglements of drugs and dirty money. But as Martha Vangelden had said, the soil of the Bahamas is thin and unproductive. Subsistence is the only reward of honest pursuits. Smuggling continues as a siren's call. The sun will bleach the blood that is spilled on the rocks; waves and tides will carry away the wrecks. Maybe "Disneyfication" is the *only* answer to the Bahamas' problems.

Or maybe the answer is to earn foreign currency by harvesting new medicines from the *baha mar* — the shallow sea.

Of course, I had to tell Dr. Broadmoore of Sir Hector's wrongdoing and of his failure to help. Dr. Broadmoore replied that he didn't know Sir Hector Pimentel all that well and that, "The chap is irrelevant, actually." It seems that calling people and institutions "irrelevant" has become part of the power vocabulary of modern diplomacy. The term is widely used by Americans and Englishmen alike.

"Give it up, Ben," I told myself. "Why make yourself sick with the world's problems on such a wonderful day?" The sky was blue, the water was a transparent shade of turquoise, and a wonderful *baha mar* landscape was gliding below us — patches of sand, grass, coral, sea fans, and a plethora of sponges. Broadmoore's company would employ Bahamian conch men to harvest them, the government would get a fee, cancer patients would have hope, and maybe those smiling children in the school yard would benefit from this, somehow.

And talking about healing, I looked to the bow of the *Diogenes* and rested my eyes on a beautiful sight: Rebecca sunbathing. She was also reading photocopies of journal articles on tropical medicine. It turned out that Prof. David Thompson of Bryan Medical School had more research money than he thought. Rebecca's position would not be dependent on the grant proposal, and she would start in six weeks. In the mean time we would learn a lot more about the Little Bahama Bank and the Abaco Islands. And we would enjoy together many salty days and sultry nights.

Of course, Rebecca is not just a beauty, a lover, and a healer. She can be fighter, too. She managed to put a deep cut in Kevin's arm before he choked her into unconsciousness in the shotgun room. She regained consciousness right before Kevin announced that his shotgun was aimed at me. And when Jay's and Wade's shots went off, she jerked the shotgun and spoiled Kevin's aim at me.

But she told me to try to forget those things, now. She is such an idealist.

I looked back again. The Caribe was doing fine. Behind it, a white dot on the horizon had grown into a cabin cruiser. It was coming our way, but there was no reason to be alarmed. We were on a traveled path — the straight shot between West End and Mangrove Cay. And that was the only shot for big boats like ours. The water to the south of us was too shallow and unpredictable for anything but small motorboats and inflatables.

"Rebecca, there's a cabin cruiser at one-eighty degrees, relative — ETA about two minutes. Shall I hand up your bikini?"

"Yes, I suppose," she said, absently. She was still a little hoarse and had bruise marks on her throat and cheeks. She was absorbed in a scientific article: "Plasmodium falciparum *in vivo* resistance to quinine: description of two RIII responses in French Guiana," by Demar and Carme.

I clamped down the wheel, pulled Rebecca's bikini from the cockpit's side pocket, and made my way along the port rail to hand it to her. Back in the cockpit, I turned my attention to a ballistic device that I'd fashioned from a hollow boat pole, several washers, and a couple of pieces of concentric steel pipe.

Rebecca got my attention with a frown. "Ben, I'd feel a lot more comfortable if you would put that thing away. You haven't tested it enough to know it's reliable. You could blow off a hand — or worse."

It was my "unauthorized boarding prevention device." It didn't look like a gun but it accepted shotgun cartridges and shot the buckshot in a pretty tight pattern. I'd assembled it a couple of days after bluffing Wade with my "shotgun-cartridge-loaded" flare gun. It didn't seem right, now, to be completely helpless.

The cabin cruiser was on an intercept course, dead on our stern. If they'd intended to pass us, they should have veered off already. I waved them off. They waved back. Two men on the flybridge, one with a light complexion and one an Islander with a funny-looking white shirt. They powered down and came off plane a couple of dozen yards behind the Caribe, making an enormous wave that kicked it from behind. Then I recognized them: Sherwin James (a.k.a. Jay Sherman) from his big head of blond hair, and Sgt. Leonard Townsend from his uniform. With his epaulettes and red-striped black pants, the Good Sergeant seemed out of place on the flybridge of a small fishing yacht.

I was sorry for all the bad thoughts I'd harbored about the Good Sergeant. He had been as much a victim of circumstance as I. He had known of Sir Hector's low-level smuggling activity but couldn't do a thing about it. He knew that the boat owners in the marina were smuggling, but it wasn't his job to stop them. And he had known for most of his life that Reggie was a wild card that would bring trouble.

By showing up with a corpse, I had put the Good Sergeant on the spot. After reporting to his superiors, he received orders to not give me any information and to delay release of the yacht by all possible means. His ASP gave the order but wouldn't go on record with it because it came from a high echelon of the DEA. Sgt. Townsend had dispatched Constable Ivanhoe Walker with orders to guard the boat and be on the lookout for anyone who showed any interest in it. But Sgt. Townsend's ASP didn't tell him that the DEA was investigating Wade Daniels as a bad apple. And he didn't even learn who Jay Sherman was until after I did.

The cabin cruiser inched its way along our port side to within hailing distance. I waved again. Sgt. Townsend looked awfully cheerful up there. Rebecca, now bikini-clad, gave them a wave and returned to her medical reading. And I have to admit to feeling overprotective of my bikini-clad physician and soul mate — and to still feeling a little resentment toward those guys.

"Hey, Sergeant, what are you chasing us for? You bringing us a special cash reward from the Bahamian Government?"

Jay Sherman supplied the answer with a smile. "What's the matter? Weren't you satisfied with the sixty thousand that the DEA paid you?"

"No, Jay, I'm not really satisfied." I had agreed to keep calling him by his alias. "I placed an honest salvage claim against the 'S.C. Corporation,' a lawfully constituted entity even if it was created by your government agency. The claim was for one hundred thousand dollars. The Agency could have given up the property and agreed to let me sell it."

Jay shook his head and gave me one of his wooden smiles. "The Government never gives up any property."

"Then the Agency could have paid me the full one hundred thousand dollars."

A frown mixed in with his smile. "Hell, they paid you sixty thousand dollars, didn't they? Do you have any idea how hard it is for the Federal Government to pay someone to get back something it got for free? The Agency got the *Second Chance* by confiscation. It was a narcotic-trafficking boat before we got it."

Maybe I was still smiling. "Yeah, it was nice of you to give the boat a second chance." I caught the Sgt. Townsend's eye. "Which reminds me, give my thanks to Ivanhoe for giving the *Second Chance* all that kind attention."

"No problem," Sgt. Townsend said. "And he did find useful prints on the boat."

"What! You *did* go over the boat for fingerprints?"

"Ivanhoe did it. He did it with great patience, under my instructions. He had to wait until Wade Daniels was away, shadowing you and Dr. Levis when you went for your bicycle excursion. I was instructed to keep a low profile around Wade Daniels and to do nothing that would raise his guard."

"And that included keeping Rebecca and me in the dark."

"Sorry, mate, but the higher-ups apparently decided that such knowledge might be dangerous for you."

"Or they decided that they could learn a lot more about Wade by letting him react to me." I paused for a reaction from the Sergeant, but he had none. "When you got prints off the boat, how did you know that they weren't mine?"

Sgt. Townsend smiled. "You were kind enough to provide me with an excellent set of exclusionary prints for all fingers when I gave you the photo to look at in the plastic sleeve." He gave me a minute to recall that he'd handed it to me after I'd come to a skidding stop in front of him on my bicycle. He laughed, now, and said, "*X* marks the spot!"

I had to laugh, too.

Sgt. Townsend continued his report. "We got a fingerprint match for one of Harold Pearce's men. He is being charged with murder. We also have a match between the gun that he threw down and the one that killed the DEA agent with the codename 'Steve.' We have a firing pin toolmark match to the cartridge you found in the cockpit."

"*Congratulations*," I said.

Yes, Sgt. Townsend had done a good job under difficult circumstances, investigating murder under the eyes of a corrupt DEA officer and maintaining professionalism while the district's member of Parliament and his son were trafficking in cocaine. Yes, Sgt. Townsend was one of the good guys, but I was still having trouble accepting it on the emotional level.

"Congratulations accepted," Townsend said.

"Sergeant, I'm developing a positive image of the Royal Bahamas Police Force. But I'm afraid that doesn't extend to Sgt. Toomey, who wanted to bust me for cocaine on my boat."

Sgt. Townsend turned serious. "Wade Daniels was a credentialed DEA agent, and Sgt. Toomey was duty-bound to make a search."

"And he was also duty-bound to ask Wade Daniels how he knew exactly where to find the cocaine. At best, Toomey needs a slap on the hand for acting as Wade's pawn. At worst, he was in collusion with Wade and the smugglers."

Sgt. Townsend's face became serious. "The matter is still under investigation, mate. It would be best not to make a thing of it."

I had to smile, how the Bahamians pick up these Britishisms, like the use of "mate" to emphasize the closeness and seriousness of being on the same ship together. Then I remembered that Sgt. Townsend had called me "mate" a few times before.

"Sure, mate," I replied, smiling as I pictured Townsend as an officer of the deck. "What else do you have to tell me?"

"I have one thing more to tell you and Dr. Levis."

"Okay," Rebecca said. She returned to the cockpit, journal article in hand. She'd been pretending to read it, but had actually been listening the whole time, sometimes pursing her lips or shaking her head when my words came out too sharp.

"This is information from the Superintendent. Kevin and Edgar have agreed to a plea bargain — five years imprisonment. We will not need you to testify against Kevin.

"Okay," Rebecca said.

"The cases against Sir Hector and his son, Reginald, have been officially closed. The file is now officially sealed. Reginald is in a rehabilitation program and will remain on probation for a long time. I am asking for your promise of silence on the matter."

"Yes," Rebecca said.

For me, it was not as easy. "Smuggling can be forgiven, but not murder. I'm sure that Rick Turner was killed because he started watching Reggie's house after talking with me about the seaplane. I'm sure that Reggie was the one who killed him."

"We cannot eliminate the possibility, but we cannot prove it either."

I replied with irony. "It must be hard for you to walk away from a homicide."

He grew very serious. "It has always been hard to do any sort of policing in the Bahamas. We are a poor country without resources. We are forced to live with many paradoxes. That is the price of living on the little acre that God has given us." He delivered his last sentence like a prayer.

For a second, an image of the smiling school children replaced the man on the flybridge. Behind my sunglasses, my eyes went blurry. Then, looking at Sgt. Townsend — vessel to vessel, man to man — I began to see myself through his eyes. And I had trouble forming my words, at first. "I understand. You have a tough row to hoe, mate. Brother."

Rebecca brightened, and so did her voice. "This calls for a toast. And I can't think of a better use for a bottle of wine that we've been saving." With light-footed grace, she exited below. And in an instant, she reappeared with a bottle, corkscrew and four disposable plastic glasses. She handed the bottle to me and took the wheel. "Ben, could you do the honors?"

Using the bench as a bar, I poured four equal glasses. With one of them in hand, I mounted the transom and offered it at arm's length, leaning out as far as possible on the port side. After Rebecca switched the Caribe's line to a starboard cleat, Jay Sherman maneuvered his boat behind me. The Sergeant inched his way to the front and wedged himself into the cabin cruiser's bow pulpit. I stretched sideways and he stretched forward. The transfer required concentration on both our parts and great skill on the part of Jay Sherman. It reminded me of when I'd jumped aboard the *Second Chance*, two short weeks ago. Rebecca handed me the second glass, which we also successfully transferred. Jay returned the yacht to a parallel course on autopilot, with plenty of leeway. Then he made his way to the bow to relieve the Sergeant of one of the drinks.

"To your success and safety," Rebecca cried out.

We all drank.

"To a rosy economic future for the Bahamas," I called out.

We all drank again.

"To the success of your client's company," the Sergeant called back.

We all drank again.

"And to your vacation in paradise," Jay Sherman called back, as three of us drank. "Just remember that the Orion turboprop has eyes. So do the Coast Guard jets."

The guys drank. Wine gurgled in Rebecca's throat and almost came up. I patted her on the back. Thoroughly distracted, I drank the rest of my wine in one gulp.

Jay Sherman and Sgt. Leonard Townsend returned to the flybridge, and the cabin cruiser started falling behind. We waved to them. They waved back. The DEA agent turned the boat away from us, then increased speed, putting it up on plane and carving a broad arc in the water. The boat straightened its course as its bow pointed toward West End.

I looked down at my hand. It wasn't holding the wine glass anymore. It was holding my portable VHF marine radio. And my thumb was twitching around the transmit button, as if begging me to continue the conversation.

"Ben, what do you think he meant by *that?*"

"He was warning us, my precious sea anemone, to be careful what we do around here in the rubber duckie — especially in daylight."

Rebecca took a long pull on her wine, then giggled. "Come on,

Sprite of Neptune! Do you think that the crew of the Coast Guard jet gave *him* video pictures of us *doing it*?"

"I don't know, darling."

Somehow, I couldn't bring myself to push that button and ask the guy. And to this day, we don't know the answer.

ACKNOWLEDGEMENTS

I would like to thank Gisela Haynes, Gregg Brickman, Christine Jackson (Ph.D.), Suzie Schultz and Doug Beckman for their critiques of the manuscript; Sgt. Victor Jeff Forbes and Constable Raymond Culmer of the Royal Bahamas Police Force for sharing their experience with police work at West End; Mr. Berkeley Kemp for offering us the shelter of his covered porch and for delightful conversation during an hour-long rainstorm; Elaine Talma of the Sir Charles Hayward Public Lending Library for an informative conversation; and Jerome Sanford, author of the novel *Miami Heat*, for reviewing illegal and marginally legal financial schemes that pop up in the story. I also thank Reinhard Motte, M.D., Assoc. Medical Examiner, Miami-Dade County Medical Examiner's Department for definitive information on postmortem changes as a function of time after death; Monika and Dr. Stanley Burg for sharing their experience and literature on ciguatera; and Fredi Schwartz for a card reading, for teaching me the details of her system (now available at www.CardSage.com), and for helping to tune up Chapter 16. Finally, I thank Betty Wright of Rainbow Books for her encouragement of my work and Betsy Lampé for imaginative cover design.

AN INTERVIEW WITH DIRK WYLE

Rainbow   Dirk, we have decided to add some pages to your fifth book in the Ben Candidi Series to give you an opportunity to answer questions on your work. Your first book in the Series, *Pharmacology Is Murder* published in 1998, validated all of Rainbow's highest expectations, receiving marvelous reviews on a national level. Your subsequent books have shown that you can sustain your high standards and continue to garner high-level reviews. How many Ben Candidi adventures do you think you can produce?

Wyle   Twenty-one is my desired number. That is the number of Travis McGee novels produced by John D. MacDonald, one of my literary influences and a kindred spirit. Twenty-one is also the number of amino acids necessary for human life.

Rainbow   Will you have enough time?

Wyle   I have written the first five books in seven years. I'm 59 years old now. According to the actuarial tables, I should be able to write another 16 books.

Rainbow   Do you have that many Ben Candidi stories in your head?

Wyle   Biomedical science generates a host of important projects that can serve as starting points for Ben's mystery-adventures. And let's not forget the contributions of Rebecca Levis (M.D.), Ben's lifetime partner. Her passion for world health broadens Ben's horizons to include the whole world. Witness *Amazon Gold*, fourth in the Series. It was Rebecca's work with the Yanomama Indians that set the story in motion.

Rainbow   Are you guaranteeing that Rebecca will be Ben's lifetime
           partner?

Wyle   Yes.

Rainbow   Will they fight, separate, fall prey to drugs or alcohol, and
           come back together like so many "significant others" in
           detective fiction?

Wyle   No, I consider such unromantic subplots to be a failure of
           imagination on the part of the author. In my opinion, the
           stale-coffee-and-stinking-cigarette-butt, workaholic, my-
           spouse-doesn't-understand-me stereotype has dominated
           detective fiction for much too long. At a national mystery
           conference that I recently attended, the discussants were
           still fueling the paradigm that the hero must be flawed and
           that society numbs the soul. I prefer a more optimistic
           mindset in my protagonists — at least at the beginning and
           end of the story. I see no reason to drag readers over cowpats
           of personal woe. The reader has worked hard for the hour
           that he or she can spend with me. They deserve better from
           me.

Rainbow   Are you saying that Ben and Rebecca are perfectly
           adjusted?

Wyle   Ben thinks that Rebecca is a "15." She has found love
           with him that is deeper than anything she has experienced
           before. Their love is strong. But a healthy love is never
           static. Problems will keep rolling their way. They will
           continue to be challenged to use imagination, intellect and
           commitment to work things out. For example, we already
           know that Rebecca would like Ben to establish himself in
           a defined career. Ben, on the other hand, seems more
           inclined to follow the opportunities that present themselves.
           A constant problem, of which Ben doesn't seem to be aware,
           is his roving eye. That has gotten him into trouble or
           misunderstandings in four of his five adventures. Rebecca
           seems resistant to inappropriate male attention, but a world
           health mission in another part of the world might prove a
           more serious seduction. The relationship parts of the stories
           deal with their attempts to stay tuned in to each other's

special qualities. Their "vacation" together in *Bahamas West End Is Murder* has shown that they can amuse each other with both humor and philosophical *shtick*. That bodes well for a long-term relationship.

Rainbow   How did you research *Bahamas West End Is Murder*?

Wyle   We sailed from Miami to Grand Bahama Island and then to the Abacos on our *Gizmo II* several years ago. An observation of a certain watercraft doing a strange thing gave me the idea for the central crime in the book. A couple of summers ago, with the book half-written, we sailed back and spent several days at the marina in West End. We sallied forth on bicycle to meet local people and to pin down geographic detail. We also zipped along the shoreline and over the sponge flats and coral reefs with the hard-bottomed inflatable. Being a novelist is a good excuse to do such things. Seeing with a scientist's eyes adds to the sense of mission. Interestingly, the West End marina and its basin had undergone a radical make-over between our two visits. That fit well with the story where the boaters were worrying about the marina becoming gentrified and expensive. My fictitious boaters were more like the old crowd.

Rainbow   You are not retracting your disclaimer that any similarity of characters in the story to real people is completely coincidental, are you?

Wyle   No, the disclaimer stands. And I stand by my claim, made privately, that boating brings out the oddball in people.

Rainbow   Do you care to elaborate?

Wyle   Sure. Take a look at the fish fry scene in chapter six of this book.

Rainbow   What other sorts of field research are you doing for the Series?

Wyle   We had an interesting time on the Amazon and in the rain forest for *Amazon Gold*. In two weeks we are going down to Campeche in the Yucatan, guided by fellow author Steve Glassman (*Near Death Experiment*) to take in Mayan pyramids and local culture. Now it seems that friends are volunteering to do research for me. In the middle of a month-long trek in India, Doug Beckman sent me a postcard that read like the back cover synopsis of a Ben & Rebecca adventure on the subcontinent.

Rainbow   What kind of research are you doing for the sixth book in the Series?

Wyle   I am investigating a venue that is quite close to home but is a lot flashier than Bryan Medical School.

Rainbow   A *Publishers Weekly* review said that your novels are "pleasing for both their intrigue and for their intellect." We agree. How do you manage that?

Wyle   I worked for over 30 years as a biomedical scientist testing complicated schemes and asking the question, "What molecule does what to what other molecule, and which molecule gets zapped for it?" Such mechanistic experience comes in handy for analyzing and constructing plots of murder mysteries. But I admit to spending several years of weekends and evenings learning the rules of fiction. Regarding appeal to the intellect, mindset that tunes in to background, undercurrent and the character traits will tend to do that.

Rainbow   Are your stories manifestly intellectual?

Wyle   I hope not. Certainly not *self-consciously* intellectual, as is the case with a lot of mainstream fiction. It is best for the intellectual energy generated in the story be emitted as overtones that resonate but do not obscure the melody. My primary goal is to tell a good story.

Rainbow   But Ben is an intellectual, isn't he?

Wyle   Not when he's getting a ragging and ribbing from Sam and Lou at Captain Walley's waterfront bar. Also, he spends a lot of time with unpretentious people, encouraging them to sing their song, so to speak. He is fluent in Spanish and used to hang out in the Little Havana section of Miami.

Rainbow   Are you fluent in Spanish like Ben?

Wyle   No, I'm sorry to say. I read and understand Spanish pretty well, but I have a long way to go toward fluency. But I am

	fluent in German for having studied it and lived there four years.
Rainbow	Are you going to send Ben and Rebecca to Germany?
Wyle	I've given that a lot of thought but haven't been able to come up with an interesting plot. Foreign stories would seem to require a more exotic location.
Rainbow	But a Klaus-Dietrich Grünhagen plays a role in *Amazon Gold*.
Wyle	Yes, he is the German pilot who owns "Amazon Touristic" and flies an amphibious airplane around the Rio Negro. As Ben commented, the guy had a Teutonic spirit that was too strong to be beaten down by the pedagogues of the Latin school. Klaus-Dietrich wouldn't let anyone box him into a narrow social category. Klaus-Dietrich is the type of strand that I enjoy weaving into my stories.
Rainbow	What can you tell us about reader response?
Wyle	I receive lots of e-mails and they are a joy to answer. Some are from biomedical scientists who are pleased to see their profession depicted realistically. Many are from mystery fans with comments on the plot. A growing number are mainstream readers who just like the story. My work has been used in conjunction with college courses. In addition to doing live readings and discussions, I enjoy doing speaker phone discussions with book groups. My website lists some discussion points for each book, organized according to type of group.
Rainbow	Thank you very much, Dirk. To close this interview, could you tell us your website?
Wyle	Yes. It is *www.dirk-wyle.com*. My e-mail is *dirk@dirk-wyle.com*. Dear Readers, I am looking forward to hearing from you.

**Titles
in the
Award Winning
Ben Candidi Mystery Series
by
Dirk Wyle**

Pharmacology Is Murder
ISBN 1-56825-038-X
Published 1998

Biotechnology Is Murder
ISBN 1-56825-045-2
Published 1999

Medical School Is Murder
ISBN 1-56825-084-3
Published 2001

Amazon Gold
ISBN 1-56825-095-9
Published 2003

Bahamas West End Is Murder
ISBN 1-56825-100-9
Published 2005

ABOUT THE AUTHOR

DIRK WYLE is the pen name of Duncan H. Haynes, Ph.D., a 30-year veteran of biomedical science with a lifelong interest in literature. Commercial success of his drug microensapsulation technology enabled an early retirement from the duties of medical school professor. Since 2001 he has devoted full effort to inventing new challenges and adventures for his youthful protagonists, Ben Candidi (Ph.D.) and Rebecca Levis (M.D.).

Believing there are no stone walls separating the realms of popular science, serious literature and formal mystery, Dirk Wyle has created stories that play out in all three arenas. Ben accepts "straightforward" projects which quickly turn perplexing, mysterious and then sinister. Shortly after Ben solves the mystery, the bad guys (and gals) strike back and he must fight for his life. In the last two books of the Series, Rebecca has been fighting along with him.

Dirk Wyle does not regard work and play as necessarily separate activities. In *Bahamas West End Is Murder*, Ben and Rebecca receive their call to action while on vacation. Dirk's research work for the Ben Candidi novels has included travel in the Brazilian Amazon and sailing the Bahamas. He is now hard at work to add a sixth adventure to the Series.

Dirk invites your visit to www.dirk-wyle.com.